PRAISE FOR
*FINDING THE WAY HOME*

"*Finding the Way Home* does not disappoint. This richly-layered novel is overflowing with real life and redemption. After only one chapter, you will want to book the next flight to the English coast just to see the world Sarah Byrd lovingly describes. I highly recommend this debut novel from Sarah Byrd!"

Jana Ford Muntsinger, literary publicist,
Muntsinger-McClure Public Relations

"*Finding the Way Home* is a gripping novel that through its wonderfully told story and vivid characters digs deep into human nature and will keep you up at night until you've arrived at the back cover! It captures humanity in its truest sense – the struggles, joys, flaws and gifts – and it will undoubtedly cause you to look internally and ask yourself some of life's toughest questions. It is absolutely a must read."

Shawn Boyer, Founder and CEO, snagajob.com

"There is love and conviction flowing through every page of *Finding the Way Home*. I found myself wanting to cross the ocean to visit this tiny English village – not only because of its beauty, but because its characters display so much charm and character. Through their lively relationships, Sarah Byrd has captured what we all experience: the tension, the tenderness, the anguish, the grace, and ultimately, the rest that comes from trusting that we are loved after all. This story is deeply satisfying."

Kim Greene, Women's Leadership Development,
West End Presbyterian Church

"In a world choking with isolation, Finding the Way Home is a refreshing, restorative reminder of the power of love and forgiveness. So descriptive, I read through many cups of tea and was ready to pack my bags for a trip to the English countryside."

Kim Newlen, Founder and President, Sweet Monday®

For discussion questions and more, visit www.sarahbyrd.net

# finding
the way
# home

## Sarah Byrd

WestBow
PRESS

*WestBow Press books may be ordered through booksellers or by contacting:*

*WestBow Press*
*A Division of Thomas Nelson*
*1663 Liberty Drive*
*Bloomington, IN 47403*
*www.westbowpress.com*
*1-(866) 928-1240*

*Because of the dynamic nature of the Internet, any Web addresses or links contained in this book may have changed since publication and may no longer be valid. The views expressed in this work are solely those of the author and do not necessarily reflect the views of the publisher, and the publisher hereby disclaims any responsibility for them.*

*ISBN: 978-1-4497-0350-9 (sc)*
*ISBN: 978-1-4497-0349-3 (e)*

*Library of Congress Control Number: 2010931001*

*Printed in the United States of America*

*WestBow Press rev. date: 6/28/2010*

To Steve

You've been the inspiration for this book from the first words to the final re-write. It's been a long road and you've never wavered. Thank you for holding me up when I faltered, for cheering me on when I doubted, for believing when I didn't, and for loving me through it all. You make it easy to write about a man of high character, deep passion, and big love. And thank you for asking if I'll write another book. That's true love.

# Acknowledgements

I've received more than my fair share of love and encouragement in the writing and editing of this book. It gives me tremendous pleasure to offer my very special thanks to the following:

Katie and Rebecca, my daughters and friends. Each, in her own way, has known how to encourage and inspire me. There has been some form of this story for most of their lives and they've born the journey with grace and love.

Sarah Cornwell, Kim Greene, and Allison Hearn for investing themselves in me, and this book, for many years. I am overwhelmed by their faith in me. And to Joyce Minor, Joanne Wallace, Kitty Witthoefft and Ursula Barravecchia for listening to the ups and downs, patiently enduring my ramblings, and consistently being for me. To Jana Muntsinger for always telling me to listen to my heart. And to Heather Angello for her wise insights into the hearts of the characters. Her gentle nudging made me dig deep for my truest voice. It was a great joy to work with her.

Thank you to Rob and Rebecca Musser, for putting their talents and passions into mine. To Townsend Hunn, for her diligence, care and attention to detail. To Sarah Doerfler for donating her photography talent. And to my dear friends in our Tuesday night group, for listening, praying, believing and cheering.

*Finding the Way Home* has also been a story of me finding my way home, into the arms of people who have loved me so well. Thank you to the rest of my family and friends who remembered, inquired, cared and encouraged—who bound their hearts to mine with kindness.

You have made us for yourself and out heart is restless until it rests in you.

*St. Augustine*

# 1

## Suzanne

I don't have many memories. Once, I described it to Edward as sleepwalking through life. I do remember a few things—momentary awakenings, I guess.

I remember the soft blue velour of the recliner in the family room and the way the foot rest clicked when I pushed the handle to raise it. I sat in that chair the first time I saw *Anne of the Thousand Days* and fell in love with another time and place.

I remember the look on my father's face when he saw a picture of Mark Jordan and me at a seventh grade dance. What began as a secondary glance became a full, head-on stare as his face hardened in a dawning understanding. Mark's dark-skinned arm lay awkwardly across my back. His white nails, resting casually on my shoulder, glowed from the camera flash. A single pulsing vein and a small twitch in his left eye were all that hinted at my father's carefully contained rage.

And I remember the jade necklace that slipped from beneath the nurse's uniform as she pulled the sheet up over my mother's lifeless body. It was a teardrop cut, set in lacy gold filigree. It swung back and forth; an upside down metronome counting off the first seconds of the life I had dreaded since hearing the diagnosis ten months before.

When I told my best friend that I was taking this trip, she asked if it was to forget. No, I said. It's to remember.

⸙

I always thought I would make this trip with Edward. Instead, Blair sat next to me on the terrace, both of us looking down at the fishing village below. Like a scene from a postcard, it was complete with stone breakwaters and bright red skiffs along the harbor. It was easy to see why Dylan Thomas called Mousehole "the most beautiful village in England." The taxi driver who picked us up at the railway station in Penzance explained that we'd been mispronouncing the village name. It would read 'Mowzil' if spelled phonetically. My ten-year-old daughter, however, would insist on pronouncing it "Mouse hole," as she had since the day I decided to come.

We'd come for a three-month respite. It took her smile to restore the confidence I'd lost during our journey from Washington, D.C. to the far southwest of England.

Joy sprang from her voice as she surveyed the view. "Daddy would be proud of us for being so brave."

No one had ever accused me of being brave before, especially Edward. I won't lie and say that, somewhere over the Atlantic, I didn't begin to wonder if my father's assessment was correct. Was I a fool for coming here? Blair's words bolstered my courage, reminding me why we had come. "Yes, he would," I heard myself say, but wondered what he'd really have thought. That was enough to push me out of my seat. I reached for her hand. "Let's unpack and find something to eat. Early to bed for us tonight."

The cottage was decorated with the seaside vacationer in mind, whitewashed walls and seaside knick-knacks throughout. Nothing sophisticated or fancy, it had a homey quality that put us both at ease. Edward had hired a decorator when we moved into the three-story brick house in Great Falls. Her motto, "A house shouldn't look lived in," meant it always looked more like a museum than a home. After years spent in a home designed to appear artful, I appreciated Wisteria Cottage.

Once Blair was tucked in, only one thing remained to be done: report in to my father in Massachusetts. I dialed the international code and listened to the hollow ring until I heard the deep, bass voice I knew so well. I took a deep breath as I closed the heavy drapes over the windows. "We're here, safe and sound. Blair's already asleep. I'm not far behind."

"I still think you're crazy to do this, Suzanne. Any decision on the company yet?"

I sank onto the bed and crawled under the blanket. "I've only been thinking of selling it for a month. I told you I haven't made a final decision.

Until then, Cathy has everything under control. I came here to get away, remember? I don't want to keep discussing it."

"I still don't understand how you can just walk away from a business you built yourself," he countered.

"It wasn't by myself, it was with Edward. And he's gone now." I hung up with the beginnings of a headache and a promise to call again next week. Dusky light still peeked from behind the curtains when I finally closed my eyes.

I awoke first the next morning, glad to have a few minutes to think about the day ahead. Sipping coffee, I stepped into the tiny garden, packed with more flowers than I could name. Mrs. Howell had left instructions about keeping it weeded. It looked small enough to manage, even for my black thumb. Along with a stocked pantry, she also left detailed notes to help us get settled. The list read like the cast of a play.

Seeing Harry Malloy's name beside *car hire* reminded me of our afternoon appointment. After our taxi ride here along a narrow, twisty road and through the maze of half-lanes and hairpin turns, I questioned my ability to drive. Continuing down the list, I shook my head at the art lessons, but silently thanked her for including a stable. Unable to ride since the accident, maybe Blair could help groom. I looked at Mousehole below me and gathered my courage to begin this summer.

All eyes seemed to be upon us as we walked downhill towards town. Did people know I hadn't purchased return tickets? Did they know we'd left our familiar life in America because it no longer was? Did they know sometimes I felt like I might burst through my own skin? I told Blair I was holding her hand to keep her safe on the blind curves, but failed to mention the security her nearness afforded me.

As we passed a shop door, Blair let go of my hand and ducked inside. I followed behind and found her bent over, perusing through thick, bright sweaters, horses galloping across their fronts. Several rows over, two women spoke. It was like looking at the elegant, aging Grace Kelly talking to a model plucked from the pages of *British Vogue*.

"...must be good for business," the older woman concluded.

Miss Vogue turned up her nose. "No doubt the invasion is in full force, half Americans, half Germans."

A thinning eyebrow shot up. "Your work sells well enough to both, doesn't it?"

"Too true. I don't know whether to be flattered or insulted." Silver bracelets on her slender wrist chimed as she stroked her glossy, honey-blonde hair.

"Hmm…" The older woman frowned. "And how is Peter?"

"Quite lovely, but far too busy. Those children would occupy him every weekend if they could."

"Well, after all, he is—."

"I know," Miss Vogue cut in sharply. She pulled up ram-rod straight and crossed her arms. "That's what he's always telling me. I'm just saying that if he had more backbone, he could say no once in a while."

"Maybe he's doing what he enjoys." Her dull response suggested they'd had this conversation before.

I realized, a second too late, that I'd been unashamedly eavesdropping. The younger woman's angry eyes locked with mine; I felt the heat rush up towards my face. Turning abruptly, I grabbed Blair's arm and dragged her from the store, protests trailing from her like exhaust. Imagining the worst of small town life, I was certain by sundown half the village would know about the rude American and her whiny child. My dreams of anonymity faded with my good mood.

Things went from bad to worse as I maneuvered our MINI from the car hire desk through town and back towards our cottage. "Stop screaming at me," I shouted the third time Blair cried out in fear.

"I can't help it. You're going to hit something."

"Just be quiet. I have to get us back to the house. You're scaring me."

"You're scaring me," she mumbled, getting the final word. Her sulky demeanor the remainder of the ride was no match for my own, and I added one more check on the list of why coming here was looking like a terrible mistake.

Once we were safely at the cottage, I calmed down enough to apologize. "Let's go exploring and find someplace fun for dinner."

Blair's expression clouded. "Will we have to drive there?"

I burst out laughing. "Not tonight. But we can't avoid driving forever. We'll have to do better. You don't scream at me and I won't scream at you."

There was a long a pause, and then she grinned. "But you scared me."

Agnes Buncle looked far different than her name implied. I guessed she was in her early thirties, though her shapely figure could belong to someone ten years younger. Lively brown eyes smiled at us. I liked her right away.

"Mrs. Howell told me she'd let Wisteria Cottage for the summer." She leaned toward Blair. "Do you like to read?"

Blair nodded furiously, and they disappeared into the silent stacks. I browsed the New Arrivals shelf and glanced through the announcements board. A flyer for graduation trips caught my eye. Suddenly, that awful aloneness snuck up on me again, like a cat waiting to pounce. I began to shiver. And just like that, my excitement about our summer vanished, replaced with numbing fear. Would Blair see her graduation day? How would I raise her alone? The distance between now and then was too far, the challenge too great.

"Are you cold?" Blair's face was wrinkled in confusion, while Agnes looked on with concern.

I forced a laugh. "Must have had a chill."

Agnes paused for the briefest of moments. "These old stone buildings hold the winter cold long past spring. There's a reading group for Harry Potter that begins in an hour. Blair said she'd like to stay for it. I'd love to have her company till then. Why don't you get out for a few hours and warm up? Come back around 3 o'clock. We'll be fine till then, won't we, Blair?" She was already envisioning Hogwarts, and I was free until mid-afternoon.

⁓

The minute I stepped outside, I knew where I wanted to go. I hopped on the local bus part of the way, then followed Mrs. Howell's directions the rest. Finding a narrow path cut into a tall hedgerow, I stepped through a green tunnel and found myself standing in a quiet cove, its rocky walls half circling a small, sandy beach. I found a spot against the rocks and spread out the blanket. I lay down, closed my eyes and let the sun's warmth wash over me. My new spot was nearly empty. All I could hear were waves rushing, singing, *de capo,* with reassuring repetition. For awhile I simply lay there and breathed deep, in and out, in and out. Filled with clean, tangy air, the fear that had stalked me back at the library simply ebbed away.

Friends and family kept telling me to take life one day at a time. Their words seemed trite until moments like these, when the prospect of years alone threatened to undo me. But then, so did the thought of a single day. Be it one day or a thousand—both felt too hard to bear. Wiping tears away, I looked up in time to see a gust of wind pluck a hat from its owner and toss it down the beach. Her dog barked and strained at his leash. I hopped up, snatching it before it escaped. As she drew nearer, I recognized her from the sweater shop.

"My dear, thank you for rescuing an old woman's hat." Turning back, she said, "Hush, Wally. Goodness, are you all right?"

"I'm fine," I croaked, before dissolving in a puddle of tears. I turned to go, but she put a hand on my shoulder.

"Now then, come sit with me for awhile." She led me to a blanket beside her chair, quietly rubbing my back until the tears stopped.

"Thank you, I'm fine now."

She looked me directly in the eye. "I don't believe that for a minute. I'm Eleanor Cavendish." A beautifully manicured hand, bright with jewels, reached out for mine.

"Suzanne Morgan" I said. "I'm so sorry, please excuse me."

"There is nothing to excuse. Clearly something has you terribly upset. I do wish I had a thermos of tea. A cup would do us both some good." We sat quietly for a few minutes gazing at the sea. With each roll of the tide, the feeling that I was imposing grew. Still looking into the distance, she said, "I believe I saw you the other day in Mousehole. In that charming little woolen shop."

Ashamed, I couldn't look at her. "Yes. With my daughter. That was our first day here."

She turned toward me with a welcoming smile. "That's lovely. Are you enjoying your holiday?"

I laughed. "Yes, although you wouldn't know it today."

"Maybe not today." She rubbed Wally, who had settled at her feet. "Where in America are you from?"

"Blair and I live in Virginia." I heard the slight quiver in my voice.

"Just the two of you?" Again, that direct stare.

"Yes…Edward…" I looked away, swallowed hard. "I'm a widow." The word still stuck in my throat.

"I am sorry. I, too, am a widow. Twenty-seven years last February." I looked away from some of the kindest eyes I had ever seen. "It gets easier. With time. How long has it been?"

"A year. In a car accident with Blair."

"How awful. Was she injured?"

I nodded, remembering the days in the hospital when I thought she might die too. Nausea rolled through me, and I grew faint.

"Oh my dear, steady on. Such a lot for you to bear. You're still so young."

"I don't feel young anymore." I hadn't walked someone through the story in a long time and was surprised at the fresh pain.

Eleanor nodded. "So you're here on holiday to catch your breath. Jolly good." She rooted around in her bag, extracted a small tin and removed the lid. "Biscuit?" The buttery shortbread melted on my tongue, a welcome relief from the salty tears I could still taste. "What made you choose Cornwall, Mrs. Morgan?"

How was it that this woman's questions could hit so many nerves? Memories of planning a trip with my mother while she raced against cancer swirled in my head. The cancer won and there was no trip. But afraid of sounding as pathetic as I felt, I left that out. "Suzanne, please." She nodded. "It's a place I've always wanted to come. There was a painting called *Cornish Morning*. It piqued my interest." I also left out the part about the painting hanging in the living room of my childhood home. "Have you always lived here?"

"Not only that, but my whole life in the same house. Penwylln. It's a behemoth, cold and drafty, but it's the only home I've ever known. Cornish first, English second. I suppose I shall die there. My daughter and grandchildren live with me. They've brought a bit of life back to the house. Before that, I kept up with my garden, book club, and local events. Not a very useful existence, I suppose, but a pleasant one."

"It sounds wonderful. My life is too hectic. Taking care of Blair and running the business." I hadn't meant to say too hectic. Leave the personal commentary out of conversation, I told myself.

"You're a businesswoman?"

"Edward and I...I mean, I own Morgan's, a small chain of women's boutiques in the Washington, D.C. area. Apparel, shoes, accessories."

"That explains why you look so lovely. Some women have an eye for those things. That young woman I was speaking with in the woolen shop has just such an eye."

I grew hot at the memory of her friend's angry eyes. Eleanor didn't seem to notice. "She's an artist. Jillian Allingham. Done well for herself. Has a shop in St. Ives and sells in London. Bit of a local celebrity."

Eleanor reached for another slice of shortbread. I drifted off, remembering how much Edward loved the spotlight. In the Washington business community, he was quite well known. "Edward, a good solid name. Tell me about him, will you?"

Her words reeled me back into the painful present. "A boring story really. Met in college, fell in love quickly, or at least I did." My finger made circles in the sand. "Edward always said I had to grow on him." I gave a hollow laugh and saw Eleanor's lips purse. "He was strong, smart and knew exactly where he wanted to go." My circles turned to hearts, which I drew and erased.

"Did he get there, wherever that was?" she asked, as though studying my answers.

"Oh, yes. He was very successful. He loved the business. I'm not sure he ever missed a day of work."

"A source of pride, indeed," she said firmly.

"It was for him. It used to annoy him when I got a cold or had to miss a day when Blair got sick. He was thoroughly dedicated."

"Mmm." She looked away briefly. I felt an odd tightening in my stomach.

"I understand how he felt. But I also felt sorry for Blair when she needed me. Once I tried...well, anyway, Edward was a doting father. He loved for her to be a class leader or win blue ribbons at the horse shows. Blair loved to make her Dad proud."

"Not all children strive to win their parent's approval." She continued to stroke Wally's head. He wriggled onto his back and looked up at her. Without a pause, she stroked his belly.

"I wouldn't say she was striving for approval. But he had very high standards, and she liked showing him she was up to them."

"And you, my dear, were you up to them?"

"Usually. I tried to be."

Eleanor was still for a moment. Then she nodded and began to pack her bag. Silence always left me unsure of myself. Had I said too much? For so long, I'd lived in confusion about what was appropriate and what wasn't. Edward always balked when I spoke of him, saying I didn't guard his privacy. He had no qualms, however, in telling people at Morgan's about my tears over having a tubal ligation or the time Blair wet her pants at a Kennedy Center premier because she was embarrassed to walk up the aisle in front of everyone. Wally barked at two gulls near water's edge. She unhooked the leash. "Go on." He took off at a run. I wished I could do the same. "We must meet again. You and Blair could come to Penwylln for a proper tea and she could meet Fredericka and Simon. I'll ring you to make a date."

&

We spent the next week getting familiar with Mousehole. Before long, an easy routine emerged. We spent mornings at the cottage; reading in the garden, puttering in the kitchen, playing games at the table. After lunch we took off on foot. Our favorite spot quickly emerged. A sandy beach on the eastern edge of town. The accident had left Blair with lingering balance problems. The first day I worried about her on the sand, fighting for steady footing. For months I'd watched her struggle through the maddeningly slow progress of physical therapy. To my delight, she worked hard at improving her balance and gaining control, even learning to laugh when she fell.

These daily beach jaunts were followed by stops in The Mouse Hole. Blair especially loved a little curiosity shop that housed the kinds of treasures 10-year-old girls seem to love. She delighted in the endless key chains, Celtic jewelry, ceramic cats, and teapots, and found more than one keepsake to share with Rachel, her best friend at home.

We explored by car close to home. Blair squealed in delight each time we came in view of the water. Laughing, I told her she wouldn't be able to keep that up all summer or we might end up in a ditch. There was loveliness everywhere; wildflowers were strewn about hillsides lined with stone walls and bright green hedges. Bare rocks lent a strong, wild feel to the countryside. Church spires peeked out in the distance, suggesting small villages tucked amongst the hills. Cattle roamed through pastures, past red farmhouses and bright, tiny cottages.

"It's hard to believe people actually get to live in a place this beautiful, isn't it, Mommy?" We were standing at the end of the stone jetty in the town harbor, looking across the bay.

"Maybe they think we're lucky getting to live in the U.S., in such a nice neighborhood."

Blair watched the sea sparkle with sunlight. "I doubt it."

&

This was a day people dreamed about. Upper 70s, clear blue sky, a gentle breeze. We'd come to Lanhydrock to tour the house and gardens.

The legendary house, restored to its entire Victorian splendor, was beautiful, but it was the gardens that took our breath away. The Rhododendrons, begonias, magnolias and yews were magnificent, but it was the towering hydrangeas that captured our hearts.

"It's as if God himself planted these here," we overheard an elderly woman say to one of the gardeners employed on the estate.

"Maybe He did," the sun-worn fellow replied, "but it's me that tends to 'em. I know that much, don't I?" I stifled Blair's giggles with my hand.

We took our time in the gardens and then entered the house for a tour. An historical re-enactment invited us to participate in a weekend party. Blair found a Victorian girl near her own age and quickly took on her identity. She leapt into the scene wholeheartedly, acting out the whole charade. By the time Blair mentioned she was hungry, it was almost noon. A small cafe was set up in one of the servant's rooms. Lovely lace curtains, little table doilies, and wait staff in full costume completed the feeling that we'd stepped back in time. Our waitress, a pretty young girl named Amelia, suggested that Blair might like the egg mayonnaise sandwiches with crisps. Eager to please, Blair ordered it immediately.

I took a good long look at Blair, seeing a girl much like the one I'd known before the accident. But I could honestly say this one seemed not only healthier, but happier, too. Bright eyes sparkled out at me and rosy cheeks shone out beneath her suntan. The relaxing pace and daily trips to the shore were working magic. But was there something else contributing to the well-being of my daughter? I had my suspicions and decided to test the water.

"It's lovely here, isn't it?" I asked.

Blair nodded, and then added, smiling, "It's positively blissful." Erupting in giggles, she confessed to having heard that phrase on an installment of *All Creatures Great and Small*. "Seriously, mommy, I love it here. I wish we didn't ever have to go back to Virginia. I didn't really like it there."

"But that's where school is and Rachel. Wouldn't you be sad not to see her?"

"Not any sadder than I already am." I knew what she meant.

"What about your school? You've been happy there."

Again, Blair shook her head. "I was, before...but it's not gonna be the same. They all had almost a whole year without me. I'll never fit back in."

Thinking how prone girls are to cliques, I thought this might be true.

"Couldn't we stay here? I could go to school here. Miss Buncle told me about the school and the principal. He has a barn and gives lessons."

"You'd have to make all new friends."

Blair grimaced, deep in thought. "I know. But I'll have to do that at home too. Everybody treats me differently, like they forgot who I was after the accident. I'm the same person. Can't they see that?"

The truth was that she was different. Not all together, just some times in some ways. A child couldn't go through this type of trauma and not be changed. "Of course they know you're the same person, but you do act differently sometimes. That confuses people into thinking that you are different. People who really know you, like Rachel and me, know that isn't true." I wasn't sure why I couldn't tell her about the differences. At least, not yet.

"You're different here, too," Blair blurted out. "You're happier and more fun. And you spend a lot of time with me. I really like that."

"I'm glad you're having fun with me, but I get to spend more time with you because I'm not working. I would eventually have to get a job wherever we lived. You understand that, don't you?"

Blair shrugged. "I guess."

Amelia brought our lunch and Blair stuffed a handful of potato chips in her mouth. She took a huge bite out of her sandwich and then turned to me, puzzled.

"Daddy always said we were rich. If we're rich, why would you have to work?"

"Like it or not, I am responsible for the company." My neck tightened in tension, and I felt like I did when I had to answer my father's inquiries. I hadn't told her I was considering selling it.

"Well, you have people running it don't you? For the summer? They could just keep doing it. Or you could sell it. Daddy wouldn't mind." That was the problem. He would mind. He would hate me for it. It had been the most important thing in his life for over 10 years. "Even if he did," Blair continued, "he isn't here to say so, is he?"

Her flippant tone puzzled me. "That doesn't mean I don't still want to do what he would have wanted."

"Why?" Blair asked. I stared at her until the lengthening silence made her fidgety. "Why, Mommy? Are you still afraid of him?"

"What in the world are you talking about?" I recognized something in my voice which I hadn't heard since we'd left Great Falls. Awkwardness filled the space between us, and we finished lunch without another word.

As we drove back to Mousehole, I reconstructed the conversation in my mind. It had begun to degenerate when Blair suggested that I was happier since Edward died. I felt alone and accused. I could barely tolerate the idea that she would be so bad at reading me. I struggled with this idea the whole way home.

≈

After Blair had gone to bed that night, I put on a sweater and went outside. Lights glimmered in the village, and I watched a motorboat approach the harbor by the moonlight. From where I sat, I could nearly convince myself that it was a quiet, peaceful scene. The problem was I'd been on a motorboat. Noisy, bumpy. It was nothing like I could pretend from here. Cathy, my father, and even Blair imagined they knew what my life was like. But their imaginings were not my reality.

*You could do what you want, couldn't you...Edward isn't here, is he?* Blair's words filled my mind and echoed those of Cathy just a month before. *...do what you want...* I could hear their words as if they'd been in the garden with me. Could I do what I wanted? What *did* I want?

Tears started slowly at first, then sobs overtook me, making breathing hard. What was wrong with me? I didn't know myself at all. I was a person living as a creation of Edward's. I'd grown comfortable with his control because he told me it was good for me. He had convinced me he knew me better than I knew myself. I'd let it become true because I gave up the right to being me. To having opinions, to getting my way, to knowing what I wanted.

But that plan fell apart, didn't it, Edward? You left me. You aren't here any longer to tell me what to do. And you made me believe any choice I'd make for myself would be a bad one. I can think of one that was a mistake—I stopped myself, and ran inside. Frantically I searched through the medicine cabinet until I found the sleeping pills the doctor had prescribed after Edward's death. I gulped two down, and in short order was sound asleep.

2

# Peter

My head was full of lists as I filled the scooper with grain: who was on for afternoon lessons, what needed repair at Oakton, and preparations for Thomas' arrival. Enough for one day, I realized, my arm heavier with each scoop. It had been a surprise when Thomas called and said he wanted to come for the weekend. It hadn't been easy to arrange a substitute for Saturday lessons and feedings. But I'd had no choice. It had been months, maybe closer to a year, since I'd seen my older brother. Wondering what the occasion was, I almost called Mum for an explanation. In the end, I decided to wait and see. Fortunately, waiting was no problem. If there was one thing I had learned in the past five years, it was to be a patient man.

The Stewart men have never been afraid of a good, solid hug. Our Da made sure of that, hugging us all our lives. Now, in the doorway of my cottage, we embraced, finding it hard to speak for all the love that sat lodged in our throats.

"I've missed you, Petie."

I thumped him on the back. "I've missed you, too. And I still hate it when you call me by that stupid name." Thomas smiled wide as the Channel. The laugh lines, etched like parentheses around his eyes, didn't belong to a bitter man.

Winston, my bulldog and companion of three years, joined me in welcoming him. Home for us was a stone cottage, hidden among a grove of trees a mile from my stable. It had a thatched roof, bright blue doors

13

and window frames; I had to duck each time I entered. It had been painted white recently enough, so it still looked fresh and clean. While the outside was tidy, the inside hadn't fared as well. The shelves, once neat and pristine, now overflowed in a jumble of books, knickknacks and pictures. Worn leather chairs and overstuffed pillows sat as an open invitation to get comfortable. After so many years, this was my shelter from the storms of the school, the stable, and life.

I handed him a pint from the icebox and we sat down together. Thomas took a long look at me. "You don't seem to find many reasons to come to Yorkshire." We settled deeper into the chairs; I could feel the strain between us.

I eyed him with suspicion. "You didn't come to—"

"Slow down. I didn't come to start a row with you. I just wanted to check in. We don't hear from you very often, now, do we? You're missed by us all."

"It does me good to see you, I'll admit that. How is everyone?"

"Managing, at least. Mum's a lifesaver. Don't know where I'd be without her," Thomas said. Raising his bottle to his mother's strength, he added, "We're blessed to have her."

"To Mum." Up went my hand.

"She misses hearing from you. It's another loss. Too much of it in a short time." He rolled the bottle in his hands, his wedding ring clinking against the glass with each revolution.

Some wounds just weren't to be avoided. "I don't know why I keep my distance. It's wrong, I know that. I just can't seem to…" I ran my hand through my hair, scratching my head.

"I wasn't saying it to make you feel guilty, Pete. But you need to know she's suffering, too."

I nodded, hating the knowledge that I had added to her pain.

When Thomas continued, his voice was softer. "How do people go through these trials without hope? I'd have gone round the bend, been a nutter, if I hadn't had someplace to take the grief." Watching Thomas deal with the death of our father five years ago, followed by the death of his wife just a few months later, moved him to hero status in my book.

Thomas' voice grew husky. "And some days it's as raw as if it just happened." I nodded, and he nodded back. "Still, the kids are good. Archie loves his sports, although winning is too important to him. He almost got banned from the league after a particularly nasty outburst following the loss of the district championship game. I begged them to give him another chance, explaining how tough things have been for him since his mum died."

"And Lily is a sweet little lamb, all smiles and hugs. Frannie can be a handful, but she's a great girl. Helped us survive. She's doing well in her studies and keeps busy with friends. No one she's keen on. Yet."

I realized that I barely knew them anymore. "I miss that brood of yours. I'll have to pay them a visit before they're grown and gone." I flushed bright red, regretting the words as soon as they left my mouth, but Thomas didn't flinch.

"What about you? Anything new in your life? Anyone?" I shrugged, but remained tightlipped. "Come on, Pete. Talk to me. Surely there's someone here that you enjoy being with."

"There's a woman I spend time with." I shifted in my seat, ready to meet any objections.

Looking pleased, Thomas pushed for details. "That's grand. Tell me about her."

"You wouldn't approve of Jillian."

"Why not?"

"You just wouldn't." I'd been dreading this conversation.

Thomas appeared to be measuring his words. "Are you thinking of marrying her?"

"Of course I'm not thinking of marrying her. Her or anyone else."

"I'm just asking because—"

I interrupted. "I know why you're asking." I grew uncomfortable under his gaze. Finally, an unspoken truce was declared, and we each sat back and relaxed.

"What are you doing then? Is this wise?" His voice mixed with fear and compassion.

"She's not serious about me. And she knows I'm not getting serious with anyone. We have some things in common, and we're spending a bit of time together. We're friends. That's all. Isn't that what you wanted?" I waited for the inquisition to continue.

He sighed, lost in thought for a minute. "What I want is for you to move on with your life, make peace with the past. I would expect that to include dating and, eventually, marrying." I looked at him as though he'd suddenly sprouted horns. We sat in prolonged silence until we both grew fidgety, another trait of the Stewart men.

And then Thomas shifted gears, speaking in his sunny voice. "I'll have to bring Mum and the kids down next summer. It's been years since we've taken a seaside holiday. I'm sure you could get us set up in a nice B&B."

Although I hadn't a clue why he'd backed off, I was happy to play along. "Right. It would be brilliant to see everyone again."

⤸

Ignoring the frown on Thomas' face, I pulled into the car park at Frederico's, the newest chain of restaurants to make it to this corner of England. The sign by the road boasted live entertainment on the weekends. I was confident Thomas would get my none-too-subtle message; this was not a place for intimate conversation. The music's deep throbbing base—boom-boom, boom-boom—blasted us as we walked in the room. But Thomas was undeterred. We placed our orders, and he picked up right where we had left off.

"I'd like to meet Jillian."

"Why?"

"Why not? If you're interested in her."

Boom-boom, boom-boom.

My eyes narrowed. "I told you—we're just friends. It's nothing serious." The motion and noise of the busy restaurant swirled around me. Each breath seemed harder to get. "Why are you going on about it?"

I had planned on being the calm one, but it was Thomas who exuded a steady, quiet control. Oblivious to the riot around us, he just smiled his big brother smile and said, "I worry about you, little brother."

"Maybe it's you we should be worrying about."

His smile faded. "What does that mean?"

"I don't see you dating anyone."

"Jeez, Peter, Liza died."

"Yeah, four years ago. Isn't it time for you to find another woman? You're ready enough for me to get on with things."

"I was married for almost 20 years. It's not the same. "

"Why isn't it the same?" I knew the answer but wasn't in a mind to back down now. Before he could speak, the waitress appeared with our food, giving a chance for both of us to sit back and take a breath.

"Don't answer," I said when she left. "I know it's different. Still, I think you've got even more reason to be in a relationship than I have. Three reasons, if I'm not mistaken."

"It's because of those reasons that I'm so cautious. Bringing the wrong woman into our family could do far more harm than good. It's not something I'm willing to rush into. I have to be sure."

"Me too," I said loudly, slamming my glass on the table. Beer spilled out over my hand and across the table, soaking our forgotten menus. I tried to clean up the mess I'd made but quickly ran out of paper serviettes. Frustrated, I looked around for more, but there was nothing in sight. Thomas made no move to help me, but watched, stone-faced, while I walked over towards the wait station and grabbed extra serviettes. Back at the table, I threw them onto the mess and sat hard into my seat. I finished what little beer remained and felt a deep sigh rise up within me. Suddenly, I felt drenched in sadness, not so easily mopped up.

I hated saying the words that sat ready on my tongue, but I was powerless to stop them. "I loved her like a wife."

"You couldn't have. You don't know what you are talking about." The sharpness of his words drew blood as surely as if I'd been stabbed.

"You don't either. You've barely seen me for five years—"

"And whose fault is that?" Thomas demanded.

I stood up with a force that pushed my chair halfway to the nearest booth. "Mine," I yelled at him. "Everything is my fault. Isn't that what you really think?"

Grabbing my jacket off the back of my chair, I fled outside. The car park was crowded and it took a few moments before I found my car—sandwiched between a Range Rover and a tiny Ford. I fumbled with my keys, finally opening the door, banging it into the Range Rover's passenger door and leaving a dent, when Thomas sprinted up to the car.

"You were going off without me, weren't you?" he accused.

Scowling, I pushed the button that automatically unlocked all the doors so he could get in. Before his shut, I'd already started the car and put it in reverse, flooring it the moment it was in gear. A furious horn blared behind us; Thomas made a strangled noise. I reversed, missing the car behind by centimeters, and sped towards the way out. Cutting the turn too close, I clipped a pole and put a dent in my front mudguard.

I went straight to bed without a word, leaving Thomas to fend for himself. Sometime in the night, I woke and made my way through the darkness into the kitchen. I turned on the light and reached for the kettle.

"Oh," I mumbled, surprised to see my brother, wrapped in a blanket and standing in the doorway. "Sorry I woke you. I got hungry."

"What's that?" Thomas asked, looking at the frying pan.

"Thursday night's supper. Get a plate." We sat across from each other, chewing silently. The clock on the wall clicked loudly, the minute hand ticking off the slow seconds. After four clicks, I pulled the clock from the wall, removed the batteries and placed it back. We finished our belated meal in silence.

"I really am chuffed you came," I said sheepishly, dropping the fork onto the empty plate.

Thomas laughed, clearly happy to see that the storm had passed. "Me too. Even considering tonight."

I saw, in the man sitting across the table, the brother who had always watched out for me, always put me first. "I guess I was a pretty nasty beast. Humiliating, really."

"Yes, well, we could have another go at talking. Maybe this time you could keep straight that I'm not the enemy," Thomas said.

"Right. I don't even know why I went off last night." I looked to Thomas for help. I had enjoyed lifelong praise from schoolmasters and coaches for my self-control. Losing it grandly and publicly like I did tonight was as frightening as it was unexpected. One of Laura's complaints about me was that I lacked a certain passion. She should have seen me tonight. "Your being here has really shaken me up. Honestly, I didn't expect it."

"I can see that. Sorry."

"Don't be." I choked up. "I've been happy here. Really I have."

Thomas nodded like he believed me to be in earnest.

"But I've also been hiding. I'm a grown man, for crying out loud. And I probably know less about myself than your Archie does about himself." I hated my weakness. "I used to be so confident, so sure."

Thomas finished my sentence. "... Of yourself."

I nodded slowly. "There's almost nothing of me left." I carried my plate to the sink. "I'm not sure I'm going to survive it. I can't see an end to the pain." I kept my back to him.

He pushed back his chair with a loud scrape. "Your family loves you, Peter. Just let us; don't be too proud." His strong arms gripped me like I was a kid again.

"I can't seem to find solid ground," I said. "And with Dad's and Liza's deaths, and then losing Laura..." My voice broke. Thomas kept his arms around me and let me grieve. "I barely know what way is up."

"Peter, when you're out on that boat of yours and waves get rough you look at the horizon to steady you. Head back, nose up, searching off in the distance. You're on dry ground now and that doesn't work. Keeping your eye off in the distance only makes you think about how far away you are from it. You need to be bowed over, looking down, watching your feet. Focus on each step, and before you know it you'll have traveled the long path to healing."

We spent the rest of the morning talking about work. When we said our goodbyes, it was with a promise to see each other again soon.

⸎

It was my favorite place, my secret studio. Wind tossed heaths and gray-green grasses to the north and blue sea to the south. I perched on a bare rock, flat enough to set up my chair and easel. A small mound protected me from passers-by along the cliff path just fifteen meters from here. It didn't take me long to make the trek from the car park to my spot; I never tired of the view here. Once, when I needed to stretch my legs after a time of concentrated painting, I walked the short distance to Eric Forbes' cottage.

I'd found Eric struggling to cut wood for heat two winters ago. His frail arms lifted and dropped the axe nearer to his feet with each swing and I'd come running before he did himself harm. We forged a friendship over cups of weak tea and slightly stale bread. I remembered the first time I'd heard about him at the pub shortly after coming to Cornwall. His people had been fishermen. Like them, he'd spent his life on the sea. He had been deeply devoted to Daisy, his wife, who'd been gone ten years. They lost two children in infancy, but no one had ever heard either of them say a word about the heartbreak of that. I found him even more wonderful than I'd expected, and our visits became more regular, both of us glad to ease our loneliness a bit.

The sky and sea this afternoon ran together like a Monet landscape; it was hard to tell where one ended and the next began. Probably meant a storm coming. In the distance, a fishing boat tossed high into the air, almost as if the water were trying to expel it. I feared for the fishermen and followed it until it made its way into a distant harbor. As I squirted a bit of the blue and gray onto the palette, I felt a sudden pang about Eric. How long had it been since I'd gone by? Last week? A fortnight? I remembered him telling me that the new vicar came by occasionally, and that the parish helped supply some of his needs. But everything I'd seen of Ian Hamilton led me to conclude that he probably wouldn't be making the trek from town unless there were blue skies overhead. Standing there, thinking of Eric, I suddenly knew I couldn't wait another minute. I took off at a run down the foot path.

Seeing no smoke from his chimney, my stomach and chest tightened. I knocked and opened the door before he could answer. Inside, it was dim and dank, without even a single lamp turned on. Eric lay huddled under a faded duvet. I rushed to him, held my fingers to his neck, and watched his eyes flicker. Relieved, I bent down to him.

"I was worried you were... What's wrong? Why is there no fire, no lights?"

His dry, thin lips trembled. "I didn't mean to frighten you. I was saving my wood for a cold day."

"Eric, *this* is a cold day." It was an unseasonable 56 degrees outside.

"Aye, but then, you never know what tomorrow will bring." He winced as he spoke. "I didn't want to get caught wanting in case the weather turned a bit nasty." There was no use arguing with him, he'd lived this way all his life.

I put my hand on his forehead. "You have fever. Does your throat hurt you?"

"A wee bit."

I wrapped the comforter even tighter around his frail body, placed a ragged blanket on top, and put the kettle on. The cupboards and icebox were practically bare. I cursed the parish under my breath. Weren't they supposed to be responsible for delivering groceries? And I cursed myself. I'd remembered to fill the boot of my motor car full of painting supplies, but not to bring a morsel of food for a helpless old man. After feeding him some tea, I laid him carefully back on the bed.

"I need to go and get food for you. I'm going to build a fire and then I'll pop out and be back before you need another log." Too polite to argue, I knew he worried about his supply of firewood. "I'll fetch more wood for you after I return."

Nearly reckless with guilt, I drove to Tescos grocery store and hurried in. Poor Eric didn't stand much of a chance of survival if he was dependent on that pompous Ian Hamilton or me. Parents of several of my students greeted me as I flew down the aisles. I hesitated at the checkout, then added a frightfully expensive tin of sweets to my basket.

The drive back was agonizingly slow. I got stuck behind a meandering tourist, and it wasn't until I pulled into the car park that I realized I should have stopped by the house to feed Winston. Carrier bags in hand, I ran for the cottage, stumbling through the door. His breathing had turned raspy and he looked even weaker than when I left. Suddenly, I was uncertain how to help him. Every instinct told me to get help, but I was afraid to leave him alone. If he got too bad, I would take him to the hospital. But knowing him as I did, that would have to be a last resort. I stopped for a minute, took a deep breath, and tried to think of what to do. And then I remembered what Thomas had done with Frannie when she was a baby.

"Eric," I called out, "I think I know how to ease your breathing." I hurried to put water on the stove and raced through the kitchen, stashing perishables in the icebox, setting the soup on to heat, and starting a pot of tea. That done, I carried a towel and a bowl of boiling water over to where he lay.

"Lean on me and breathe as deeply as you can." I pulled his fragile body into a sitting position, the bowl in my lap and the threadbare towel over our heads. "Now Mr. Forbes," I said with mock-seriousness, "I imagine you are wondering why I've arranged this meeting."

The corners of his mouth turned up slightly as he breathed in the moist air. After only two refills, it was clear that he was worn out from sitting up. His breathing had improved slightly, so I laid him down and brought over the soup and tea. Something nagged at me, though. I'd forgotten something. A faint voice interrupted my thoughts.

"I'm sorry for the bother," Eric whispered.

I looked down into his eyes and put my arm across his bony shoulder. I didn't like to put people out either. "You are no bother. You're my friend." Feeding him was painstakingly slow, testing my reserves of patience and compassion. It reminded me that plenty of people had been patient with me as I muddled through life.

"Have you had any other visitors lately, Eric?"

"Rector Hamilton came by."

"When was that?"

"Now let's see. It was before that terrible storm."

"That's a month ago." Indignation flamed in me.

"Aye, I think that's right. It's so very much trouble to get here. The roads get bad you know." Apparently Eric didn't know that Rector Hamilton drove a car known for its off-road capabilities. A bit of rain in Cornwall wasn't even a hiccup for him.

"Yes, well, anyone else?"

"Now and again, someone walking the moors waves hello. If I needed anything, I suppose I could ask them."

"Oh Eric, I've not been the friend to you that I should have been. I'm ashamed to find your cupboards bare and you almost out of fuel for heat." I put my hand atop his. "Please forgive me," I pleaded. "You deserve a better friend than me."

"That's rubbish. You are as good a friend as I've known." If that was true, my heart broke over a lifetime of dismal friendships. "I'd forgive you if there was anything to forgive. In truth, you are an answer to an old man's prayers." Uncomfortable with physical affection, he withdrew his hand. "God's been gracious to me all my life. I've not wanted for anything, except maybe some company. And here you are." He struggled to swallow, wincing in pain.

"You need to stop talking now. I've brought some lozenges from the market. Let me get one." I sat beside him, studying his pale, weary face. I realized I'd forgotten to give him something for the fever when he was eating. He was almost asleep now, so I just got a cool cloth and laid it on his forehead.

Washing up and putting away groceries didn't take long, and then I settled into the rocking chair. I would arrange a firewood delivery, no matter how much he protested. What a wonder Eric was, with his beautiful, simple faith. He wasn't simple-minded, not at all. Just simple-hearted. I was jealous. He had a peace and contentment that constantly eluded me. His simplicity was foreign to most people. Jillian thought him a bit daft.

*Jillian.* Oh no. What time was it? I had a date with Jillian. Tonight. An hour ago. What could I do? I didn't bring my mobile and I couldn't leave Eric. She'd be livid, but I had to believe she would understand once I explained. Or would she? Suddenly, I wasn't so sure. But there was nothing I could do now. I checked again on Eric. His sleep had turned fitful. I brought another cool rag to lie on his forehead.

It was a long night as Eric suffered with chills, fever, and restless sleep. I worked at keeping him comfortable, sponging his head, coaxing him to sip tea, tucking the covers in around him. He laid there in a hazy fog, never fully awake. I wondered what would have happened if I'd not come.

I woke, disoriented, to light streaming through the windows to the east. A moment's confusion until I saw Eric on his bed, pale and weak, but sitting up, bright-eyed.

"Good morn'n to you. You must be right worn out from playing nurse to me."

I smiled and stretched, relieved. "You kept me busy, but I managed some rest too."

"My throat's not burning and I'm improved all around." His lips trembled. "Thank you, son."

⸎

Winston was sitting by the door when I opened it. He waddled across the lane to the woods while I checked the house for evidence that the time had been too much for him. Pleased to find none, I caught up with him, rubbing his head and back vigorously.

"Good old dependable Win."

"At least someone is dependable." I hadn't heard Jillian approaching, but smiled at seeing her.

"Oh Jillian, I'm glad to see you."

"Are you?" Her body wore the tension reflected on her face.

"Of course." She looked at me blankly. I continued, "Let me explain—"

"Yes, do." Her voice was taut.

"I went out to the cliffs to do some painting yesterday after lessons. Realizing it had been weeks since I'd checked in on Eric, I went to his cottage. I found him there sick, chilled, and almost out of food. I ran to the market straight off and then spent the rest of the night tending to him."

"Yes. And?" Her hardness stunned me.

"Eric was sick and there was no one else." She looked at me, uncomprehending. I wondered if I'd stopped speaking in our mother tongue. She knew Eric was old and alone.

"Why didn't you just take him to hospital?"

"He's frail and he wanted to be home. As it happens, he is much improved this morning."

"A relief, I'm sure." She brushed away something from her sleeve.

"It is a relief. I care about him."

"Clearly." She said, without passion or sympathy.

I jammed my hands in my pockets and started back, Winston lumbering beside me. Jillian's angry steps weren't far behind. Inside, I put the kettle on and joined her in the living room.

"Jillian, I would have phoned, but I didn't have my mobile. I really had no choice. He lives alone; there was no one else to help him. Can't you see that?"

"I do, I suppose. But I think you should have found a way to ring me. You said you went to the market. Why didn't you try me then?"

I rubbed my face and sighed. "I forgot."

"Forgot?"

"I was worried about Eric."

"You forgot that we were to meet altogether?"

"Yes, and then to call. And I am sorry. Won't you forgive me?"

A shadow fell across her face. "I'm not sure it should be that easy, really. You stood me up, making me look the fool, and then expect that with a quick apology, I'll just say everything is fine. Well, I don't think it is."

"I don't know what else to say. I'm sorry I didn't ring, and especially sorry that your feelings were hurt, but I did the right thing, and I'd do it again," I said, my voice rising. After a moment's pause, I added, "Eric needed me. I expected you would understand."

Jillian's eyes were cold, locking into mine as if to try and stare me down. "You made your choice, Peter."

When it became clear to her that I had nothing more to say, she left, furious, rocks spraying out from her tires. As angry as I was at her cold heart, I knew only one thing would break through it. And it was the same thing that had once broken through to mine.

# 3

# *Suzanne*

"…didn't like him. Did you?" Blair squeezed my hand. It was Sunday morning and we were walking up Duck Street from the harbor.

"What did you say?"

"I didn't like that minister very much. He was mean."

"He wasn't mean. You were stepping in his flowers," I explained to my half-limping, half-skipping child.

"Only because I tripped."

"But he didn't see you trip; he only saw you standing in the flowerbed. Anyway, he wasn't mean about it."

"Well, he wasn't nice," she scowled. "He yelled at me to get off his Primlas or something. Some lady tried to tell him it was an accident, but he didn't believe her."

Inside the cottage, Blair disappeared to her room. I went into the kitchen to make lunch and take a mental inventory of the morning. We visited St. Stephen's Anglican Church, the only one in Mousehole. Cathedral-like and majestic, its stained glass windows told the story of a crusader knight venturing off to fight the infidels and of his triumphant return. It seemed a bit grand for this little village. Embroidered kneeling cushions brought some warmth to the medieval building. We'd failed to realize the stone floors and cavernous architecture would make it a good ten degrees cooler inside the church and wished we'd brought sweaters.

I was grateful the short sermon did not test Blair's endurance, as a long one would have. At the completion of the service, Dr. Hamilton went to the door to greet his parishioners. When it was my turn, he offered his hand, as soft as kid leather. His perfect face looked as though it had been sculpted, but it was his sapphire eyes that jolted me.

"A visitor? And you are?"

"Suzanne Morgan."

"An American on holiday. Where to next?"

"We're here for the summer, at Wisteria Cottage."

"How delightful for you," he said, suddenly interested and taking a hurried inventory of me. "I hope you have felt welcome thus far. Actually, I should like to take tea with you. I'll ring you. I have the number." He didn't wait for my response but turned to greet the man shuffling behind me. I would enjoy having another adult to talk to, but something about him made me nervous.

I caught up with Blair on the sidewalk. Still wobbly from descending the front stairs, her weak foot dragged as she tried to keep step with me. I was distracted looking for Eleanor, who'd said she might be at the service, and didn't realize Blair had lost her balance and tripped into a flowerbed. By the time I turned back, she was struggling to extricate herself. I was sure that Blair's dislike for Dr. Hamilton was rooted more in her embarrassment than any supposed harshness. Over a lunch of tuna sandwiches and potato chips, we agreed to disagree about the rector.

❧

We woke Tuesday morning to a gray flannel sky. Blair bounded into the kitchen and came to a sudden stop.

"And here's the lady of leisure herself. Good morning." Ian Hamilton glanced at his watch.

"Morning," she answered curtly. Eyeing him suspiciously, she tramped over to where I was sitting and gave me a kiss on the cheek.

"Honey, do you remember Dr. Hamilton?" I asked. Oh, right. The episode with the flowerbed. "Why don't you sit here and visit while I fix your breakfast? I was just telling him about you."

Blair looked at me imploringly, but took a seat. Ian watched her with a puzzled expression and then seemed to recall something. "Blair, I understand you're a horsewoman."

"Yes sir." She offered only a flat voice and downcast eyes.

"And that you ride hunter/jumper."

"I did."

"I see." He took a bite of his coffee cake. Blair studied her fingernails, ragged from constant chewing. I'd given up trying to rid of her the habit, at least this year.

"Why don't you tell him what you got blue ribbons for?"

"Equitation," she mumbled.

"Aha." There was a long pause, and I thought that might be the end of their conversation. Ian cleared his throat. "Will you miss it very much while you're away from home?"

"I haven't ridden since the...since last year."

Ian looked helpless, so I jumped in. "But Mrs. Howell left the name of a someone who owns a stable. I thought we might visit."

"Peter Stewart," he said sourly.

I reached into the drawer for the list. "That's right." Turning to Blair, I said, "Would you like me to call him?" She nodded, excused herself, and fled.

There was no certainty that she'd ever get back on a horse. It would require the right horse and instructor, and bales of patience and courage. Until then, Blair would have to be satisfied with being near her heart's desire, yet having it constantly out of reach. I didn't think I could do that.

"Sometimes," I told him, "I'm amazed by her strength."

"Who?" he asked, as though new to the conversation. It reminded me of when Edward would ask an obvious question to indicate his desire for a change of subject. I disliked it when Edward did it, and I couldn't help but wonder at Ian's motive.

"Blair, of course. She's come a long way since the accident."

"What accident?" Something in the way he asked caught me off guard. He was a different person from the one who had been sitting here just a few moments ago. His eyes were softer and his voice more soothing. This time, I believed he didn't already know the answer to his question.

Picking up the kettle, I asked, "Would you like more tea?"

"Only if I have reason to stay a while longer," he said, without a hint of teasing.

"You do." I handed him the cup. I gave him the facts, carefully avoiding mention of my fear, anger, grief, and relief. Though my voice still quivered. He put his hand on my arm. His expression changed very little as I continued. When I got to the part about meeting Eleanor on the beach, he gave a nod.

"Eleanor has done a lot of grieving herself," I said. "She understood my wanting to get away for a while and have the time with Blair."

"Blair seems to be recovering well enough."

"She still has problems with mobility and balance but improves almost daily." I hesitated, and then decided to set the record straight. "On Sunday, when you looked up to find her standing in your flowerbed, she had just lost her balance and fallen back. She was terribly embarrassed when you spoke to her."

"I had no idea," he admitted. "I thought she was just another of those selfish brats who doesn't care whose flowers they trample." He reminded me of my father, to whom order was the stuff of life.

"She wouldn't do something like that. Edward and I have always been very strict about manners." The words echoed in my mind. "I continue to be."

My discomfort appeared to go unnoticed as he said, "She looks quite healthy. I think Cornwall agrees with her."

"I think so, too. Blair likes it here more than I'd dared hope she would."

"And you? Do you like it here?" He was eager, holding his breath.

"Very much. It's a comfortable place and I feel at home." There were aspects of talking to Ian that reminded me of talking to the Edward I first met. Interested, focused, sometimes sympathetic. I found myself relaxing more and more.

Ian told me about his quiet upbringing as an only child to an older couple. Then he talked of going to seminary, graduating first in his class, his first parish in Oxford, and finally, his assignment to Mousehole. "It seemed like a nothing little village when I first came. I was still unsure until I met Eleanor. She reminded me of my mother. She didn't mince words and encouraged me to look below the surface of Mousehole. I did, and I found what I needed. I've been here ever since."

"What did you need?"

"A place to stand out, where my talents would be noticed."

I couldn't imagine anyone wanting that.

I loved the stark, mysterious beauty of Cornwall. Discovering the English are fanatics about their footpaths, I consulted the Ordinance

Survey map and Mrs. Howell's notes. One afternoon, I put my reluctant daughter in the car and set off toward Zennor.

Thirty minutes into the walk, Blair started whining. "Mom, I'm really tired. My leg is hurting." She exaggerated her limp to make the point.

I knew she could do this, so I pressed on. "Let's slow down then. It isn't that much farther and I really want to see it today." I had read about a particularly dramatic stretch that also was the home to a historic cottage.

"Why do we have to see it today?"

"I told you. The woman who lived there died recently, and it's been deeded to the National Trust. She was a local poet."

"Ooo, that's creepy."

"What are you talking about?"

"I don't want to go in where someone just died."

"That's ridiculous. We still live in our house, even though Daddy died."

I regretted the words as soon as I said them. Blair's mood always darkened at the mention of Edward.

"Well, if it's so nice at the house of a dead person, why are we over here for the summer?"

I stopped and grabbed her shoulders. "I am not asking for the moon. I want to see the cottage, and I thought you might enjoy it too. I know it's tiring for you, but I also know that you didn't complain when we walked to and from beaches for the past two weeks. I would appreciate it if you would cooperate with me."

Blair mumbled her "yes ma'am" and kept walking. I kept the pace easy for her, and we didn't speak again until it was in view.

"Look honey, isn't it pretty?" The tiny stone cottage was plain and square, with a row of flowers across the front.

Blair scowled. "I guess it's okay." Fed up with her attitude, I walked ahead and peered in a window. Though sparsely furnished, it still looked inhabited. Then I reached for the doorknob. "What are you doing?"

"Going inside."

"I don't like it here."

"If you don't want to come in, stay here. I won't be long."

"But Mom—"

Ignoring her, I tried the door. To my delight, it opened.

I entered the cottage and was immediately transported to another era. An old basket, probably used to gather eggs, sat on the kitchen table. Picking it up, I held the basket close to my chest and thought about the life lived in a place like this. One filled with humble pleasures and pursuits. I stood still, savoring the thought of a life of such beauty and simplicity. And then it occurred to me that Edward would have characterized it quite differently—a life of destitution and humiliation.

I'd begun to see how Edward had convinced me that eating in the right places, even eating the right food, mattered to others and should matter to me. He convinced me that possessions were the measures of people. I felt ashamed of myself and who I'd become. He could never have seen the grace and dignity in this life, and I was angry with him for it. I replaced the basket and walked over to the faded curtains. Keeping your hands off the artifacts was a basic rule of tourism, but I couldn't help myself. Standing here, inside this quiet, primitive little place, something shifted in my heart. And touching these things made that shift, whatever it was, more alive to me.

I stood by the window, stroking the rough blue cloth, and looked outside. I didn't see Blair by the path. The spell broken, I ran outside, calling out several times before seeing her return over the rise of a hill.

"Come look," Blair called, pointing back where she had come from. We'd happened upon a wide field of flowers, each outshining the other. I recognized the bluebells but couldn't name the pink ones. To the south was a sudden drop to the sea. And to the west were rolling farms, their hedgerows separating one man's kingdom from another, until even they had to bow to the sand and sea.

In the distance, a single sailboat danced upon the waves. Blue hulled and gleaming white, she moved with grace and ease. It was a mesmerizing sight, a vision too beautiful for this flawed earth. Neither of us spoke. Finally, when the sailboat disappeared from sight, we reluctantly rose to leave.

"It's nice here, like you said." Blair reached for my hand as we walked back towards the path.

"I'm glad you like it. Could you imagine living here?"

She pulled her hand away. "I don't want to live here. I didn't mean that."

"I'm not making plans; I'm just asking you how you feel."

"Why are you changing things? We had everything figured out." Blair started to cry, her face contorted in frustration.

I fought to control mine, mostly at myself for ruining a nice moment. "You're being silly."

"We'll have to move and we'll go where you want to go, just like we always did what Daddy wanted to do," she shouted. "What about what I want?" She turned and went in the direction of the car, her gait a pathetic combination of limping and stomping in a sort of *Mouse that Roared* moment. She turned a corner and was out of sight.

Immobilized by her outburst, I stood rooted to the ground, angry and bewildered. What did she mean we always did what Edward wanted? Did everything really revolve solely around Edward? How could she say I didn't care what she thought? Tears sprang to my eyes, but I pushed them away and hurried to catch up and set her straight.

The path hadn't seemed so narrow and curvy when we were first approaching the cottage. I kept expecting to find Blair around each bend. But my hopes were dashed with each successive step, and the path began to torment me. Anger, hurt, and frustration swirled inside me, a storm fueling itself. Was this a reaction to Edward's death or to coming to Cornwall for the summer? I didn't know if I should give comfort or correction. I rounded the corner by the field of flowers and nearly tripped over Blair and Agnes, sitting in the middle of the path. Blair was alternately holding and rubbing her left ankle.

"What happened?" I asked, bending down to look for myself.

"Tangled feet, right Blair?" Agnes answered for her. "Let's get you up, shall we?" She slipped her arm underneath Blair's and helped her up. "I often take an afternoon walk, and this is one of my regular routes. I'm surprised to find you here. Blair says you're wanting to move in." This was said more as a question than a statement.

"No, of course not. I was just saying this type of life appeals to me."

"Blair said she doesn't like it. Can't understand that myself. I've always loved the remote setting."

"Yes, I do too." Uncertain about what else Blair might have said, I was anxious to get her to the car and be on our way. Blair tried to put weight on her foot, but pulled up with each step.

"You'll want to put ice on that ankle and keep it elevated for the rest of the day. Probably be right as rain tomorrow."

After my difficult exchange with Blair, I realized that I wanted a friendly face at dinner tonight. Surprised by the invitation, Agnes accepted immediately. Blair and I rode back to Wisteria Cottage in betrayed silence.

∽

Agnes arrived at 7 o'clock with a bottle of wine in hand. I screwed the opener into the cork, watching tiny bits of cork spill out the top and onto the floor. I could feel the heat rise in my face. "I've never been good at this. That's why Edward... well anyway, I've made a mess of it. I'm sorry."

Reaching for the bottle, Agnes said, "No bother. Let me." She filled the glasses halfway, and we sat at the kitchen table and worked our way through a block of Gouda.

Agnes had known most everyone in the village her entire life. She'd gone off to Oxford to study English Literature, vowing never to return to what she viewed as an "inbred little village."

"I hadn't expected to want to come home, but things happen you don't expect." Her eyes clouded over. "But then, you found that out, didn't you? No one plans to be a widow, especially a young one."

A chill ran up my spine as it did every time someone called me that. Not long after Edwards's death, I'd sat in the doctor's office and stared at the *Marital Status* section for five minutes before checking the 'single' box with a shaking pen.

I must have looked surprised, so Agnes continued. "Eleanor told me that your husband was killed last year."

"It's been difficult, but I'm doing fine now." I used my practiced smile, the one I'd learned to use with my father and had perfected with Edward. It had served me well through the years, preventing many a fight. I hoped Agnes, like both of them, would be satisfied with the surface answer.

"That's brilliant. I remember when my mother died—I seemed to be tossed about by my emotions and memories for quite a long time. Then there was peaceful acceptance, followed by guilt, regret and general torment. It seemed to go on for years. I hope you'll have an easier time of it; maybe not everyone goes through those stages of grief that doctors prattle on about." She seemed to see through my carefully constructed answer straight to my heart.

Wanting to keep that subject off limits, I quickly asked Agnes about her life. "Is this what you'd always wanted to do? Be a librarian?"

Her face reddened. "No. I'd planned to stay at University and get my teaching credentials. Thought about going to London to teach underprivileged children."

"That's a noble plan. Why didn't you?"

"It didn't work out. It would have meant staying at Oxford another year and I preferred to be done. And hasn't it turned out smashingly?" The flat tone of her voice suggested something quite different.

While I put the finishing touches on dinner, Agnes went to check on Blair, who was sprawled out on her bed with a book and an icepack. "She's a sweet child," Agnes said as she came down the stairs. "And she seems to be happy here."

"Yes, we both are. I've already begun to dread returning to work," I said, explaining the demands of Morgan's. "Business wasn't my first choice. I've done well enough, but I changed my plans when we got serious so that we could do something together." There didn't seem to be any point now in admitting that I'd always planned to stop working all together once we had children. "So the strain of being in the world of business was manageable when Edward was alive because he kept me going. It's different now."

"What would you rather be doing?" Agnes asked in earnest.

"It's funny. I don't really know." I took a gulp of water and picked at my plate of spaghetti. "Haven't given it a thought since Morgan's is waiting for me."

"Sounds like a punishment." She mopped up sauce with her last piece of bread and then leaned toward me, in the way friends do when passing secrets. I followed her and leaned in. "Couldn't you sell it or hire someone to run it for you?"

I pulled back. "Edward would never want me to do that."

"Hmm. Well, yes, I can see that you might want to consider that, but then it's really your life, isn't it? He isn't there anymore, is he? I mean you *could* do what you want to do, couldn't you?"

∽

There was a steady decline in the number of shops and houses as we drove west with Ian. He said he'd chosen this outing especially for Blair's enjoyment. She chattered about all she saw, an indication of her excitement. When we reached a house standing alone in a treeless field, Ian said we were within a mile of the end of England.

"Surely you'll want to stop talking a moment and appreciate the majesty of this terrain."

He almost sounded lighthearted but the words were tinged with anger. I wondered how Blair would react, but she turned to look out the window.

"Let's walk awhile before worrying with the hamper," Ian said, turning off the car.

"But I'm really hungry," Blair cried. Our early lunch had worn off long ago.

"Ian, do you think we could give her a small snack to hold her over?"

"That won't be enough. I'm *really* hungry," Blair whined. Ian got the picnic hamper from the trunk of the car and pulled out an apple. Without a word he handed it to Blair.

"It's my fault she didn't have something before we left. We ran out of time," I said feebly.

We took off in the direction of the cliff's edge and the swirling water below. The rocky ground was hilly and uneven, testing Blair as she struggled to keep her balance. I offered a hand, but when Blair noticed Ian watching her, she refused the help. Within a few steps, Blair's left foot caught a ridge in the ground. She tripped, falling forward awkwardly, but managed to catch herself. We continued on without comment. As we approached the edge of the cliff, there were no guardrails or anything else to keep us from tumbling over the edge to the rocks 300 feet below.

Ignoring the sudden creeping pace with which I now moved, Ian strode past both of us and stood not two feet from the precipice. "Blair, come see this," he called over his shoulder.

"No," I shouted.

He turned and shot me an angry look. "I'll take care she doesn't slip. She really should see the gulls and the waves. It's why we came, isn't it?"

"I'll be careful," Blair said as she moved forward. I didn't know what to do and looked to Ian for help. He allowed her to hold onto his arm and they kept moving. He pointed out rocks and other obstacles on the ground until they stood at the edge. I joined them, feeling a bit dizzy. Ian talked sweetly to Blair, pointing out birds and boats and a lighthouse on a small island off in the distance. Blair listened attentively and asked questions. I think they forgot I was there.

After awhile, Blair needed to rest. She settled down among a group of large, moss-covered rocks. "Ian, won't you come sit with us?" I asked.

"I'd rather not take the chance of soiling my clothes," he answered stiffly. "And I could use a moment of quiet."

Blair laughed. "Wow, that's like…" She turned away. After a time of studying the sea she looked back at me. "Look at the shimmery V on the water." Her voice quivered and her eyes were wet. I gazed at the vast expanse, comforted by its stretch to infinity. Blair seemed small and confused. Grief surprised both of us in such unexpected ways. Often what triggered it in one didn't affect the other. Ian continued to keep his distance, apparently engrossed by the view.

After a lengthy silence, he suggested to Blair that they keep walking along the edge to where the cliffs started curving sharply away from the sea and then back out again. "People often repel down the sides of the cliff. We might be lucky enough to see some of them."

Neither consulted me before they set off. I could see uncertainty in Blair's eyes, the same look she often had with Edward when she thought he was holding a grudge for an offense she didn't realize she had committed. She would wait for the storm to pass and then gratefully accept his attention. I stayed several steps behind, feeling an unwelcome chill from Ian.

She enjoyed Ian's attention, full of dramatic stories of shipwrecks off this coast. A couple of times Blair began to stumble. I instinctively reached for her, but Ian always caught her and reminded her to be more careful. Being careful had nothing to do with why she was having trouble walking, but he didn't seem to remember that.

Eventually, Blair grew tired and her hunger returned. "Could we have dinner now?"

His eyes darkened, but he agreed readily enough. We circled back to where we began and claimed a picnic table. Blair waited while I walked with Ian to get the basket out of the car. As soon as we were out of hearing, I put a hand on his arm. "Ian, have I done something to make you angry at me?"

"I can't imagine why you are asking," he answered, his tone clipped.

"Because you seem to have stopped talking to me."

"Nonsense. I was focusing on Blair to make the time more interesting for her. You can't object to that." He seemed like a soldier at attention.

"Of course not."

"Then I cannot understand your question." Without any further conversation, we retrieved everything we needed and returned to find Blair singing to herself. Ian continued telling her stories about pirates, criminals, and oddities that washed up on the shore after big storms, while making no attempt to draw me into the conversation. I was being punished and I knew it. I didn't understand what I'd done wrong, and going over it numerous times in my head didn't make it any clearer. Over time, Ian seemed to get over his mad and began including me. Reticent at first, I eventually joined in, grateful for the thaw.

By the time we packed up, I'd all but forgotten the punishing silence I had endured earlier. We chatted and laughed most of the way back to

Mousehole. Blair fell asleep ten minutes before we turned in the drive and was as hard to awaken as if she'd been asleep for hours.

Ian helped me guide her into the house and up the stairs. He stepped out into the hall while I got Blair ready for bed. I'd expected him to go downstairs and jumped slightly when I found him lurking outside the bedroom door. We made our way downstairs, where I hinted that I was ready to say goodnight. Ian lingered in the hall until I realized he was waiting for me to offer him a nightcap. I did, though a familiar nagging feeling had drained my energy.

"I'm pleased we were able to get together today on such short notice. I did try to reach you two nights ago." He stopped, as if waiting for me to say something. I didn't. "I called once," he continued, "and when there was no answer, I actually came by to make certain that you weren't lying in a heap at the well of stairs." Again I offered nothing, aggravated by his need to know where we were. "It seems you are going to make me ask. Where did you find to go in this quiet little corner of the world?" His lighthearted tone stood in contrast to the intensity in his eyes and jaw.

"Agnes Buncle joined us for dinner. We took a stroll afterwards and got ice cream for Blair." He visibly relaxed and leaned back, his hands clasped behind his head.

"Brilliant. One can't get into trouble with Agnes. Dull as dishwater, isn't she? I approve completely."

"Not at all. I like her," I sputtered. A sort of paralysis of the mind came over me and I took a sip of water. But before I could piece together a thought, Ian stood and put his glass by the sink.

"Must go, I'm afraid. Duty calls tomorrow. It's my rotation to visit the hospital. Miserable job full of petty requests for ice or books. I'm always glad to get the day over with. But it's part of the role I play."

His choice of words surprised me. The hospital chaplain who had sat with me for hours as Blair fought for her life didn't seem to be punching a time clock. He was eager to help me in any way he could. I couldn't quite picture what Ian would have been like during those dark days.

He took my hand when we got to the door. "I think it best if the next time we are with Blair you don't challenge me openly. That type of behavior can be quite confusing for a child." He sounded haughty and sure, like the parent talking to the babysitter. I started to withdraw my hand. He gave it a squeeze and strode through the door. I closed it softly behind him and sank to the floor. Everything was silent except the growing noise in my head.

# 4

# Peter

I'd had to move the morning appointment from Muirfield to Oakton because of the school's uncooperative plumbing. The woman on the line sounded confused when I asked her and her daughter to meet me here, but I knew I could explain it well enough in person. Not certain who else might be here today, I told her to ask for the Headmaster. Old and sturdy, the stone house was embraced by dense, overgrown ivy. Ancient windows of lead glass and a weathered oak door stood sentry in front.

My head was under a sink to repair a leak when, to my left, I spied a rather small pair of blue Nike trainers, their polka dot laces neatly tied. The left shoe was considerably more scuffed than the right one. "Hallo. Could you reach into my toolbox and hand me a spanner?" I asked.

"What does it look like?" She had the same American accent as her mum.

"It's a sort of U shape with a large screw that you can turn. It gets smaller as you tighten it," I explained.

"I don't see it. Are you sure it's in here?" Her voice grew anxious, shrill.

"I am. Take your time. You'll find it." After another moment of fumbling through the box, I made a suggestion. "Why don't you take things out one at a time and lay them on the counter? I'm sure it's hard to look through a box that is so full."

"No, that'll make a mess. I don't want you to get mad at me."

"Now why would I get mad at you for a little mess? You could clean it up, couldn't you?"

"I guess so." Her hesitant voice made me curious. Was she naturally fastidious or was it something else?

"Then you have nothing to fear from me."

I heard metal clanking, and then a delighted squeal. "Here it is." She stretched to hand it to me and watched while I tightened the valve.

When we stood up, a woman had joined us in the kitchen. A woman with sun-kissed skin, kind green eyes, and the most delicate countenance I'd ever encountered. "You must be with this young lady."

She extended her hand. "Yes, Suzanne Morgan." Mesmerized, I was slow to respond.

"Blair, why don't you introduce me to...?"

"Cause I don't know his name," the girl said plainly. Turning toward me and smiling, she said, "I'm Blair. Who are you? We're looking for the principal."

"Headmaster," her mother corrected.

"Yeah, the Head Mister. Do you know him?"

"I'm afraid you've found him," I said, laughing. "Pleased to meet you Blair Morgan." I shook hands with both of them. "And you, Mrs. Morgan."

"I thought you were the janitor," Blair explained.

"I am that, and a lot more. Would you wait for me in my office? It's in the main hall. You can't miss it. I'll just tidy up."

They were sitting quietly on the faded divan when I joined them. "You've moved here permanently, then?" I asked.

"No," Blair's mother answered, looking at the rug. "We haven't made plans past August." I couldn't stop staring at her, even when it got awkward and she flushed red.

I turned back to Blair. "You're a rider, then, are you?" I asked and reached for the barn schedule. She nodded, but her lack of enthusiasm was palpable. I wondered if the mother was pressuring her into a hobby she didn't enjoy.

"Blair was in an accident last year. She used to ride and misses the horses terribly." I stopped what I was doing and gave Mrs. Morgan my full attention. She was trying to be bright for Blair, but I could see a deep sadness about her. "We were hoping Blair could visit the horses, maybe even help with some grooming. She has some balance issues that need to be resolved before she can ride again." Blair blushed and turned her face away.

No pressure there. In fact, just the opposite. "Of course. I could use the help." I touched Blair's arm. She turned her face back towards mine. "There's always something to be done at a barn," I said. "But then you know that, don't you?"

~

Mrs. Morgan dropped Blair off at Muirfield the next afternoon; it was arranged that I would take her home afterwards. "Get the curry comb from the large tack box and start on the large gray over there. He's a gelding named Ferguson." Blair headed willingly to the far stall.

I wanted to see how she was with the horses, so I busied myself with odd tasks in and out of stalls. If she was fearful and timid, they would know and it would affect their behavior. Blair stuck her hand out to rub the horse's nose and introduce herself to him. He nickered and she put her face to his. She brought Ferguson out of the stall and put him in the cross ties. Slowly and lovingly, she rubbed the currycomb in a circular motion, starting at his neck and running the length of his body. All the while she talked to him, pausing every few minutes to look him in the eyes and kiss his muzzle.

After she was done currying him, she took a grooming brush and started to clean off the dirt she had just loosened from his coat. When her right hand got tired, she switched to her left and then back again. She reached for another brush from the tack box.

"Hallo, Fergie. How's the boy?" A ginger-haired girl called Margaret stroked Ferguson's face. Blair stepped forward to see who she was.

"Isn't he pretty? I've got a lesson on him later today."

"You're lucky," Blair answered. "Do you want to help me?"

Margaret rooted around the tack box until she found a comb for his mane. "I'm Margaret Heston. I've never seen you here before. You sound American. Are you?"

"Uh huh. I'm Blair. My mother and I are staying here for a few months."

"What about your father?" Before Blair could answer her, I interrupted.

"Just checking in, Blair. Everything okay? Hi, Margaret."

Blair snapped to attention. "I haven't picked his hooves yet."

"Should you wait for me to do that?" I asked, concerned with her balance.

"No, I can do it." Her face reddened.

"If you're sure. Shout to me if you need help." I hoped she was right. It wouldn't get her on a horse any faster if she got stepped on. I checked on the riders outside warming up and then quietly slipped into the barn again. I wanted to stay close to Blair this first visit, but didn't want to hover.

Margaret focused on combing out Ferguson's mane while Blair took a hoof pick from the box. Her foot dragged just enough to make a distinct scrape with each step. Walking to Ferguson's right front leg, she reached down and lifted up his hoof. He stood patiently, letting her work; she had just gotten it clean when it slipped from her hand and fell with a heavy thud on the concrete floor. Margaret jumped from the sudden noise. "Are you okay?"

"Fine," Blair answered, undeterred. She went to the other front leg, but as she lifted that hoof, she lost her balance and fell against him. Again, the hoof spilled from her hand, this time narrowly missing her foot. Margaret rushed over to see what happened. Blair's face was red with anger and her eyes were filling with tears.

"C'mon. Let me help you." She took the pick from Blair's hand and waited for her to move away from Ferguson. "What's wrong with your hand and foot, anyway?" Margaret kept working on the hoof as she waited for Blair to answer. "It's okay, you can tell me. I won't tell anyone."

"I don't care who you tell," Blair spat at her.

Margaret looked up from the hoof and smiled sweetly. "Well good, then. That's settled. So what happened?"

I wanted to stay and listen, but I had riders waiting for me in the ring. And since it seemed that Margaret had things under control, I resumed the lesson. 45 minutes later, my students dismounted, and I returned to find the two girls deep in conversation. Not wanting to interrupt, I went back outside and delayed as long as I could before calling Margaret's name.

Blair came and stood with me at the rail. She wore a velvet hat from the tack room and gave me a satisfied smile. "I see you met Margaret. She's a lovely girl. It's her lesson that's next. Can you wait through it before I take you home?"

She nodded enthusiastically. "Sure. I'd love to watch."

Margaret walked Fergie to the gate and mounted effortlessly. I adjusted her stirrups, and she began to trot around the ring. I rejoined Blair, who now hung from the lowest fence rail. "You did a smashing job grooming. I came and checked on you once or twice." Blair froze in alarm.

"Don't worry, I didn't eavesdrop on you and Margaret," I laughed. "Why would I care what two little moppets are chattering about?" Blair gave me a grateful look and I felt a keen sense of my guilt. I would have stayed in the barn to hear her explanation if it had been possible. "I'm glad to see that you and Margaret hit it off. She'd be a great chum." We talked in fits and starts as I called instructions to Margaret and periodically ran alongside her to explain something.

When the lesson was over, the girls un-tacked Ferguson and rubbed him down. Blair helped me feed and water the horses. And although she moved more slowly than she had earlier that afternoon and was nearly blanketed in dirt, Blair radiated happiness. She met Margaret's mum and the girls talked of getting together the next day.

"Have you got time to see something special?" I asked as we climbed into my car.

She nodded vigorously as we turned toward the sea. It was late afternoon and the sun was beginning its slow fade. The roads narrowed as we drove. Our destination was a cliff, overlooking rocky fingers pointing hither and yon. I pulled the car off the road and we walked to the edge. Blair looked down, seeing the tiny footpath carved through the rocks and leading to the water.

"Do you walk down there?" she asked.

"Sure. Sometimes I go down there to get closer to the sea, and sometimes I stay up here where I can take it all in at once." I drank in my favorite vista in all of Cornwall.

"Do you come here a lot?"

"Almost every day."

"Why?"

"I need to. The truth of it keeps things in proper perspective."

I concentrated on the sounds: the percussion of the surf as it pounded its rhythms, the shrill calls of the seagulls as they pursued their prey, the voice of the wind first whispering, then shouting. The waves grew bigger and angrier with each landfall.

I noticed Blair hugging herself and offered my sweater. It hung down to her knees, the arms extending beyond her hands. She pulled it close around her. "It's perfect. Smells like horses."

"Can you feel the storm coming in? We'll have a good rain tonight," I said, scanning the horizon. I pointed to the winding path leading down to the sand. "Do you think you can make it down there?" I stepped down and reached my hand out to her. Gripping hard, she started a slow decent, careful not to lose her footing while I helped direct her steps. We found a spot in the sand and leaned against a rock wall.

"This is really pretty. Mommy would like it."

"It's my favorite. You'll have to show it to her sometime." We soaked in the view for a bit longer. "Was it a good day for you at Muirfield?"

"It was the best day since we got here. I really like Margaret. She's a lot like Rachel."

"And who is Rachel?"

"She's…she was…she's my best friend at home."

"What happened? Did you have a row?"

"A what?"

"A disagreement. A fight."

"Oh. No. We hardly ever fight. We just…she sorta…I'm not sure we're still best friends. Well, she's mine. I'm just not sure if I'm hers." I'd spent enough days with school age children to become well acquainted with catty little girls. "I used to see her everyday at school and we spent the night together a lot. But after the accident, I wasn't in school and then we hardly…it's just different, you know?"

I nodded. That wasn't quite what I'd expected. We sat quietly for a time, watching the waves and gulls, and later, fishing boats that were coming in for the night. When the last boat was past the break wall, I turned back to Blair.

"Would you mind telling me about the accident?"

A trace of pain fluttered across her eyes. She picked up a piece of shell and started digging in the sand beside her. I kept silent as she focused intently on making patterns in the sand. "Daddy and I were on the way home from my lesson." Her voice grew tiny and her eyes started to blink rapidly.

"What kind of lesson?" I asked, trying to keep my voice light.

"Riding. You know, like today." I nodded, but my heart grew heavier. "Mrs. Galloway was my teacher. Anyway, the lesson ran long and Daddy was going fast because we were late for dinner. And then the car went off the road and ran into a tree. I don't remember anything after that. They took me to the hospital. I was in a coma. You know what that is?" she asked politely. I nodded.

"Daddy died. I had hurt my brain bad and so I couldn't go back to school and I had to go to a special teacher to learn some stuff I already knew but kept forgetting. And I don't walk as good now."

"I'm very sorry about your father. You must miss him." I gave her arm a squeeze.

"Yes, sir."

Her sterile reply stunned me. I waited, expecting her to say more, but she just stared at the sea. "How did you end up here? And before you answer let me tell you that I'm awfully glad you did."

She smiled and a light returned to her eyes. "Yeah, me too." Blair tugged at the sleeves, wrapping the long ends around her.

"If you're cold we can go."

"It's okay. I like it here."

Blair looked out at the sea, making me wonder if she remembered she hadn't answered my question. Pushing her hair back from her face, she looked up at me and continued. "Mommy wanted to get away. She said she'd always wanted to come here."

"Do you think you'll stay past August?"

She shrugged. "Mommy really likes it here, and she says she isn't ready to face the store."

I grinned at how she'd adopted her mother's phrasing. "Is that where she works?"

"Yes, but she's the boss. It's hers and Daddy's. She says she doesn't want to go back there yet. Sometimes I think I'd like to stay longer. But I don't know. And really, we just got here, anyway. I mean, like a couple of weeks ago. When I ask her if she likes it here, she just says it's complicated."

"I'm sure it is." I stood up and brushed the sand from my legs. "We should get you home."

I watched Blair weave slightly and struggle with the spots where the path was uneven, but she managed to get to the top without falling.

"Maybe you'll get to stay. If you came to Oakton, I would be one of your teachers. Now, tell me about your riding."

As we drove off, Blair took one last look at the orange and pink and lavender of the sunset, painting the sea and sky.

⌒

Mrs. Morgan was pacing in front of the cottage as we drove up. She grabbed Blair as she stepped out of the car and gave her a rough hug.

"Thank God you're okay. I was terrified something happened to you."

"Gosh Mom, I'm fine. What are you talking about?"

"I'm talking about you coming home so late. I expected you an hour ago. I've been worried sick." I got out of the Rover and joined Blair.

"You worry too much. You knew I was with Mr. Stewart. I don't get what the big deal is." Red splotches were beginning to cover her neck and cheeks.

This was my fault, and they shouldn't be in a row over it. "Blair, she's right. I should have brought you straight home."

Blair glared at me and I turned to her mum. "Mrs. Morgan, I am sorry. We stopped along the coast for a bit. I should have talked to you about it first."

"Yes, you should have. I wouldn't have expected you to be so thoughtless." She spat her words at me, and I knew I deserved them.

"Mom, he was doing something nice for me. Don't be so mean to him."

"Blair, your mum isn't being mean. She was worried about you. That's natural." Blair's face was frozen in anger. Now I'd managed to make both of them angry with me.

"Mr. Stewart, I appreciate your help, but I really don't need you defending me. I'm quite capable of handling this." She measured each word out with extreme self-control.

Blair stormed toward the house, but as she reached the door, she turned back. Her expression had thawed enough for her to offer me a weak smile. "Thanks again. I had a great time."

"The pleasure was mine. I enjoyed talking with you."

Suzanne jumped as the door slammed behind Blair. I felt terrible for causing all this and rushed to get the first word in.

"Mrs. Morgan, Suzanne, I really am very sorry that I caused you such distress. I didn't expect it to take us long, and Blair thought it would be alright with you if we were a little late."

"It wasn't Blair's decision. You're the adult." The anger and the cool air overtook her and her teeth started chattering. "You're supposed to be responsible."

Turning toward the house, she took several steps and then paused. "Thank you for bringing her home safely, Mr. Stewart. Goodnight."

The truth of her words leveled me. I stood there long after she had gone inside.

⌒

I needed a hot cup of tea. I had to hunch to get to my favorite table by the fireplace in The King's Guard. Here I could stretch out my legs, lean back against the wall, and not be in anyone's way. I closed my eyes and put my head back. Her green eyes immediately came into focus. I felt my throat tighten. There was more than anger in her reaction. She'd been ashen, a look more akin to suffering than fury. I knew that look all too well and was sick at heart knowing I'd caused it. And even more sick not knowing what I could do to fix it.

"You're looking far too comfortable there. Those horses wear you out, did they?" I opened my eyes to find Harry Turner taking a sip of his beer. Harry owned the local chemist shop.

"That they did Harry. And how are you faring these days?"

"Couldn't be better. Especially glad to get the rain for my roses. The little lovelies were getting thirsty."

I nodded. Harry's roses were regular winners at the Truro flower show.

"Speaking of lovely, where is Jillian this evening?"

"I couldn't tell you." In fact, I'd not given her thought today.

"Have a row, did you?"

"No. Why would you think that?"

"When I saw her at the shop today, she mentioned wedding bells. It sounded to me as though it was only a matter of time. You're a lucky man."

This wasn't the first time I heard talk like this, but I saw no need to humiliate Jillian. I'd made it clear to her that our relationship wasn't leading there. "Summer business good for you?"

"Oh yes, just like always. I've been noticing more Germans this year. Can't figure out what they're asking for half the time. Could be wanting to buy me out so I can go on holiday for good, but I wouldn't know. It's a bugger."

Laughing, I agreed. "It is, indeed, a bugger." Harry wandered back to his favorite seat at the bar and had another pint. I felt a sudden need to be alone, so I paid and left for home.

When I got there, Winston and I went out for his nightly constitutional. In the quiet of the day's end, I had time to think. Sometime shortly after we met, Jillian decided that she wanted to marry me. She mentioned it to one or two people in the village, and it didn't take long for me to start receiving congratulations. Not wanting to embarrass Jillian, I answered vaguely whenever people tried to engage me in conversation about it. I remembered talking to Jillian the first time someone bid me good luck.

*Jillian, the oddest thing happened today. Eric Young, at the market, offered me good luck on our impending marriage.*

*Hmm?*

*Do you know where he would get the idea that we are getting married?*

*No, maybe he just thought we should. Anyway, don't be mad at me for something someone else said.*

I'd been inclined to believe her until the next time it happened. I tried to ease off from the relationship more than once. But for some reason, even though I'd told her I wanted nothing more than friendship, I'd always managed to get dragged more deeply in than I meant to be. Funny what we put up with when we're lonely.

The odd thing was that she barely noticed the difference. As long as I was available to listen to her complaints on a regular basis and take her to dinner once in a while, she seemed content. Well, not content, really. She did want a future with me. She had made that clear. But at least she wasn't always talking about it. She could be fun, but more than once I asked myself why I didn't just end it.

Back inside, I changed into my sweatpants and poured a brandy. Winston sauntered over and licked my hand. I picked up a book and settled into the easy chair. Things with Jillian were a muddle, and now things with the Morgans were, too. I couldn't seem to get things right with any women. The warmth of the brandy spread throughout my body, and I nodded off after three pages.

⮑

Two nights later, Jillian and I sat facing one another in a back corner of our favorite Indian restaurant in Penzance. "I don't understand you. I waited until eight o'clock, but I finally had to go." She always took this tone when she reprimanded me. I was beginning to tire of it.

"I told you I would come if I could. The veterinary ran late and then it took a long time to feed and muck. I was exhausted by the end of it all. Surely you can understand that."

Jillian studied her French manicure. I was growing weary of this mea culpa she required. I would say it one last time. "I'm sorry that you were disappointed. But I know you understand it had been a long day and I was tired. It really is as simple as that."

A slight pout lingered on her lips. "I guess you can make it up to me." She paused, probably to let me think how I might do that. "How was today, then? Any frights with the horses?"

"They were fine. Did some work at Oakton, then spent the afternoon at Muirfield giving lessons." Our order arrived, and I savored the spicy meat and curried rice. "I met a new student the other day."

"Hmm?" She covered her mouth as she yawned.

"The girl is ten. Americans here for the summer."

Jillian arched a single eyebrow. "Eleanor told me about them. Saw the mother actually. A week or two ago. Didn't like her. Nosy sort."

I sighed. "They seemed nice enough. The girl walks with a limp, drags her foot a bit. Result of an accident. She'll help me out, grooming and mucking until she's ready to ride again."

"God, they'll probably want you to make all sorts of special arrangements for her. Watch they don't take advantage of you. I read about some Americans who..."

I nodded, pretending I was listening. When I couldn't take her prattling any longer, I asked, "What have you been painting lately?"

As Jillian launched into the inspirations for the newest additions to her collection, I considered how to get back into the good graces of Suzanne Morgan.

# 5

# *Suzanne*

The storm between us finally passed. Saturday morning dawned clear and bright; Blair stood at the window, watching the gulls as they twirled and dove in search of food.

"What do you want to do today, Mom? We could go to the beach."

"Would you like to call Margaret to see if she wants to go with us?"

"I just want it to be you and me." I guessed she wanted to make up for days of pouting. I hugged her, acknowledging the apology. We packed lunch and gathered our things. Out of cookies, I said we would stop at the grocery. On the way, Blair chatted non-stop filling me in on everything that had passed through her head during the week, leaving me both dizzy and delighted.

We turned down the cookie aisle, avoided a head on collision with Peter Stewart, and burst into a fit of giggles.

"Hello ladies. What's got you full of beans this morning?"

"We're going to the beach," Blair squealed.

"You've a beautiful day for that. Are you going to show your mum where we went?"

Her face fell. "I don't know how to get there."

"Right. Well, all the beaches around here are worth your while."

"No. I want her to see our beach. Why don't you come, too? You could take us there." She looked back and forth between us, eager and hopeful.

I tensed from head to toe. Our last meeting had ended so unpleasantly, with me shouting at him like a fishwife, that I wasn't sure either of us really wanted to be forced to be together for hours. "I'm sure Mr. Stewart has a full day ahead of him. And besides, you heard him say that all the beaches are nice."

"Oh mom.,. Please...I know he'd have fun with us."

"I don't think this is a good day for it. Some other time, okay darling?" Blair was quiet for a moment. "Okay." The sparkle that was so hard to come by was gone.

"Actually, I guess there's no reason you couldn't join us, Peter. Unless you have other plans, of course." The sun came out on Blair's face again.

A slow smile spread across Peter's face and crept towards his eyes.

❦

He led the way through a maze of hedgerows, overhanging trees, and lanes the width of a single car. Eventually, he pulled off the road into a tiny car park already filling up. Parking beside him, we got out and began to unload our gear.

"I'll get this. You ladies go pick out a spot."

We crossed the road, and Blair showed me the path leading down to the beach. It was steep, uneven, and rocky. "Honey, I'm not sure you should do this."

"Why not? I did it with Peter."

"He let you climb down there? You could have gotten hurt!" I felt my anger returning. Not only had they been late, but they'd been here? Again, I questioned his judgment.

"But I didn't. He held my hand when it got a little slippery. I'll show you." Blair started down the slope, letting her foot drag a little more than usual to slow her down. Only once did she need to reach out to me for help. By the time we got to the bottom, Peter had caught us.

Several families had claimed their territory. Blankets, umbrellas, baskets, coolers, and a variety of toys staked out each individual settlement. It wasn't until we found our own spot and spread out our blanket that I stopped to notice the beauty in front of me. I breathed deeply of the salt air, pulled forward into the scene before me.

Vivid, aqua water, more like the Caribbean than the North Atlantic, lapped onto the shoreline. Off in the distance, it grew darker, less friendly. I could only imagine how much colder and deeper that was. A light wind blew my hair in my face, and a smattering of whitecaps danced upon the water. I couldn't help but smile as I looked at the wide, blue sky and shining sun. It made me glad we'd come.

"It's hard not to be peaceful in a place like this." I started at the sound of Peter's voice as he took a place beside me.

"Umm-hmm." I was still struggling with remnants of the anger I'd felt only a few days ago.

"I wish you could believe how truly sorry I am for bringing Blair home late from the barn. I am sick that I caused you such anguish. It's no excuse, but by way of explanation, we were having a lovely time talking, enjoying this spot, and we lost the time. She told me about the accident and your decision to come to Cornwall. You've both been through a terrible ordeal." I could hear his sincerity.

His pause gave me time to consider the situation. If she'd been confiding in me, I wouldn't have been quick to end it either. I turned to him. "I accept your apology." His kindness filled me with warmth… until I began to wonder what Blair had told him about me. We gazed at the sea awhile, until the silence between us grew awkward.

I walked over to Blair, squirted sunscreen lotion in my hand, and began rubbing it onto her shoulders and down her back, loving the gentle caress of my daughter's skin. She was all I had.

Peter sat on the blanket beside Blair. "I'll wager you won't get in."

"Why not?" The edges of her mouth fought a grin.

"Too cold for Yanks, and city girls besides."

"Not for me. I can take it." Blair jumped up and ran straight for the water, followed closely by Peter, tearing off his shirt behind her. She shrieked as she hit the frigid water but wasn't about to turn back.

I sat in the sand, watching the two of them laugh and play. Not once did Blair whine nor make any of her usual excuses to stop. I loved watching her play like the other children at the beach. I watched Peter, as well. Muscular and tanned, he moved with the confidence and agility of one very at home in his body. Looking up, he caught me spying on him. I felt myself blush, but his smile was easy. I turned to the seagulls overhead, but managed to steal one more peek before laying back and closing my eyes. I dozed off to the concert of my daughter's laughter.

Frigid drops of water woke me. Blair stood over me, all blue lips and chattering teeth. I pulled her towards me, wrapped her in a sun-warmed towel. Over lunch, Peter offered sightseeing recommendations; I didn't tell him Ian had already given his. I worried Blair might blurt it out, but she'd grown drowsy under the warm sun. Soon she lay stretched out across the blanket, still wrapped in her towel and snoring lightly.

I cleaned up, then went to the water's edge. I could feel Peter's eyes following me. I sank my toes into the sand and inhaled deeply.

"I'm sorry about your husband," said Peter, coming up from behind.

Startled, I turned and looked into those disturbingly intense eyes of his. "What did Blair tell you?"

"That they were in a motor accident because they were late for dinner. I'm sure it was awful for you."

"Yes."

"I didn't make the connection the other night. Dreadful of me."

His kindness touched me. "It's all right."

He nodded, but didn't look at me. Strangely, I felt a strong desire to relieve his guilt. "It's been a difficult year, but Blair is doing wonderfully. Rough at first, not knowing if she would live. Then there was the concern about permanent damage. And then watching her struggle just to be herself." My voice grew quieter as I spoke.

"Has she made it back?" he asked softly.

"Almost. Do you know anything about the personality changes that can occur with head injuries?"

"No." He guided me to a place on the rocks where we could sit and still keep an eye on Blair.

"It's called an affect change. The personality gets turned upside down. Someone who is quiet becomes loud, someone loud becomes quiet. Frightening for the victim, and terribly difficult for family and friends."

I remembered the first Christmas after the accident. We kept our annual tradition of attending the Nutcracker Ballet. We got to the theater early and made our way to our seats. Edward had always liked to sit in the first balcony, but I'd gotten tickets in the orchestra section so Blair wouldn't have to navigate stairs. I remember looking at her sitting beside me, and grieving for the girl she'd been. The child for whom the world held possibility and promise. The girl who wanted to be the Sugar Plum Fairy when she grew up. I thought that child had died with Edward.

The lights had flickered and anticipation rippled through the audience. I'd looked over at Blair and saw an angel smiling back at me. I'd wondered then, consumed with guilt, how I could have seen death on such a night? Haunted by my thoughts, I'd fought to enjoy the performance. Blair seemed lost in it, though, occasionally having to be reminded to whisper when asking a question, never taking her eyes off the stage.

The evening had seemed like a success until *The Waltz of the Flowers*. Blair noticed one of the dancer's timing was a beat off those of the others. *That girl over there isn't doing it right.*

I hushed her, reminding her to whisper. But again, and louder, Blair complained about the dancer. A few heads turned and I reminded Blair again. She ignored me. Then the giggling began. With each successive dance step, Blair's giggles grew louder and more offensive. I took Blair's arm, turning her toward me. *Stop it!* I had whispered sharply. *You're bothering everyone.*

She sobered momentarily and then the giggling began again. I was horrified. Blair had never behaved this way before. More heads turned, more faces frowned. She was losing control by the second. The only thing to do was leave. Quickly. We pushed past the others to get to the aisle. We made our way to the doors, Blair's loud voice demanding to know what was wrong. Once inside the lobby, I jammed Blair's coat through her arms and pushed her towards the door. She seemed genuinely confused and kept shouting, wanting to know what was wrong. The more time passed, the louder and uglier her tone became. It wasn't until we reached the car that I stopped and turned to her.

*What in the world were you thinking? I've never seen you behave so badly. How could you continue to bother everyone even after I said to stop? You're ten years old. You know how to behave at the theater. What is wrong with you?*

And just like that, I realized what I had said. Blair's face told me that it had registered with her, too. For a split second, her mouth fell open, agape. And then, tight-lipped, she looked down at her newly scuffed patent leather ballet flats. Time seemed to stop. Then I heard her small, wounded voice answer my awful question.

*Everything.*

It had been difficult to handle, and I'd failed on a grand scale. I didn't know if I would ever stop feeling the shame of it. "What happened to Blair?" Peter asked.

I shook the memory away. "She went from being an angel to fighting me on everything, making scenes in public, arguing with her friends."

"I haven't seen any of that here."

I smiled. "She's improved a lot. Just happens occasionally now. The lasting problems for Blair are diminished strength in her arms and legs, and lingering balance problems."

"Ahh, that's why no riding. She'd not given a reason."

"Yes. That's her biggest loss in all of this." Wait... "Beside her father, of course." I wished it was dark then, my face too exposed in the sunlight. I got quiet for a while and picked up a handful of sand, letting it fall through my fingers, damp and silky.

His voice broke through. "What about you? How are you after all of this?"

Sand fell from my hands to the ground. I tried to hide their shaking. "One always finds new strength in those times. But it takes something out of you to watch your child suffer. You never get over that." You also never get over the weaknesses that emerge under pressure. Impatience, judgment, loathing.

"And the sudden and permanent loss of someone you love," Peter added in a hushed voice. "I know about that."

I was puzzled. "Are you a widower?"

"No. I just meant..." He grew quiet, his brown eyes turned towards the horizon.

I wanted to know more, and yet also to put him at ease. "Since the accident, I haven't seen Blair happier than when she is talking about Muirfield. Mrs. Galloway didn't have the time or patience to have her at the barn if she wasn't riding, so Blair was completely cut off from the horses. It devastated her. You can't imagine what joy she has in just being able to touch them, love them. It's all she talks about. I can't thank you enough."

I felt a flush of affection for him, grateful for his kindness to her.

"Are you certain that riding is completely out of the question?"

"I can't see any other way. Can you?"

Blair began stirring. We stayed until late afternoon, when Peter had to return to the stables for feeding time. Blair begged to be allowed to help, Peter readily agreed. I knew he wanted a second chance at bringing her home on time. And I was glad for time alone.

My face slowly emerged through the steam. It had been a long time since I had looked in a mirror critically. The events of the past year had aged me considerably. I no longer looked the 36 years I would turn in five months, but at least the bags under my eyes were smaller since we arrived. I wondered what Peter saw when he looked at me.

Peter. Unlike Ian, he seemed to prefer asking questions to talking about himself. I wondered about this, then thought that if I was going to compare him to anyone, it should be Edward. But that was the problem, wasn't it? I was a widow, a recent one. How could I justify being attracted to Peter? What did that say about how much I loved Edward? I flopped on the bed, my mind scurrying about like a squirrel.

My thoughts tracked back to Peter. What did he mean about losing someone he loved? I was intrigued that he didn't tell me everything. Edward would have. So would Ian. They liked being an open book. Not so with Peter. He would take a while to get to know.

I remembered hearing Jillian Allingham talk disdainfully about a man named Peter—something about being too devoted to "the children." It had to be him. Even after the brief encounter, it was hard to imagine someone as nice as Peter being involved with Jillian. They were so different. Someone had once said a similar thing to me about my relationship with Edward. I knew that the person talking just didn't know the real Edward, the one I loved... I trembled, breaking out into a light sweat. Despite having just showered, I no longer felt fresh.

I finished getting ready and ran downstairs. I decided on a light jazz CD, just right with the fresh breeze flowing through the room. The warm, bright day had transformed into something soft, ethereal even. Standing still a moment, I let the peace of the evening settle over me, calming the anxiety which so often lived in my heart. This cottage, with its tiny rooms and big views, had quickly become my haven.

The dinner menu would be ratatouille and spinach salad. I still had zucchini bread left over from yesterday to round out the menu. I finished early, poured myself a glass of Merlot and wandered out to the garden. The array of plants in this tiny space, their colors woven seamlessly together, still took my breath away. I stood there, drinking in the sweetness, when I heard a car pull up in the front.

Walking out to greet Blair and Peter, I reached up and smoothed my hair. I turned the corner toward the front of the house to find Ian getting out of his car.

"Hello, Suzanne." He eyed me seductively. "You look positively bohemian."

Suddenly self-conscious in my sundress and bare feet, I dearly wished I wasn't holding the glass of wine. "How nice of you to drop by." I fought to keep my voice light. "What brings you here?"

"I was just over the hill visiting Mrs. Kentworth. She loses track of the days. Needs reminding services are tomorrow morning. I thought you might, too."

I didn't appreciate his assumption that we would become regular attenders. But before I could say anything, we heard a car. Ian's eyes narrowed when he saw Peter.

Blair climbed out of the car, was flushed with excitement and talking a mile a minute. "I told Peter we wanted him to stay for dinner. Gosh, you look beautiful in your new dress." I wished she'd not called attention to that.

Ian looked at me disapprovingly, and then at Peter. He was freshly showered and looked handsome in faded jeans and a white polo shirt. I'd done nothing wrong, was doing nothing wrong, but felt Ian's judgment nonetheless.

"I'm sorry for interrupting. I didn't realize you were having company."

I put my hands on Blair's shoulders. "Say hello to Dr. Hamilton."

Peter extended his hand. "Hello, Ian."

"Good evening, Peter. I just came to see if Suzanne remembered what time the services are tomorrow."

"They're the same as last week, aren't they?" Blair asked, clearly exasperated.

His voice tight, he said, "Yes, yes they are."

"Then we know when they are. You didn't need to come."

"Blair," I said sharply.

Ignoring me, Blair continued. "Mom, what'd you fix us for dinner? I told Peter what a good cook you are."

Ian looked back at me. "I hope you'll forgive the intrusion into your evening," he said with exaggerated politeness.

"Ian, please excuse my daughter's poor manners. It was very kind of you to come by. We'll be there in the morning."

"Right. See you then." Looking at Peter, he said, "Give my best to Jillian."

"Good night, Ian," Peter said.

The corners of Ian's mouth turned up slightly as he drove away. Why was Peter being so nice to me if he was involved with Jillian? Why had Ian looked so smug when he said it?

"Who's Jillian?" Blair asked Peter as Ian drove off.

"Peter, I'm so sorry for that. Blair, go upstairs. I'll be there in a moment to talk to you."

"What did I do?" she demanded. Then to Peter she asked again, "Who's Jillian?"

"Go." I was humiliated, and now angry with myself for rushing to speak. I would have liked to hear his answer. Blair looked at Peter, then back to me. She stormed off, slamming the door behind her.

This was not how I'd expected the evening to begin. Defeated and frustrated, I said, "That is a little of what we were talking about this afternoon. A complete lack of seeing what is inappropriate behavior." It looked like Peter had something to say, but changed his mind. Instead, he held the door for me as we entered the kitchen. "Blair was right about one thing. We want you to stay for dinner, if you're still interested."

"I'd love to. I spent a good part of feeding time hearing about your gourmet cooking."

"Good. Blair will be pleased." I turned the heat on low under the pot of vegetables. Motioning toward the wine, I added, "Help yourself while I go up and talk to my daughter." I felt like a bad hostess leaving Peter alone for very long, so I told Blair she wouldn't be seeing him anytime soon if she didn't show better manners. She understood me.

Back downstairs, Peter had found his way to the garden. I stole a brief glance through the window. His weathered face was evidence of a life lived outdoors. Some wrinkles, but no frown lines. Sun bleached hair, just a touch of gray at the temples. I picked up my glass and joined him. "There you are."

"Everything to rights with Miss Blair?"

"I think so. She'll apologize to Ian tomorrow and to you at dinner."

"If you think it's necessary."

"I do. We've taught her...I've taught her better manners than what she showed today. She'll have to learn to manage her increased impulsiveness. I am unwilling to let it be an excuse for rudeness."

Dinner went well. Peter raved about everything, and Blair cleaned her plate without incident. While I cleaned up, I could hear their voices in the living room but not the words. I looked up just as Blair reached out to give Peter a hug. Her sweet smile said it all. When dessert was ready, we sat around the kitchen table chatting comfortably. I trundled a sleepy Blair off to bed, and Peter and I settled in for another round of coffee.

"Of all the places you could have gone, what made you chose here?"

We were back in the living room, watching the sun set from the huge chintz sofa. Orange light danced across the pale walls. I thought for a moment before answering. How much did I want to tell him about myself? My experience with men told me to keep my comments to a minimum, even when asked a direct question.

"We've had a hard year. Adjusting to Edward's death, then dealing with Blair's health issues."

"Were you caring for her alone?"

"She alternated between therapy and school in the mornings. In the afternoons, I picked her up and continued to work on whatever they'd focused on that particular morning."

"How could you leave your company for the summer?"

"I've left it in able hands." I tucked my feet under me. Peter had stretched his legs out but was still angled towards me. I found his intense focus a bit unnerving, but I kept on.

"So you chose Cornwall because…"

"I saw a painting. It looked peaceful. I guess I needed some peace in my life, so I came here to find it." I could have talked about the grief and how Edward's death had left me without a compass. Instead, I said, "I've always loved the sea, growing up in New England. I need its rhythms and predictability to keep me sane. And yet I love the way it looks different every day. Different colors, different waves. Never boring."

"Yes, but you could have found that in America," he said. "Why go so far from home? From memories?"

"Because it *is* so far from home and memories," I blurted. My words hung in the air like a guillotine over my head. "What about you? What brought you here?" I asked.

"That's a rather messy story." I wondered if it had to do with the unexpected loss he'd alluded to, but he didn't offer any details. "It was five years ago. I threw myself into Oakton and Muirfield. Made good friends. I guess I've planted my roots. Just like you and Blair."

I was embarrassed to tell him that the roots I planted threatened to strangle me, that every time I thought about going back to Great Falls and Morgan's my stomach tightened into a thousand knots. So I asked him about his love of horses and found out that he grew up riding. His mother was an instructor.

"But, of course, it's difficult to make a living with just that, so I do it on the side. I'm a good teacher; I get that from Mum. My father died in a fire a few years ago. He was trying to get a neighbor's wife out of their burning house."

"Oh, I'm sorry to hear that. It's a terrible loss. What a hero he was. Maybe that's where you get it from."

"What do you mean?"

"You've been a hero to Blair. Letting her come to Muirfield. Being with the horses breathes life into her. And she's quite taken with you."

"Ah, and I with her, I assure you." His entire face broke into a smile. Again, I got the impression he had something else to say. Instead, he cleared his throat and stood. "I should go."

We walked to his car. "Thank you for an unexpectedly wonderful day. All of it."

"We enjoyed it, too."

"Could we go out for an evening? Dinner somewhere? Maybe a walk on the beach?"

He wanted to spend more time with me. The prospect excited and flattered me, but I knew I couldn't. "Thank you for the kind offer, but no. I need to be...."

"I know. You need to be with Blair."

"Uh-huh."

I was going to say faithful.

⮾

The organ music reverberated from the stone floor to the beamed ceiling. Blair was in high spirits after yesterday, providing a running commentary on the parade of hats walking down the aisle. Ian, presiding again, brightened when he saw us. I fervently hoped no one else noticed. The sermon was long, something to do with one's duty to attend the weekly service; Blair grew restless, fidgety.

As we stood for the Benediction, I saw Jillian. Being somewhat of a local celebrity and a friend of Eleanor's, I wanted to introduce Blair to her. However, just enough people separated us to make it awkward.

When we neared the doors, I heard Ian greet Jillian in the narthex. "A picture of loveliness today. I hope Peter gave you my regards last evening."

"What? Actually, I don't know where Peter got off to all day yesterday."

"Maybe this lady can tell you that," he said, glancing back at me.

Jillian was surprised to see that Ian was referring to us. "I beg your pardon?"

Before I knew it, Ian had taken hold of my hand. "Jillian Allingham, I don't believe you have met our American visitor. You ladies have several things in common."

Jillian's face tensed. I did too, remembering last night with Peter. I withdrew my hand from Ian's.

"You are both friends of Eleanor Cavendish, of course," Ian laughed. "Jillian met Eleanor upon her return to Mousehole and found in Eleanor, a patron, and of course, a friend."

"My mommy told me about you this morning," Blair blurted out. Jillian glared at me. "You're a painter." Over breakfast I'd answered last night's question about Jillian, explaining she was a local artist and friend of Peter's. I'd done it only so that she wouldn't put Peter on the spot again. I never anticipated this scenario.

We moved to the bottom of the steps. "I understand from both Eleanor and Ian that you are quite talented."

"Thank you," Jillian replied blandly. She looked at me squarely, directly, taking an account of what she was seeing. She had just begun to excuse herself when Ian rejoined us.

"So have you discovered who your other mutual friend is?" He was bursting to say it.

"I know," Blair said enthusiastically.

"Peter Stewart," Ian answered, looking directly at Jillian. "I ran into Peter last evening, just as he was arriving at Wisteria Cottage for a gourmet dinner in his honor, I believe."

Jillian's gaze went from frosty to pure ice. I had become the enemy. Why, I didn't know.

"He was bringing Blair home from Muirfield," I said, looking to Blair for confirmation.

"He lets me take care of Ferguson and work at his barn."

"Eleanor told me that you'd be leaving at summer's end," Jillian answered, as if that settled everything.

"We haven't made plans past August, actually." I don't know why I felt the need to add this.

"I see." She kissed Ian on both cheeks and bid him farewell.

After she left, Ian looked at me innocently. "She can be high strung, artistic temperament and all that. But she really is a lovely person. I'm so glad you came today. We must think of another outing. Have you been to

St. Michael's Mount?" We shook our heads. "It is a breathtaking spot. I must escort you ladies there. We could pack a hamper again."

"A what?" Blair asked.

"A picnic lunch."

"Oh. We just had one with Peter. We don't need another one."

"Blair!" I took hold of Blair's elbow and started pulling. "That's a very nice offer, Ian. I'll talk it over with Blair and call you later this week."

"Til then, I shall keep hoping," he whispered in my ear.

# 6

## Peter

The cove had been empty for hours. That suited me fine. Stark and desolate, as if sculpted by our own Barbara Hepworth. Rocks set in earthen mortar smoothed flat by centuries of predictable tides. I was absorbed in mending a sail on my 17' dingy when I heard a woman call out. I looked up to find Suzanne Morgan walking toward me, a friendly smile lighting her face.

"What a great surprise!" I said. "What brings you here?"

"I spent the day at Thom's Cove and needed to stretch my legs a bit. I followed the shore until it turned the corner into this little cove. How picturesque."

"Yes, it's often photographed," I explained.

"Even painted. I saw a painting of this in a local shop." I knew it. It was Jillian's. I remembered the day she had come here with me to sketch. It was early in our friendship and one of the last times I remember her honestly inquiring about me. It had been a pleasant enough day, but I recalled feeling rather flat afterwards. When Jillian wasn't the center of conversation, her attention drifted off quickly.

"And where is Miss Blair?" Already, I'd found in Blair a vulnerability I hoped to someday find in Suzanne.

"She's off with Margaret for the afternoon. Plans to spend the night. I'm glad you introduced them. Blair needs a friend, and I like her. They're planning to go sailing. Blair's never been on a boat before."

"There's nothing to bother about. I've gone out with Ronny for years. He's an old salt. He'll keep a close watch on her."

She relaxed a little, taking in what I was doing. "You're a sailor, too?"

"Too right. A man can't live at the coast and not love the water. I learned to sail the first summer I was here. I took her out earlier today, in fact. That's how my sail got torn." I gestured at the rip with my needle. "So you've spent a blissful day at the beach. You weren't lonely?"

Suzanne laughed. "Well, I wasn't exactly alone."

I thought immediately of Ian. "Oh?"

"I had a country vet and a town of interesting people with their quirky pets to keep me company." I laughed in relief. Dr. Conway encouraged the owners to bring their pets to the beach one Saturday a month. His one-man crusade to help ensure the animals were being exercised thoroughly had grown immensely popular.

I turned back to my work, then looked up to catch Suzanne studying my face. Our eyes met, but I held my gaze steady. It was she who became self-conscious and looked away first. This woman charmed me, and a plan was forming in my mind.

"What have you scheduled for this evening?"

"More adventures with the vet, I guess," she laughed.

"May I suggest, instead, an adventure with a sailor?"

Her smile faded. "Thank you, really, but I don't think..."

"I'm only suggesting a friendly evening together. Surely you need friends. Like Blair." I hoped I sounded casual, feeling anything but, my heart thudding inside my chest. I held my breath, and when she nodded, it pounded even harder.

"Of course I do. What adventure did you have in mind?" Though her voice was hesitant, I detected a slight twinkle in her eyes.

∽

I dithered over what shirt to wear, almost making me late, but managed to pull up to the cottage at 6:45 sharp. I took a deep breath and got out of the car. How long since I'd felt this kind of anticipation? Suzanne greeted me at the door, looking beautiful and relaxed, a sweater thrown over her arm.

"This should be fun," she said. I felt myself relax. It should, indeed.

We headed towards Treen and turned south, the roads becoming narrower with each curve. We soon found ourselves on a one-lane road, flanked on each side by ten-foot hedges. Suzanne held her breath as a car drove straight towards us. We both pulled as close as possible to our respective lefts, folded in our side-view mirrors, and without a single word, maneuvered our cars past one another, never more than six inches apart. Once I had the lane to myself again, I turned to Suzanne.

"Worried?" I teased. She let out something between a sigh and a laugh. Climbing still higher, we finally pulled into a field marked off by a flimsy rope barrier. Suzanne gasped at the scene ahead. Carved into the granite cliff, a backdrop of Porthcurno Bay's turquoise water, sat the Minack Theater.

We spread our rug on grassy seats atop the stone tiers. *The Pirates of Penzance* was due to start in 45 minutes. We took our time, enjoying the cold supper I'd thrown together. I regaled her with antics of the pre-adolescent boys and girls at Oakton. "They're all in need of grace to get through these tough years. I am too, dealing with them every day. In the end, I'm grateful for the opportunity to give them some of the love they so desperately need. Still, they can be a trying lot."

Suzanne frowned, maybe remembering her own childhood. Then, in a bright voice, "Tell me about your family."

"My people are from Yorkshire. My brother is a widower with three children. Mum lives with them. Thomas lost Liza to cancer four years ago. I hated being so far away. We had a good reunion here a fortnight ago, but it's been too long since I've seen the rest of them." I wasn't ready to tell her that there were other reasons I'd stayed away.

"It must be hard to get away, what with having to look after Oakton and Muirfield." She was generous to give me an out, but I didn't deserve one. It was hard to admit, but the truth was that I'd not made an effort.

I enjoyed the cadence of conversation with Suzanne. I liked how she was slow to pass judgment and quick to extend sympathy. Except for that night I brought Blair home late. But that night, it was due.

Suzanne looked out towards the bay while I finished eating. "Do you think Thomas will re-marry?" An interesting question. I couldn't help but wonder how she would answer that one, herself.

"Yes, if he was convinced that his children loved the woman as much as he did. He would never risk bringing someone into his family who wasn't best for everyone."

"Of course not. That would be choosing his happiness over theirs. No good parent would…" Her voice trailed off, leaving me to wonder what she'd been thinking.

Suzanne excused herself just moments before the show began. I watched her make her way through the crowd, struck by her sheer loveliness. It was silly, but I couldn't wait for her to return. I wanted her next to me, and

I wanted to share every minute of this beautiful evening with her. At intermission, I went for tea and ice cream. I stood in the queue and looked at Suzanne, who sat surveying the audience. Couples nestled up to one another and families sprawled out on blankets, relaxed and happy. The queue moving slowly, I returned with our ice cream just before intermission ended.

It didn't take long to notice the light had gone from her eyes. She sat stiffly beside me, offering one-word answers when I tried to engage her in conversation. She was clearly upset. I wanted to ask her about it, but the show started again. I would have to wait.

I spent the second half of the night wondering at the change, wishing the show would end. Finally, it did. Families hurried past us, mindful of bedtimes already missed. Several couples poured themselves more wine, lingering under the warm, starry sky. Suzanne stood as soon as the applause ended and began cleaning up. Our walk back to the car was quiet.

Once we were on our way, I tried to break into the silence. "Did you enjoy the evening?"

"Of course," she said, her voice level. "The performance was wonderful and so was the food. Thank you for all your trouble."

"It was no trouble," I mumbled, confused by her formality. Keeping my eyes on the road, I worked to sort out how to say what was on my mind. Twenty minutes from town, when I thought I couldn't stand it anymore, I finally spoke, doing my best to keep my voice measured, even.

"Suzanne, I'd like to ask you something. I had a wonderful time this evening. The show was grand, of course, but mostly I mean with you. But I'm not certain you can say the same. Did I offend you in some way?"

"Of course not. I'm not sure why you're asking," she said like one practiced at controlled responses. She would not reveal herself that easily.

"You were different after intermission. You grew quiet, guarded." I glanced over at her.

She shifted about in her seat, but refused to look at me. "I don't know. I'm probably just a little tired. I'm sorry."

I felt as if I'd been punched. That was a lie and we both knew it. What I'd wanted her to say was that it had been as wonderful as I thought it had. That she hoped we would do it again. Instead, she didn't move or speak for miles. When the quiet became unbearable, I tuned into Radio2 and let Haydn, Liszt, and Chopin accompany us the rest of the way. I'd hoped to come inside and talk, but Suzanne cut the good-byes short and hurried into the house.

≈

I was out of sorts for days and quickly tired of my own company. Sure that Eric could help me out of this fog of disbelief, I went to see him on my first free night. We sat down at his table, devouring the shepherd's pie I'd brought.

"The vicar came by to see me yesterday," he said.

"Did he? I wonder why."

"Said he'd heard I was feeling poorly. Vicar thinks I'm a project, thinks he's earning his way to heaven by helping an old man. Brings me a terrible sadness, knowing how blind some men can be."

"What makes you doubt his sincerity?" I asked, already suspecting the answer.

"Said he wanted to help me because, 'Faith without works is dead.'"

I laughed loud and long. "Sorry, Eric. It's just that the one time I had a talk with him about anything of significance, he quoted the same scripture."

"Could be the only one he knows," he said, a gleam in his eye. I got up from the table and carried over the dishes. I washed and Eric dried. I asked him once why he didn't let them air dry. He answered with all the nobility of the highest born. "My Daisy kept a good house and just because I'm old and bent doesn't mean I should disappoint her."

Eric spoke of Daisy, his wife of 65 years, as though she was just in the next room. When I first met him, it took me a while to work out that he'd been widower for three years. I wished I'd had the chance to know this woman he spoke of with such tenderness and devotion. They had no children, a sadness he said she bore with great dignity. But they always had each other and God, he said, and it got them through. His mouth trembled when he spoke of her, his grief still fresh and real.

We washed up in companionable silence, but my mind raced with thoughts of Ian Hamilton and his little St. Stephen's parish. As if reading my mind, he said, "I'm telling you now; I'll not be one of his good works." I laid the towel across the sink to dry.

"Of course not. But perhaps you could make him your project. You know, turn the tables on him."

He considered this. "True. He's in need of a good dose of love." Thinking about how to show love to Ian Hamilton was something I was loathe to do. "Now, I'm not saying it's easy," he continued, again the clairvoyant. "I'd have to pray a goodly amount to be able to receive things graciously from him, knowing his motives."

"Maybe he'll bring you one of those treacle tarts you're so fond of."

"Well now, I could receive that without an extra measure of prayer," he said, laughing impishly.

We sat down together on his ancient sofa; I pulled a few books from my rucksack. I'd come to talk about Suzanne Morgan, but something held me back. "Any of these interest you?" I asked.

He squinted to read the titles. "I think the one by C.S. Lewis. It gladdens my heart to know of an Englishman who shares my faith."

"Right you are. Are you ready for some tea before I start?"

"Are you sure you want to do this? It could take more of your time than you mean to be spending with an old man." He asked sincerely, wouldn't have flinched if I'd suggested I had better places to be.

"Who do I have to spend time with other than you?"

"That pretty artist has her cap set on you." He didn't look pleased.

"We're friends, nothing more. I explained that to Jillian. She understood me." I should have said I wished she did. A nagging worry told me I would have to talk to her again.

Eric nodded. "Time will tell. It must be difficult for you with so few women around of marrying age, and ones with faith, too."

"Eric, my heart's been broken once. I'm not looking to have it broken again."

"Who said anything about you getting a broken heart? If its God's will and you aren't acting all stiff-necked, there won't be any break'n. Might get a bruise now and again, but noth'n last'n." Looking into my eyes, he said, "I will make it my business to pray for a wife for you, one you'll be willing to risk your heart on. That's when you'll know God sent her for you, and you'll remember that I prayed her to you. In the meantime, I could use that tea now and then would surely enjoy time spent with you and Mr. Lewis."

Talk of Suzanne would wait for another day.

The next evening, after a full day at the barn, I remembered to check messages. I saw "9" flashing on my answering machine; they must have been accumulating for almost a week. Several were to reschedule riding lessons. Two were from Jillian.

"Peter, it's me. This is the third time I've called today. It's now 7 o'clock. Where are you, darling?" I deleted it and went on to the next.

"Peter, it's me. I really am rather put out by you. I think you owe me an explanation. I'll be here a little while longer. Be a lamb and ring me up." The sweetness in her voice could not mask her ire. It did nothing but stir me up. Really, the woman was too much. She thought she could keep me on a short leash, and I was fed up with it.

I stormed from the house and headed to The Kings Guard for a pint. Driving to the pub, I realized that I must talk to Jillian about our relationship, and soon. I dreaded it, knew she was more attached to me than I to her, but this could not continue.

And then it hit me, took the wind right out of me. Is this how it was for Suzanne? I worked to remember some hint of interest from her during the few times we'd been together. At the beach, eating dinner, at the Minack—lovely times, but woefully platonic. Not that it should have progressed much further yet, but she gave no indication that it might. She seemed no more interested in me than, well, I was in Jillian. I drove slowly towards the pub with a heavy heart. As I pulled into the car park, I saw Jillian's car. I didn't have the strength for a row, so I turned around and drove along the coast instead.

Forty minutes later, I arrived home to find Jillian's car outside and the cottage lit up. She'd intruded like this before, ignoring me when I told her I didn't like it. I paused and asked for forbearance.

No sooner had I stepped away from the car than she appeared at the door. "Hello, darling. Where have you been?"

Immediately annoyed, I took a deep breath. "Jillian, what a surprise. What brings you here this evening?" I said, trying to keep my voice light, coming inside.

"You, lamb. I've missed you. Didn't you get my messages?"

"Just this evening. It's been a full week."

"So busy you couldn't even check your messages?" Un-phased by my silence, Jillian continued. "I saw you leave the pub. You didn't notice me waving, so I came straight away."

We stood face to face in the living room. I stepped away and sat in the armchair. This left Jillian only the couch across the room. She hesitated, then perched herself on the edge, ready to pounce. Her fingernails dug into the cushion.

"Peter, I'm at a loss to understand your behavior. Care to explain it to me?"

"I was just taking a drive and thinking about that." I paused, hearing the coldness in my voice. This was going to be hard enough without sounding mean. "I'm convinced that we see our relationship differently."

"What are you talking about?" she asked, her nails nearly piercing the cushion.

"Jillian, I believe you are more serious about me than I am about you. It's just that simple." I knew she wouldn't let it be.

"That makes no sense. We want to get married."

"No, you want to get to married. I never said I did."

"Of course you did. We talked about it. I remember with perfect clarity." She paused, watching me. Her eyes narrowed. "It's that American, that Suzanne Morgan. She's chasing you, and your mind's in a jumble."

"That's ridiculous. I'm her friend and nothing more. This is about you and me. We want different things for our lives; have important differences in our core." She looked at me with such a blank expression, I erupted. "And with regard to our friendship, I find your possessiveness wearing. I'll not have it anymore."

She pushed my feet aside to make room on the ottoman and sat down. Then she put her hand on my leg and gently rubbed it. "If I've been possessive, it's because I thought you belonged to me and that I belonged to you. Isn't that what love is about? Belonging."

Pushing her hand away, I sat up. "There's the problem. We're friends and we have fun together, but it isn't love and it never will be. I'm sorry."

Her face contorted in rage. "Brilliant! Really! I spend months giving myself to you, and waiting for you, and you say you don't love me and never will? So where does that leave us? Why are you telling me this now?"

"Because things must change. I don't want what has been a pleasant friendship to end up ruined. You can't keep hoping for something that is never going to happen, and you can't keep telling people we're to get married."

"A pleasant friendship? Is that all this has been, you dolt? I think something different, not better, mind you, came along from America and that your curiosity has got the better of you. Plain and simple. Once you've tasted the little treat and found it's all just a sugary coating, and nothing more, you'll remember when you had gourmet and gave it up for a holiday trifle."

She got up and paced in front of me. I had glimpsed her meanness before and pretended I didn't, but I wouldn't ignore her insults about Suzanne. Standing up, I took her by the shoulders.

"Jillian, do you really want to destroy the friendship we have built because it didn't turn out according to your hopes? Does the friendship itself have no value to you? Do I have no value to you except as a husband?"

As though a switch flipped, she stood on her tiptoes, and in a coquettish gesture, kissed my cheek and ran her fingers through my hair. "You just need time. You are worth the wait." She took her keys from the table and strode to the door. Then turning, her face full of confidence, she said, "You'll love me. And soon."

 

 

"Oh dear. That is most distressing and so disappointing. I had hoped—well, you know what I'd hoped." We sat in the library of Eleanor's house; I had just finished telling her of Ian's visit to Eric. Wally lay curled up by the fireplace. I left my wing chair to join him. Rubbing his ears, I realized that Winston was probably lonely for me at home. I needed to be on my way soon, but we still hadn't had the conversation I'd come to have.

I met Eleanor when I first arrived in this village, which, like so many others, could be unwelcoming to newcomers. The first time I attended church, Eleanor approached me with an invitation to lunch with her after the service. She'd heard that a new headmaster was due at Oakton and supposed I was he. In no time, she put me at ease and won my trust. I found myself disclosing more to her than I expected to, but I never regretted it. Eleanor was discreet, wise, and loyal. Sitting here now, I knew I needed to put my pride in check and listen to her. I cleared my throat.

"Eleanor, I'm in a muddle with Jillian."

She nodded. She had warned me months ago about befriending Jillian. *Be sure to watch yourself. She's a lovely girl and it may not be wise to set yourself up to temptation.* Now she looked at me. "Oh dear."

"It's not what you think. I've not fallen to temptation. No, the problem is she's become demanding and possessive. She thinks she loves me. Says she thought I loved her."

Eleanor's eyebrows shot up. "Why did she think that?"

"I don't know. I only ever meant to be kind and enjoy a friendship, to have someone to do things with. She's jumped to conclusions, told some people we were planning to marry"

"What have you done about it?" Her tone was urgent.

"I've talked to her more than once and again yesterday. I told her I didn't love her, that I'd never marry her."

"And how did she take that? Not well, I imagine." This was not a cursory comment. Eleanor knew Jillian's obstinacy when she set her mind on something.

"First, she got furious. Then, in no uncertain terms, told me that I would love her. And soon."

One of Eleanor's qualities was the care she took with her words. I'd learned to be patient when we spoke. Finally, she responded. "My goodness. She's quite determined. I daresay she's not one to value friendship. Rather 'a means to an end' focus. She'll not be easily dissuaded."

I hung my head; the weight of my problems felt so heavy. "I've come to talk to you about someone else too.

"Who?" she asked. I was glad to see her surprise, proof that the rumor mill was slow.

"Suzanne Morgan." Slowly, I lifted my head. Eleanor's eyes were wide in surprise.

"I didn't realize you'd met," she said.

"Her daughter was a rider before the accident that killed her husband. Lydia Howell left my name on a list of area contacts for Muirfield. Blair's been coming to the barn to groom the horses. One thing led to the next, and we've spent some time together."

"The three of you?"

I nodded. "And the two of us. The other night we went to the Minack while Blair spent the night with a new friend." This was the real reason I'd come to talk, but the words didn't come easily now. She let me fight with myself, with my pride, with what I knew was true, but she didn't demand more than I could say.

"The truth of it, Eleanor, is that I'm quite attracted to Suzanne. It's taken me by surprise. But it seems rife with problems. How my feelings can be so strong when we've only been together a few times? One minute I think she's feeling something, too, and then it's gone. I only want to have the possibility of more. Something to hope in, but she keeps wavering back and forth. It's terribly confusing."

I took a deep breath. "Eleanor, it's getting the better of me. Jillian's too headstrong and Suzanne's too timid. What is wrong with these women?"

Eleanor placed her hands on mine, her skin dry and warm. Then, in a tone I'd heard from my father, she said, "Peter, the problem in both of these relationships is you."

# 7

## Suzanne

Clouds stirred the sky into pinwheels of color. Cornflower. Powder. Robin's egg. What a pleasant distraction from my own shades of blue. Downcast. Pensive. Troubled. I hadn't bargained for having my heart twisted in knots. This trip was to be a retreat, a respite from the load I carried. Instead, it seemed I had exchanged one set of burdens for another. At home, the constant juggling, invariable guilt, and unavoidable reminders exhausted me. Here, the dizzying confusion, unwelcome surprises and inevitable changes left me tired and worn. I hardly knew what I felt, or even what I should feel.

Ian's call brought me back to earth. Blair was spending the afternoon at Muirfield, and I had no reason to say no when he asked to stop by. He showed up with a handful of pamphlets, then looked annoyed when I wouldn't commit to an outing without consulting Blair. Nevertheless, I held firm.

As we walked to the door, he placed his hand on the small of my back. "I am pleased we were able to get together today on such short notice. I tried to reach you last Monday night." He looked at me expectantly. I squirmed, remembering the evening with Peter.

"I called," he continued, "but when there was no answer, I came by to make certain that you weren't lying in a heap somewhere." I fell into a stubborn silence. "It seems you are going to make me ask." He tried to sound playful, but failed completely. "Where did you find to go in this quiet little corner of the world?"

"I saw a delightful play at the Minack."

"I'm impressed. Tricky driving, getting to that isolated little spot. Did the roads give you any bother?"

I knew he wouldn't stop probing and surrendered to the inevitable. "I rode with Peter Stewart." Saying it aloud opened the door to unexpected feelings.

I had liked it. A lot. Peter didn't need to prove anything, especially by putting others down, Edward's method of choice; or shutting people down with lectures, my father's. Trouble was, I barely knew how to relate to someone like Peter, leaving me awkward and on edge when we were together.

A vein pulsed in Ian's neck. "Rode with him, you say? You already had tickets then?"

"He had an extra ticket. It's wonderful. Have you seen it?"

"No," he answered coldly.

I forced a smile. "Well, I can recommend it. It was great fun."

"And did Peter say how he ended up with an extra ticket? Was Jillian suddenly taken ill?"

I blushed, resenting this inquisition and realizing I didn't much like mention of Jillian. "I don't know. He didn't say anything about her."

"I see," he said disdainfully. I felt like a fool and hardly knew why. I had nearly pushed him out the door when he stopped. "Suzanne, this may be none of my business, but I feel I should caution you. Going out with Stewart might cause some confusion, and I would hate to see you put in an awkward situation. He and Jillian are practically engaged. You don't want people to talk, especially since you are new here. It would be such a shame for anything to cast a bad light on your judgment."

He kissed my cheek and left. I held the tears back until the door closed behind him.

≈

It was Blair's eleventh birthday. She and Margaret chose a window table. Blair had picked this place from our guidebook, and it turned out to be immensely popular. We had to take a late reservation and weren't seated until almost 8 o'clock.

Margaret and I listened to Blair tell us all about the home DVD Rachel sent. Silly and stupid and wonderful, it showed everything from her messy room to her little brother covered in mud to the pool where she competed on the swim team. Her mom filmed her practicing a back dive, then laughing hilariously when she kept flubbing it. At the very end, she leaned in close and whispered, telling Blair how much she missed her. She ended with her own rendition of "Tomorrow" from *Annie*.

Margaret's face fell. "I guess that means you wish you were back in America for your birthday."

"Not really. It was super nice of Rachel, but I'm really happy to be here." Servers fanned out across the room, lighting votives on tables. The girls were delighted. Eating dinner by candlelight, ordering whatever they wanted, just like grown-ups. The review had been right about the slow service, but the food was better than I expected. We would have cake at the cottage, so didn't linger after dinner.

I was herding the girls out when the door was abruptly pulled out of my hand. I nearly crashed into Jillian, followed closely by Peter. "Watch out," she snapped.

I couldn't hold my laughter inside. "Oh, I'm sorry," I choked. "I didn't see you coming."

"The door was closed. How could you?" Peter offered good-naturedly, seeming unsure at whom to look.

Blair came to the rescue. "Peter, it's my birthday! I wish you could have joined us." Her face lit up, and a smile stretched from ear to ear. I felt a pang of hurt.

Peter gave his full attention to Blair, ignoring the awkwardness he had to know I was feeling. "Me too. Did you have something special?"

Before she could answer, Jillian tugged at his arm. "Peter, love, we'll lose our res. Let's hurry, shall we?"

A look of extreme discomfort came over his face, and I wondered whose feelings he was concerned about. I heard his trailing voice as we hurried off, "Looking forward to seeing you girls tomorrow…" No such message for me.

The girls chattered all the way back, oblivious to my silence. I replayed Ian's comments in my mind, and then the strangeness I experienced upon seeing Peter with Jillian. What should it matter, I wondered? I was merely Peter's friend. Perhaps I did think about him otherwise from time to time, but that didn't change what was real. Or what was right.

I spent a restless night tossing and turning. What little sleep did come was littered with anxious, fearful dreams. Finally, in the early morning hours, I fell into a restful sleep, only to be awakened at 7 o'clock by a hungry daughter, wanting pancakes for breakfast. I crawled out of bed and stumbled towards the kitchen.

Distracted and upset, I grabbed the griddle handle without using the hot pad. I screamed, dropping it in the middle of the floor, pancake batter and oil spilling into a slimy mess. Blair and Margaret came running, but I kept them from entering the kitchen, assuring them I was okay. I tried putting ice on my hand but nearly fainted from the pain. I grabbed a dishtowel, ran it under the cold water, and wrapped it around my hand. It was obvious; I needed to get to the hospital.

I told Blair I was going out and got her promise to stay out of the kitchen. "I'll finish the pancakes as soon as I get back," I promised.

I had a general idea of where the hospital was, but couldn't think straight and ended up making several wrong turns. Near panic, I finally found it and followed signs to the Casualty Department, which I sincerely hoped meant Emergency Room.

After a quick check in, I was directed to the waiting room. I took a seat in the back and leaned my head against the wall, fighting tears and trying to concentrate on not screaming. Lost for a while in the deep, black pain, a familiar voice pulled me back to the present.

It was Ian. Walking out of the treatment area, his arm about a tearful elderly woman. He led her to a seat, then approached the desk. When he turned around, he saw me and ran over.

"What are you doing here?" He stared at the dishtowel covering my left hand; his eyes and voice all compassion. I explained. He told me, reluctantly, that he needed to rejoin Mrs. Harris until her family arrived. I understood, even though I hated being left alone with my pain. A little while later, Mrs. Harris' daughter hurried through the door, freeing Ian to join me.

Finally, my name was called. Ian guided me to a bed and then offered to check on Blair and Margaret. The doctor came, and he quietly slipped into the hall. When he returned, the nurse had wrapped my hand in gauze and obtained a prescription for more of the salve she'd applied to the burn. The doctor gave me a dose of pain medication, accompanied with a warning that it could make me light-headed.

"You'll want to show extra care this afternoon. Musn't spend much time on your feet. And eat lightly. Stomach could feel rather wretched from the medicine." I mumbled my thanks, already feeling woozy.

Ian helped me climb off of the table and kept me steady as I shuffled to the door.

"This is really quite frightful," he declared. "I wish I could spend the afternoon with you, but it's my day in the rota at the pensioner's home."

He eased me into the car with a worried look. "I'll talk to Blair when we get you home. Make sure she nurses you properly."

I awoke in my bed a few hours later, momentarily confused about why I was there. Then the dull throbbing reminded me. My last memory was of driving away from the hospital with Ian. With slow, wobbly steps, I made my way to the kitchen. The girls were sitting at the table, eating sandwiches and trading stories from horse shows.

Blair rushed toward me. "Are you okay? Dr. Hamilton said I couldn't bother you."

I nearly fell into the chair she pulled out for me. "You wouldn't have been a bother, but I needed to sleep. I'm sorry I can't take you to the barn," I said with a pasty mouth. I tried licking my lips. Margaret saw and got a glass of water. Just a few sips and my stomach reeled.

"It's okay. Dr. Hamilton is coming back soon. He's taking us, and Margaret's mom is bringing me back. He'll be here in 25 minutes." They raced from the room to get ready but didn't get far before returning. "Oh yeah, we're supposed to make you a sandwich. What do you want?"

I chose the easiest thing for them to make, with no thought of what sounded good. I choked down half of the peanut butter sandwich before lying on the couch in the living room. I awoke to a jolt of pain shooting through my hand and up my arm. Must have knocked my hand in my sleep. Whatever the reason, I needed another pain pill. I shuffled down the hall and looked at the clock. I didn't remember hearing Blair leave, but the house was silent. Not due back for hours, I had time to sleep off the medicine. In no time, I succumbed.

An hour later, a wave of nausea woke me. Maybe I could quell it with food. I forced down the rest of my sandwich, which helped a little. Lying down on the couch again, I thought how stupid I was for all of this. Time crept by, measured only by swells of pain. I tried watching television, some detective show, but even that was too much. Concentration of any sort was impossible.

My stomach finally decided to be done with it, sending me tearing for the bathroom upstairs. A relentless cycle of choking, heaving, and vomiting followed. Between episodes, I laid on the cool tile floor. Eventually, I pulled myself to the bed, sinking into the duvet. After almost an hour, and back on the bathroom floor, I heard the door open. Blair called out. In between heaves, I answered. I was crawling back to bed on my one good hand when the door opened. I almost fell over. It wasn't Blair entering the bedroom.

"Blimey, Suzanne, mind yourself," Peter exclaimed. Before I could respond, he picked me up and carried me to bed. "You should never have been left here alone."

"I'm alright, really. Forgot to eat something before I took a pill."

"It doesn't matter why... How long has this been going on?" He pulled a blanket around my shoulders.

"I don't know. A few hours?" I couldn't even lift my head to look at the clock.

"You've got to go back to hospital."

"No," I said with surprising strength. I would not put him out of his way for this. "I'll be fine once my stomach settles down and I can eat some toast. The doctor said today would be the worst."

"Blair said you'd hurt your hand, but this was not what I envisioned. How did this happen?"

"Stupid carelessness. I picked up the griddle without using a hot pad." Just then, Blair called his name. He gave my shoulder a squeeze before hurrying from the room.

Horrified, I realized what I must look and smell like. I forced myself to the bathroom sink and, fueled by the power of vanity, managed to brush my hair. But when I started to brush my teeth, the nausea hit again and crumpled to the floor.

"What happened?" Peter rushed in, instinctively reaching for me.

"No, I'd better stay here. Go downstairs. I'll be down later."

"Certainly not. I'm not leaving you alone again." I couldn't believe my ears. I was not about to have this man near me while my head was in the toilet.

"Really, Peter, I appreciate your help, but I'm a big girl. I'll be better soon."

"That's not the point, is it?" He looked at me with certainty, not an ounce of reticence in his face. He would not be easily dissuaded.

Mustering my strength, I tried my most forceful look. "I need you to go downstairs. This is humiliating." I held my stomach and rocked slightly. "I'm going to be sick again. Please go."

"There's absolutely nothing for you to be embarrassed about. If I were a doctor, you wouldn't think twice about me being here. I'm not going to leave you to be sick alone."

Suddenly, I lurched up over the toilet, retching and vomiting. Peter steadied my shoulders so I could use my hand to pull my hair back. It was a good thing that I didn't have real hopes of us being anything more than just friends, because this would put an end to any romantic illusions he might have had. Finally done, I started to fall back onto the floor when Peter, for the second time that day, carried me to the bed, gently laid me down. Then he went back into the bathroom and got two cold washcloths. With one he carefully wiped my lips, the other he folded across my forehead. I closed my eyes and mumbled thank you, finally devoid of pride or protest.

He went into the bathroom and opened the closet. Then I heard him go downstairs. I drifted off to sleep but awoke to the sound of running water. Peter came in and sat down on the corner of the bed, smelling like cleanser. I was too exhausted to object.

"Go to sleep. I'll be downstairs with Blair."

The rattle of dishes woke me up. I'd been asleep for three hours. I felt weak, but better. Even the throb in my hand had dulled. I pulled on my robe. From the top step I heard Peter and Blair talking in the kitchen. Neither had noticed me yet, so I came down a few steps and sat.

"You have to tear the lettuce." Blair was telling Peter how to make his first American-style salad. "Daddy told Mom it takes too long and to just cut it but she said this is the right way. And she cuts all that dark green off and all the seeds out of the middle, too. Oh yeah, put cheese in the salad. Dad liked the yellow cheese but sometimes she used the white."

"Your mother isn't bothered about being independent, is she?" Peter asked.

"I don't know. What does that mean?"

"She likes to take care of things herself. Without help from anyone else."

"Maybe. I can remember when she would ask my Dad for help, but he was usually too busy," she answered. "Now we have to find some dressing. Mommy likes to make hers from the cupboard. Oil and something. I can't remember. I'll ask her," she said. I heard a thump, the familiar sound of Blair jumping off the counter, where she often perched for a pre-dinner chat.

"Hold up, there," Peter said. "She's probably asleep. Let's sort it out ourselves."

More conversation about the dressing ensued. Then he said, "You looked smart last night. Did you have fun?"

"Mommy let me pick out the restaurant and I got to order whatever I wanted. I had spaghetti. And she let me invite Margaret. If we'd been at home it would have been Rachel. Except for how much I miss her, I could stay here forever," Blair declared.

Peter laughed. "That's quite a statement. What do you think your mum would say about that?"

What would I say? Before I had time to consider it, Blair answered for me. "She likes it a lot here too. She told me that if she didn't have the store to go back to she wouldn't bother going back at all." I winced, wishing Blair hadn't put it quite like that.

"She wouldn't miss family and friends too much?" Peter asked. I wondered if there was something else behind that question.

"Granddaddy fights with her a lot. And I don't think she has many friends except Cathy, 'cause she was always working and doing stuff for Daddy. Plus she's happy here. It's nice. I like doing things with her."

The truth of her words pierced through me. Blair was right. I was happy here. I heard water running and guessed they were cleaning up. In case they felt the need to check on me, I stood up, straining to hear over the noise.

"Do you want to see what Rachel sent me for my birthday? It's really neat. I'll show you when we're done."

"Sure. But what can I give you for your birthday? Just because I missed it doesn't mean you won't get a gift."

"Really? How about lessons on Fergie?" she asked without hesitation.

"Hmmm…we'll see what we can work out." It was nice of him to let her down gently.

"I won't be very good since the accident. I lose my balance easy now. When I asked Mom about it, she said she didn't think I'd be able to ride again. But I miss it so bad. And I'm doing better."

"I don't mean to contradict your mum, but are you sure there's nothing we could do that would get you back on a horse?"

"I don't know of anything," she mumbled.

"Right."

Then, in the way of young girls, Blair flitted right to the next subject. "I don't like TV over here. It's weird. I can't find anything I can even understand, except for *All Creatures Great & Small*, caused I watched that at home."

"I'd fancy a talk then. I live alone so it's a treat for me to have the company." I sat back down on the step, eager to keep listening.

"What do you want to talk about?"

"Tell me about your father. Were you great friends?" Blair paused, and moments between Edward and her flashed through my mind. I worried, wondered how she would describe their relationship.

"No. I... well, he...he scared me sometimes, and he was always sort of mad at me." Her voice was small. "I don't think he liked me very much." I could picture Blair biting at her nails, something she did whenever she was nervous or unhappy.

"Knowing you the way I do, I can't imagine that your father didn't like you. But, you know, some people have a hard time showing others how they feel." It was a generous thing to say. I'd said it too. Many times. She never believed me.

"Yeah, maybe... But I don't think so." Blair got quiet. I admired her honesty.

"Tell me what fun you had together," he persevered. After what he'd told me about his father, I don't think he could fathom such a strained father-child relationship.

"Once he let me go with him to New York on a business trip. He took me to a play and we got dressed up and went to a fancy restaurant on top of a big building. It was really cool. You could see the whole city. And I ordered ginger ale that they brought me in a special glass so I could pretend I was grown up. Everybody treated Daddy so nice and they did everything he said. It was neat. I felt sort of like a princess."

Edward's description of the trip was somewhat different. He had spent a good deal of the time being annoyed with Blair's chattiness and relentless curiosity. Hearing Blair's fond memories of it broke my heart. It's a shame Edward had missed what had been magic to his daughter.

"...And some mornings, when he was driving me to school, we'd talk about stuff. And that was fun. He wasn't yelling at me for something I'd done wrong, he was just talking to me about what his day was going to be like and asking me about mine. I liked talking like that." Those had been sweet times for Edward, too, at least on those days when he didn't have the pressure of an early meeting.

"Sure, I know what you mean. Our days are made up of the ordinary things of life. They don't seem so ordinary when we talk about them with people we care about."

I heard some rustling around and, afraid that they might catch me, I rose to sneak back up the stairs. Then I heard Blair's next question.

"Can I ask you something?" He must have nodded, because she continued. "What about that lady, that artist? Is she your girlfriend?"

Everything stilled, even the beat of my heart.

"Jillian? A good friend is all." I let out my breath. "Why do you ask?"

"Just wondering," Blair said. "How come you aren't married? Can't you find anybody who'll marry you or are you too old?" Peter laughed long and loud. Just then the phone rang. Fortunately, Peter was still laughing, so I was able to get back upstairs undetected. He burst into the hall, and I turned around, giving every appearance of having just started to descend.

"Hello," he said into the phone. He saw me, his smile wide and encouraging. Then, to the caller he said, "This is Peter Stewart. Who is asking?" The smile froze as he listened further. "She's here, just out of her sickbed." He covered the phone, handing it to me just as I reached bottom. "It's Ian in need of a report."

I took it from him, returning the smile. The strain around his mouth deepened, and I realized he might have thought I was smiling because of Ian. There was no way to set that straight without over blowing it. I was mad at myself and irritated with Ian's timing.

"Hello, Ian. It's kind of you to call." I wanted Peter to stay, to hear my businesslike tone, to know that I'd rather have been talking to him, but he turned around and walked towards the kitchen. Dishes clanged loudly, his movements swift and efficient.

"I see you're well enough for visitors. Quite an improvement, that."

"Peter's been keeping Blair company. I believe he fixed her dinner while I've been upstairs sleeping off the medication. Thank you again for your help. I couldn't have managed without you."

"But you can now, can't you? Yes, well, I was calling to see if you needed anything. But since obviously you don't, I won't keep you. However, I feel I must warn you again to watch your reputation. I question whether it's appropriate for Stewart to be there while you don't completely have your wits about you. I'll check in with you tomorrow." He hung up before I could respond.

I hung up the phone, feeling confused, and somehow both guilty and angry. Only later, after I had eaten a light supper and convinced Peter that he didn't need to sleep on the couch, I realized that he'd never answered Blair's question. I fell asleep wondering what he would have said.

The next morning Blair bounded up the steps, turned the corner to my room, and stuck her head through the door. "There's a pretty lady downstairs." I pulled my robe over my shoulders and followed her into the living room.

Eleanor's face contracted when she saw me. "Your poor hand. Come sit." She moved toward the couch. "I didn't mean to disturb. I came to see if you were wanting for anything."

I sat down, cradling my injured hand. "How did you know?"

"Ian told me. Saw him at Boots. He said you'd had an accident but thought you'd be quite fine by today. I decided to see for myself."

"It's healing. I think a couple of days will make a big difference."

"I thought as much. I'll return this evening with your supper. Shall we say 7 o'clock?"

I couldn't help but think how Edward would have been horrified to have someone like Eleanor bring us dinner. He'd have said it was beneath her, or me, to need help. Funny, nothing about her indicated she felt that way. So I accepted, enjoying the freedom I felt to be on the receiving end of such graciousness.

"It's so kind of you to come. Have you had a nice morning?"

"I have." Her face relaxed. "I like to start each day reminding myself of something true. Then I reflect upon it a bit and record my thoughts. It's a lifelong habit; I'd sooner go without breakfast than my bit of morning quiet. Do you do anything similar?"

Did reading the Business section of the Washington Post count? Edward had insisted on it before we went to the office each day, lest we fall a step behind the competition. Since his death, I'd continued out of respect, but it had turned it into a thing I dreaded. I'd not thought of it since being here. "I used to, at home."

"Ah," she smiled. "It's a joy, is it not? It keeps me rather sane." Her laugh was so warm and light, I wanted it, too. But, if I were honest, I really didn't know what she meant. And I felt ashamed to ask.

Blair's voice cut into my thoughts. I'd forgotten she was in the room. "What do you mean true? Like the sky is blue? That's true."

Eleanor turned to Blair. "That's true some days, isn't it? But not every day. I have in mind things that are true, no matter the weather, or where you are. Things that are always true, despite what may happen."

"Like what?" I was thankful for Blair's questions, though slightly ashamed for hiding behind them.

"Today I thought, when I know the world is not as it was meant to be, it's good that I long for a day when it will be set right." She sat so still and peaceful, almost other-worldly

When neither of us said anything, she added, "Yesterday, I pondered this: an anxious heart weighs people down, but a kind word cheers them up." Her smile was gentle, easy. "Isn't that so true? People need to hear kind words when they are worried."

Blair nodded emphatically. "Yeah, like when Rachel thought Kara told Kevin Wilson that Rachel liked him, I told her that Kara was too afraid to talk to Kevin and she was just saying that to be mean. And I was right."

Eleanor snuck a wink at me and laughed. "That's very much like what I'm talking about. You were thinking of what would make your friend happy." Blair beamed. "Suzanne, you look tired. I'll be off, but back soon enough." She kissed us European style, which always got Blair giggling. With lighter hearts, we saw her out the door.

Blair found *National Velvet* on television and soon lost herself to dreams of owning a horse. I tried watching with her, but I couldn't stop thinking about what Eleanor had said. I wished I'd had the courage to ask what she meant. When the world isn't as it was meant to be… She said she knew it. I didn't know it, but I certainly felt it. When I tried to express this to my father, after Mom died, his terse reply was, *That's just how things are.* *Well, right*, I remember thinking, *but is it how they should be?* A woman dying before she reached 50 years? Too many years of my life lived without my mother? Mom never knowing Blair? And what about Edward? Things *aren't* how they should be. Thank you, Eleanor, for saying it.

# 8

# Peter

Sometimes the only thing to do is run.

I ran along the sea, the cliffs, and the labyrinth of country lanes that meandered through our little spot in the world. Day after day, hour after hour. Before going to the barn to groom and muck, and at the end of a day of lessons and bill paying. But I couldn't run far enough to leave myself behind. Though Eleanor's words stung, I knew my nature, the hard truth. There was no ready defense, nothing with which to argue. I was, however, still working out her full meaning.

Eleanor hoped I'd work it out on my own, but I needed help. Eric was already worn down, and I feared tiring him even more. Ian wasn't an option. When I first heard about the new vicar, I thought we might have some common interests, but it took just one meeting to see we were cut from different cloth. I wanted to get to know him; he wanted to know the local gossip. A man needs a best mate, but mine wouldn't be found in the West Country.

∾

"Thomas, it's me. Can you spare a few minutes?" I'd worn a path pacing round the cottage, working out how to start the discussion. Now I sat on the bench by the yew bushes, buoyed by the bright, clear day.

"I can't believe it's you. I planned to ring you tonight with my news." His voice ran over the edges with wonder, something I hadn't heard since Liza was expecting their third child.

His joy lifted me out of my own troubles. "Say it, man. What's the news?"

"I'm in love." The joy I felt quickly dissipated, and confusion and anger overwhelmed me so I couldn't speak. "Did you hear me?" he asked, his feet now a bit closer to earth.

"Yeah, I heard you," I groused. "But I don't understand. Did you just meet her in the last month?"

"No, I've known Gemma for awhile. She's been a friend, a good friend. But something has changed."

"Weren't you just here saying you didn't know if you'd ever remarry? I can't work out why you didn't tell me."

"Because I never expected it, was satisfied with the friendship. I hadn't dared to hope it would be more. But, the more we knew of each other, the more our feelings changed. It's been the perfect progression."

How could I stay a scrooge when there was something to celebrate? "Well, I'm chuffed for you, man. It's brilliant news. I can't wait to meet her."

"She feels the same about you. We're all raving about you—she can hardly believe you're not a super-hero." His innocent joke cut straight to my heart.

"Yeah, well, that's why I rang you. I need to ask you a question."

"Go on then."

"Eleanor said something unsettling. I've spent a week sorting out her meaning. But I can't quite lay hold of it."

"What's it about?" He'd always been there for me, so I don't know why I found this so hard. I stopped the posturing and blurted it out. "Jillian and Suzanne."

"Hold up—who's Suzanne?"

"She's an American. I met her just after you were here."

"Divorced, is she?"

His assumption irritated me. "Widow," I snapped. "She's here for a few months, at least."

"Ah." Something was lining up in his mind, but I didn't know what. "What did Eleanor say, then?"

I relayed the conversation I'd been replaying in my head all week long. When I got to Eleanor's conclusion, Thomas laughed.

"Oh Pete, I think things are coming full circle for you." I braced for where I guessed he was going with this.

"How so?" I asked.

"It's time to look at what happened with Laura, full in the face."

I guess a man can only run for so long.

⌒

Blair searched the tack box for a brush while I lost myself in thoughts of her mum. I'd tried to greet Suzanne when she dropped Blair off, but she sped away before I could get there. We did manage to wave at each other, but I couldn't help but notice an odd look on her face. Embarrassment, maybe? I could understand, remembering the last time I saw her. Seeing Blair had the tools she needed, I felt fine to leave her with Willow, a dappled brown a bit too tall to be classified a pony.

Margaret was halfway through her jumping course when I'd left to greet Blair. When we resumed our lesson, Blair came to the gate in time to see Margaret and Fergie clear the brush box, a clean 1.2-meter jump.

"Right, Margaret, that's the way. Clean and aggressive." I turned to Blair. "Did you see that?" When Blair nodded, I added, "Pretty, wasn't it?"

"She's good. She didn't hesitate at all. I would have." She kept her eyes on Margaret, who was approaching the next jump.

I did, too. We watched them float over the brush box. I turned back to Blair. "Would you? Why?"

"I always got a little afraid just when Midnight would start the jump. I was nervous I'd lose my balance and fall off." Pleasure slid from her face.

"That wouldn't have been the worst thing, would it?" What kind of instructor had she had?

"Daddy didn't like it when I fell off. He said it looked like I didn't know what I was doing." Such rot. I paused and tried to control my rising anger. I didn't have the right to judge this man, despite the confused brown eyes looking back at me.

"Did your father ride, too?" I asked.

Blair giggled. "No. Daddy didn't like all the dirt out at the barn. I don't think he even really liked horses. He only helped me brush down Midnight once, and when we finished, he seemed kinda upset."

"Oh, then that explains how he could be so off."

She pulled a face. "What do you mean?"

"Well, the saying around here is that you aren't a good rider if you don't have some dirt on your breeches. Do you know why?" Blair shook her head eagerly. "Because that would mean you're too careful and not willing to learn new things. I'm not talking about being wild and reckless. Margaret fell off the first time she tried a 1-meter jump. But you saw her jump today. She kept working on it, and now it's brilliant."

Blair thought for a moment. "That's what Mrs. Galloway meant when she said the cleanest rider in the ring isn't always the best rider in the ring." I was relieved to learn her instructor had her head on straight, though she'd failed to sort out Blair's confusion.

"Yes, that's exactly what she meant," I said. "Right-o, when we're done here, I've got something to show you in my office."

"I wish Mrs. Galloway had explained that to my Dad," Blair sighed. Wistfully, she turned her attention back to Margaret. When the lesson was done, Margaret circled the ring to cool Fergie down. I motioned to Blair to follow me inside. I sat at my desk, and Blair settled herself on the giant sofa that nearly filled my office. This was going to be fun.

"I've got a surprise for you."

"Oh," she exhaled. "I thought I was in trouble."

I waved my hand, swatting away her concern. "Why would you be? Here's the thing. I have a mate who helped me make a special saddle for you. It's got extra straps to keep you from falling off the horse if you get dizzy."

"I thought you just told me that it's okay to fall off of a horse."

"Right you are. It depends on why you fall. Falling because of balance problems isn't the same as falling because you're learning something new."

She sat still and straight, her body rigid with anticipation. I reached beside my feet, pulled up a saddle, and placed it on my desk. She sprang up to touch it, taking no notice of its obvious age. "It's for me? Really?"

She threw her arms around me, hugging hard. My throat tightened; the words stuck inside me. Again, I wondered what kind of father could have been so hard on this sweet child.

"I thought we would surprise your mum with a little horse show just for her. Can you keep the secret?"

An hour later, an exhausted but exhilarated Blair grinned up at me, her helmet under her arm, her hair plastered against her head. I'd gotten her up on Willow. Her smile, shaky at first, turned blissful as they walked, even trotted, around the ring. After we finished, Blair put Willow in the stall. I was at the far end of the barn when the phone rang, so I asked her to answer it. She disappeared with a fast limp into my office.

I reached the doorway and heard her say, "But I'm not ready. I still have things to do." I went in and sat on the edge of the desk. "There's always stuff to do," Blair blushed and smiled conspiratorially. "I've worked really hard today. You'd be proud of me. Can't I stay just a little while longer? Peter could bring me home." Blair pulled back from the phone, and I could hear Suzanne's voice. Though I couldn't make out the words, her tone was clear. "What's wrong, mom? Why couldn't he bring me like before? Besides, I'd be back in time to go out with you and Dr. Hamilton tonight."

The joy I'd felt just moment ago vanished. And why was Suzanne so adamant that I not take Blair home? Blair hung up the phone, pouting. "I've got to hurry. She's coming right now."

I wanted to talk to Suzanne when she picked up Blair, but got stuck holding a nervous horse for Reggie Shields, the blacksmith, when she arrived. I've never been a chatty sort of fellow, so Reggie took no notice of my silent brooding. The last couple of lessons seemed to drag on. By the time I left the barn at 7:30, I felt completely deflated.

I stopped by the pub for some dinner, but a few minutes in and I knew I needed to be alone to think. I rushed through my steak and kidney pie and then returned to my car. I sat there a moment, deciding. The thought of sitting at home didn't feel right, either. It was a beautiful night; the stars were beckoning. I stopped by my cottage to get Winston, then went in search of a quiet cove and clear perspective.

Eleanor's words chewed at my heart. *The problem in both of these relationships is you.* I couldn't tunnel my way through this alone. I'd been groping in the dark for years, ever since my happy life imploded. First when Da died, followed so cruelly by Liza, and finally Laura breaking our engagement. Terrible events that seemed to snatch me out of the haven of truth that had been my life's foundation, and then thrust me into darkness.

I'd felt alone, discarded even. Thought my only recourse was to take back the reigns of my life. I tried to live by the Golden Rule, but it wasn't enough, not unless it was tethered to a greater truth. One I knew, but on which I had turned my back. What was becoming increasingly clear, both in my troubled heart and strained relationships, was that this half-truth life I was living wasn't sustainable.

⌒

Jillian invited me to attend an art show in St. Ives Friday night. It featured several contemporary artists new to the St. Ives community. She was in full force, working the room like the professional she was. This was Jillian at her best: clever, charming, in top form. Afterwards, we chose a restaurant with a harbor view. She immediately launched into a discussion about our relationship. We'd not spoken since the night of our row in my cottage.

"I've thought about our last confab. I meant what I said, you know. And I know what to do to set things on fire. You, darling, should move in with me. We need to be sharing a bed."

She nearly purred as she spoke, rubbing her leg against mine. I jumped in surprise, then tried to hide my discomfort. I looked out onto the harbor, at the small, black and white lighthouse standing at its mouth, thinking through how to respond in a way she might understand.

"I'm flattered by your feelings for me." Her eyes flashed alarm, but she held steady. "But I have to ask, what do you think it would accomplish?" It was obvious that the question confused her.

"Relationships are changed forever by sex. But not for the good." As awkward as this felt, I suddenly knew I needed to talk to Jillian about what I believed. And so I added, "Outside of marriage, of course." I shifted in my seat, trying to find a comfortable position under her glare. "I'm not saying this very well. What I mean is that I'm convinced that sex should be reserved strictly for marriage. I honestly think that's best for both people. Out of its proper time and place, it can spoil things."

"Rubbish. Do you mean to tell me that you and Laura never slept together?" she asked, her voice coming at me like a machine gun. "I mean, really Peter, I've not gone completely daft. You were together for years, weren't you?"

I felt the heat rise to my face. I was the accused sitting in the dock. "I'll not deny it, but it was a huge mistake." I let go a sigh.

The pain of that compromise still stung, along with the repercussions to the relationship. I knew whereof I spoke. I hated how I'd betrayed all that mattered most. A fog moved into the harbor. Not unlike the one taking form, I suspected, in Jillian's head. I knew this was foreign to her, odd even.

Her bewilderment changed to disdain. She pulled at her earring. "Honestly, you sound like you're from another century."

"I learned the hard way what happens when I make choices that are not true to what is most dear to me, to what makes me who I am. Whenever I am able, when I can see those choices plainly, I'll not make the wrong ones again." I did sound like a throwback. Few people thought this way anymore. But I didn't know any other way to be. I stopped for a breath.

Sitting back in my chair, I searched her face. She looked, well, gobsmacked. I wished I'd spoken this plainly sooner.

"Jillian," I said as tenderly as I could, "I've not meant to lead you on. I've been unfair. I'm deeply sorry for it. I've been lazy. Worse, cowardly, in not being clear with you." She continued to stare at me, her eyes vacant. Could it be that she still didn't understand me? I was quite thrown, realizing this. She didn't seem to be able to take in what I was saying. Maybe the fault was mine, in not being utterly, undeniably clear.

"You are a beautiful and talented woman. I've enjoyed having you as a friend to spend time with. But I've never considered you more than that. I came to Cornwall to recover from the wreckage of the breakup with Laura. I never intended to jump into something serious. In hindsight, there were signs that you felt differently. I was wrong to not address them when I took notice of them."

Jillian moved not a single muscle. She looked to be made of stone. It was a protective reaction, one I'd seen before, though she'd never quite pulled it off as well as this. But I understood. She'd offered herself to me, and I'd turned her down. I felt sorry for her, knowing it stung.

"Jillian, don't be quick to give yourself away. You deserve better."

The fog lifted, and she turned clear eyes on me. "Of course I do."

≈

"...I said, are you okay?" Suzanne looked up distractedly, blushed red and turned her face away. I'd spotted her at the market, her trolley nearly empty, as she stood motionless and blank in the middle of an aisle.

She quickly wiped her eyes. "I've been negligent in thanking you for spending time with Blair at Muirfield," she stammered.

"I can assure you, the pleasure was mine." I spoke brightly, trying to hide my nervousness. Why was she crying? She was off, and it worried me. "I tried to catch up to you, though, to see how your hand is faring. It seems like too long since we've been able to talk."

"It's better. Thank you for the concern," she answered stiffly. She might as well have been talking to a stranger. Then she looked down the aisle, first one way, then the other, before saying quietly, "I am overdue, also, in thanking you again for helping me while I was so sick. I'm not sure you should have..."

"Why not?" I interrupted, expecting the usual objection one gets from people who are terminally independent.

"Well," she stammered, "I think it may have been inappropriate."

Her reply stung. "Nonsense. You were sick and needed help."

"Well, I, Ian said...I wouldn't want to give anyone the wrong impression..."

"Who would get the wrong impression? What did Ian say?" I tried to hide my agitation.

"It doesn't matter. I shouldn't have mentioned him. I would just hate to do anything to adversely affect your reputation...or mine..."

Inwardly, I fumed like a snorting bull. Realizing I was in danger of saying something stupid, I closed my eyes and tried to gain a measure of control. Then, mindful that I might be stepping into the ring with red flag, I inquired gently, "Is it because of Jillian?"

Suzanne froze. "Jillian, no. Of course not. Well...I don't...no...of course not."

"Because if it is, we recently agreed that there not be any more confusion regarding the status of our relationship. We are friends. Only."

I watched, waiting for this to provide some relief, but it didn't appear to.

"I see. Regardless, I am very uncomfortable with the memory of your having helped me at such a vulnerable time. And I *am* concerned about impressions."

"I'm sorry, but who was there to get a wrong impression? Blair certainly wouldn't have." Suzanne shifted her feet, checked the aisle again. "I don't know what Ian said to you, but I am, and have been for quite some time, unattached." I heard my voice grow sharper, but I couldn't help it. "So there is no one in my life to read something questionable in the simple act of one person helping another. And it offends me that something like that could become twisted in anyone's mind."

Suzanne had no response. But I could see understanding dawn in her eyes. I should have stopped to let her respond, but the bull reappeared in my mind's eye. I'd have gone straight at Ian if he'd walked down the aisle at that moment.

"Really, Suzanne," I continued, "How could you let Ian put ideas like that in your head?" As soon as I said the words, I wanted them back. I'd gone too far.

Suzanne snapped out of her haze, gathered herself resolutely. I'd just given her the excuse she needed to discount all I'd said.

"I can think just fine for myself, thank you very much. These are my concerns for me and my daughter, who, by the way, I've just dropped at Margaret's. I thought they were meeting you at the barn."

"They are. I just popped in for a few things. We're low on carrots and apples for my boarders. I only stopped because it was you." My friendly attempt to lighten the mood failed.

"You'd better be on your way, then." She jerked the trolley in the opposite direction and marched down the aisle.

～

I hauled myself into the shower after a full day at the barn, letting my muscles relax under the hot water. Most of the tension, I knew, came from being worried about Suzanne. Our exchange this morning gnawed at me. That, and Ian. Than man had an ability to worm his way into vulnerable people's lives, to manipulate them. He'd done it with Suzanne, and I didn't like it.

As I dried off, I realized that I didn't see Blair leave the barn. Or more accurately, she didn't say goodbye. And that was completely unlike her. Aside from being unfailingly polite, Blair liked me, liked being my co-conspirator. We grew closer with every lesson. She would have let me know she was leaving, as sure as she said hello with each arrival. And Margaret, who arrived with Blair, left alone. I distinctly remembered watching her climb in her dad's car.

A cold dismay crept over me. This just couldn't be. I couldn't have left her there. In the five years I'd owned Muirfield, this had never happened. For a moment, I considered ringing Suzanne. I could end my misery in a moment, hearing she'd gotten safely home. But what if she hadn't? I couldn't admit I didn't know where she was. I couldn't admit to a failing like that. I had to be sure. I had to search every inch of Muirfield. I tumbled through the bedroom, throwing on clothes and shoes, and fled like a madman.

The relief I felt when I discovered Blair was not at Muirfield ended abruptly. Ian was the last person I wanted to see. He sat on the stoop,

93

holding Winston by the collar. When I got out of the car, Winston broke lose from Ian's grip to greet me. Ian followed.

"Hello, Ian, what has you skulking around here tonight?" If he were here to discuss Suzanne's honor, he'd be sorely disappointed.

"I almost ran over your dog," he said with contempt.

I glanced at Winston. "What are you talking about?"

"On my way home from visiting the Abbott's, I came around a bend in the lane, and there he was. Fortunately, I have excellent reflexes and am a dog lover myself, or he'd be dead."

"I wonder how he got out." I recalled my frenzied departure. "I did rush out, but—."

"Your door was open when I arrived." He confirmed my suspicion. "If you don't mind my asking, where were you rushing to?" His attempt to make it sound like an innocent question failed. Who was he to think he could manipulate me?

"Why do you...?" I said, more sharply than I meant to. Though I had more than enough reasons to start a row with him, I didn't want to. There had been enough drama for one evening.

"It doesn't matter. I'm just grateful you came along and were kind enough to see that he got home safely. Thank you." Taking hold of Winston's collar, I walked to the door.

"Oh, Peter, one other thing." I looked back at him. "Blair told me how kind you are to work with her everyday at Muirfield. I just wanted to thank you. It's really so charitable of you to go out of your way to help a child who is, shall we say, challenged. It means a great deal to me."

His words were tempting me beyond what I could endure. "Means a great deal to you? Why should it mean a great deal to you?"

"Sorry. I don't get your meaning," he answered smugly.

"Why should what I do for Blair Morgan mean anything to you?" I asked through clenched teeth. It was the slight chuckle that brought me to a boiling point. "What is so funny?" I demanded.

"Really, Peter, I don't understand why you should be asking the question. You must know that I am quite close to Suzanne and feel, among other things, protective of her...and Blair, of course."

I was dumbfounded. There was no mistaking the meaning in Ian's declaration. I took a deep breath, ignored the retort on my lips. Tempting as it was, I would not be goaded into a prolonged conversation with Ian, especially one about Suzanne Morgan.

"Yes, well, Blair is a good little rider. Now if you'll excuse me, it's late, and I haven't had my dinner yet."

"Jolly good. You'd best be more careful with that dog of yours. You're lucky it was me that came upon him."

Ian sped off, and I entered the kitchen, thinking luck wasn't what came to mind. I slammed the refrigerator door shut, then the cupboard, and finally, the larder. No food. Nothing to eat. When was the last time I'd been to the market? Right. This morning. Suzanne. My mind reeled with thoughts about her. And then with Ian. Hungry and agitated, I left for The King's Guard, then on to a late night run to Tesco.

The light on the answerphone blinked in the dark. Winston was insistent about going out, so I slapped his leash on and all but ran him to his spot behind the cottage. Once back in, I tried to convince myself that I was thirsty, and turned on the cold water tap. Realizing I was being stupid, I pushed the PLAY button.

"Hallo, Peter, it's your friend, Jillian." Pause. "And you know I *am* glad you are my friend. I hope you'll ring me so I can apologize for getting snippy with you last time we talked. You're such a lamb, you've probably forgotten about it already. So ring me, darling, I mean, well, please ring me, won't you?" Before I had time to think about what to say to Jillian, the next message began.

"Peter, it's Suzanne." Every nerve ending was on alert. She sounded odd. "I hardly know where to start. How could you leave Blair at Muirfield by herself? Anything could have happened... Well, she's not coming back. I never expected...I thought...well, I don't need a response. In fact, I don't want one. Don't bother to call me back."

Shocked. Leveled. Angry. Guilty. I fell heavily to the floor. So Blair had still been at the barn. Where could she have been on my last walk through? How could I have missed her? I retraced my steps, over and over, but it hardly mattered. It didn't change anything.

After a few moments, I replayed the message, this time concentrating on the fear in her voice. It shook all the way through. She sounded on the verge of breaking down. This was horrible. Unforgivable. I felt sick. How would I fix this? What could I say to her?

I turned out the lights, laid on the bed, and with Winston at my feet, felt the weight of what I'd done.

# 9

# Suzanne

Blair looked healthier and happier than I'd ever seen her. Her appetite back in full, she rooted through the kitchen to see what was for breakfast. The therapists had said that increased activity would strengthen her muscles. Time and use would heal most of her physical deficits. I was committed to finding ways for that healing to continue. Ways that didn't involve Peter Stewart.

"Mommy, I gotta go to the barn early tomorrow."

"Sorry, honey, I don't know when you'll be going back to Muirfield," I said, setting a plate of eggs in front of her.

She pushed it away. "Why not? Wha'd I do?"

I smoothed her hair, still wet from the shower, and kissed the top of her head. "Nothing. It's just that you've been spending a lot of time there, time we could spend together. Here we are on a three month vacation, and we're already in a rut." She crossed her arms, stuck out her bottom lip. Ignoring her, I pressed on, trying for an extra dose of cheeriness. "Where would you like to go?"

"The barn," she whined. "I have to. Peter's expecting me."

Anyone could see she liked Peter, but I was unprepared for how attached to him she'd become. "I already told him you aren't coming. But we'll find other great things to do."

"I don't want to do anything else." She stared at the egg. "And Margaret's there."

"You don't have to be at the barn to see her. We can invite her over anytime."

"But I'm working on something important." Her voice was full of panic, making me uneasy. I went to the sink and grabbed a glass to rinse. I couldn't understand what could be so pressing. She was, after all, only mucking and grooming. Pulling the towel from under the sink, I slowly dried my hands. I turned back to see her scowl. I took a breath. "Whatever you are working on, I'm sure Peter can get someone else to help with."

"No," she shouted, "he can't. It's—." She popped up from the table. "You can't stop me."

I'd expected resistance, not complete defiance. Frustration boiled up in me. Couldn't she see that I was the only one left to protect her? I was doing what I was supposed to do, what good mothers do. I threw the towel on the counter and walked over to her. I put my hands on her arms and bent down to be at eye level. "I don't need you to like it or understand it, but I am telling you how it is going to be. It's my decision. Not yours. Do you understand me?"

"Yeah," she muttered.

"Excuse me?" I said through clenched teeth. We glared at one another.

"Yes, ma'am," she said.

◇

Blair was sullen and distant for the next three days. We went to the library and she didn't check out a single book. We went for tea and scones and she wasn't hungry. We toured the Royal Cornwall Museum in total silence. I put away the guidebooks, surrendering to her mood. The only thing left to do was wait her out. On Wednesday, Margaret invited Blair to a movie, giving both of us much needed relief from each other. I sat nestled in a chair, happily lost in Holyrood Palace, trading my problems for those of Mary, Queen of Scots. A chipper knock at the door brought me back to Mousehole.

Ian thrust a bouquet of Dahlias toward me. "I've been remiss in checking on the patient. Ah, a smaller bandage. Well done, you." None of the previous judgment remained in his open smile.

I laughed. "I don't get credit for that. It was the salve that did the trick." He followed me into the kitchen while I searched for a vase, settling instead for a pitcher. Ian watched my pathetic attempts at flower arranging, then nudged me aside and did the job himself. He took a glass from the cupboard and helped himself to water. We went into the living room; he sat first, motioning for me to join him on the couch.

"I'm happy to see that you are mending, but I've come to inquire after Blair. I thought I would take her on a surprise expedition tomorrow." He seemed quite proud of himself, and I was glad he'd thought of it. Maybe Ian's attention would fill Peter's void. "How fun. Where do you want to take her?"

He wagged his finger at me. "I said it was a surprise, didn't I?"

I bristled at his superior tone. "Look, Ian, I don't mind you taking Blair out, but I need to know where. She could need special care depending on where you are going, and I might need to give you instructions. I won't ruin your surprise."

"You insult me," he said haughtily. "Do you think I would not be aware of how careful I need to be with someone who is handicapped?"

I pulled back as though I'd been slapped. "Handicapped? Is that how you view my child?"

"No, not handicapped. That was an unfortunate word choice. But she isn't completely normal, is she? I realize she can't do everything that normal children do. I will be very careful."

"Not normal?" I was aghast at his callous words. Thank goodness Blair was gone.

"Her balance, she's wobbly and her foot drags some, doesn't it? That's all I am saying. I don't know why you are being so tetchy. You are deliberately misunderstanding my words."

I got up and walked over to the window. Maybe I was overreacting to poor word choice. I couldn't ignore how difficult the strain between Blair and me was. It sickened me to realize how much like Edward and Blair's relationship ours had become. Ian came toward me, reaching out with a hug. "Please don't do that," I said, taking a step back. "It makes me uncomfortable."

He looked bewildered. "And why is that?"

Though I appreciated the gentle, undemanding note in his voice, I crossed my arms and hugged myself tightly. "It's inappropriate."

Now he was the one who looked like he'd been slapped. He thought for a moment. "I see I should tread more carefully." He lifted his eyebrows. "Are you sure it has nothing to do with Peter Stewart? Has he said something to upset you?"

"Of course not." Exhausted, I sat in my reading chair. This conversation needed to be steered away from Peter Stewart for more than one reason.

"Ian, please let's start over. I'm happy you want to take Blair somewhere special. I'm sorry for picking at your every word. I'm sure she will enjoy it. But I would still like you to tell me where."

The lines in his face smoothed, and he smiled again. "I will tell you this. It is to a place rife with *in idipsum*, beauty for its own sake." He paused with a flourish, seemingly impressed with his use of Latin. "If you would just trust me, I promise to bring her back safe and sound. No harm will come to her. I will treat her as my own."

As that really was my most pressing concern, I agreed. We walked to his car, finalizing the plans. "I'll be here tomorrow at half-nine. She should be dressed demurely."

I nodded, thinking that was how she always dressed. Once again, I realized I was dissecting his every word. We said goodbye, and at the last second, before slipping into the seat, he reached up and kissed me. Shocked into silence, I couldn't utter a protest before he sped away.

❧

I was still troubled by the interaction with Ian. Why hadn't I insisted he tell me where they were going? What made me shrink from my role as Blair's sole protector? When I reached the top of the hill, I saw Peter's car in front of Wisteria Cottage. I almost turned around, but decided I would enjoy giving him a piece of my mind in person. Here was someone else who failed at caring for her. Neither of us should be let off the hook. Each step filled me with confidence to do battle. I saw him in the garden, slumped in a chair. It was late afternoon on Friday, and the sky had threatened rain all day. The colors around us were muted, mirroring how he looked and how I felt. Dark circles rimmed his eyes, his hair in dire need of a wash and a comb. He looked like he'd spent the past week in his own slough of despond. Pity mixed with the anger I was feeling.

"Hello, Peter."

"Suzanne. It's nice to see you. Could we step inside?" His hoarse voice was urgent, his eyes intense.

He glanced around the cottage, searching for something. "Blair is at the library with Agnes." He nodded. "I'm expected back in a little while. What do you want?" Much of the fight in me had dissipated at the sight of him.

"To tell you how sorry I am. To tell you I've never done something like that before. To tell you that I would never do anything to harm her." He rubbed his eyes, his face. He looked away but kept talking.

"I got your message. In fact, I listened to it several times. About Blair, I'm sorrier than you can imagine. I have no excuse. But I must tell you that I thought she'd gone. Thought I'd checked the barn thoroughly. After I got home, I began to wonder. I knew they'd arrived together and remembered Margaret leaving alone. I hurried back to Muirfield. You must have come in the interim." He looked at me with pleading eyes. "I would never have knowingly put her at risk. You know that, don't you?" His voice was completely sincere, his face full of real pain. I believed him and owed it to him to say so.

"Yes, I do. I'm glad to know you gave her a second thought, but why didn't you call me, rather than go back yourself, when you'd realized she might still be there?"

"If she wasn't, you'd have known I left her there and I couldn't stand the thought of that."

"So you put your pride ahead of her safety?" I asked, hoping I'd misheard.

He closed his eyes. "Aye, and I'm more sickened by it than you are."

In that second, every bit of compassion and pity I felt for him vanished. "I doubt that," I thundered.

"I was an idiot. And I beg your forgiveness. To begin with, I failed you by not checking the barn more thoroughly, by being certain she'd left. And then I let your opinion of me keep me from doing what was best for Blair."

I waited for the justification that inevitably followed apologies. I held my tongue until I realized he had no intention of saying anything more. I couldn't think of the last time that someone apologized, took responsibility, and didn't try to worm his way out of it. I enjoyed the power I felt as he explained and apologized, but I hadn't expected this new twist. He was guilty, and he was admitting it—without excuse. It was strangely humbling, cracking the door to my compassion back open. As I sorted through it, Peter held his breath. I could see what he needed. I was angry, not cruel.

"Yes, of course, I forgive you. It doesn't mean I'm going to act like it didn't happen though."

"I know it's hard. I accept that." He reached for my hand. Giving it to him, in that moment, was like a peace offering. It felt generous and right.

Thinking we were through the worst of it, I thought I could safely ask what I really wanted to know. "Why did you wait so long to come?" I said, sotto voce.

"I don't know," he said, looking out the window. Something in his voice didn't sound right. "I came on Wednesday... I'm sorry—I got confused about things between us and I let it influence me. That was wrong."

I flushed, grabbing my hand away. "What things between us? What do you mean? We're friends."

"And what about you and Ian?" he asked, an edge of accusation in his voice.

"What about him? He's been a wonderful friend. He's trying to help Blair deal with the disappointment of not coming to the barn anymore. I don't know how I could repay him for all his kindness," I continued.

"I think you already did." No longer the guilty, he became the judge.

"What do you mean?" I wasn't going to play word games with him. He would need to speak more plainly if he was accusing me.

"I saw him kiss you, Suzanne. That's the payment he's after. He's a user. Don't let him play you for the fool." Though the kiss had made me uncomfortable, angry even, I wouldn't let Peter know that.

"You don't know what you're talking about."

"I saw you kiss. I told you I came by once before. Why would you—?"

"You are the most arrogant man I've ever met. Were you spying on me? That sounds like something ..." I swallowed the end of that sentence and caught my breath. "You had no right."

"I wasn't spying. I told you I came to apologize. How was I to know he'd be here?" The volume of both of our voices had become high and shrill.

"Nothing wrong happened. I don't know what you think you saw," I said, my lip starting to quiver.

"I know what I saw, and so do you," he said, strangely calm. "And I know why you're lying about it now. You are ashamed." I spun toward him but he continued on. "You know what kind of a person Ian Hamilton is. He is only out for himself."

"And you're not?" I spat.

A stricken look came over him. "No, well, not completely," he said, with less bravura. "I'm...I care very deeply for you Suzanne. In fact, I think I'm—"

I gasped. Before he could finish his sentence, I yelled, "Don't you dare say that to me. You don't even know me." And then, falling back on what I knew most about love, I said, "You just want to control me."

"No, I don't. That couldn't be further from the truth. How can you think that about me?" His anger gave way to hurt, and he suddenly looked like a vulnerable boy.

"How can I not? You are no different from any other man I've ever met."

"I know you think that now. Maybe it even looks that way today. But I am different. I want what's best for you."

I cringed at those words. They'd been used against me more than once in my life. "You mean what's best according to you! What if I think Ian is best for me? Would you be happy then?" The words choked in my throat. I hated talking about this. Abruptly, I said, "I want you to leave."

He frowned. "No, let's work through this. It's important." His voice was gentle, but determined.

I leaned forward and said in slow, exaggerated syllables, "Let me say this in a way you will understand. It would be best for me if you leave."

"We both know there is more to say." He looked and sounded both discouraged and deflated. He opened the door to leave, then turned around to add one more thing.

Before he could say anything else, I punctuated the conversation. "There is nothing else to say. Stay away from my daughter and me. Do you understand?"

"You wouldn't keep Blair from Muirfield, would you? She needs it, it's good for her."

"Get out!" I could barely contain my rage. I knew I sounded like a fishwife, but I didn't feel like one. I felt like a warrior, a protector, the only one Blair had, what I should have been with Ian. "And don't you dare presume to know what is best for Blair too. She is my daughter. Mine. I know what is best for her, and it isn't you."

"Maybe not, but it isn't Ian Hamilton, either," he said quietly, before shutting the door.

❧

The blanket felt like a straight jacket. I was tangled in it, and in my weariness, couldn't find an escape. The thrashing started small, then built until it wasn't about the blanket anymore, but my life. I sat bolt upright. Hot, tired, and bursting with fury. How could things have gotten like this? Why did men always think they knew what was best for me? I spun through my history—Dad, Edward, now Ian and Peter. The constant was me. I got up and began to pace. What do I do that makes them treat me like this?

What about my life? What did I want? I thought about Blair. Her life had changed too much; her friends hurt her too deeply. She wasn't at all eager to go back. I couldn't face the thought of returning to a life that had been entirely about Edward. But it wasn't only the returning that troubled me; it was also the leaving. We were better versions of ourselves here. Back in bed, I stared at the ceiling, wishing that somewhere beyond it lay the answers I needed.

And still my mind wouldn't rest. What made Blair happy? Peter, for one. But the change in his behavior sent a chill down my spine. Edward's behavior had been equally confusing. He'd been loving and attentive until a few days into the honeymoon. I still didn't know what I'd done to cause his change. Peter's sudden transformation from kind and generous to suspicious, controlling and wanton in his care of Blair felt hideously familiar. I was so discouraged to find I'd been wrong about his true nature, too, that he was so like... Tears slid from the corners of my eyes, making a wet descent into my ears. I'd toyed with the idea of agreeing to stay, at least a few more months, and letting Blair begin the school year at Oakton. Now I just didn't know.

Still, there was no denying that Peter got into places of her heart that only I had ever reached before. Though he infuriated me, I put that aside to think about Blair. After this incident, I suspected he would take every possible care with her to win back my trust. But would I be able to give it? And how would I ever fully trust his motives again?

Surely, this was an example of what Eleanor meant. Things weren't right. I couldn't change Peter or fix me. And yet I wanted, what was Eleanor's phrase, longed for them to be different.

Amidst all the longing and confusion, I fell into an exhausted sleep.

The stacks of books at the church bazaar, or fete, as Agnes corrected me, reminded me of the spires along the Cornish countryside. Agnes walked row by row, filling her arms with treasured out-of-print editions, emptying them into the growing pile at my feet, then going back and filling them again. Her library budget exhausted, she was soon shopping for herself. She checked with me more than once, making sure I didn't mind the time this was taking.

"That's what we came for," I reminded her. "Besides, it's fun watching you act like a kid on Christmas morning."

Thirty minutes later, we carried our loads to her car and went to the food tent.

"I can't get enough of these," I said, finishing the pasty.

"American's don't usually go for them. Don't know why. Not at all good for their figures, I'd imagine."

I laughed. "I guess I should be more concerned about that, but it's nice not being nagged about it constantly." I saw an uncertain look on Agnes' face, quickly adding, "And of course, I could get lazy about it, so I can't deny I needed the reminders."

"Yeah, my mum and dad have always made it their business to make sure I didn't turn into a 'right round blimp,' to use their words." She laughed, albeit hollowly, at the memory. "It wouldn't have been the least bit funny if I actually ever got heavy. As it is, I've always been pretty slim, so I didn't take any notice of them."

"I suppose it's some peoples' way of showing they care." My dad had claimed that was his reason for monitoring me so closely.

After the meal, we went from table to tent, perusing dishes and silver and every kind of knickknack imaginable.

In a tent of estate pieces, I inspected a Wedgwood vase. "Have you settled on how long you're staying?" Agnes asked.

"I thought I had, but—I don't know anymore. It's just the longer we stay, the harder it will be on Blair to settle in when we go home. And I'm afraid of her growing bored here. She's begun to act out a bit."

"Bored here? How could that happen?"

"I don't know. She's having fun with Margaret, but there are still too many hours in the day. When she was spending those hours at—." I stopped short.

"At Muirfield," Agnes finished the sentence. I nodded. "I'm not a mum, and don't mean to speak out of turn, but I don't see why you can't let her go back." I'd told her about the incident over lunch. "Is it just to punish Peter?"

"Don't be ridiculous."

"It's not so ridiculous," Agnes answered knowingly.

"Well, that's not it at all," I said, feeling defensive. It was so much more, but I didn't want to draw her into that part of the story. Agnes let it drop, turning her attention to an anchor-shaped lamp. We carried on in silence, speaking only when we found something useful for Wisteria Cottage or the library.

I would have liked to simply enjoy Cornwall's wild beauty during our ride back, but Agnes had something on her mind.

"Suzanne, I'm sorry for questioning you about Muirfield. I've watched you with Blair; I can see that you're a smashing mum. I'm sure you've got a perfectly good reason for keeping her away from the barn."

I pulled my gaze from the hedgerow border we were passing. "Thank you." We continued in silence for several more miles.

"Let's stop there," I said, pointing to a charming little tea garden.

Agnes rolled her eyes. "It's a bit twee, but…okay."

"I'm not due to pick up Blair yet, and I don't really want to get back early." We chose a table next to a meadow full of wildflowers. I ordered scones with "lashings of cream." I slathered it on and raised the scone to my mouth. Seeing Agnes face, I burst out laughing and took an enormous bite.

"I guess I'm getting carried away," I said with a mouthful.

She grinned. "You can't be in the West Country and not eat scones with cream. I think they'd run you out straight away." The tension between us disappeared with the last taste.

"I'm not mad at you. It's just more complicated than punishing Peter. Blair's gotten attached to him, and when I saw how much like…" I swallowed hard, dropped my hands in my lap and started clenching and unclenching my fists.

"Blair and Edward weren't close," I said, continuing my nervous habit. "He never had time—he was under enormous pressure at Morgan's. Of course Blair loves having the attention of a man, and they share a love of horses, but…"

I looked at Agnes, whose earnest friendliness put me at ease, reminding me of Cathy, who I realized I missed more than I'd admitted to myself. Cathy would have asked the same hard questions. "I'm saying this badly.

Edward was a good provider, but a man can't do everything. He meant to make up for it later." I detested the pleading I heard in my voice.

"I don't get the connection to Peter," Agnes said.

"Sometimes Edward's preoccupation with work put her at risk. He didn't pay close enough attention. I'm afraid Peter is the same."

"But his life is devoted to children," she protested.

"Not to mine," I countered. "He left her at the barn." Why couldn't she see the problem?

"Once. And he went right back. You can't hold one mistake against him."

"She's all I have," I cried. "I can't let anything happen to her."

"Of course not. But you can't protect her from everything. Don't you think there are more benefits to letting her go to Muirfield than there are risks?"

"I thought so at first. Now, I'm not sure," I admitted.

"I'm just saying I know Peter. I know he will do everything possible to make this right. I can't believe there isn't some way to sort this out." I didn't know how we would, and I was out of ideas. I attempted a weak smile and sipped at my tea. She did the same.

Then she grew excited. "Maybe you could go with her. It's only a few hours a couple of days a week, isn't it?"

"No, I don't think it's a good idea. I'm not a barn person."

"Do you have to be? You'd just be there for Blair."

But she wouldn't be the only one there. "I don't want to." I finished my tea, which had grown cold and bitter.

❧

"Are you completely daft? How could you look at my daughter and think she could read something this difficult? Is it your job to devastate her confidence? How did you get this job without a bit of common sense?"

I recognized the woman from a picture at Eleanor's. Her daughter, Hillary, and her two children had recently moved back to Penwylln. She was filleting Agnes, who stood stock still, bleeding and shocked. The other library patrons stole uncomfortable glances at one another. I whispered in Blair's ear. She quickly went down the steps to the children's stacks. Agnes looked at me, ready to speak, but Hillary continued.

"Don't get distracted. We're not done. Don't you have anything to say for yourself?" Hillary barked. Agnes remained mute.

"Let's move into Agnes' office," I suggested.

Agnes moved toward the door, but Hillary stood her ground. Swiftly, she glanced around the room and found that everything had stopped. All eyes were on her. Her countenance crumbled and she fled through the front door.

"What was that all about?" I asked over the slamming door.

"I hardly know. A girl was in earlier this week wanting something her mum could read to her. I asked her if she thought she'd try to read it by herself, but she said no. She wanted it to be special time with her mum. So we picked out some books, nothing horrific, and the next thing I know her mum is here shrieking like a mad cow."

"I'm so sorry. She's Eleanor's daughter, in the middle of a divorce, I think. I feel sorry for her. Do you mind if I try to find her? Blair will be fine."

"Sure, take your time. Maybe you'll make sense of this."

I scanned the square, and then up and down High Street. I peered in the window at Chaucer's; there, in a corner table, was Hillary. Wondering if I had any business doing this, I pushed the door open.

"Mind if I join you?" I asked, my voice quavering a bit. "I'm a friend of Eleanor's." I reached out my hand. "Suzanne Morgan."

Hillary looked at me blankly, then offered a limp one in return. "Right. Suit yourself."

I ordered coffee. When it came, I stirred in the sugar, clanking the spoon against the cup. Clink, clink, clink, clink. With a sudden, irritated motion, Hillary reached her hand out and put it atop mine, stopping me instantly.

My head flew up, and I caught Hillary on the verge of a collision of anger and tears. A timid smile from me was all it took to persuade her that she was safe. Anger stepped aside and made way for the grief underneath. Hillary put her head in her hands, not coming up for air for several minutes.

"I don't know what came over me. I'm not normally a barking lunatic," she said, fumbling for tissues. Wiping her face, she looked imploringly at me. "I don't even know who I am anymore." Suddenly laughing, she added, "God, what a pathetic woman I am. I sound like I belong on one of those pop psychology shows on the telly. It's a new low, really."

I laughed with her. "I've had those same thoughts this summer. I must be as pathetic as you."

Our eyes met, and we saw something in each other, an immediate and deep connection. Warmth and understanding replaced the judgment and hostility.

"I don't know what's happened to my life. I never thought I'd be facing life alone, and with children to care for," Hillary said. I shuddered, knowing I'd said the same thing to Cathy shortly after the accident.

"Me neither," I admitted, feeling the raw sting of it.

"Good grief, I'm thick. I'm so sorry. I didn't even think—."

"Don't say it. How could you know? The truth is we are both dealing with the death of our marriages. But are you certain yours is over? Is there no hope for reconciliation?"

Hillary shook her head. "I don't see any. I'm not sure I even want it. But the awful thing is, I don't want this, either. I don't know how to be a single mum. I'll be terrible at it. My kids will probably end up on BBC one day because of me. You know, the show called, My Mother was a Nutter, or something equally awful."

I laughed, finding her far less scary than before. "We all have that fear. You'll settle down after a time," I said, thinking how different my life was now than just last winter.

"Hillary, why did you get so angry with Agnes? She just did what your daughter asked her to do."

She appeared to have forgotten the reason for her outburst. "Fredericka? What's that?"

"Pick out a book for you to read to her."

"You mean I was meant to read the book and not Fred?"

I nodded. "She told Agnes she wanted something for special time with you."

Hillary put her hand over her open mouth. "I really am losing touch. Fred didn't mention anything when I found it in her stack of books. I knew it was too difficult for her, so I assumed—well, you can work that out for yourself. I'll have to go back and apologize to that poor woman."

"Oh, what time is it?" I checked my watch. "I've got to get Blair. I didn't mean to be gone so long."

"I've kept you. I'm sorry."

"I'm not. You're so like my best friend. Tell your mother hello for me. And stop by the cottage sometime. We'll get Blair and Fredericka together." I rushed to the library, already planning to call Cathy later tonight.

✎

Cathy Lawrence and I met in freshman English at Georgetown University. A mutual preference for museum hunting over bar hopping and a decided fondness for foreign movies sealed the deal. We'd been sisters ever since. When she answered the phone, my heart soared. Thrilled to hear my voice, she brought me up to speed on Morgan's and all the fun she was having. She'd left a competitor to join me at Morgan's six months ago and had quickly made herself indispensable, shoring up my weaknesses. Her agreement to become interim CEO had enabled me to take this trip. The job provided an outlet for her skills and suffused her with energy, the exact opposite of what it did for me. And she told me, so happy, that she was dating Mark Riedel, the manager of the largest of our six-store chain.

"It's amazing. He's got character. And kindness. And intelligence. He can admit when he's wrong. And he can accept an apology. Humility's a rare quality."

It was indeed a rare thing. I knew that from experience. Edward relished being the one to bestow forgiveness, loving the upper hand, but, as far as I knew, never admitted a fault.

"He's not perfect, mind you, but he is quite special."

Like Peter, I thought.

"Cath, time for brutal honesty." Although superficial interests brought us together, it was our willingness to talk honestly—more honestly than with anyone else—that bound us together. Nothing was meant to be off limits, from parents to eating habits, politics to faith, though I didn't quite keep to this when problems arose with Edward. I never quite knew how to walk the loyalty tightrope.

I hesitated, wishing we were sitting in our favorite booth at Caféspresso, sipping cappuccinos. She caught the pause. "Just ask, Suze, whatever it is."

I took a deep breath. "Do you think there's something seriously wrong with me?" A light sweat broke out on my forehead.

"What are you talking about?"

"I just feel lost, so displaced. I feel like I wander around inside myself, looking for a place to rest. And I can't find it. The truth is I don't know where I belong."

"Brutal honesty?" she asked.

"Yeah," I whispered, then held my breath.

"Okay. I think you've been lost for a long time, been restless in yourself for years. But you're just seeing it because you've finally slowed down enough to notice." She couldn't see my forlorn nod. "But I also think you're asking the right question. Rest will come when you find your home. You just need to figure out where that is."

# 10

# Peter

Wally and Winston were odd bedfellows. They'd met before, but still went through their funny doggy ritual, sniffing and barking like strangers. Now they lay side by side in the morning sun. With a busy day ahead, I'd requested this breakfast meeting with Eleanor. We chose to meet near the harbor at an outdoor cafe. I told her about leaving Blair at Muirfield and of my row with Suzanne.

"You were right. I could only see what I wanted from her. There are bigger things at stake here. I'll tread wisely from now on." I tossed a stick toward the quay. Winston, too lazy to fetch, allowed Wally the honor. He went back again and again, while Eleanor clapped in delight.

I could see Eleanor had something on her mind. She was adept at hearing what wasn't spoken, and the diversion with Wally gave her time to work it out. "I believe what you say, but you have to be very careful. You could grow impatient and end up pressuring her. It will challenge you." Thomas had also warned me of trusting in my resolve. *You know what's in a man*, he'd said.

"I know. If left completely to my own, I'm bound for failure. I'll need you in this, Eleanor, to be an advocate and a friend. For her sake and mine"

She squeezed my arm. "Of course I will. I want the best for both of you. And of course, you know what else you must do."

My steps felt heavy. "Laura." She nodded and took my arm. We strolled toward the water's edge. Low tide had left the sand brown and spongy, full of crabs and seaweed. Skiffs and fishing boats cluttered the harbor, listing for want of the leveling water and taught lines to hold them steady.

"Suzanne made quite the impression on Hillary. They're becoming friends. She showed surprising strength in defending Agnes from one of Hillary's tirades." I wasn't surprised, having been on the other side of her protectiveness. "Her loyalty is commendable," Eleanor concluded. Wally nipped at my heels, so we played fetch until the wind caught the stick and carried it to sea.

"I don't know how to put things to rights. I betrayed her trust, and she can't stand the sight of me."

"I doubt that," Eleanor said, brushing dog hair from her dark pants. "Still, it will be a challenge to win it back. I gather that was a big issue between her late husband and her. She'll not give it easily again." I nodded. She stretched up on her tiptoes, kissed my cheek, and collected Wally's leash.

⌐

I heard the clamor of voices in the background and realized I'd rung during supper. Mum was calling to Archie. Lily was talking to Frannie.

"I'm not usually such a dolt," I said to Thomas, hoping he was paying some measure of attention. "I don't know how I could have let my pride lead me to such wretched behavior. I am so awfully ashamed. So sorry."

"Have you told her that?"

"I have. She's hurt. She's trying to forgive, but she's not ready to offer me a second chance."

"Then I don't know what else you can do. Hold there, Peter." Sounds grew muffled as Thomas put his hand over the phone. After a pause, "I'm back. Lily got too near the cooker and nearly reached the frying pan. Go on then."

"That's it. How are you? Busy week?"

"I'd say that. Yes. You won't forget the wedding this weekend, will you? You're pretty distracted these days. Is that what this woman does to you?" In one swift and stunning act, Thomas and Gemma had announced they were getting married. They planned to have it by the brook at the edge of the garden. Archie would stand up for Thomas, Frannie and Lily were the attendants, and I would give the bride away. Gemma was an only child, her parent's long dead. To give mum a rest, I planned to bring Frannie and Archie back with me while Thomas and Gemma honeymooned in Corfu.

Thomas couldn't see the heat rise to my face, but the annoyance in my voice was undisguiseable. "My distraction is from school and the barn. It's the height of show season. Remember? I spend two nights a week and every weekend as groom and trainer. I'm giving more lessons than ever before, and Muirfield is practically as busy as Waterloo Station."

"That's a grand thing, little brother, so long as you don't use it as an excuse."

I already knew the answer, though I asked anyway. "From what?"

"From what you know is most important."

"This is cool, Uncle Pete. Which one can I ride?" Archie asked.

Archie sailed right through the wedding, offering back to Gemma every bit of attention she showed him. Frannie seemed to endure it with all the duty of a good Englishman. Gemma seemed quite nice, really. Enough so that I was actually looking forward to getting to know her. But it was Thomas' smile that day that finally silenced my concerns.

"I think we'll put you on Fergie, a particular favorite of mine." An image of Blair grooming Fergie sprang up. I coughed, trying to clear the sudden catch in my throat... "What about you, Frannie?"

"Not interested. Don't want to get dirty and all that." She gave me a bored, why-am-I-here face.

"Blimey," Archie exclaimed. "You can take a bath when you're done."

"Bugger off, Archie. I just don't feel like it, okay?" This wasn't the Frannie I knew. But then, it was the little girl I remembered. I'd barely seen this adolescent.

Archie rolled his eyes at me. Then, forgetting about his sister, he found Fergie's stall.

"Come help me, Uncle Pete. I forget how to get this on," he said, looking at the jumble of reins and straps in his hands. Frannie wandered outside while I helped Archie tack up. "Is Frannie okay? She doesn't seem like herself," I asked him, while tightening the girth.

"Dunno. She's been different since Da and Gemma told us. I don't get it. I thought she liked Gemma." Archie was a simple, big-hearted boy. Gemma would have a sure ally in him.

"Can you handle this yourself? I'd like to check on her." I patted Fergie's flank and gave Archie a thumbs up on the way out.

The last thing I wanted was for her to think I was playing psychiatrist. I didn't pretend to understand her feelings. She was dealing with real pain and change; losing her mum to cancer, watching her father remarry. Still, I knew the benefit of airing feelings and dealing with them honestly. She had a friend in me; I only hoped she knew it.

Frannie didn't look up when I joined her. "How are you, Fran?"

"Just grand." She picked at tiny splinters of wood as I leaned back on the fence. I looked down at her hands, noticed the pale pink nail varnish chosen to match the garden roses Gemma had carried down the aisle. She saw me looking at them and started picking at a chip in the varnish.

"Right. Are you mad at your Da?"

"No." She pursed her lips together, as though that might keep the truth inside. I knew this family trait well. Deny, pretend, ignore.

"Gemma, then?"

Frannie turned away, hiding her face. "No."

"You know it's okay to feel upset, don't you, lass? It's big changes you're dealing with. You probably worry about Gemma replacing your mum. I don't think she means to."

She turned back, angry. "Of course it isn't. They're all happy, aren't they? And besides, you don't know how I feel. I've hardly seen you since Mum died." The truth of her words leveled me. I hardly even knew my own reasons for staying away. What was I doing talking to her about hers?

"Frannie, love, I didn't mean—."

"Just leave me alone," she shouted, leaving me to stare into the empty ring.

⌒

Jillian rang before Winston's morning constitutional, just as I was finishing washing up. I reached over to pick up the phone, felt the tickle of a single bead of water on its journey from hand to elbow. "I thought we might see what's on at the Minack and make an evening of it with Archie and Frannie. I could bring the hamper."

It wasn't Jillian I wanted with me at the Minack Theatre, and I felt irritated at the mere suggestion. "I don't know if that's quite the place for them." Winston ambled to the door, looking back at me with impatient eyes.

"Oh, come on. There's a lovely fluffy musical of some kind. I can't think what the name is, but I recall thinking it would suit them perfectly." I had some making up to do to both of them, especially Frannie, so I agreed, hoping it would prove to be a good diversion.

We went early and had a marvelous dinner before the show started. Jillian outdid herself, packing an assortment of sandwiches and main dishes, taking into account each of our particular needs. Frannie would only eat sesame chicken skewers. Archie consumed two turkey and avocado sandwiches, and I savored a Huntsman. Jillian nibbled at her Thai Chicken wrap. Archie loved the terraced seating and begged me to let him do some exploring. Frannie, happy to be left alone, agreed to accompany her brother.

"It's nice to have a few minutes to ourselves," Jillian said, pouring another glass of wine.

I really didn't want a minute for just us, so I stood and scanned the crowd. I spotted the kids on the stairs near the visitor's centre. I gave a wave, encouraging their return. "It's been great having them visit. I'm going to miss them when they leave next weekend. They're terrific kids."

She took a gulp. "I'm sure it has. But it does cramp your social life, if you get my meaning." I knew exactly what she meant and kept my eyes trained on Archie.

"...Something about Blair Morgan getting forgotten at the barn."

Like a marionette on a string, the mention of Suzanne's name pulled me back. "What did you say?" I felt on a tightrope, wanting to know, but not giving her the satisfaction of seeing it.

"I said I was having lunch with Agnes Buncle.

"Did you?"

"Yes, well, I've never spoken to her. On purpose, anyway. We ended up chatting on the green together one particularly keen afternoon. She's much brighter than she looks."

"You know, don't you, she has an English degree from Oxford? Not exactly a dull knife," I said.

"Right," she said peevishly. "The important thing is she told me about Blair Morgan getting left at the barn."

I shuddered at the memory. "Aye. I thought she'd gone with Margaret. But she was back with Fergie. She was alone at least 30 minutes before Suzanne picked her up."

"That's all? Why do you think Suzanne is playing the protective mother part?"

"She's not playing a part at all Jillian," I said, annoyed with her barbs. "She's a good mum with reason to be protective. Blimey, she's had enough loss, hasn't she?"

"Yes, of course, anyone can see that. But, the child being alone for a few minutes at the barn—really, I can't understand the fuss."

"That's the point, isn't it Jillian? You can't understand it. You're not a mother."

I regretted it as soon as I'd said it. I sat back down and tried to give Jillian the full attention she so desperately wanted. "I'm sorry I said that." I squeezed her hand. "She's being protective because she relied on me to make sure Blair was safe, and I let her down, didn't I? However well-intentioned I was, it doesn't change the fact that I was responsible for her safety, and I failed."

"Yes, but nothing happened to her," Jillian continued, almost flippantly.

"Doesn't matter." I found a small pebble, tossed it several rows down, looked at Frannie and Archie, willing them to return.

People were beginning to fill in the seats while the orchestra warmed up. It was a sound I loved; the tuning of multiple instruments, dissonance and perfection dancing about. I closed my eyes and drank in the sounds.

Jillian leaned into me and said softly, "I gather your reckless care of Blair reminds her of her late husband, and finding you to be so like him keeps her from being able to trust you again."

A pain shot through my chest. I opened my eyes to find Jillian smiling and waving at Archie and Frannie, who were ten steps away. Before I could respond, she was offering sweets and hot tea in advance of the show commencing. She was a stealth bomber: in and out under radar. I'd been her target and she'd hit a bulls-eye.

Time changed for me. Surviving the first two acts until the interval might as well have been forever. My heart pounded; I sat in growing frustration. I was quick to send Archie and Frannie to the line for ice cream cups, despite Frannie's objection that they'd already had their dessert.

"What do you mean?" I asked Jillian the minute they were out of hearing.

"About what?" She licked strawberry from her fingers. I wanted to grab her wrist and pull it down from her mouth. Jillian's control of her emotions was pure art. She kept a puzzled, yet faintly interested, look on her face.

"Wherever did you get an idea that I was like Edward Morgan? What do you know of him?" I tried my best to hide the urgency I felt.

"Not so much, really. I just had an enlightening conversation with a friend of Suzanne's, who mentioned—oh look, Archie, you got a Neapolitan. Those are lovely. Can I have a bite?"

The conversation turned to ices and everyone's favorite flavors; I kept conspicuously silent.

"What's wrong, Uncle Pete?" Archie asked. I couldn't quite fathom how Jillian could look at me with those innocent eyes.

My mumbled "nothing" didn't satisfy Archie.

"That's not right. You're different," he insisted.

The sound of applause drew me back, and I joined in just as it was dying down. Frannie kept Archie talking in the rear seat on the way home, while Jillian switched on the radio. I dropped Frannie and Archie at my cottage and then ran Jillian home.

Knowing I couldn't stay, she didn't make the usual offer, but instead acted in a hurry to say goodbye. She could see she'd upset me. If I were a betting man, I'd say she had some satisfaction in it. I didn't care.

∽

I wondered if after-shave was a bit pushy. Deciding it probably was, I finished toweling off, threw on my clothes, and left the house in record speed. Suzanne had called and asked me to stop by. Said she wanted to try and sort things out. I drove down the lane, sheltered under a dappled, green canopy of leaves, realizing I hadn't the faintest idea how to start this conversation.

A sweet, gleeful face met me at the doorway. "Peter," Blair cried, throwing her arms around my middle. "I've missed you."

"Same here, moppet," I said, hugging her back. "How've you been getting on?"

"Okay. Not great." She took my hand and led me down the hall. Her limp was barely noticeable. "I got a letter from Rachel. She and Kara are going to riding camp together."

"I thought your friend Rachel didn't ride."

"She didn't. But now I think she and Kara are best friends. She wants to do what Kara does. I hope she falls off the first day." She peered at me, looking for approval.

"What a good friend you are," Suzanne said from behind Blair.

I hadn't seen her sitting in the chair. Suzanne stood, brushed back her hair, smoothed her skirt. A bit nervously, I thought.

"How's Fergie?" Blair pressed.

It was hard, but I turned my focus towards her. "He's always a good old chap. Misses you though." I'd done it again. Said the wrong thing.

Her face grew wistful. "I know. Me too. I wish—."

"Blair, why don't you get Peter something to drink?" Suzanne interrupted.

Jutting out her lower lip, she said, "I helped mommy make iced tea. You want some?"

As soon as we were alone, I mouthed that I was sorry for my stupid comment. I needed to relax. Crashing and banging emanated from the kitchen. "Do you need help?" Suzanne called.

"Nope." Giggles.

Suzanne offered me a seat on the enormous couch, where we sat in painful silence, awaiting Blair's return. We laughed out loud when she appeared in the doorway, balancing a tray full of drinks, each sitting in a very large puddle.

"So why are you here?" Blair asked, mopping the drips from her glass.

"Your mum invited me over to talk to her," I said, looking at Suzanne.

"What about me?" Blair demanded.

I gave her an affectionate punch in the arm. "Of course, you too. I have some visitors you might like, my niece and nephew from York."

"You have relatives in New York? That's cool."

"Not New York in America. York. England. Where I was born."

"Oh," Blair said, disappointed. "Well, they still might be nice." As we drank our tea, I told them about Thomas' wedding. Suzanne sat, mute and pinched, as Blair peppered me with questions.

Suzanne reached for Blair's hand. "Honey, I would like to talk to Peter alone a few minutes. Would you please find something to do outside?"

Blair looked at me, dismayed. "Why should I? You don't even like him. You've been telling everybody." I felt like I'd been punched in the gut, every hope I had in coming evaporated.

Suzanne turned red. "That's ridiculous, Blair. Don't go too far. I'll call you when we're done." Suzanne stood up to shut the door behind a very pokey Blair.

"I don't know what she was talking about. I don't really have anything in particular to say, but I would like to see if we could mend things. For Blair's sake." She sat back down and waited.

"I want nothing more. Let me apologize again for leaving Blair at Muirfield. It was an aberration in my behavior, but I'm afraid it leaves you thinking I'm careless, self-involved, untrustworthy." I was going over old ground, but a tight mouth and narrow gaze told me this was still the problem. I paused, then added, more quietly, "Maybe you know someone from your past that this reminds you of."

She shifted in her seat.

"You know you've painted your late husband as a man who was quite occupied with being successful. I wondered if that preoccupation, however well-meaning, had ever led him to give Blair less than superlative care?"

"What are you implying?" Alarmed, she stretched her neck to be sure Blair was visible outside.

"Just that I understand how, if you'd been let down previously, that might be a sore spot."

Her voice quivered in anger. "I don't have a sore spot. I am not the problem here. I am not the one who neglected Blair."

"No, of course not. I'm not saying you have the problem." I stopped and put my head in my hands. I couldn't believe what a blundering dolt I was. I sighed, heavy and loud, in complete exasperation of my own stupidity. But I'd opened this door, and I couldn't leave it swinging.

"I'm saying this badly. I'm not trying to take away any of my own guilt and responsibility. I was trying to suggest that I could understand how especially hard this would have been for you if it had a…a…déjà vu feeling about it."

She stared ahead, pokerfaced. Maybe I wasn't being clear enough.

"I thought that maybe if your husband had been a source of disappointment to you… Well, then my doing so, too, could have magnified the pain even more."

"Sorry to disappoint you, but my husband was exemplary in his care of the both of us."

"I thought—."

Suzanne flinched, as though she'd been slapped in the face. "Did Blair say something to you?"

I shook my head. "No, well, not about this."

"Then where did you get the idea—?" My face burned. I felt, suddenly, guilty and humiliated. "I can't believe you would listen to gossip. Get out." She bounded from the chair to the door and threw it open. I followed her step for step.

"I suspect I'm near the truth Suzanne. And I understand that you don't want to talk about it. You've had more than enough reason to be angry with me and that's the last thing I want again. This conversation hasn't ended the way I'd hoped it would, with me offering to take you and Blair out for dinner to make up and be friends again." She stared back at me, her face pale, her eyes ice-cold.

I said, in the warmest voice I had, "I want to be your friend Suzanne. It would make me very happy." I paused, hoping to penetrate the wall I'd helped erect... "You are very special, and I'm grateful you came to our little part of England this summer. Please let Blair return to Muirfield. It is good for her there. I'll not let you down again."

∽

And so while I waited to see what Suzanne would decide, I did my best to concentrate on Archie and Frannie. We brought in take-away Chinese, went to the cinema, and picnicked at the beach. Though full, the days crept by. Each passing day drove home the diminishing chance of recovering from my disastrous conversation with Suzanne.

"There's that lady." Archie said, looking in the direction of the car park.

Jillian approached with something in hand. When she got to the door of the barn, she wrinkled her nose. She'd come in the middle of mucking time. A large bucket was filled to the top with manure, flies swarming about.

"What a beastly smell! Can't you put that somewhere?" She took an exaggerated swath around the pail.

"We're getting to it. What do you have there?" I asked, looking at the plate in her hands.

"I've brought you an afternoon treat, lemon and ginger biscuits. I'll set them in your office." Archie made a sour face.

"That's brilliant." I followed her inside; she dodged an oscillating fan to avoid getting mussed.

"Where's Frannie this morning?"

"She stayed back at the cottage. She's out of sorts, so I thought it best to give her a bit of space."

"That was probably wise. Shall I stop round and talk to her?"

"It's a kind offer, but I think the grief for her mum is fresh. She needs to do it in her own way."

"It's not been so very long since my mum died, you know. I just may have some helpful words."

"If you like then, but I'll warn you to not to be offended if you're rebuffed."

"I've got thicker skin than that," she assured me. That was certainly true. But maybe this time she'd put it to good use. "And I'm not a push over like some people. I'll not let her use her sorrow to manipulate me."

I put my head back and took a deep breath. "Whatever can you mean by that? How in the world could she manipulate you? To do what?"

"I don't know. I'm just saying I'll be on my guard against it." Why had I thought for a moment she could be tender with Frannie? "You know, on second thought, maybe this isn't a grand idea."

She waved a perfectly manicured hand at me. "Oh bosh, of course it is. I'll be sweet Aunt Jillian."

I ignored that. "And what do you mean you're not a push over like some people? Who?"

"Eleanor and Ian, of course. You do know, don't you? It appears Mrs. Morgan twisted her ankle right in the middle of Duck Street and had to be helped home by Ian. The next thing you know, she's got Eleanor fixing her dinner, of all things, and, this is the richest part, Ian went to the market for her." If smugness were currency, Jillian would have been Croesus.

The last time I listened to her gossip, I'd paid a heavy price. And yet I couldn't stop myself from asking, "How do you know all this?"

I could see the gleam in her eye. "Well, it seems Eleanor was serving the dinner to Morgan and her child when Ian appeared, bags in hand. Eleanor even helped him unpack the groceries. Must have made for quite the domestic picture." She laughed, but there was no mirth in it.

I was running out of patience with Jillian's jealousy. "Is she all right?"

Jillian pulled a face. "Eleanor?"

"No, not Eleanor," I snapped. "Suzanne. Did she need to go to hospital?"

She rolled her eyes. "For a charade? Are you mad? She'd have been found out as a fraud if she'd done that. And if she's not, she's absolutely the feeblest woman on the planet. Let's recount all her mishaps since she got here and how many times the three of you have had run to her aid."

Talking about Suzanne with Jillian was fraught with dangers and no good could come of it. I chose, instead, to eat more biscuits. Jillian watched, waiting for a verdict.

"Very good," I said reaching for a third.

"And now, I'll have a look-in on Frannie and give her a cheer up." She smiled triumphantly, turned, and flounced out the door. It served as another reminder for me to tread carefully.

# 11

# Suzanne

"Can I have seconds?" Blair held out her plate. She filled our dinner conversation with chatter about Fredericka and Martin. Fredericka, a smart, funny twelve-year-old, was fast becoming a good friend.

"Freddie and Martin are going to Oakton next year. They're so lucky."

"Why are they lucky?"

"That's Peter's school. Remember that's where we met him." His kind way with Blair that day was only part of what I had appreciated about him.

"Of course. I just didn't know what you meant." I had no energy to apologize for the exasperation in my voice. We finished our meal in silence.

Blair carried the plates into the kitchen and put the kettle on. "I'm making tea," she called out.

"No, you might burn yourself. I don't want you picking up the kettle."

"Mom," Blair replied, turning it into a two-syllable word, "I can do it. I'll be extra careful."

I listened closely. A few minutes later, Blair entered with a tray. "See, I told you I could do it," she exulted. She carefully poured the tea, adding two lumps to each cup and stirring slowly, making certain nothing escaped over the edges. Beaming, she handed me my cup.

While at Eleanor's, Blair had developed a fondness for the Scottish show, *Fully Booked*. She turned on the television and curled up on the couch, laughing uproariously every time they said, "foooly boooked." The show ended, but she kept switching the channels hoping that somewhere, hidden in the recesses of the BBC, were American re-runs. Finally, she threw herself onto the floor and sighed deeply. "I'm so bored."

My usual suggestions: puzzles, drawing, reading, sounded dull even to me. "Why don't you write a story?"

"What would I write about?"

"I've always heard people should write about what they know and love. What do you love?"

"Horses," Blair said quietly.

Of course. I felt colossally stupid for setting that trap for both of us. "That sounds great. Lot's of girls share your love of horses."

"I don't want to." Her enthusiasm evaporated like a morning mist in the hot sun. She went to her room and returned with a book in hand. A James Herriot story about a cat. She poured herself more tea and climbed under the afghan. Already, Blair had learned the art of burying her emotions under a façade of indifference. It was a painfully familiar pattern, one I had mastered years before.

I left my chair and joined her. "Can I ask you something?"

She looked at me with guarded eyes. I swallowed hard. Peter's words had been stark and jarring. What's worse, they were true. I didn't know why Edward acted the way he did. It probably had to do with me. Maybe I needed to support him more. Maybe I needed to challenge him more. I honestly didn't know what I did to keep Edward from being the man he needed to be. But what I did know, beyond a shadow of a doubt, was that Peter was nothing like him.

I hated thinking people were gossiping about us. I hated swallowing my pride in what I was about to say. But mostly, I hated seeing Blair so unhappy. I put my arm around her, pulling her close. "Would you like to go back to Muirfield?"

She looked up at me, amazed. "Really? You said you'd never let me."

"I know. I was mad, and that made me too hasty. But anyone can make a mistake. I know he's sorry." For all the other things Peter and I had fought about, I knew, at least, this was the truth.

"Do you forgive him, then?"

"I guess I do. All I care about is how unhappy you are when you don't get to see the horses and your friends at the barn."

"And Peter. He's kinda like a... he's really nice and he isn't always mad at me. He's really special."

"I can't deny that," I said, remembering how hard it was to breathe when he was near. Even when I was furious with him.

Blair gave me her warmest hug. "I can't wait to tell him."

⌒

Peter rushed out of his office, a red-headed boy trailing behind, toting a dressage saddle. He stopped when he saw me and gave a wide smile. "Clive, tell Blair her mum is here."

His open expression loosed the knots in my stomach. Back at the house, I'd taken my time getting ready, and now I was glad. My hair was back, sunglasses rested on top of my head. Denim Capri's, sleeveless top, and lizard sandals gave me what I hoped was a clean, casual look.

Approaching the barn, I heard Blair's voice. "You're doing that wrong," she said, with the full confidence of a seasoned equestrienne. "He likes it smoother."

A boy was beside her. He set his jaw and dug in. "I'm doing it like Uncle Pete showed me." Ah, this was Archie.

"Then why are his ears back?" She sounded smug. "He doesn't like it. Do it right." I cringed at her bossiness.

He threw down the brush and left in a huff. Blair smiled and scooped it up, setting to work as though brushing down the next Derby winner. She leaned in, following each stroke of the brush with her hand. His warm skin and silky coat were medicine to her, the cure for an injured heart.

"I won't let that boy near you any more," she reassured her four-legged friend.

"I'm afraid you can't make that promise, little one," Peter said.

Blair turned around in surprise. "I know. I just like to pretend he's mine," she said burying her face in Fergie's side.

Peter walked around the horse, giving him a slap on the rump as he went. "I think you and Archie make a smashing team. He looks brilliant."

"But, Peter, he—," she protested.

"Darlin', Archie likes Fergie too. You've got to share him." Blair pouted. Peter put his hand under her chin and turned it up as he squatted down, bringing them eye-to-eye.

"Archie and Frannie will only be here one more week. In the meantime, as a favor to me, be nice to him. Remember, he took good care of Fergie while you were away." Her solemn nod was rewarded with a hug. "You know, moppet, we need to talk later. We have some decisions to make." That piqued my curiosity. I would have to remember to ask Blair about it later.

"C'mon, Uncle Pete," Archie interrupted. "Some girl just fell off Prince Arthur." Archie and Peter ran from the barn. Blair followed them to see who it was, but when she didn't recognize the girl, she returned to Fergie and resumed brushing. A minute later, Peter entered with Connie in his arms.

"It's just a scrape. Ice will keep the bruising down," he reassured the crying child.

"Will I be able to go to Sparkings on Saturday?" she asked between sniffles.

"You've got to. It's your first week over rails." They disappeared into his office. I wondered if Blair was remembering her last show before the accident. She'd gotten three blue ribbons on Midnight, and Edward had taken us out to dinner that night.

"What are you smiling about?" Archie asked, his voice surly.

Jolted out of her reverie, Blair looked over at Archie. "Have you ever ridden in a show before?"

Archie shook his head. "Never did do. Sounds awfully fun. Have you?"

"Yeah, a couple. Mostly mini-shows. But I did ride in one real show." In one magical moment, she was that girl. The one who stood in center ring with a handful of ribbons and the admiration of her peers.

"Did you win anything?" Archie looked at her suspiciously. I could hear the skepticism in his voice. I hoped it was lost on Blair.

Her head bobbed up and down. "I was on Midnight. Maybe I can come back and groom for you before you ride." Blair remembered I was there. "Mom, this is my friend, Archie. Can I come back tomorrow? It's really important." Peter returned with Connie in tow.

I brushed Blair's hair back from her eyes. "What time?"

"Mid-afternoon. About two o'clock ," Peter answered.

"Aw, Uncle Pete, why so late?"

"You forget, my little friend; I teach lessons. I'm booked all morning, but tomorrow afternoon is quiet." He turned to me. "If you're free, why don't you stay when you bring Blair?"

I was surprised by how quickly I said yes.

❧

"Mom, are you coming? I'm gonna be late."

The pile of shirts on the bed was growing. After several years of washing Blair's barn clothes, I knew full well there was some dirt that never came out, so I wanted to choose carefully. Blair came to see what was taking me so long.

"You look really pretty mom. What did you do?"

"Nothing." An hour on hair and makeup had paid off.

Blair shrugged. "You did something different."

Peter was talking to the farrier when we arrived. He waved to us from the end of the aisle and pointed to his office. Archie was inside looking through *Horse and Hound*.

"Look at this," he exclaimed. Blair joined him on the couch, their heads bumping as they poured over pictures of horses flying over fences in pursuit of trophies.

The only remaining seat was at Peter's generous oak desk. A fine layer of dust settled over the rest of the office, but the desk had recently been wiped clean.

"Sorry," Peter announced, breezing in. "I'd forgotten Ambrose was due today." He looked at the kids. "You two can be about your business. Choose between Prince Albert, Fergie, and Lizzie."

Blair held her breath, head bent down, hands clasped tightly, while Archie pondered his decision.

"I choose—," he paused for dramatic effect, "Fergie." Blair exhaled loudly and shot out the door, jettisoned by love.

"Oh, my," I said laughing. "She's got it bad, doesn't she?"

"She does, indeed. She's set her cap on Mr. Ferguson, but he'll not disappoint her." He cringed. An awkward pause followed; his words seemed to hang in the air.

Keeping my voice light, I said, "No, I know *he* won't disappoint her." His silence bore witness to his confusion, not sure how to read me. I stood and smiled at him. "I'm optimistic about the future. Now, I've got work to do."

Blair was picking Fergie's hooves. She handed me a brush and showed me the correct motion to use. Each time Blair leaned against Fergie, she forced up his leg to get to his hoof and her whole body shook with exertion. I must have been as white as the salt lick on the wall. Once Blair finished the hooves, she stood atop a stool to clean his ears and nose. I watched with amazement at her deft handling of such an enormous animal, immensely proud of her competency and comfort.

I felt ashamed about how long I'd kept Blair from the barn. Now I understood why she had fought me so stringently, grieving when the battle was lost. She'd been separated from her greatest joy. Peter was right to keep challenging me. Our eyes met in unspoken understanding.

"Mom, can you get his tack? It's on the hook under his name."

"I'll get it this time, moppet," Peter answered. I helped Blair put away the grooming tools. Archie, who had disappeared, returned with a secretive smile.

"Where have you been?" Peter asked, returning with full arms.

"Talking to Frannie."

Blair put the saddle and tack on Fergie, each time climbing up on the stool to make sure that they were placed in just the right spot. She took the bit, and after forcing it into Fergie's mouth, pulled the reins back, securing the head-piece between his ears and the throatlatch under his chin. Once, she swayed wildly atop the stool, but she grabbed Fergie's mane to steady herself. I shot a glance at Peter, who nodded, almost imperceptibly, that he'd seen it.

"Whoa, Blair, you okay? You almost fell," Archie cried.

"At least it wouldn't have been very far," she said, laughing. "I just turned too fast."

"You'll slow down a bit?" Peter asked.

"Yep, if I'm gonna fall, I want it to be in the ring, not the stupid old barn." I had newfound respect for the fine balance between protecting and teaching that Peter provided. And I realized I could trust my daughter to him.

Archie got a leg up from Peter. Blair adjusted the stirrups and led Fergie outside.

Archie beamed as he walked, then trotted, around the ring. Blair hung on the fence, offering occasional instructions, having promoted herself from groom to teacher. As Archie began to canter, a girl came toward us from the barn. Lanky and thin, her legs looked like they'd grown faster than the rest of her. She had sad eyes and didn't smile easily.

"Frannie, what a nice surprise." She stiffened as Peter hugged her.

"Archie wanted me to see him ride," she said, her voice flat and lifeless.

"Great," Peter said, pulling her toward us. "I'd like you to meet some friends of mine."

Before Peter could say our names, Archie trotted over to us. "Blair's dad died last year, so she knows what it's like," he announced to Frannie.

Frannie and Blair turned red; my mouth fell open, along with Peter's. "What?" Archie asked, looking at everyone looking aghast at him.

Frannie turned crimson. "Archie, you dolt. You don't say things like that to people out of the blue. Crikey, don't you know anything?"

"I didn't say anything wrong." Archie frowned at Frannie. "It's true. I was just telling you so we could talk about it if we wanted."

"Well, I don't," Frannie said defiantly.

A silence as big as the barn paddocks hovered over us. Then Peter started to laugh. "Archie, your heart's in the right place, but sometimes your brain is tucked in your pocket."

Archie shrugged, then tilted his head to one side. "I didn't mean anything. It's just, you know, sometimes you think no one gets how you feel."

There was an uncomfortable silence while we all considered the veracity of this observation. I looked at Archie. "You're right. My mother died when I was still in high school. From that day on, I felt completely different from my friends."

"You did?" Blair asked. "You never told me that." I don't know why I hadn't thought to tell Blair about it before, feeling a bit lost in my thoughts.

"Yeah," Frannie joined in, "and my friends are odd now, too, afraid if they mention their mums I'll break down in front of them. I'm sick of it."

"My father was like that," I admitted. "It was hard to talk with him about practically everything."

Tired of the talk, Archie resumed his riding. Our attentions shifted back to the ring, but something existed now that hadn't just minutes ago.

Frannie and I fell into small talk while Peter and Blair focused on Archie, who was learning to two-point in preparation for a low jump. Thirty minutes later we were still talking. At the end of his lesson, Archie dismounted with a thud and a satisfied smile.

"I have an idea," he announced.

Archie and Blair took turns hanging onto Winston, who pulled at the leash in an uncharacteristic display of athleticism. Peter carried the basket. Frannie walked with me; her hair swept up in a ponytail like mine.

Breaths were getting shorter and silences longer as we made the ambitious trek from the car to the edge of the cliff. And then we were in a spot of green, every bit as emerald as the Isle across the sea. We looked down the face of the rock into a palette of turquoise, jade and olive. The soft light of that mystical time between afternoon and evening fell upon our eyes, threatening to lull us to sleep. A committee of seals lay on the warm rocks below, while birds of differing tribes spun and twirled above us.

"Didn't you get Lizzie somewhere around here?" Archie asked.

"I did indeed, just over near Mullion. She's named for the Lizard Peninsula, since she was the first mare born at that stable." We walked on till we were only fifteen feet from the edge. "Here's a good spot," Peter said. "We'll make sure no one goes any closer to the edge where the footing isn't as sure."

"You mean me, don't you?" Blair asked.

"Sure, but not just you. People have been known to slip on this moss and tumble down. It's a nasty landing, and I, for one, don't want to make a run to hospital when I could be enjoying the company."

"Me too," Archie piped in.

We laughed as we pulled out the odd assortment from Peter's pantry and fridge that would be our dinner. We played a few rounds of I Spy during dinner; Archie had us in stitches, calling out "I spy something green" every time his turn came round. He and Blair wanted to walk back up the rise to see how far into the distance they could see. Peter followed a few steps behind.

Frannie and I were putting leftovers into containers when she asked, "Did your dad remarry after your mum died?" Then, in a flash of concern, "Do you mind me asking that?"

"Of course not," I smiled at her. "No, he never did. I sometimes wish he had though, for both our sakes."

"Why?" Frannie asked, clearly not expecting this answer.

"When mom died, the heartbreak was unspeakable. I didn't think it could get any worse, but somehow it did. Time does heal, the rawness of the pain is lessened, but the years of missing her took their own unique toll." I stopped my clean up. "All I'm saying is that I think, in time, I would have welcomed another woman. Not to take mom's place, but to have her own place in my life. And in my father's."

I could see my words had reached something in her. She rubbed her nose, the way you do to stop the itching that precedes tears. "I see what you mean." I stuffed the last few containers into the hamper and held up the coffee thermos. Frannie nodded; I poured two cups. She blew into hers. Little puffs of steam floated up, landing on her cheeks and nose.

"I like Gemma. Even thought I was happy about their marriage... Then, I don't know," she paused, searching for a way to explain, "I just got mad."

I listened patiently, but when she seemed stymied, I tiptoed in. "It's important for you to remember that you like Gemma. I think you'll discover that your anger and confusion have far less to do with her than it does with you."

Frannie listened intently, even sliding closer a few inches. "If you're anything like me, and I suspect you are," I said, giving her hand a little squeeze, "you don't like the unknown that change brings. You've worked hard to adjust to all the change your mother's death brought, and now you have to adjust again. It's hard work, and tiring, and scary. But you have people who love you, who will help you through it."

Frannie nodded. "I'm sorry you never got another mom."

We sipped coffee, watching boats return home for the night, drawing deep breathes of the clean, salty air. Shouts and squeals interrupted the chorus of bird's calls, causing us to turn and look. What had begun as a sightseeing expedition had turned into a wrestling contest.

"Can I ask you something else?" Frannie said. "Do you think you'll re-marry? You know, cause of what you said. You don't want to end up like your father, do you?"

I hadn't seen this punch coming and it was a stunner. I looked away, unsure of what my eyes might reveal. How could I have expected this young girl to understand the nuances of individuality that granted me dispensation from my own advice?

In an unexpected mercy, Blair called my name, begging me to join them. I leapt from the blanket then turned back to Frannie, encouraging her to come, too. When everyone's energy was spent, Archie and Frannie taught Blair their favorite card game to the soft glow of Peter's lantern. Peter and I lay on the blanket, watching stars appear like candles in the darkening sky.

Propped up on his elbows, he asked, "Are you reading anything interesting these days?" Only Cathy asked me questions like that. I loved how it suggested wanting to be known.

"Agnes introduced me to some local authors. They make the area come alive." I was grateful for the luxury of time to read. I realized now how much I'd missed it. Knowing only a reader would ask that question, I had to ask, "What about you?"

He named several British authors he'd recently enjoyed. I recognized a few. "And I like philosophy and biographies. But it takes me forever because I make notes as I read. I get more out of them when I do. It's worth it, though it slows me down."

"Do you keep a daily journal, too?" I asked. I remember Cathy telling me that she started every day with a pen in hand.

He nodded. "For years now. Got into the habit when I was at university. How about you?"

"No." I shook my head. "I wasn't any good at it, so I didn't stick with it."

"I don't think there's much skill involved, just putting your thoughts and feelings on paper. Developing it into a habit, that's another thing."

I took a moment to consider why I felt like I did. Suddenly, I sat up.

He sat up, too. "You've made sense of something." I nodded. "Something upsetting," he suggested.

"Or something insanely stupid, I'm not sure which." He made me feel safe to continue. "I think the reason I've been unsuccessful at journaling is—." I wasn't sure I could say this. Or why I wanted to. I'd never bared my soul this much, even to Edward. But I saw compassion, not judgment, in Peter's face as he sat there quietly, ready to listen.

My voice dropped to a whisper. "It's just my thoughts and feelings. Who am I? No one important." I stopped, continuing to work it out. "I guess," I said haltingly, "I don't believe I'm worth the paper and ink."

His mouth grew tight with indignation. He leaned towards me, making certain I was paying attention to his words. With a quiet intensity that scared me, he said, "You think you aren't worth spilled ink. I think you are worth spilled blood." I had no idea what he meant. The words were shocking, but they moved me, as well.

"Mom, look," cried Blair, "there are so many stars. Isn't it beautiful? Where'd they all come from?" The sky was alive with twinkling lights, as if home to a million fireflies.

"God made them on the fourth day," Archie said with certainty.

Later, at home, I lay awake, looking out the window, considering Peter's words. As I drifted off, my last conscious thought was of his penetrating compassion.

∽

Tuesday was a perfectly lazy day. We stayed in our pajamas until mid-morning, then went to our favorite beach a few miles away. It was a blue-bird day and playing in the surf wore us out. After an afternoon nap on the couch, I let Blair have her favorite dinner. French toast. "I wish they didn't have that funny bacon here."

"It's not so bad. Why don't you give it another try?" I asked, cracking eggs into a bowl. I was showing Blair how to whip her wrist around, the trick to good stirring, when we heard a knock at the door. Blair ran from the room, returning with Agnes in tow.

"We've missed you," I said, hugging her. She was stiff, and didn't offer one back.

"I've missed you, too," she said, clearly uncomfortable.

"Come see what I'm reading." Blair dragged her upstairs. When they came back,

I invited her to stay for dinner. She ate three pieces and held out her plate for more. "I've never had American French toast. It's quite good."

"Yeah, and we don't eat gross bacon," Blair added. I gave her a look.

"I'm sure there are lots of things you've had to get used to being so far from home."

"Yeah, but they're almost all better here. I don't want to go back; I want to live here from now on and go to Peter's school."

"Oh surely you don't mean that," Agnes answered. "You'd miss your friends and your family and all the things you used to do."

Blair shrugged and stuck the last piece of toast with her fork, sinking it into the lake of syrup on her plate. She finished and went to call Margaret.

"I'm so sorry. I didn't mean to start all that," Agnes said, when we were alone.

"Don't worry. Blair didn't know what she was saying." We took the dishes to the sink, and I started washing. "She's certainly been happier here than I ever thought she could be. I even think about staying, but..."

"Do you think you might? That would be wonderful."

"I don't know," I laughed. "I've dreamed about it, but working it out practically? I'm not sure I could make it happen."

The dishes finished, Agnes got serious. "I need to talk to you."

"Sure," I said, rubbing lotion into my hands. I offered her a squirt.

A flush covered Agnes' face. "Could we go for a short walk?"

"All right." It was getting dark; rain clouds were forming on the horizon. A breeze was born in the coming weather and the barometer was falling. Agnes walked slowly, looking more uncomfortable with each step.

"Really, Agnes, I wish you'd just say whatever it is. You're making me nervous."

"You're right," she agreed, but continued in silence.

A little further, I stopped and faced her. "What is it?"

"Okay. I did something—I feel awful about it. I need to tell you, and you've got to forgive me."

Why was this word suddenly the centerpiece of every other conversation I was having? We came to a low stone wall and sat down. She reached down and picked a handful of grass from a crack in the pavement. It fell through her shaking fingers.

"I don't know what got into me. I just feel so insecure sometimes, and when I give into it, well— Ugh." Agnes sighed, then squared her shoulders. "I said something about you to Jillian, to ingratiate myself with her. I actually thought there was a person behind all that makeup and hair color, and I momentarily lost my head."

Jillian? I felt queasy. "What did you say?" When there was no reply, I grew insistent. "Tell me what you said."

She looked pale. I would have been sorry for her if I hadn't felt so nervous. She took a deep breath and closed her eyes. "I told Jillian what you'd said about not trusting Peter and not letting Blair return to Muirfield."

I waited for her to continue. When she didn't, I let my breath out slowly. "That's not so bad. I told Eleanor and even Peter himself. I wish you hadn't pulled her into it, but I don't think it affects much."

My words brought no relief to her. "There's another thing." She looked pained, and I felt a frisson of fear. "I suggested there were similarities between Peter and your husband. You know, the stuff we talked about at the church fete."

I bolted upright. "You said that?"

"I'm so sorry, Suzanne. I don't know how I could have betrayed you like that. I get all strange around her and—." She stopped ranting and looked me squarely in the eye. "I have no excuses. I'm so ashamed. All I can do is admit how sickened I am by my own behavior. I know my actions don't prove it, but I really do value your friendship."

The gulls, preparing to rest for another day of play, called to one another in clear, piercing voices. I looked up at them and envied their flight. I wanted to run, but the weight of betrayal held me in place. "I would never have expected…this." Slowly, my heavy legs carried me back to the cottage. I slammed the door behind me. Blair found me in the hall. Ignoring my tear-filled cheeks, she looked past me.

"Where'd Agnes go? Is she coming back?"

I shook my head and then pushed past Blair and went into the bathroom. Pouring bath salts into the steamy water, I sank slowly into the hot sanctuary. Eventually, I was able to breathe deeply again, my mind no longer an explosion of pain and anger. I laid my head back against the cool porcelain. And then clarity came.

I should have expected this. It was my fault. I knew better than to open up. People let you down. That's just what they do. I'd experienced it my whole life. Being in England didn't change human nature. What an absolute fool I was.

# 12

## Peter

I was ready to go. The kids would spend the evening together while Suzanne and I went out. We gave final instructions and left. Our twilight picnic was only two days ago, but already Suzanne seemed different. A light had gone out of her eyes, her expression guarded. I tried to keep my hopes up for the evening, but the change in her countenance made me nervous.

She agreed to stop by Jerry Livingston's shop so I could drop off a saddle. The few extra miles would give us more time to talk. Only we didn't. Instead, she sat stiff, expressionless, and silent. After a failed attempt to draw her out, I gave up. I wanted to know why she'd retreated behind her walls again. Afraid I'd offend her, I didn't ask. Maybe she'd tell me in time.

Quickly back on the A394, we turned at Marazion. At the final curve before reaching the northern end of town, Suzanne gasped, and I knew she'd seen the jewel of Cornwall. St. Michael's Mount, the crowning fortress of the St. Aubyn family, was an imposing granite presence rising up from the sea. The artist in me couldn't see it often enough. I'd brought Archie here recently and watched him transform, like every lad before him, into a medieval knight. At low tide, visitors walked the short distance across the causeway. High tide forced us onto a ferry. I had planned for us to just enjoy the gardens and the view, but Suzanne spied a picture of the house's interior, and I knew she'd be disappointed if she didn't get inside.

I would have been, too, I discovered. I'd forgotten the drama of the Chevy Chase Room, the elegance of the Blue Drawing Room. The tour through the house ended too quickly; a docent ushered us outside to the tropical gardens. There we found a stone bench. "Thanks for bringing me," she said, looking out to sea. "I can't wait for Blair to see this. Ian offered, but we never scheduled it."

I managed to avoid commenting about Ian. "Are you disappointed Blair's not with us?"

"No," she answered quickly. "You saw her; she felt like she'd been summoned to the royal court of Queen Frances." A bit of the missing sparkle returned to her eyes.

I laughed. "I just hope they don't leave Archie out of their hen night." We watched the boats and birds move about the blue water. Even after five years, the activity of life at the sea held a fascination for me. My years in the Yorkshire dales, with their fixed markers of barns and fences, stood in stark contrast. The differences fed my homesickness for a long time. Perhaps Suzanne felt something similar. "Do you ever feel how far you are from home?"

She wrinkled her brow. "I don't think about it much. After all, I brought the best part of home with me."

"Yes, you did." She folded her arms over her growling stomach. Taking the cue, I said, "I thought we'd eat in Marazion, enjoying the view of the Mount. Would you be bored, I mean, since you've seen it close up?"

She looked from the sea to garden and up at the house. "How could looking at something this beautiful ever get boring?" I looked over at her and wondered the same thing.

Twenty minutes later, we were seated on the patio of the Marazion Arms. "I had a brilliant time Monday at our little picnic." I held out my glass for a toast. We clinked our glasses together so lightly they hardly made a sound. "Did you?"

"Yes," she answered shyly. "It was a lovely spot. And Blair's infatuated with Archie and Frannie." Questions lined up in my mind like soldiers standing at attention. Why was she talking about Blair when I asked about her? Was I causing this distance between us?

Though it was hard, I wasn't about to be an idiot again. This time, I wouldn't ruin a perfectly pleasant time as I'd managed to do before. "Getting reacquainted with them has been grand. I'm sorry to see them go." I thought of Frannie's suffering when Liza died and of the girl she is today. Light had returned to her eyes. I was ashamed that I'd let unfinished business with Laura keep me from my family. It was time to be done with the resentment I felt toward Laura. And it would require the best of me.

A family with three teenagers was being seated at an adjacent table. I watched, momentarily distracted by their silent communication as they worked out who would get the seats with the best view. Running both a school and a stable, I'd had ample opportunity to reflect upon the mysteries of family dynamics. "I worry, though, how they'll manage with all the adjustments awaiting them at home."

"They will," she said confidently. Some little piece of her wall gave way when she talked about my niece and nephew. "Frannie opened up to me Monday night."

"That's smashing. What did she say?" Suzanne hesitated; so I rushed to reassure her. "I'm not prying. I worry about them." I gave what I hoped was my most pleading look. "They're my family. I want to help."

"I know," she said. She paused, taking a sip of wine. "Frannie likes Gemma. But she's nervous about all the changes this marriage will bring."

"Sure, she's already had to deal with a lot of it. What did you tell her?" I could sense myself rushing the conversation again. The server appeared with our food. I was grateful for the interruption.

She took a bite of salmon and nodded, "It's good." She took a few more bites, leaving me to wonder if she would continue. Finally, she put her fork down. Looking across the causeway, she said, "I told her change is inevitable. Trying to avoid it is like trying to stop the waves from reaching the shore." Her eyes grew moist, and she took a drink. "I wanted her to see that, even with the changes that come, it's what's best for her dad. She needs to remember Thomas' loneliness."

"Your father didn't remarry, did he?"

She shook her head. Her brown hair showed streaks of gold, distracting me. "No. And I think he's suffered for it."

Her unselfishness touched me. She would have opened her heart to a stepmother in order to keep her father from more pain. "Thanks for talking to her." This conversation intrigued me at several levels. But all of them tied into Suzanne's circumstances, threatening to mire us in quicksand if I wasn't careful. Before the question I most wanted to ask burned a hole in my brain, I needed a diversion. "Tell me about Morgan's. Did you love being a shopkeeper?

A strained look crossed her face. Did I blunder again? Then it passed, and she launched into a description of Morgan's and insightful observations about the managers and staff. "They were dedicated to Edward. It's been difficult for them to have him gone." Again, the look appeared on her face;

she took a sip of water. "I'm fortunate Cathy's there. She commands the respect Edward did."

I wondered if it was respect that he commanded. Fear, more like. "Tell me about her."

She smiled. "She's my best friend. We met as freshmen in college. After graduation, we both stayed in Washington. We've always been competitors. Until now. You'd really like her."

"Why is that?" I was chuffed she'd given a thought to me.

"She's smart, loyal, self-sacrificing." She said it with conviction. "She's always quick to put others before herself."

I sensed something else, something unfinished. "It sounds like you've been fortunate to have her as a friend. Certainly, she's fortunate to have you."

"She's a much better friend than I am. I worry there will be a day when she'll grow tired of the inequity of our relationship."

"She could, I suppose, if she was selfish—needing to be repaid. But it doesn't sound like that's what motivates her."

She paused, her eyes moving about as though in search of something. Then she took another bite of rice. "No, I'm sure it isn't," she said with surprising confidence.

"What do you think motivates her?" I asked.

"Her convictions, her faith." Again, she answered with certainty.

I nodded. "Visible faith is so rare as to be memorable."

She stared down at her plate, thinking hard. This would have been an ideal time to give her the gift I brought, but I'd left it in the car. Not wanting to lose the momentum we'd found, I needed to think of something else to talk about. "Blair's made several good friends, Margaret for one, and Eleanor's granddaughter.

"Yes, Fredericka. She's a delight. She's a little older. Blair feels quite special having her attention."

"And what about you? Do you know Eleanor's daughter and our wonderful librarian?"

"I wouldn't call either of them a friend. I've only met Hillary once."

"I understand she's separated from her husband. That's quite sad. Tell me how you found her."

"It's not my place to say," she snapped. Her eyes grew angry and dark. "I don't gossip."

I shuddered. "Of course not. I didn't mean to ask you to. I was merely concerned about her."

She smirked at me. "In my experience that kind of language is used to cloak bad motives." That was strong language. I sat in numbed silence while she fumed. And then some of the puzzle pieces moved into place, enabling me to see how I may have played a part in something that felt threatening to her.

"You're right," I said, evenly. She let a wary gaze drift back to me. "It's true that some people hide behind the language of concern to get information. I agree caution can be good, but it might be a mistake to assume bad motives are always the case. Sometimes people are genuinely concerned. Maybe knowing the person asking helps with the judgment to know the difference." I was met with silence, albeit less inflamed.

A blue dusk was settling over the English coast. As we sat there, sipping coffee, I tried to work out how to prolong this lovely evening. Attempting to find safe ground again, I shared stories from my youth. Eventually, the hands of the clock nudged us from our seats; it was suddenly quite late.

Once in the car, I reached past her for the glove box and handed her a bag "This is for you." She pulled out a book, covered in soft blue leather, filled with tiny embossed flowers. Opening it, she put it up to her face and drank in the aroma. Then, she rubbed her hands over the velvety leather. I reached for a second bag. She pulled out a pen, turning it over and inspecting it.

"A Waterman. It's lovely." I could see her looking closer; seeing a spot where the gold finish showed signs of wear.

"It was Da's."

She drew back, pushing it into my hands. "I couldn't take your father's pen. It's your treasure."

Thinking of my father brought me peace, like sinking down into an old, overstuffed chair. "It is a treasure. That's why I want you to have it. He'd be pleased by that."

She looked, again, at the pen and rolled it over her fingers, into her palm, back over her fingers. "I...I don't know what to say."

"I'm the one saying it, and this pen will remind you." I waited until she looked at me again. I closed my hand over hers. "You are worth spilled ink."

We drove back to the cottage, the air soft, ethereal; I felt lifted from my seat into another realm. I wondered if she felt it too. There was so much I wanted to talk about, so much to ask about her. I focused instead on enjoying her presence. I knew I needed to reign in my need to plumb the depths of who she was. I wanted to charge in, throw open her heart.

But getting to know Suzanne was more akin to savoring each chapter of a book than rushing to the last few pages.

It was a short drive back. When we got there, I carried a sleeping Blair to Suzanne's car and set her in the seat. Just as Suzanne was getting in, I stopped her with a light touch on the small of her back. All the warmth of my body flowed to those fingers. "I enjoyed the time with you tonight. Thank you for going with me."

She looked at me with eyes that always seemed to be brimming with unspoken emotion. "No, thank you. For everything." Her voiced faltered and I began to reach for her. Taking a tiny step back, she clutched the bags to her chest. I held her eyes with mine, hoping she could see what my heart was saying. Was it thirty seconds or three minutes? I didn't know. But when she said she needed to get Blair, it hadn't been long enough. As she drove away, I knew something changed for me that night.

~

The waning light settled on Eric's face, casting spidery shadows behind us. We'd enjoyed a fish dinner, and now lingered over tea and stories about his days at sea. But before I could ask for another tale, he cut me off. "I've had my fill of hearing about me, even if you haven't. You're a Yorkshireman. What did you leave behind to come here?" I knew that deceptively innocent look of his all too well.

"I needed to start over and couldn't do it in a familiar place. I wanted to live at the coast."

He looked at me with wry eyes, shaking his head. "I'm old, but I'm not out of my head. You didn't answer my question."

"Ah, Eric. You like the heart of the matter, don't you?" I said, feeling penned in.

"I didn't always. But I've learned a thing or two. Most of men's troubles start, or end, in their hearts."

I let out a long, slow breath. "Aye, they do." I wanted to answer his question, but I didn't know how. I was still thinking when he lifted his arm toward me. Dry, paper-thin skin hung loosely on his shrunken frame. I helped him out of the chair. We walked haltingly toward the path. "I'll tell you when we're there. Now, talk."

I sighed. He'd asked the question I'd avoided answering for five long years. "I was Assistant Headmaster in a school in York. My fiancée, Laura, was a catering manager for a hotel. Busy with wedding plans for the following autumn." My chest grew tighter, my heart suddenly pounding furiously. I'd walked through this regularly since it happened, but it felt the same with each telling.

"It was January. The 17th. My father got a call. A fire. When he got there, the man was outside, but his wife wasn't. He didn't know where she was. Da ran in." Anger and sadness rose up in me, threatening to burst through like some leviathan from an old Norse myth. I hated talking about it. I took another step and stopped.

Eric clasped my arm. "He died." I nodded. "A great man, your father."

"Aye." We kept walking. "My brother, Thomas, also a great man, moved his family in with Mum. The kids had to change schools, but they knew it was the right thing. Mum hadn't lived alone. Ever. She'd married young. She wouldn't have coped." I looked at the heather blooming all along the path, mixing with gorse across the heathland. A blanket of thick moss filled in a strip near our feet. "Do you want to rest?"

"I'm fine lad. Keep on."

"They'd only been with Mum for two months when Liza found out she had cancer. Four months later, she was gone." I still wondered at the purpose in it all. "And still Laura planned the wedding. The pain of it, the grief. It was too much for me. I told her we needed to delay. I needed some time." I shrugged, attempted a smile. "That was the beginning of the end."

"The end of what, would you say?"

My head swung round. He certainly knew how to go for the heart, didn't he? "The life I had. Laura broke things off. I left my home and family."

"She wasn't keen on the delay?"

I shook my head. "Found someone else. It was all too much. I didn't handle it well."

"What would that have looked like, that good handling of your life?" He was forcing me into places I didn't like to go. His relentless questions made me angry. And this slow pace made me angrier. It gave me too much time to think about each word. Each feeling. If it had been anyone else, I'd have marched off and left him there. But it was Eric. I knew him. He was without guile. He asked because he cared.

"I wouldn't have walked away from my family when they needed me most. I let them down, left them to heal on their own. And…" I needed to think how to say this. "I wouldn't have left things with Laura like I did."

"And how was that?" I burst out laughing; I'd walked right into that one. He was going to keep asking until he was satisfied that I'd been completely honest. Behind his weather worn exterior beat the heart of the truest friend. As true to me as Thomas. "Here's the spot," he said. I'd been so consumed with my story that I hadn't noticed where we were. Our path had turned toward the sea. Just beyond us, cut into the rolling earth, was an opening. Wide enough for a bench, missing more finish than remained. I leaned forward to read the small brass plaque. *For Daisy*.

"It comforts me to come here," he said, and sat down. The sun set quickly, taking the day's warmth with it. A cool breeze came off the water. The air grew misty and the bits of light on the top of the water dimmed as the water turned from blue to gray.

"I said something terrible to her." I looked to him, expecting disappointment. Or shock. But the truth was, he never made me feel judged. And now, here with him, the bench became my confessional. "She'd changed toward me, but I didn't know why. I suspected the delay made her doubt my love. I tried to reassure her, but I just couldn't move on to something so joyous when my family was suffering. While I was suffering." I put my head in hands and closed my eyes. "We were in her kitchen. She pulled the ring off her finger. 'I've met someone else. He's everything you aren't. Everything you could never be. I need more of a man.'" I could still hear her voice, still smell the candle burning. A chill run through me.

"I'm not perfect. I get as angry as anybody else. But I'm not usually mean. I looked at her, Eric. I looked at her and said, 'Maybe I've let you down during these terrible months. Maybe I'm not the man you need. Couldn't ever be. But what I know is you're not worth my trying. You're just not worth it.'

I sat there, immersed in guilty silence. And good old Eric, he let me. "You asked what I left behind. I left the scene of the crime."

I watched the waves lap against the rocks that jutted out down the coast. Every once in awhile, the wind caught the spray, casting tiny rainbows through the air. I was thinking about granite, a defining characteristic of Cornwall, and what I'd learned about it since being here. Tors, large mounds, formed at the site of previously erupted volcanoes. Durable, immovable, hard. Like my heart. Eric cleared his throat.

"It sounds like you've spent a good bit of time since still living in those moments you've described. They're weighing on you as much today as the first day you came. So I'm wondering, what can you do that would free you up to be living life now?"

We stayed until just a thread of light remained to help us find our way back. The walk had tired him, and he seemed ready for sleep. When I left him, book in hand, his eyes were already growing heavy.

I thought about his question all the way home. I would not be able to move on until I freed myself from the past. I'd been stuck in the fact that Laura didn't believe I was enough of a man to her. I realized even I didn't believe it for a time. And in that moment, I realized something else. I didn't need to convince Laura of anything. I needed to set the record straight.

∽

Two days later, I brought Blair home after another good day at the barn. Our excitement grew as she improved with each ride. We huddled beside the car, talking and laughing. When Suzanne opened the door, we jumped to attention, trying our best to hide our guilty grins. "What's going on?" she called out.

"Nothing," Blair squeaked before turning to laugh into my side. It was getting harder to keep Suzanne in the dark.

"I'm off to London, then Yorkshire. Leaving day after tomorrow. But," I added, making sure I had Blair's attention, "I still need you at the barn. The work continues whether I'm there or not. Margaret's brother will be looking out for things while I'm gone."

"How long will that be?" she whinged.

I squeezed her thin shoulder. "Not even a fortnight."

"A what?"

"Oh sorry, I forgot you don't speak proper English. Less than two weeks."

We dropped Blair off with Fredericka, then sped away on the A390, toward Padstow. Memories of the evening in Marazion gave me hope for tonight. We walked a few blocks from the harbor, finally stopping in front of a three story stone building. Hanging baskets and window boxes poured out their flowers, and a green and gold sign said *The Rusty Anchor*. The blurry, undefined interior betrayed the age of the windows we peered through. I held open the oak door, and we stepped into a modern restaurant, full of stainless steel and black marble.

I had reserved one of the few tables which afforded a view. We looked out toward the water where three boats rested side-by-side, bobbing different rhythms. Eventually, our easy banter ran its course, and Suzanne looked uneasy. She squirmed about in her seat, nervously grabbing the serviette. She rearranged the utensils, and then folded and refolded the linen serviette, finally settling it onto her lap.

"Traveling on business?" she asked politely. I didn't want her to be polite. I wanted her to be interested.

"Seeing an old friend." I grabbed my glass and gulped some water. I wasn't ready to talk about Laura yet. "Shall I visit some shops? Investigate the London trends? I could bring you back a report. For Morgan's."

A muscle in her cheek began to twitch and she turned pale. "You don't need to do that. It's just a store."

"Of course it's not. It's your shop." What had started out playful had taken a serious turn. She shook her head.

"It was always more Edward's than mine." Her eyes were hard, but her jaw trembled slightly.

"I can't imagine that. I've seen you bring life to everything around you. Look at Blair. She's changed since you got here." She stared at me as though I was speaking a foreign language, but I went on. "And Frannie. You said yourself that you connected with her. That you helped her with her fears about life with a step-mum. And Hillary. Eleanor said she found a friend in you." She blanched with each word. The truth I offered, meant to encourage and console, threatened instead. My words bounced off her, like arrows off a shield. Lies held more power than truth.

"I'm not sure it's quite like that," she countered. Of course it is, I wanted to scream. You brought life to me. I felt a thrust of pain in my chest. She wasn't ready to hear that. In fact, she might never want to hear that from me. Memories of all that went wrong with Laura crashed in, leaving me feeling even more bereft. But I knew why that was. My unfinished business with Laura kept me from being the man I was meant to be. The man Suzanne needed me to be.

"Blair said something surprising to me the other day." Her smile returned. "Said she was different here. She wants to go sailing with Margaret. She also said she wanted to stay and attend Oakton, even if it meant having Rachel as a pen pal. It surprised me to hear her weigh the cost of a decision like that." I waited for her to agree with me. To see her happiness in how well Blair was doing.

Instead, she frowned and took a deep breath. "I'm not surprised by it."

"So, you've talked about it?"

"Of course. She's my daughter," she snapped. "She talks to me, too."

She'd grown decidedly chilly, while I grew completely confused, increasingly afraid of opening my mouth. Time to say something completely innocuous.

"I noticed the buddleia beside your cottage was thriving. Did you do anything in particular?"

"I have a black thumb. I don't know what a buddleia is and care even less."

"I see," I said, completely deflated, feeling like I was stumbling about in the dark. Thankfully, the waiter appeared with a breadbasket. As soon as it was placed on the table I took out a piece, reached for the butter, and slathered some across the length of the roll. I swiftly licked off the bead, which rolled onto my finger. She smirked at me.

"I didn't realize you had such a fondness for butter," she said. I realized I'd been rude. And my discomfort turned me into a 12-year-old boy, red-faced and stammering. Generally thinking girls were the enemy.

"I... I... I should have offered you some. Guess I was hungrier than I realized."

We limped through our main courses, my attempts to restore the evening completely in vain. The server suggested dessert. "No thank you," Suzanne answered quickly. "Just the bill."

"I don't understand what the rush is. I thought Blair was spending the night with Fredericka."

"She is. I'm just ready to go home." Blank. Dull. Done. Her face said it all. I sat back and waited for the server to return.

The trip home was painfully quiet. When she and Blair drove away she was clearly as eager to say goodnight to me as I was to her. Archie wanted to tell me about the movie they watched, but I'd run out of patience. I was relieved when he mumbled good night.

Suzanne was under my skin and driving me mad.

# 13

## Suzanne

Blair went sailing with the Hestons, leaving me time for errands. And to think. And all I could think about was the other night. I was ashamed of myself. Peter hadn't done anything to provoke me. And still I was moody, mean even. It was ridiculous. I liked him. A lot. But he was getting too close.

I'd just emptied the last bag of groceries when there was a knock at the door. It was Margaret Heston, chewing her lip, and her dad, Ron, looking worried. Ron had taken the girls out for an afternoon sail. I'd been nervous about it. "What's happened? Where's Blair?" I said, trying to keep calm.

"She's okay. With Agnes Buncle." He rubbed his face. "I got a bit hot with Blair when she got in the way of the boom. I'd told her to watch when we came about but she didn't listen. I didn't want her getting hurt, you understand. I guess my fear got away with me. Well, she got upset." My heart sank for Blair, thinking of her dashed excitement. "We were bringing the boat in, you see. She made such a ruckus it caught people's attention. Miss Buncle was eating her fish and chips but she came runnin'." He looked at Margaret but she kept her eyes on her feet. "Miss Buncle said to tell you she'll bring her home in a bit."

I could see how hard this was for him. I had no interest in making it worse. "Thanks for coming. I'll talk to Blair when she gets home. The important thing is that no one got hurt." Margaret gave me a strange look, sending a shiver down my back.

There was nothing I could do now but wait. I sat down in the rocking chair to think. Each rock forward seemed to loosen memories bound by something I couldn't name.

I thought of the Saturday morning two years ago when Blair raked the leaves. She knew Edward hated the messiness of autumn and wanted to surprise him. She'd waited in the garage until he left for the office. To reach the rake, she had to climb on a shelf. Shortly, piles of leaves polka-dotted the yard. She came inside to ask me where bags were. I showed her and when we came out of the garage, Edward was standing in the driveway. He'd forgotten his sales forecasts. *Leaving a job unfinished is worse than never starting it*, he'd said, angrily. She explained she'd needed bags, but he chided her for her lack of preparation. She had accepted his censure with a hurt face but no tears. But when he saw where she had climbed on the shelf, leaving a few pots askew, he bellowed at her. We waited out his anger. I made his apologies as he drove away.

I continued to rock. A little faster now. Another memory came. Two months before the accident, there was a school fundraiser at an ice cream shop. We were dumbfounded when Edward agreed to go. *It's important to appear supportive of these events*, he'd explained. It had turned out to be stellar night for him; he saw a senator from Connecticut whose children were also at Great Falls Academy. Everything was fine until Blair's cone began to drip on the way home. Edward yelled at her for not eating it fast enough, then at me for not getting enough napkins. When it dripped onto the leather seat, he screamed at her to clean it up. She used her sweater to wipe it, but the ice cream smeared across the seat. Panicked, she handed me the cone, and panicked, I threw it out the window. Edward berated us the rest of the way home, saying we didn't value his possessions. *We could only think ahead as far as we could see*, he'd said. We walked into the house in a defeated silence that hung over us the rest of the night.

Backward, forward, backward, forward. Why hadn't I thought about this before? How had I managed to avoid this part of our lives for so long? My 30th birthday. It was a Sunday. Edward was watching The Master's golf tournament. He'd said more than once that he'd turned down tickets, resenting anew his decision to stay home. I was upstairs folding laundry when Blair ran into Edward's office. He followed a few minutes later and began yelling at her. He'd found Blair writing something, the paper sitting on the desk, not the blotter. He called her careless, accused her of scarring the wood. With words and tone reserved for four year olds, he explained the function of a blotter. When he paused, I asked her what happened.

She explained that she'd made Edward mad by stepping in front of the television. *Ernie Els was lining up his putt*, Edward said, as though that explained everything. He left the room before she answered me. *I was writing Daddy a letter, telling him I was sorry.*

I stopped rocking. I didn't think I could handle another memory. I closed my eyes and saw Blair's face. With each attack, the light in Blair's eyes dimmed until all she could do was stare back in defenseless resignation. Repeatedly, she'd been called *stupid, careless, irresponsible*. And I hadn't protected her. I'd made excuses for Edward. Explained his actions away. But I'd never said he was wrong. Never told him he couldn't speak to her that way. A cold, clammy sweat swept over me. I might as well have been the one breaking her in pieces, word by word. Of course she screamed back at Ron Heston. If no one else would fight for her, she'd do it herself.

The next hour slipped away in a haze of memory and regret. Finally, I heard Agnes and Blair coming up the path. They were singing. I jumped from the chair, ran to the door, and threw my arms around her, knowing I didn't deserve the hug she gave me. "I want to hear all about what happened, but first I need to talk to Agnes." Blair disappeared up the stairs. Before I could say anything, Agnes did.

"Suzanne, I know you're mad—."

"Ron and Margaret told me what happened," I interrupted.

Agnes bit her lip. "Did either of them tell you what she said exactly?" I shook my head, wondering why it really mattered.

"She said *you always call me stupid. You always say you won't do it again but you do.* She yelled at Ron as though he was Edward."

I leaned against the door and let that sink in. "Ron didn't pick up on that at all."

Agnes shook her head. "No, and I think it's just as well. I'm not sure Blair even understood. I don't think she heard herself."

I took a deep breath. I didn't know what to say to her. She'd been so kind, but I didn't like her being so close to Blair's vulnerability. I didn't trust her. "Thanks for giving up your lunch to help her and for bringing her home." I ignored the hurt and confusion in her face and pushed open the door. I couldn't think about her right now.

I left Blair alone for a few hours; we both needed time to think. Over dinner, I heard about the good part of the day. "I loved it when the wind pushed my hair way back and it was hard to open my eyes. Like the wind was making me close my eyes so I'd listen. The water is really loud. But kinda peaceful, too. It's weird. You'd like it."

We finished eating, and I carried the dishes to the sink while Blair poured soap onto the sponge. I'd drifted off to thoughts about Peter. I was wondering if he'd ever invite me to go on his boat, when Blair's voice broke in.

"I thought you would be mad at me for having lunch with Miss Buncle," Blair said, practically rubbing the design off of a dinner plate she was washing.

"I'm not," I said, rinsing the plate.

Her face filled with relief. "Good, cause we had fun together. She's really nice." Blair wanted to talk about Agnes, but we needed to talk about her outburst.

"Follow me," I said, drying my hands. We sat back down at the table. "Mr. Heston yelled at you on the boat, didn't he?"

Blair started chewing on her fingernail. "Yeah, it didn't matter. I'm not mad at him."

"Maybe you should be," I said. Blair shrugged and looked away. "Maybe you wished you could have yelled back at Daddy sometimes." She covered a quivering mouth with her hand. "It's okay. Your daddy was harsh, even mean, sometimes. I don't know why he acted that way, because I know he loved you." I put my hand under her chin, drawing it up until her eyes followed. "He was wrong. No excuses. He was wrong. And I was wrong for not making him stop." Tears began to fall from my eyes, too. I pulled her to me. "I'm so sorry," I whispered. "So, so sorry." A thousand years later, she hugged me back and said in a tiny voice, "It's okay, Mommy."

A weight fell from my heart, shrank into a little ball, and rolled away.

⤖

Ian arrived just when he said he would. I greeted him in a simple skirt and blouse, pearls and heels.

When he saw me, he took my hand and kissed the back of it. "You look lovely. I feel most honored to have you by my side."

"Ian, I don't—"

"Stop. I won't be argued with." His tone was playful. I did a quick curtsy, and he laughed aloud.

"I hear Stewart is off to London soon," he commented as we circled a roundabout. "I do hope he isn't abusing school funds." The playfulness was gone. And with it, my good mood.

"That's ridiculous," I said sharply. "What a thing to accuse him of."

"Just voicing concern for fiscal responsibility."

"I don't think you need to concern yourself with how Peter runs Oakton."

"And why not? Several parish families have children that attend there. I'm just looking out for their best interests. Do you know what his business is?"

I shook my head and looked out the window. "I don't have the foggiest idea." Visiting an old friend was all he told me. All I let him tell me.

"Do you know when he's due back?"

The questions were beginning to annoy me. Why did he think I would know? "Not sure."

"No matter," he said.

Ian turned northwest and I found myself in an area of Cornwall I'd not yet discovered. Although I liked the coast roads best, there was still much to enjoy. Whitewashed houses tucked into groves. Narrow lanes winding off to nowhere. Meadows of grass and stone. I was lost in a daydream about a small village in the distance when Ian broke in. "Really, Suzanne, I wish you'd join me."

"Oh sorry, was I ignoring you?"

"Yes, in a manner of speaking. You certainly weren't acting as though I'm here."

"I just got lost in the countryside. My imagination got carried away. I was picturing life over in that village," I said, finding it again out the window.

"For heaven's sake, Suzanne. You're a grown woman. Surely you've done with girlish imaginings. What a ridiculous waste of time."

I burned with humiliation. "Edward thought I daydreamed too much," I admitted, eyes fixed on the green distance.

Ian thought for a moment. "He looked out for your best interests, as do I."

It didn't feel that way. The opposite, in fact. A sort of vigilance crept into me, a sense that I risked constant correction if I didn't watch every word. I was glad when St. Ives came into view, diverting my thoughts.

We browsed in several galleries before dinner. Ian's droning commentary started to wear on me after awhile. Closing time finally came.

The restaurant Ian chose had an obviously romantic ambiance, plushy pinks and golds, candles and flowers. I worried about his expectations, but had to admit I enjoyed the pampering. I'd ordered one of my favorites, scallops in white wine. I was enjoying the lingering taste they left in my mouth when Ian's voice called me back. "Suzanne, I must say I was pleased you accepted my invitation. I thought you'd quite forgotten me." Was I imagining it or was he always accusing me of something?

"I didn't," I said, trying to keep my voice light. I didn't want to be blamed for being defensive, too. "Life got busy while Peter's niece and nephew were visiting. Blair was always finding reasons to go to the barn to see them."

"I see. It was Blair's fault. Well, I'm certainly big enough not to hold a grudge against a child." I nodded, remembering instead a question I wanted to ask. The waiter appeared to refresh our glasses, giving me time to gather my thoughts.

"Suzanne, you look as though you have something to say."

"I do."

"I imagine it has to do with the whole fiasco with Heston." He pinched off a corner of his roll.

"Very indirectly. Blair and I had a difficult conversation that afternoon. I felt so empty afterwards. That led to a sleepless night." This was harder than I expected. I wished I'd saved the question for Cathy. But I'd begun and his growing restlessness was making it worse. "Have you read the Psalms?" I blurted.

He stiffened. "What kind of vicar do you think I am?"

"I mean, what do you think when you read them? Do you believe them?"

"In what way?" He sounded skeptical, reminding me of my father whenever I asked about anything spiritual.

"Do you believe what they say?"

He chuckled. "Are you asking me if I believe the Bible should be accepted as literal truth? All of it?"

"Well, at least, the Psalms."

"Of course not. Heavens, imagine that. Next you'll ask if I believe in miracles or evil spirits. This is the 21st century, after all."

A titanic sense of disappointment washed over me. "I think David was lonely a lot."

"Goodness, Suzanne, everyone's soul is lonely in the dark of night." His dismissiveness left me speechless. I was still deciding if I wanted to ask anything else when Jillian walked up.

"You two don't appear to be having a smashing time. What's wrong, a lover's quarrel?"

I burned in embarrassment, but Ian just laughed. "What brings you here?" he asked, delighted to see her.

"I met an art dealer for a drink. He's going to set me up with a mate from school. Cambridge, I believe. He's got big plans for me. Thinks the dealers in Cornwall are provincial and unsophisticated. Says my talent is wasted here. I need better representation and exposure in London."

"London? That reminds me. Peter's headed there. Suzanne doesn't know what the occasion is," he said, a smile creeping onto his face. "Do you?"

Her smile slipped. "I've been so busy with my art; I've barely had two minutes for him." She leaned toward Ian, and in a low, conspiratorial voice. "His ex-fiancé lives there. He spoke of her recently. Went on about her for quite awhile. I expect he's looking to rekindle the flame."

To my horror, I turned away and blushed. Ian glared at me, and I tried not to look as disconcerted as I felt. "Well, I guess it's just a lucky coincidence that you picked the same spot for tonight. You've been most helpful. I hope the art connection proves profitable. Let me walk you out."

I sank down in the miserable knowledge that I'd betrayed myself in every way this evening. He returned, and self-satisfaction wafted from him like bad cologne.

"I daresay Jillian's always got her pulse on what's happening. So good to be current."

≈

I peeked out the window when I heard a car. Ian. Our conversation from last night still left me cold.

"Hallo! How did you sleep last night?" He was cheery when I met him at the door.

I mustered what I could. "Fine."

"Yes, well, that's grand. Look what I've brought you?" He held out a box from Whitechapel Bakery. "Have you had their lemon sponge?" I shook my head. "Right. I can see you're angry with me. This is my peace offering. I might have been a bit harsh yesterday." He thrust it at me. When I made no move to accept the box, his lips curled in anger.

Fury rose in my heart, but before I got a word out, he burst out laughing.

"Oh my, you should see the color of your face." He continued to laugh. "I was teasing you. I thought maybe I could take you and Blair for a picnic. There are gardens not far from here, and it would be a lovely place to set ourselves to rights."

Reluctantly, I agreed. On the way, Ian made a stop at Conrad's Pie Shoppe, which to Blair's disappointment sold meat pies and pasties, not meringues and creams. Feeling ambivalent about the day ahead and still chewing on last night, I had little to say. The quiet must have bothered Ian. In an act of unusual interest, he looked at Blair in the rear-view mirror and asked, "Are you in a furor trying to think what you might want to do in September?"

"No. Not really," Blair answered nonchalantly.

"Oh, why ever not?"

"Because—"

I interrupted. "I'd rather we didn't talk about this just now. Do you mind?" I glanced at Ian.

"Well, no, but I can't imagine—"

"I so appreciate you humoring me." And then turning around, I said, "Blair, why don't you tell Ian about some of the wonderful books you've been reading this summer?" Turning back to Ian, I added, "Agnes has been such a help in picking out books that interest as well as challenge Blair."

Blair was slow off the mark, but I managed to lead her through a recitation of her summer reading. Ian eventually joined the conversation, surprising me by asking Blair some very astute questions about plots and characters. I was glad for the chance to step back and be a bystander, the thing I'd wanted all along. Eventually, we turned down a winding lane, ending up in a parking lot surrounded by tall, fragrant pine trees and bursting purple rhododendrons.

"Here we are," Ian exclaimed.

"Where?" Blair asked, looking confused.

"At Dartington Gardens. Surely, you've heard of it."

"Why?" Blair challenged him.

"You'll see. I'll get the hamper and rug."

Blair and I walked hand in hand along a tree-lined path to the gardens; I noticed her increased steadiness with delight. Between hours at the barn and all of Cornwall being uphill, Blair's balance and strength were steadily improving. A buttress of clipped yew prevented us from seeing what lay beyond until we got to the end of the gravel path. Magically, a wondrous garden opened up before us. We came to a stop, taking in the barrage of color, texture and scent.

"Oh, it's…" Blair's face softened.

"What a wonderful place to bring us to. Thank you," I said to Ian. He beamed back at me.

"I thought it would work its magic on you." Taking the lead, he said, "Follow me." He led us past the field of showy peonies and around the holly topiaries sculpted into rabbits and squirrel. Then through the roses, enticing us with perfume, and into the Elizabethan herb garden. In the southeast corner two benches sat perpendicular to one another, providing a cozy spot for picnickers. Even in the summer, the stone benches were cold, so Ian spread the blanket across one and motioned for us to take a seat.

"If this spot is all right with you, Blair? I thought you'd like it."

"It's great," she said, helping to straighten the blanket. Ian emptied the contents of the hamper onto the bench. "That smells funny," Blair said, pointing to the Cornish pasty.

"Yes, I didn't bring that for you. It's an acquired taste. I brought you this." He handed her a cheese sandwich wrapped in wax paper. She smiled gratefully.

"This is our second picnic. Do you remember the first?" he asked Blair

"Yes, at that Land Ahoy place." I was relieved to see Ian laugh at her mistake this time.

"No, no, Blair. It's Land's End. I seem to recall you couldn't remember that name even when we were there." I held my breath, waiting for the dressing down. Instead, he asked pleasantly, "Do you remember why I told you it was called Land's End?" Blair thought a moment before nodding her head.

"It's the end of England. So I guess the Lizard Peninsula looks like a lizard?"

"Oh, have you been to the Lizard Pen?" He tilted his head in surprise and glanced quickly at me. As soon as she said it, I wished I could force the words back into her mouth. Now I felt nervous about what she would say next.

"Peter took Mommy and me there for a moonlight picnic. It was really fun, and scary. Archie and Frannie were still here, so they came, too."

"Yes," he said a bit slowly, "I understand you became good friends with Stewart's niece and nephew. Shame they live so far from here. I imagine you'll not see them again."

"Oh no, Peter promised I get to visit them sometime."

Ian nodded slowly. "I see. That's grand. Everyone needs friends." He took his time finishing lunch. Then he stood. "Blair, do you know your cookery herbs?"

"Herbs?" she repeated, exaggerating the way he pronounced it with a strong H.

"Blair—," I reprimanded.

"Not to worry, Suzanne. I realize Blair is still adjusting to proper English." He took her by the hand and led her across the garden. At his instruction, Blair closed her eyes, leaned forward, and breathed deeply, quickly identifying mint.

"Let's do another," she begged. She soon ran out of ones she could name but continued to enjoy the different scents. Happy to let her wander from row to row, smelling blossoms and leaves, Ian returned to the bench and handed me a sprig of lavender he'd just picked up from the ground.

"A moonlight picnic on the Peninsula. You must have been near Kynance Cove. It's a particularly lovely spot. Good choice. I'd have made the same."

"I suppose. I'm not completely sure where we were."

"Hmmm." He lifted the hamper and set it back down, exactly perpendicular to the bench. Then, in a light, breezy voice, said, "It doesn't seem very smart to be somewhere at night, especially with a child, children really, and not know where you are. What if something had gone amiss?"

"We were fine."

"Well, if you're satisfied then… Just, it's so remote. The car could have broken down…"

I felt a pinch of worry. Had I been foolish? It hadn't seemed that way at the time. But hearing it described like this, I wasn't sure. I waited for him to say more, but instead he called to Blair to get a piece of cake.

Afterwards, he took the hamper back to his car and returned with a camera.

"You seem to love the gardens, so I thought you'd like to have pictures to remember it." We mimicked topiaries and posed amongst blossoms. Ian asked a few passers-by to snap pictures of the three of us. One of the men commented on how lovely Ian's family was. He answered thank you without missing a beat, making no effort to correct the man. Before I could voice my disapproval, he winked at me.

When Ian offered to cook dinner for us at the Vicarage, Blair jumped at the invitation. And seeing her so happy, I couldn't say no. But I also didn't want a late night with Ian. I was still feeling a bit worn out from the night before. And if truth were told, feeling upset at the possibility of Peter in London with his old fiancé. We stayed in the car when Ian stopped at a fish market in Newlyn, giving me a chance to talk to Blair. "I don't want to stay late. It's been a long day."

"I'm having fun. Plus, shouldn't we stay as long as he wants us? To be polite?"

"I'll decide when its time to go home, and you won't argue with me." Ian returned to the car to find Blair with arms crossed, frowning in stony silence.

All that disappeared when we got to the vicarage. She loved the big rambling house, trying to explain to him why it was the perfect place to play Sardines.

"It's like Mrs. Cavendish's. Tons of rooms. And big curtains to hide behind and stuff. I really like it." He stopped short, a smirk playing at his mouth.

"It's very kind of you, but even I know this house in no way compares to the elegance of Penwylln. You don't have to try to puff me up with comments like that."

"What does that mean?" She looked at me.

"Ian, you're off base here. She's just saying she likes your house. That's all."

"Right." He looked at Blair. "Thank you. Feel free to explore a bit more. I shall go prepare dinner." He left us in the hallway. I felt confused and uncertain, but Blair took him at his word, going in and out of rooms. I left her to her fun and joined him in the kitchen.

Ian was a genuine chef, preparing fish and vegetables with confidence. "Where did you learn to do this?" I asked peering over his shoulder.

"At university, I worked in a restaurant. I love roast and potatoes as much as any other Englishman, but I don't cook that way. I prefer to watch my waistline and my arteries. Enough of the men in my family have died of heart ailments. I don't plan on repeating their stupidity." His voice grew hard.

"What can I do to help?" I asked, taking an apron from a hook.

"Stop. That's Mrs. Danvers. She'd never recover."

I laughed. "Is that really—?"

"No," he grinned. "Jillian called her that once. She got so angry we've not been able to help ourselves since. One can't be in Cornwall and not enjoy DuMaurier references."

They kept calling her that even though it made her angry? "I guess not. Put me to work."

"Actually, I've got rather high standards in the kitchen. It's best I be left alone."

That didn't surprise me at all, so I went off in search of Blair. I found her sitting in a window seat in the library, fingering an old atlas. "Is everything okay? What are you doing in here?"

Blair gave a half smile. "I like this room. It's very quiet. And I like the smell. It reminds me of being in Agnes' library."

Speaking of Agnes, I still needed to talk to her. "Dinner looks good. I think you'll like it. Do you want to come with me into the kitchen?"

"No, I like it here." I didn't blame her. I would have stayed, too, if I could. I kissed her head, told her we'd be ready soon, and returned to the kitchen.

Over dinner, Blair was subdued, reminding me of old dinners at home. Eventually, Ian managed to get her talking about horses. That led to the barn and friends and, finally, to Margaret.

"And I went sailing with her, and her Dad. But he kept yelling at me. I was glad Miss Buncle was there when we were getting done cause I wanted to get off. It wasn't fun at all. I don't care if I never go on a boat again. How am I supposed to know what to call everything, and what to do with the sails and ropes and stuff?"

"Blair, let's find something else to talk about, shall we? I'm sure Ian doesn't want to hear any more about this."

"Of course I do," he said. Turning back to Blair, "I can see why you were anxious to leave. No one likes to be yelled at. Where did Agnes take you?"

"To eat lunch. She was really nice to me, she always is. Even after she and mommy had their fight."

"Did you and Agnes have a row? What was that about?" He seemed eager for a good tale.

My stomach turned sour. "I'd rather not get into it. Suffice it to say, it was more of a falling out than a disagreement."

"You two had become fast friends. I'm sure you can settle your differences if you try." One minute he was counselor, the next he was accuser. I was out of energy for both.

"You're making a huge assumption, Ian."

"And what's that?"

"That I want to try."

He seemed nonplussed by my response, and the rest of the evening dragged on like a bad movie. I said a terse goodbye when he took us home, not turning at the door to wave as I normally did. Blair soon tired of my distracted, half answers and gave up trying to talk. What a relief to finally stretch out in bed. I was completely exhausted, but I lay awake for quite awhile, wondering why my life was so full of difficult relationships.

# 14

# Peter

Eleanor was the only person who knew what I meant to do. "Wonderful! So glad you are getting on with it. You'll never be able to move on to other relationships till you've cleaned up the spillage from this one."

I arrived at Paddington Station, her words still playing in my head. The bus to Oxford Street was easy to find. I enjoyed the short ride from the train station, watching Londoners speed walk through life. I got off at the intersection of Oxford and Regent and consulted my map. Thomas had gotten the information I needed from Laura's mum. He wanted to know more, but I told him I'd explain after seeing her. Risky though it was, I decided against calling Laura, believing she would not turn me down in person. It was already mid-afternoon; I hoped we could meet for dinner.

Even a confirmed non-shopper like me could be persuaded to spend money in London's plethora of stores. In part because they all made me think of Suzanne. It was hard to picture the quiet woman I knew as a hard driving executive in a fast-paced company. Her discomfort when talking about it, her constant references to it being her late husband's company, seemed like her way of saying she never fit in. Then why was she there?

I checked the time and realized the shopping had distracted me. It was time to go. My heart raced as I closed the distance to her office. I slowed down a bit and breathed deeply; the tightness in my chest began to loosen. I felt like an emissary of peace, olive branch in hand as I approached a hostile nation. Would she embrace me and accept the offering or rise up in anger, extending hostilities?

Laura looked up from her desk. She'd changed her hair and was dressed more smartly than I remembered. She stopped for a moment, then ran around the desk and threw her arms around me. "What are you doing here?"

"I came to see you. To talk."

"Brilliant. Oh, I wish I could leave right now, but I can't knock off till six o'clock. Can you wait that long?" Though warm and effervescent, I didn't fully trust her. I had memories of her from the past, conversations with her leaving an aftertaste as bitter as fizzy water.

"Of course. I came all the way from Cornwall; a few more hours won't make any difference."

"Cornwall? Do you live there now? We have so much to catch up on."

We arranged a meeting time, and I went in search of a hotel. I couldn't put my finger on why I found her bubbling delight so off-putting. Would I have preferred sharp annoyance or cold indifference? Maybe I would have, because that's what I imagined she'd felt toward me for the past five years. Before I knew it, I was pressed for time and sprinting down the hotel stairs.

Laura chose an Indian restaurant in Soho. She'd arrived at the restaurant before me and sat at a table in the front window. I saw the back of her head with its mass of dark brown curls, and years of memories flooded back. She looked up and smiled; my stomach tensed just as it had before our first date.

"This is a delightful treat. I can't imagine why you would have come all the way to London from Cornwall just to see me." A familiar feeling came over me, taking me back years. I was surprised to find it wasn't altogether unpleasant.

"It's wonderful to see you, too. I do want to catch up, but I also have something specific to talk about."

"Of course you did. I expected it."

"Why?" Had Thomas said too much to her mum?

"Do you ever do anything that's not deliberate?" This phrase rang a very old bell with me, but the tone didn't. Accusation and judgment were missing. The waiter arrived with a starter. "I took the liberty of ordering this. You can order what you like for dinner," she said playfully. We'd had more than one row over who would order our Friday night take-outs.

Her bright green eyes were as beautiful as I remembered. I'd never met anyone whose eyes expressed more than Laura's did. "What's that look?" she asked in between ordering extra na'an to go with her Tandori.

"Just admiring your lovely eyes, as always. Laura of the Emerald Eyes." I was surprised to see her blush. Maybe this wouldn't be as hard as I'd thought.

"Well, business or pleasure?" she enquired. She always was one to plunge into the water quickly.

"Pleasure first. Tell me what you're doing in that office."

I listened to the saga of her life since our parting. One year in an overseas internship. Then two years in York before finally landing her current position for a large hospitality chain. "I can't imagine what else I could possibly bore you with. Oh, except that I'm engaged to someone I work with. He's called Roger. He's a very agreeable chap and quite willing to move to Geneva if I get a promotion. You're quite similar actually."

"I thought—" I stopped sharply. *You're not man enough...*

"What did you think?"

"Never mind. Doesn't matter. Is the date set and all that?"

"Working on it," she said, between bites. "What's your story?"

I told her about Oakton and Muirfield, sticking with the skeleton of the story. By the time we ordered coffee, we were nearly caught up. At least with what I'd wanted her to know.

"Okay," she said, "shall we get on with the business part of the evening?" A shudder ran through me, and I was humiliated to discover that she'd seen it. "Really Peter, is it as bad as all that?"

I smiled sheepishly. "I want to talk about what happened between us. That last conversation, really."

"I'm game. Go ahead." Her bright eyes dimmed.

The feeling this most resembled was of jumping off a bridge tethered to a bungee cord. You know it will stop you from crashing into the rocks below, but you fall an awfully long way till it's stretched to its maximum. "Things ended badly between us." With the first word, I felt myself career toward the rocks. "I've not been able to forget that last night."

"Oh, Peter, everyone has rows and says things they don't mean," she said, laughing dismissively.

"Are you saying you didn't mean what you said?"

Her hand stopped in mid-air, chicken Tandori dangling precariously from her fork. "About what, precisely?" she asked cautiously.

"You know what you said to me, Laura. Let's not completely relive it." We stared at one another, and I grew impatient. "Did you mean it?"

"Yes, well, I might have done." She looked around at the rapidly filling restaurant, distracted by noise coming from a table of students. Then, with a bit less warmth, "Actually, well, I did. I meant it then. I would mean it today."

I was shocked to discover that her words could still draw blood. I'd come on a mission of peace, but she'd have none of it. And I felt pathetic. Why was I still giving her power to still inflict pain? I could barely tolerate myself at this moment. Then I thought of Suzanne and remembered why I was here.

"As I recall," she went on, "you wouldn't commit to a wedding date because your family needed you. But then how odd that you moved away from them. Couldn't give much help long distance, could you?" Her tone sharpened like steel on flint. This sounded more like the Laura whose words had echoed in my head for five years.

Out the window, people were hurrying down Frith Street towards Leicester Square. "You've quite summed it up. I did fail them. Disappointed them and myself. I'm heading there next." She raised an eyebrow. Looked a little less certain. "The reason I've come to see you is to tell you how sorry I am for what I said. It was wrong for me to lash back at you, no matter how angry I was. And with lies."

"What lies?"

I almost laughed at her. She'd make me earn this. She wouldn't be Laura if she didn't. "I believe my exact words were, 'Maybe I'm not the man you need. But what I know is you're not worth my trying. You're just not worth it.' It was terrible of me. And it wasn't true."

"Rubbish. You were heartbroken. I barely gave it another thought." Her face was still and set, but I could see pain underneath it. She blinked quickly, fighting back tears.

I reached across the table, taking her hand in mine. She pulled back, but I held on. "If you have given it another thought, then I'm sorry. It was cruel. I hope Roger will be all the man you need him to be. That he'll treasure you."

A tiny tear slipped from the edge of her eye, ran down her cheek and perched on her jaw. "Thank you. He is. He does."

As unexpected as rain from a blue sky, healing settled over me, starting at my head, flowing through my heart, pooling at my feet. I looked at the beautiful, vivacious woman across the table and finally, with a sincere heart, was glad she'd found a good man.

❧

On the moors of Cornwall one smells the ocean, on the dales of Yorkshire the earth. I drank in the scents and felt the tensions of life slip away. Thomas' house was 30 minutes outside York, far enough away from the city to be considered country but without livestock or crops. A suburban sort of country, I'd teased Thomas. Thomas, Gemma, Mum and the kids lived in the house Thomas had bought with Liza after years of living in a three room flat. They'd saved and scrimped and loved having the shared goal. It had been their haven until the armies of cancer infiltrated it. As we turned into the driveway, I wondered how Thomas could stand to live in a place in which her spirit was so present. And why Gemma would agree to.

The moon was high in the sky before I reached the house. It was a lovely spot, nestled between two hills, with gardens front and back. The clock in the hired car said 10:30 P.M. I'd taken a late train from London, needing a bit more time after yesterday's conversation with Laura. Archie and Thomas gave me a warm greeting at the door

"We're glad to see you," Thomas said. "Mum is too, but she fell asleep in the chair at half nine. Lily had her running today. Gemma and Frannie went to the cinema. They'll be back shortly."

Archie bounced with excitement. "It's good to see you, Uncle Pete. How's Fergie? I'll bet he misses me."

"Your Archie here," I said, clapping Thomas on the arm, "learned how to groom with the best of them. No one can pick hooves as clean as he can."

Thomas laughed and tousled his hair. "So he told me."

Archie beamed. "I sure did a better job than those girls."

We were in the kitchen getting something to drink when Frannie and Gemma arrived. Frannie greeted me with the deliberate detachment of adolescent girls the world over. She hung back in the doorway, looking vaguely bored. "Hi, Uncle Pete."

"Hello, Fran. Was the film good?"

"Yeah. Sure. Ewan McGregor was in it. Couldn't be bad, could it?" She looked over at Thomas, a little smile playing on her lips. He turned a bright red.

Before he could react, Gemma came in from the hall. "He is lovely. It was fun." Then coming forward, she said, "Welcome Peter. Your visit's a wonderful surprise."

It was odd to be welcomed into Thomas' home by this woman who was still practically a stranger to me. I'd only met her two days before the wedding and said a brief hello on the phone twice since then. We chatted about my trip awhile, but eventually, a yawn escaped me.

"You're in with me, Uncle Pete." I followed Archie in and fell asleep while he was talking about playing soccer with his mates.

The weather had turned overnight, and we awoke to a gray, drizzling rain. After breakfast, I invited Mum to go into York with me. We were able to park near the Minster, my favorite place in the city. I never tired of the soaring Gothic cathedral, finding something new to love each time. We pulled open the heavy door. It whooshed shut behind us, pushed by a gust of wind. Awed to a whisper, we walked quietly to a row of pews and sat down. I let my eyes drift around the room, settling on the huge round window that filled the south transept, a masterpiece of stained glass. The Rose of York.

"It was quite a shock to get your call. It was all Thomas could do to go to work yesterday. I know he'll want some time with you this evening." She adjusted her jacket, ill at ease in her town clothes. "I don't know why you've come back so soon. Course, with all the wedding festivities, there was no time to visit. But you're not just here to visit, are you? I can tell by looking at you that you've news to share. You look different." Her weathered cheeks flushed with anticipation.

"I feel different." I did too, I thought, marveling at the power of absolution to give life. What had Eric said? I needed to be freed.

"I need to say something to you, Mum." Taking my hand, she moved closer. I hadn't practiced how to say this. So I said the truest thing I could think of. "I let you down."

"How did you do that?" she asked.

"By being a coward. By going off to grieve on my own. I should have stayed. You deserved better from me. I should have been more like Thomas." That had been true much of my life, hadn't it? I turned my shoulder so I could look at her more directly. "Mum, I'm sorry."

She stood up. "Come with me." She tucked her arm in mine and walked us out of the Minster and around the corner. We stood in front of Little Betty's Café, a cozy tea-room well loved by our family. We found a table tucked into a corner. I had a fondness for their homemade scones, Yorkshire Fat Rascals. We ordered, but when they came, I had little appetite.

Mum poured for both of us. "It's been hard. I'll not lie about that. I miss Augie every minute of every day. But I'd be daft to think I was only one who lost him. And then poor Liza. Well, you remember how awful that was."

She buttered her scone and took a bite. I stirred my tea needlessly. "What I'm trying to tell you, Peter, is it's not for anyone to judge how another handles grief. You were already suffering from Augie and Liza, and then you got dealt another blow. I'll not have you saying you should have been like Thomas. You could only be you. And if you needed to go away, then that's what you needed to do."

"But Thomas took care of you when I didn't," I protested.

"Do you know why I brought you here? Because you love those scones. Thomas can't stand them. You're different men. I never expected you to be the same."

"You're too kind to me and you know it." I remembered that first year in Cornwall when I didn't know a soul. I'd liked the anonymity, needed the unrelenting quiet. With nothing and no one, I was able to be still. Then the loneliness set in. And it wasn't the sanctuary it had first been. "Maybe I did need to go at first, needed that distance to get myself sorted out. But I stayed away too long."

She put down her half-eaten scone and breathed deep. "Maybe you did." I studied her tired eyes and gray hair, remembering a better day. She'd aged more than five years since Da died, the sadness of each one plainly visible.

"Staying away too long. That's what I apologize for."

She nodded. "Accepted." She buttered a scone and handed it to me. "Augie would never have looked at one of you and thought the choices you made, the paths you took, weren't all part of a grand scheme that was all working together for your good. And I don't either. But I know you love me—." She stopped, too choked up to keep talking.

That was the moment I realized how deeply I'd hurt her. I knew that feeling—saying the thing you know is true but struggle to believe. And Mum just struggled with the words *I know you love me.*

"Now listen to me," she ordered. "There's something that just came over your face. It looks an awful lot like guilt. I said I accept your apology. So it's done." My dear, sweet mum grew fierce, reminding me of my brave Da. "And I'm the one who decides it. You apologized to me. I'm the injured party. So if I tell you it's over, then you believe that. You don't get to keep accusing yourself if I don't."

Smiling, she handed me another scone.

❦

After dinner, I roughhoused with Archie, read to Lily, and tried to get Frannie to talk about, well, anything. Archie and Lilly finally settled into bed; Frannie was watching the telly; and Gemma, Thomas and I sat around the kitchen table, sipping coffee.

My first impression of Gemma had come just two days before the wedding just a month ago. At our first meeting, she'd sat on the divan like a fine porcelain figurine: exquisite in the details, beautiful to look at, but her demeanor was cold. Perfect posture, ankles crossed, tailored clothes, and a designer haircut. I couldn't imagine how Thomas, who'd been drawn to Liza's fresh-scrubbed wholesomeness, could be attracted to this magazine perfect image of a woman. Then she turned to butter when Lily climbed into her lap. They snuggled there awhile, Lily eventually popping off her lap to return with a picture book. Gemma took her by the hand and led her off to bed.

Thomas saw my dismay that night. "I thought the same things when I first met her; we all did. The posh façade isn't who she is. She's just more reserved than most people. But you'll soon see that she's a darling." He was right. She quickly won me over with her easy friendliness. She cuddled Lily, teased Archie, and gave Frannie distance but not avoidance. She was part of the family now, and I needed to get used to talking to them together.

Tonight they sat close together on the bench, shoulders meshing. Thomas picked up his cup with his left hand to keep from disturbing their position.

"This whole trip is about me owning up to some things. Setting things right. Yesterday, I started with Laura."

"And how was she?" The edge in Thomas' voice reminded me that he'd always be my protective big brother.

"Good." Then, to Gemma, "We'd not seen each other since the night she called off our engagement. Five years ago." I was a little surprised to see this wasn't news to her. Then I realized Thomas had probably told her my history.

"I went to apologize for things I said that night. All these years," I said, blowing into my mug, "I've carried the failure of that relationship like a rucksack, and I'd grown stooped from the weight of it. I've chewed on that last row for a long time. It was time to be done with it."

"And are you?" big brother asked.

"I am. And it feels great. She's met a nice chap, sounds like a good man."

"Right. That's done then." He took a left-handed sip of his coffee.

"And so is talking to Mum."

Thomas drew his brow in. "Mum? What was that about?"

Sighing deeply, I sat back and stretched my arms up. I drew them down, and clasping my fingers, settled my hands on my head. "I needed to set things right with her, too. And with you."

Thomas looked at Gemma, who gave a little shrug. "I don't know what you'd have to set right with me. I don't have a problem with you, Pete."

"It was hard for Mum to admit, too. But she did." I put my arms on the table and leaned forward. "I let her down. Maybe not by leaving." Thomas leaned forward, also, ready to object; Gemma drew up straight, leaning away slightly. "But by staying away as long as I did. It hurt her. And she owned up to that."

Thomas sat back and settled hard into himself. His shoulders drooped forward, some of the weight he'd carried alone finally evident. "I left it all for you, Thomas. And being the man you are, you'd never complain to me about it. But my conscience has been. When Laura ended things—it just proved to be one too many for me. I had to get away to nurse my wounds."

"I don't begrudge you that," he said.

"I know. Neither does Mum." But shame still owned me, and I looked away. "But then a time came when I was better. I could have come back. By then you were taking care of everyone; frankly, I was happy to let you do it. And I was wrong."

When I finally found the courage to look back, he had turned away. I braced myself for the anger I expected. I glanced at Gemma. She looked nervous, uncertain. This will be bad, I thought. Then he looked back.

"Maybe you were, and maybe you weren't. I know who raised us. I know what we believe is right and true. And I know your character, the man you are." He emphasized those last four words. The meaning wasn't lost on me. "So maybe you could have come back. But I'm thinking you didn't come because you weren't ready." I started to object. He stared me down. "You're here now, aren't you? You've sorted a few things out. I've no argument with you."

"But when you came in June, you said—"

"I said she needed to hear from you. Look, I don't think you've done anything wrong." I tried protesting, but he reached across the table and grabbed my arm. His eyes bore right through me. "But if you aren't at peace, then know I forgive you."

I clasped his hand. "Thank you."

☙

I was leaving tomorrow and this was our last chance to talk. The visit had been more than I'd hoped for, helping me shake loose many of the fetters that had tied me to the past. I looked forward to telling Eric and Eleanor about it when I got home. "I saw Laura. That's why I was in London."

"I guessed as much. Or should I say hoped." Mum's eyes darted up at me.

"You don't mean you hoped we'd get back together?"

She shook her head. "Of course not."

"Then what?"

"You had unfinished business with her like you did with me." She'd always had keen intuition. "It was time."

"Aye. For both of us."

The weather had been cold and rainy. The earth was dark green, the water rushing swiftly. Mum had chosen this spot, though I wasn't sure why. We'd walked through muddy meadows to get here and now stood on the little bridge, listening to the brook as it jumped and slid over the rocks below. "Your father used to tease me about my love for this spot. Said I'd as soon go here as I would Paris or Rome." She grew softer as she talked about him. "He was right, too. Do you know why?" I shook my head. "This is where I first met him."

"I never knew that." I looked at the bridge a little more closely.

"I was coming from the churchyard. I used to visit my grandfather's grave to put flowers on it. And to tell him about my life. Your father had run to a neighbor's for his mam. He was skulking around here instead of going back. When I saw him, my heart leapt out of my chest. I'd seen him around the village. But we had just come to live with Gran and I'd not talked with him. I was still a stranger here."

I pulled my coat tighter around. Though the rain had stopped, it was cool and dreary. "Mum, would you rather take this somewhere else? It's getting colder."

"I like it here." I'm not sure she felt the cold.

I put my arm around her. It was cold, whether or not she felt it. "So, your heart leapt out of your chest. Then what?"

"Then he started talking. The kindness you knew in Augie, all your life, I first saw in him that day. He knew I was nervous, so he made it his business to put me at ease. I only nodded or shook my head. Could have thought I was a mute and never said another word to me. Years later, he told me he saw something in my eyes. He was willing to wait for me to get past my fright. So, for awhile, he did the talking for both of us."

I could see that. He'd filled in enough gaps for me. "That's a wonderful story, Mum." I still choked up when talking about him. I wondered if that would ever change.

She looked off to the church on the hill. "You and Thomas are your father's sons. You have his character. He knew the nature of love is to give your self to someone. To help be for her what she can't be. Aren't we all crippled, every one of us? Some of us wear it under our coats better than others. Some pretend it isn't true."

I leaned back, hands in my pockets, and thought about this. But she wasn't done. "I expect one day you'll meet a woman who has a hurt of some kind. Maybe uprooted from a dearly loved home, as I was. Or maybe she'll have a deeper hurt. And you'll be the one to give tender care. The one to talk for her."

"How will I know her?" Suzanne's face filled my mind's eye.

"It's the heart that does the choosing. And the heart that's willing to see beyond what others are seeing." She let me have time for that sink in. Someone needing tender care. Someone feeling displaced. Suzanne's story came to mind. "You can't control who you love, Peter. It's as powerful as the moon pulling the tide in. You can't control that anymore than you can control who loves you."

Suzanne's sweet face made way for Laura's striking one, and I felt that old, familiar, pang. Though I knew Laura wasn't right for me, hearing it from her sounded like a betrayal. "I loved her the best way I could."

"Sure you did. But some people can't accept the love that's offered to them."

And some, I thought, can't offer a deep love. No matter how many excuses Suzanne made for Edward Morgan, he hadn't loved her well.

Seeing beyond what other's see. When I looked at Suzanne, I saw a woman who'd not been offered enough love. A woman crippled by a hard father and a demanding husband.

A heart doing the choosing. I wasn't just attracted to her; I loved her.

# 15

## *Suzanne*

Am I the only woman in the world who doesn't know how she feels? After days of going round and round, this was my question. No one else could possibly be as confused as I was. Why do I feel relieved when I should feel sadness? Why do I feel insulted when I should feel protected? And why do I feel jealous when I should feel nothing at all? Head, heart, will, soul—each part seems to be working independently, leaving me tossed about by every wind, like a kite on a string. I feel like a house without a foundation, like a tree without roots, like a boat without a keel. I need something sure and stable to hold all the parts of my life together.

～

Blair looked Fergie in the eye. "I've told you a zillion times. It's not my fault." I stood beside her as she stroked his coarse hair, trying to hide the discomfort I felt at being so close to the huge animal. Handing me the brush, she stood on her tiptoes, laying her head against his thick neck. "I know you're mad at me, but you know I'd ride you if I could."

"He knows."

We swung around; Peter stood in the aisle. Blair smiled like it was Christmas morning, then rushed forward and threw herself against him. "I missed you," she cried. I wanted to do the same thing. So, to protect myself from embarrassment, I stepped closer to the wall. Seeing him, hearing his voice, confirmed my fears about my heart.

Abruptly, Blair dropped her arms. "Oh, I shouldn't have... I'm sorry."

He leaned down, took her by the shoulders. "Not another word about your fine welcome," he said, looking into her fearful eyes. Turning to me, hesitant, he said, "It's good to see you."

"Thanks," I mumbled, wondering if Jillian had been right. I'd been on pins and needles since talking with her.

He walked around Fergie, patting his flank. Blair matched him step for step. "Did you come over much while I was gone?" he asked.

"Almost every day," Blair said. "And I went sailing, but I didn't really like it."

"Didn't like it? I need to take you sailing sometime. Show you how wonderful it can be. Just you, me, the wind and the water." She gave just the faintest hint of a shrug and then stole a glance at me.

"It's like getting back on a horse, isn't it?" I said. "You don't want to give up after one bad incident."

"Right you are," Peter added, winking at Blair. She turned red and giggled. I wondered why, but wouldn't ask. I realized, to my horror, that I felt a bit jealous that they shared a secret. What kind of mother felt that? "What other mischief did you get into while I was gone?" Though optimistic and playful by nature, he seemed lighter, freer than I remembered. Because London had gone so well?

"Nothing special. I spent the night with Fredericka once."

"And left your mum all alone?" he teased.

"No, she went out to dinner with Dr. Hamilton. And then the next day all three of us went on a picnic in a big garden. I never knew you could have so much fun in one."

"Really? That's great." His voice faltered. Fergie nickered softly. "Better finish with him," he said. "We'll talk more later." Looking strained, he retreated to his office.

I stayed with Blair until she finished grooming Fergie. Then, when she took him to the paddock, I stepped into Peter's office. He was going through his mail. "Was your trip successful?" I asked, trying to keep the right mixture of interest and passivity in my voice. I wasn't any good at games but couldn't ask what I really wanted to.

He looked up, his eyes soft and warm. "Smashing. Turned out better than I could have imagined."

"Oh." I paused, surprised by the crushing disappointment I felt. And immediately afraid it was obvious. "I'm happy for you." My voice sounded flat and empty to my ears. Exactly how I felt. Jillian had been right.

❦

It nagged at me, keeping me from a sound sleep. Since talking to Peter, a sharp, present sadness pierced each breath. The sun had been up for awhile, but I'd only been able to lie in bed, watching the shafts of light spread across the walls.

"Hi, Mommy." Blair ran into the room and jumped on the bed. "I already had my Frosties and watched part of a movie. Now I'm bored. What do you want to do today?"

I pulled her in for a snuggle. "Anything with you." Anything to help me avoid thinking of Peter.

While I ate breakfast, we decided on the beach. Blair's summers had all been the same, spent in day care or organized field trips. Her unending pleasure in a day outside reminded me of my childhood along the coast of Massachusetts. Summers full of carefree days when the clock wasn't watched and the only rule was safety. So why did I feel heavy? Why did each heartbeat hurt? Determined not to let it ruin the day, I turned my focus to Blair. She moved around the cottage with just a few remaining remnants of the accident, faltering just once when turning to reach for her hat. Another time she required only a touch on the bed to keep her balance when picking something from the floor. I remembered Dr. Randall's words. *Some head trauma victims recover 95% of function.* I hadn't believed it then. Could barely believe it now. But this was what he was talking about. She was nearly back to normal. I reached out and swallowed her with a hug.

"I'm so proud of you and all your hard work." I held her at arm's length, inventoried her from head to toe. "You've endured a lot, and been changed by it, but you never gave up." Thinking I might cry any moment, I let go and put on my happiest voice. "Let's go celebrate."

At Thom's Cove, we sat just out of reach of the morning tide. Though early August, the ocean was still frigid. Blair dallied at water's edge but couldn't force herself into the chill blue. I thought of the time she'd followed Peter in. Her loud cries of delight, how they'd played in the water. How I'd felt—wait. Stop it, I told myself. Remember what Peter said. … *better than I could have imagined.*

In unspoken accord, we picked up the sand with cupped hands and watched it rain down through our spread fingers. It became a rhythm between us, in perfect unison. This shared quiet stirred me, allowed what was taking shape inside my heart to make its way into my consciousness. I had fallen in love with Cornwall, with it's rugged cliffs, patchwork meadows, and the sounds of the sea. All of it worked together to feed something primal and defining in me. I felt more alive here than I felt anywhere else.

And it had provided nourishment for my starved relationship with Blair, growing it into something more precious than I thought possible. She had transformed from a girl limping away from vitality and life into one who ran towards it with hope and abandon. The truth was I wanted to stay here. I wanted to feel that same freedom and possibility. I wanted to call this home.

"Remember what you were saying this morning?" Blair asked, pushing back the silence. I nodded. She rubbed her hands together in double time, sending sand spraying in every direction. She hesitated a moment. "I think part of why I changed was because we were here. I don't think I could have done it at home."

"Why not?" I wiped sticky hands on my shorts.

"Because people there knew me before."

"Well, that's good, isn't it? To be known?"

Blair scrunched her forehead. "Yeah, I guess. But they were watching me all the time to see when I would get better. Like they wouldn't like me again till I was the same as before." She was right. I felt that way, too. Quietly, she added, "I don't think I'll ever be exactly like I was before. Not completely. And I don't even mind so much anymore."

"And I don't want you to."

She looked up at me. "Peter and Margaret and Fred have only known me like this. And they like me. Right now."

"I know." I had a list of people like that, too. We lay back against the warm sand and closed our eyes.

Blair's tiny voice floated up and fell upon me. "I don't want to leave."

≈

Blair and I were outside saying goodbye to Ian when Peter drove up. "Peter, look," Blair exclaimed. She ran to his car with a handful of photographs. "This was so funny." She thrust a picture at him through the open window. "It's when we were at the big garden. Pretending we were those—what are they called?"

"Topiaries," he said flatly.

Blair giggled. "And look at this, I like this one too." She showed him the photo of Ian posing between us with all the coziness of a nuclear family. "Mommy looks really pretty here."

He cleared his throat while he got out of the car. "Quite pretty," he said with conviction. Though embarrassed, I liked it.

"Yes," Ian threw in, "it was a memorable day for the three of us. Great fun." He flashed a smile worthy of a magazine cover. Peter's mouth hardened.

"Look," I pointed to the late afternoon sky. Clouds hung low in a raspberry and lemon sky. "It's like the heavens reaching down to earth."

"You're a romantic, Suzanne," Ian said, dismissively.

"No, she's a realist," Peter said, glaring at him. Ian rolled his eyes.

"I don't—," Blair was saying to Peter when Ian cut in.

"Suzanne and Blair, thank you again for the special time. I'm already counting the days till our next outing." He crossed his arm over his waist and bowed with a flourish. Blair giggled. I blanched. Then, with an unashamedly triumphant look at Peter, he drove away. Blair, boomeranging back to Peter, grabbed his hand and dragged him inside the cottage.

"I've come to ask you two lovely ladies to join me for a special dinner." He looked back and forth between us, seeming equal in his attentions. He was so genuinely kind; I couldn't tell what was said for Blair's benefit and what, if anything was for mine.

"Where?" Blair asked.

"It's a surprise. Bit of a drive, but well worth the trouble."

After a dinner at Kate's American Café in Port Isaac, Blair fell asleep in the back seat. "What made you think to take us for an American meal?"

"Though I was only in London briefly, I found myself missing Cornwall. So I put myself in your place. Thought about the adjustments you and Blair have had to make being here. I guessed you might enjoy eating something familiar."

"We did. Thank you." The vast expanse of darkness was a reminder of how rural and wild much of Cornwall still is. Which reminded me of the long, quiet ride home from that awkward evening in Padstow. "Peter, I owe you an apology."

"I'm sure you don't." He answered so quickly, I wondered if he didn't want one.

"No, I do. I don't know why I was so unpleasant the last time we had dinner together." I took a deep breath, my pulse quickening. "I'm feeling very confused these days. About a lot of things." I flushed hot with discomfort. "You seem so good at knowing your feelings, but I'm not. I've never given much attention to them. Demands of life and all that. I seem to be all stirred up about whether or not we're going to stay awhile longer."

"It's a big decision," he said.

"And if we decide to leave, I don't want it to hurt any more than it has to. So I guess, I…" I stopped, searching for the right words.

"You guard your heart."

How did he know? "Yes, I do. Strange, isn't it?"

"I don't think it's strange at all. I understand."

This was one of those moments when time freezes. You know for an instant that you have the chance to say something. And you weigh it, knowing that you might always regret passing up the opportunity. I closed my eyes and dug deep.

"Do you guard your heart?" The dashboard lights cast a blue hue on his face. He sighed, the edges of his mouth curling up.

"I think we all do, Suzanne. And it's not unwise. But the important thing is to know when it's safe to let your guard down. And it's hard to know, isn't it? Because we've all got a history of making wrong decisions. Trusting people. Being vulnerable, only to be hurt."

Was he talking about his old girlfriend? I closed my eyes. Time froze for a second time. In a meek, and frankly, pitiful voice, I heard myself say, "Someone said, well, Jillian, actually, that you'd gone to London to see your ex-fiancé. To get back together with her. To reconcile."

I opened them again to see that we'd just gotten off the highway onto a dark, curving road. Peter kept his eyes on the road. "Jillian? Did she?" And then he didn't say anything else. The seconds ticked by. Humiliated, I pressed myself against the door. Wished to be anywhere but here. I'd pried. I'd betrayed myself. There had been no guarding with a question as blatant as that. I put my head back and closed my eyes. A minute, two minutes, eons passed.

"I did go to London to see Laura." I turned, opened my eyes. He looked so serious. He didn't sound angry, but he looked it. It was as if

I'd opened Pandora's Box. Except what flew out wasn't all the evil in the world, just my own. Nosiness, lack of self-control, gossip, jealousy, general stupidity. Now I wished he wouldn't answer. I didn't need or deserve one. What in the world had possessed me to say something when he'd never even mentioned her to me before?

"There had been unfinished business between us since our breakup, five years ago. It's interesting that you asked. It was because of what still needed to be said between Laura and me that I've been guarding my heart a little too closely. It's been holding me back." I felt his face turn towards me, but I could only look out in the black night. "So, yes, Jillian was right. We did reconcile. Just not in the way she meant." It didn't matter that I didn't completely understand; I would not say another word.

❧

This really was a new low. A schoolgirl crush gone bad. I'd misread signs. I'd let myself get carried away. I played my hand. Hadn't I learned anything in 34 years? Time to marshal the forces of my will, just like I'd done for all those years. Take myself out of the equation. Think about Blair. Make up for all the hurt inflicted on her for the past 11 years. Push thoughts of Peter to the ocean floor.

It had been several days since our evening together. I tried to keep us busy and entertained, but a spark was missing in me. I needed time to think, so I called Hillary for help. She invited Blair to spend the day and night at Penwylln. Blair shimmered with anticipation until Hillary arrived. Immediately, I felt calmer. But there was also something daunting about facing hours of unscheduled time. This called for a plan. Item number one was to talk to Cathy. Because of the time difference, the day would pivot around that. I emailed her to arrange a time when she got off of work, and we agreed I would call late tonight.

I decided to give the cottage a thorough cleaning. I worked furiously throughout the tiny space and finished in only ninety minutes. I sat in the living room and looked through crystal clear windows, thinking about our enormous house in Great Falls. I'd been so excited when we first moved in. Excited to make it our home. And yet I loved this little cottage, a third the size of my house, more. Every surface sparkled, sand tracked in from so many happy hours vacuumed up. I was satisfied with my work, but still had hours left.

I leafed through the travel brochures, but all it did was confirm my first impulse. Within the hour, I was turning off the A30 towards St. Ives. The guidebook suggested starting at the Tate Gallery. I was unprepared for the modern white building. Its curving entrance and massive stained glass window faced Porthmeor Beach. I laughed out loud, thinking of the gutsy architect who designed it. It looked so preposterous, a low, round spaceship in ancient Cornwall. Yet I loved it. It won me over, beckoning me in. My only disappointment was the small collection; I was through the whole gallery and browsing the gift shop thirty minutes later.

A map in the gallery pointed me to the Barbara Hepworth Museum just around the corner. I decided to walk there, passing houses with names like Tremorveen and Barnawoon, past gardens filled with palm trees and overflowing flower boxes—geraniums seemed particularly happy here—and lives lived in tiny, angular houses. I stood in front of one and imagined what it would be like to call it home. I wasn't so foolish as to imagine it wouldn't feel cramped or inconvenient. Still, I would take this over Virginia's suburban sprawl without a second thought. The museum had been Barbara Hepworth's home and studio for 25 years. Smocks hung on pegs and tools lay on tables. Walking through the rooms, looking at the elemental sculptures and monoliths, I could only imagine the hours she'd spent walking the moors. It was so true to Cornwall—I understood why she was widely loved. I ambled outside with no clear plan in place. When my stomach growled, I headed towards a cluster of art galleries just off the harbor and kept my eyes open for a lunch spot. I zigzagged through town, moving downhill with each turn, until I found myself standing in front of Bumbles Tea Room.

A little box of a place, it had a wonderful bow window across the front; sugar bowls and creamers crammed the ledge. I stepped inside and immediately loved its dowdy charm. I sat at the last open table and read the menu. Just as I'd hoped, egg mayonnaise and cress sandwiches. Creamy, sweet, benign—food without ambition, happy to comfort. I enjoyed the luxury of eating alone, soaking in the surroundings. Old advertisements on the walls for products I'd never heard of. Accents that spoke words in English I couldn't understand. Smells, not unpleasant, but unfamiliar. And then, so suddenly I didn't see it coming, I felt overwhelmingly cold and lonely. Hit by the stark realization that I was an outsider. As much as I believed I could adapt to life here, there would always be things to remind me I was an alien. I would never share their history or worldview. I wouldn't understand their inside jokes or cultural references. Maybe I could fit in. But I didn't know if I would be accepted. Would I be doomed to feel as much on the outside of life here as I did in Virginia?

And that brought me to what Blair had said. She wanted to stay. She felt more loved, more comfortable in her own skin than ever before. She was at home here. How could I even think of taking that away from her? But I couldn't base the decision about our future on that alone. I had to think about everything. I had to decide what was best for us in the long run. There was just so much to consider, so many details to work out. And it seemed to always start and end with Morgan's. How could I leave the business Edward had built? But how, I asked myself a thousand times, could I go back to it? And even though I knew the decisions about staying in England and owning Morgan's didn't have to be related, they always seemed that way to me. But the decision had to be about more than Edward or Morgan's; it had to be about Blair. It even had to be about me. Who were we? Where did we belong? Sitting here, wanting this to be home, and knowing it wasn't, brought me back to the defining question. Could it be?

While I was inside, the sky had turned ominous. Dark clouds rolled in, a cool wind began to blow, and the water changed to a palette of grays and greens. The lighthouse that Virginia Woolf wrote about was no longer visible through the mist. I was leafing through my guidebook when raindrops landed on my map. Bulging, gunmetal clouds opened up and let loose. In a vain attempt to save my hair, I held my little guide over my head and looked for a door.

Three of us had the same reaction. Nothing subtle about the entrance, we pushed through the door like The Three Stooges. Our loud, slapstick entrance brought a woman running from the back of the gallery. "Whatever are you doing?" She stopped when she saw me.

"Can't you see it's raining?" said the older woman in a thick Scottish accent. "We didn't burst in to be a bother. The sky opened."

"She was just startled, weren't you, lass?" said the other, shaking her arms so that a puddle formed around her. "It won't last. We'll be gone once it eases up."

"See that you are." She turned with a flourish. The women exchanged looks before huddling close to the door and exchanging rainy day stories. I'd been in search of art before the rain started, and there were some beautiful paintings on the walls, so I strolled through the shop at a leisurely pace. Jillian looked up to find me making my way down the aisle and quickly disappeared into another room. A little bell tinkled on the door when the women left, bringing her from the back in a Pavlovian response. She looked at me and frowned. Tired of Jillian's antics, I chose right now to stop being afraid of her.

"Are any of these yours?" I asked, leaning in to read the signatures.

"Obviously. I wouldn't be here otherwise, would I?"

"Which ones?" I stood back, ready to be directed.

"Really, Suzanne. Do we have the play the charades?"

"Which ones please?"

She stomped past me and pointed a long, elegant finger at several oil paintings. I recognized several of the scenes; they were all places Peter had taken me. Porthcurno. The Lizard Peninsula. Marazion. I felt an immediate, visceral stab of jealousy. Did he take everyone to the same places? Did he have a set order? Was I a complete fool? Jealousy, perhaps because it's from a constricted heart, always produces the same feelings in me- labored breathing, pulsing blood in my head, and a thick, choking throat. It made me feel weak and puny, but only for a moment. Then anger came, like a girl popping out of a cake. It became something to break out of.

"I saw Peter the other night. He took us to dinner." Her wary, but interested, look fed the beast in me. "We got to talking about his trip to London. I told him what you'd suspected about his trip." Her wariness turned to seething annoyance.

"You gossiped about me?" I became the target of that finger.

"I didn't think of that way. Really, I was asking a question. But it was easier, more accurate, to quote you and then ask him if what you guessed was right."

She stared at me coolly, working out a response. She wanted to know as badly as I had, but she was smart enough not to make it obvious. "I wouldn't think Peter approved of your gossip. He feels quite strongly about that."

"Like I said, I didn't see it as gossip. Nor did he appear to." Her eyes widened in surprise. But she deftly moved on.

"You must have brought it up because you're dying to tell me."

I couldn't deny that. Or how fun it would be to see you squirm when I do tell you. This harder, colder version of me brought a feeling of power. "Or because I thought you'd be pleased to know you were right. I believe his exact words were 'Yes, Jillian was right. We did reconcile.'"

❧

"I never thought I'd be talking to you about this." I was in bed, in a dark room- where I felt like I belonged after today. I clutched the phone like it held the power of life and death.

"I did. Suz, I've known you for fifteen years. For the past month, maybe more, there's been something in your voice that I never heard before." From the background noise, I could picture Cathy rummaging around her kitchen to make a late dinner.

"What?" I whispered. Why was I afraid of the answer? Silence from her end. She was probably sitting in her tiny living room, looking out the window of her Georgetown condominium.

"Happiness. Rest. Home. Do you remember the last time we talked?"

I nodded, relieved at her answer. "You said I wouldn't find rest until I found my home."

"Right. And I think you're on the way to finding it. So why would you want to leave now?"

"Cath, months ago, I told my dad I would consider selling the store. I only told him that to get him off my back. But now, I'm actually considering it. But if we stay and I sell the store, it would mean cutting my last ties to Edward."

"Not exactly. Blair is your last and best tie." I swallowed, letting her words sink in. "I think, if you sell the store, it will release you from Edward."

Her words felled me, like a woodsman with an axe. "What?" I could have answered it. I was just too afraid to.

"We're sisters, right?" Her tone grew even more serious.

"Always."

"Time for brutal honesty?"

I laughed. Cathy's honesty was always so filled with love and compassion—calling it brutal was absurd. It was like calling a morning dove a falcon. "Yes."

"Edward changed you."

"But not for the good." I ventured.

"No. He snuffed the light out of you. And you let him do it."

"I couldn't help it. He was just such a strong person."

"Bullying and belittling isn't a sign of strength," she said. "It's a sign of weakness and insecurity. It's sick to put people down so you feel bigger and better."

I held my breath. I'd believed that, even when I was a willing accomplice. I'd told myself time and again that it wouldn't happen anymore. My will, as it turned out, was my very own Maginot line, quickly falling at the first sign of resistance.

"Strength," Cathy went on, "is wanting to see the best in others brought out. Wanting to build them up. It turns away from itself and looks to another. People who are kind, who are patient, who serve, are strong people."

I sank under the duvet. Literally. Ridiculously. Like it made any difference.

"Suz, you still there?"

"Yeah," I croaked.

"I know you've never said this to another soul, and I know you probably have barely been able to acknowledge it in yourself. But I would bet anything that you feel some relief that Edward is gone."

From my dark, silent hiding place, I agreed.

"And then you feel guilty for that." I did.

"And for having a second chance at life." I did.

"And maybe even for falling in love."

I threw off the cover. "Why are you saying this now?" I demanded.

"Because you are at a defining point in your life." She must have sat up too. She sounded like I did when I felt desperate for Blair to understand something important. "You're facing a decision that will shape the years that follow. I love you too much to sit silently and watch you make a bad choice out of fear. Or guilt. Or misplaced loyalty."

"What do you think I should do?"

"I'll tell you exactly what you should do."

"Okay," I said, reverting to old habits.

She belly laughed. "Boy, I wish I could see your face. I don't mean I know what you should do in the future. But I do know you can't begin to make this decision until you are completely honest with yourself. About Edward. Blair. What you want. What or who makes you happy. And knowing you as I do, my dear friend, this will be difficult for you. Do you have a notebook or a journal?"

The journal and pen Peter gave me was by the bed. I thought of his words when he gave them to me. "You should try writing things down. Keep digging deep until you've gone through all the layers of guilt, lies, and fear. Get to the very center of your heart and figure out what you feel."

I hung up the phone and picked up the journal. With trembling hands I pushed open the cover.

I feel like I can breathe for the first time in years, I wrote.

# 16

# Peter

Blair leaned up against the fence, dusty, sweaty, and exhausted. She couldn't have looked happier. "That last jump reminded me of Midnight. He got skittish at the brush box, too. I always had to talk extra nice to get him over, just like Fergie. Mrs. Galloway told me to treat him like a friend."

It felt the same with Suzanne, who had been skittish since I got back. Still sorting out when to tell her my feelings, I decided the best course was to treat her like a friend. The horse show for Suzanne was in one week. Perhaps that would provide an entree into the conversation. When I suggested that to Eleanor, she reminded me to move slowly.

"In general, you're more sure of yourself than she is. And you should be. You're on familiar ground, in a comfortable life. You have a set of truths that guide your life. Suzanne is still wandering. She's taking steps, finding her way, but it would be a mistake to rush her. She's got to know her own feelings before she can begin to deal with yours."

So I spent what time with her I could, looking for ways to walk alongside her.

∽

"I can't wait to show mommy. Thank you so much for helping me. I never thought..." She stopped, swiped away a few stray tears, smearing her dirty cheek. I stopped scraping the sweat off Fergie's back.

"Moppet, you know there is no one I would rather be teaching. I appreciate your gratitude; it's a precious quality. You are welcome from the bottom of my heart." I bowed deeply; she erupted in a volcano of giggles. "Now, I have something I want you to do for me."

"Okay." Always eager to please, she turned serious.

"Stop thanking me. You forget that I've had as much fun as you. You're my most improved pupil. My favorite, but don't brag about that to anyone. I couldn't be more proud of you." She took a brush from the tack box and started brushing Fergie's legs.

"Does this make you miss your dad a lot? He'd surely be prouder of you than I am."

She flinched as thought I'd stuck her. "He…he wouldn't. I mean, if I was getting a ribbon, or something. He just liked to see me win."

"Surely that can't be right. You must have it wrong." My words filled the tiny stall, nearly suffocating both of us.

Realizing what I'd said, I bent down on one knee. "I'm sorry I spoke without thinking. And I couldn't be sorrier that you feel that way." I still couldn't get it fully round my head that her father didn't delight in this sparkling child.

A wan smile crossed her face. "It's okay." We continued working in silence while I cursed myself for my stupidity. After Fergie was turned out to the pasture, Blair came into my office.

"I need help with a few things at Oakton and thought you'd be just the person to assist me. Are you up for it? I've already checked with your mum."

Standing at my door, small and defenseless, she nodded her head.

Blair was a sunbeam, emitting rays of joyful light. After weeks of preparation, she was ready. Every time she tried to thank me, I said, "It's you and Fergie who've done the work. I wouldn't steal your credit." Finally, the day arrived. Suzanne dropped Blair off with encouragement to return in work clothes. I'd told her I was behind on chores.

"I don't think I could be of much use," she'd protested.

"Oh, Mom," Blair wailed. "Everyone's helping. You have to, too." Succumbing to the friendly peer pressure, Suzanne agreed. She would be back in an hour.

Shortly after she left, Eleanor arrived wearing her gardening clothes. "You said to be prepared to get dirty." The sky had turned threatening.

"Might end up muddy, too." Glancing around, she asked, "Does Suzanne suspect anything yet?"

"Not a thing. I think we'll actually pull it off." A nervous excitement had been building in me since we'd embarked on this crazy plan. But today, I felt calm and confident. It would be a day to celebrate for a long time. And I hoped they'd be here to do it.

"A conspiracy of love. How delightful." Her grandchildren raced up behind her. "Hillary and the children begged to be included. They wouldn't have missed this for the world." Fredericka and Martin flashed expectant looks at me.

"Is Blair really going to ride?" Martin demanded.

"Not only that," I said, "she's jumping too." Their eyes grew wide. The children looked to Hillary, who deferred to Eleanor.

"You're certain about this?" I could see how much she wanted to trust me, but her better judgment was making it difficult. We'd all watched Blair trip and slip for months. It was hard to imagine she could actually do this safely.

"Wait till you see her. She'd been taught well in America. I've just helped her make some adjustments for balance. She'll be smashing." I checked my watch and looked down the lane. "Now off with you," I said, to everyone except Eleanor. "Suzanne will be here soon. You can't be in plain site when she gets here."

I dispatched the kids to the barn, Hillary trailing after them. As planned, when Suzanne arrived, Fredericka and Martin had taken Dusty to the far paddock; Hillary was in the stalls helping Blair. Eleanor was with me at the fence; both of us had to work at appearing nonchalant.

"Eleanor, what a surprise. What brings you here today?" She looked at me questioningly.

"She's also come to lend a hand." I smiled at both of them. "Right. Let's go then. I'm putting you two on the paddock fence." The same stricken look appeared on each face. "Don't worry, it's easy. Follow me."

To Eleanor's credit, she gave nothing away, although she seemed surprised I was taking the charade this far. And despite any misgivings, they were being great sports about it. I could only imagine what their conversation would be once I'd left them to their work.

Back in the barn, I found Blair busy giving orders to Hillary. Fredericka and Martin snuck in on the other side of the barn. There was a flurry of activity and conspiratorial smiles. I hoped Blair could see how much we all wanted her success. We were nearly ready, so we sent them outside to join Eleanor and Suzanne. Martin was to run in and warn us if Suzanne made moves to come back. But all went smoothly, and before they finished hammering, Hillary and I joined them.

"Goodness, everyone's here," Suzanne said warily, looking around for anyone else.

I took the hammer from her hand. "Follow me." She looked to Eleanor, then Hillary, but they simply stepped aside. I took her hands in mine, looking far beyond her worried eyes. "This is a gift of love from your daughter."

"I don't understand." She looked on nervously as Fredericka and Martin ran into the barn and stopped in the center aisle. Blair leaned down on Fergie's neck and whispered in his ear. Then she sat up, smiled at me, and tapped her heals into his side. Head high, ears forward, Fergie walked out of the barn, Blair proudly straddling his back. Fredericka and Martin followed along on either side.

Suzanne's hands flew to her mouth. "Oh Blair," she screamed. "You shouldn't be—." She looked at me, frantic. "Is she safe? You won't let…" She covered her eyes for a split second, and then returned her hands to her mouth.

Eleanor threw her arm around Suzanne's shoulder, speaking with motherly authority. "Steady on."

A fearful looking Blair halted Fergie at the gate. I stood beside her and put my hand on her knee. Slowly, calmly, I said, "You can do this. You've done this twenty times. Your mother is afraid because she doesn't know that." Blair's lips started to quiver. She shot a glance at Suzanne. "But you do." She snapped her eyes back at me. "I'll be right here if you need me. But you won't. Now, go show your mum what a brave girl you are." Her fear receded, replaced with clear-eyed determination.

"I never thought…" Suzanne said to no one in particular. Blair clicked her tongue and Fergie walked into the ring. I took my place beside them. She halted Fergie directly in front of Suzanne.

I'd told Blair she had to ask her mum for permission. If Suzanne absolutely refused, we'd have to respect that. She'd argued with me. But in the end, knew what I required. "Mom? Is it okay? Can I keep going?"

There was a long, painful pause. Suzanne nodded, looking first at Blair and then me. Her eyes expressed that wonderful mixture of wanting to see her child safe and wanting to see her soar. There was a collective sigh of relief. "Good, cause we worked on this real hard," Blair said. Then, with a click of her tongue and kick of her heels, she turned him around.

I walked to the center of the ring while Blair took Fergie to the rail. They walked the circumference once, then started to trot. I looked over at Suzanne and saw her hands clasped against her chest, eyes locked on Blair. As they neared the jump, I heard her gasp. Eleanor squeezed her shoulder and leaned in closer. "They've been practicing for weeks," she assured Suzanne. "Peter told me she's a good little rider."

Suzanne nodded, still not taking her eyes off Blair. "I know. Look at her, Eleanor. That's what she used to look like."

Blair's face was radiant. She moved with confidence, taking the turns without any hesitation and handling Fergie as though she hadn't been a year out of the saddle. I signaled to her. She brought Fergie to the center of the ring, where a short jump was set up. Fergie glided over the ground, while Blair remained perfectly at ease.

When I signaled to take the jump, Suzanne cried out. "She's not ready."

Suzanne, Eleanor, and Hillary held hands as Blair approached the jump. I continued talking to Blair, keeping my voice firm and even. Exuberance turned to resolve; her eyes focused on the ground just beyond the jump, her lips pursed together. Time stopped as she sailed over the jump. The take off was smooth, the landing fluid. When Fergie's hoofs touched the ground, the women cried, my heart pounded wildly, Freddy jumped up and down. Then we were all clapping and screaming. And in that moment, Blair was transformed from victim to victor. She brought Fergie around and Suzanne ran towards her.

"You're not mad I did this without asking, are you?" Blair asked, despite her mother's smile.

"How could I be mad?" Suzanne laughed. "I've never seen anything more beautiful in my life." Neither had I, I thought, looking at Suzanne's shining face.

❧

Blair insisted I join them for dinner. Suzanne readily agreed, although she blushed when I accepted. Blair answered the door, her hair freshly washed, smelling of kiwi and melon. Over dinner, Suzanne heard all the details of how our plan progressed. By unspoken agreement, we let Blair monopolize the conversation. After dinner, finally running low on energy, she went to watch *National Velvet* again. We left the unwashed dishes in the sink and, ignoring heavy gray clouds overhead, headed outside. We walked down winding lanes, ending up on a little sandy beach just beyond the quay. I scanned the water for boats trying to get in before the storm. Suzanne squatted and, using a stick she'd found, wrote Blair's name in the sand. I squatted beside her, stirring the small, smooth stones at my feet.

"I didn't think I'd ever see her look like that again," Suzanne said, turning to me. A thousand emotions flooded her face.

"I know you didn't. She didn't either. It was wonderful to watch her confidence grow with each lesson." I tossed a handful of pebbles at the approaching water. "And it wasn't easy." I laughed, remembering. "The first time she took a jump she was white as a sheet."

Suzanne shot up, anger flaring. "Then why—?"

I came right back. "Because she could do it. I knew the first time would be the worst. And it was. But then, you should have seen her. She was so proud of her self, convinced she could do anything she set her mind to." Suzanne's face softened, then filled with pride, as if seeing today's scenes in her mind's eye.

But then a cloudy confusion passed across her eyes. "I just can't understand why you went to so much trouble. Fitting the saddle, all that time, not getting paid." Her voice trailed off. I had to look away. I'd thought about this moment since I stood on the bridge with Mum. I knew what I wanted to say, how much I wanted to tell her what I felt. But I remembered Eleanor's warning.

"Why did you do it?" she asked, her voice like one walking a tightrope of hope and fear.

"You must know." My eyes searched hers; wanting her to know what I still didn't feel completely free to say. I feared she wouldn't like what she'd see and pull back. To my great relief, she didn't shrink away.

A tentative smile played at her lips. And very softly, she said, "Yes, I think I do." Looking in her eyes, every cliché, every bad poem about eyes mirroring the heart, came to mind. But in that moment they were neither bad nor cliché. They were true. In that moment when we weren't ready to put the weight of words behind it, I believe our eyes were saying what neither of us could.

I took her in my arms, and she laid her head against my chest. My heart was pounding madly; I was sure she could hear every beat, but I didn't mind. It wasn't a betrayal. It was a declaration. Gingerly, she let her arms circle my back. I squeezed her tighter. I could have stayed like that all night. I don't know how long we stood there, but I knew it wasn't long enough. When she drew back, it felt like my oxygen supply had been cut off.

⌒

Some opinions matter, some change us. What if he didn't like Suzanne? What if she didn't like him? Sure, I was my own man, made up my own mind. But I'd been raised to have wise people around me. People to trust and heed. Here in Cornwall, those people were Eleanor and Eric. I already knew what Eleanor thought.

"My, it's rustic," Suzanne said, as the cottage came in view.

"Does that bother you?"

"Not at all. I'm just concerned for him. It must be trying with the changeable weather. I imagine he's grateful for company anytime."

"To be sure." I remembered countless trips out here in every manner of Cornish weather, especially the cold, wet winters. We were just a few steps away when I stopped. "Thanks for coming. He's very special to me."

The door opened. "Dennargh," Eric said with rare gusto, in something like a growl.

"What's that, Eric?"

"I'm saying a proper Cornish welcome, if you don't mind?' He tried to look affronted, but couldn't hold the face long. "I was showing off for your friend from America."

"No need. I'm already impressed that you live in this beautiful spot. It's so remote and quiet. You must be a man of simple pleasures." She could certainly turn on the charm, but best of all, it was genuine.

"I don't know about that. It's just my home. The only one I've known most of my life. You become a part of where you are."

"And it becomes a part of you," she said, extending her hand. "It's a pleasure to meet you, Mr. Forbes. I'm Suzanne Morgan."

The Eric I knew was uncomfortable with physical affection. So I was surprised when he placed both of his gnarled old hands around hers and held on. He guided us inside. A cup of wildflowers sat in the center of the table. I looked at him, eyebrows raised. "Daisy loved having flowers indoors," he said.

"I do, too," Suzanne said. "Thank you for going to the trouble."

So comfortable with one another, so amiable, it was as if they were long lost friends. We sat around the table while he put on the kettle. He tried calling her Mrs. Morgan once. "I'm more at ease with Suzanne," she'd explained.

"Good. Well then, Suzanne, tell me about you, your home. What has become a part of you?" Eric had one way of relating. Ask the important questions. He didn't waste time on surface things. I cringed inwardly. I should have prepared Suzanne. She'd been clear that she was a private person.

"Eric, maybe you should go easy on her. She's not used to you yet."

But she brushed that aside, nodding eagerly. "Part of that question is easy to answer. To tell you about me is to tell you about my daughter. She's 11. She was in a car accident last year and suffered a brain injury. It left her with some problems - balance, weakness, a limp. She'd been a horseback rider. Avid, obsessed, a barn rat. It was horrible when she couldn't ride anymore and wasn't even welcome as a helper."

Eric frowned, "Poor child A terrible grief for her."

Suzanne's face grew pale. "And, of course, losing her father at the same time. Nothing in life was the same."

"Terrible, terrible. When my Daisy died…" He stopped and looked at the posies on the table.

Suzanne reached across the table and touched his arm. "I'm sorry for you." He turned misty eyes towards her. She waited a respectful amount of time before continuing.

"We needed a change from our normal routines. Needed time together. A new perspective. Since we've been here, she's spent hours playing in the ocean, walking up and down hilly Cornwall—"

"Working at Muirfield," I added. "She grooms, mucks and cleans tack with everyone else."

Suzanne grinned. "Once a barn rat…"

The kettle whistled, beckoning Eric from the table. With shaking hands, he poured the boiling water into a ceramic pot and added a large spoonful of loose tea. Watching intently, Suzanne kept talking. "She's healthier, improving steadily, and as it turns out, riding again." Eric turned around in alarm, but relaxed when he saw our smiling faces.

I was keen to join in, to share the great story. "She was so eager to get back on a horse, I couldn't refuse her. She did everything exactly as I asked. She'd not have risked a bad outcome. This girl needed to do this."

Looking less alarmed, Eric concluded, "Good thing it was with you at Muirfield. Could have been a disaster with someone less caring."

"Just a few days ago, Peter and Blair surprised me by showing me she could ride and even jump again. Peter had a saddle rigged for her and they'd been planning the surprise for weeks."

I got up to help Eric. I handed him the plate of biscuits I'd brought, then followed him back to the table with the teapot and three mugs. I poured as they talked. "Stopped your heart, I imagine," Eric said.

"Yes, at first. But it started it again, too." Suddenly self-conscious, she looked away. Eric had a habit of drawing things from people that they'd not intended to say.

"That's a happy story about your daughter." He offered us more biscuits. "I wasn't blessed with children, but it always gives me joy to hear parents speak of them with full hearts. It's a sad thing when they don't show it well enough to the young ones. Daisy's father was that way. Stingy with love. Left a hurt in her that would never truly be healed on this earth." I thought of my last conversation with Blair. How I'd blundered in bringing up her father, her stricken face. Because of her openness, it was easy for me to forget she was still a wounded little girl.

"You said part of the question was easy. Now, which part wasn't?" Frail old Eric was beguiling, but Suzanne was suddenly wary. She looked at me before momentarily receding into her thoughts. Eric, I noticed, watched her closely out of the corner of his eye. He liked her: I was certain. And that meant he would keep probing. It was his own special kind of love.

"Just recently, I was writing down some thoughts about this. Peter gave me a lovely journal with a special pen." Happy to hear her say that, I'd wondered what she'd done with it. "I spent many years in the suburbs of Washington, D.C. I followed my husband into business. We had Blair. The company grew. There were things about the work I was good at. Enjoyed even. But when you ask me to tell you about my home, about what's a part of me, I don't have a good answer."

She stopped. I knew this was dangerous territory for her. I was struggling to figure out what would serve her best- a light-hearted comment, a gentle touch on the back. Then I remembered my father's words after I'd told him about a row between Laura and me. I had finished and was waiting for his opinion. But he didn't say anything. Left to my own thoughts, I thought about what I'd just said. And I saw something different- where I was at fault. I asked him why he'd not pointed it out himself. Clearly, he saw it.

*Silence gives us time to hear ourselves. You didn't need to hear from me. You needed to listen to what your heart had to say. Not your will, nor your*

*pride, mind you, but something that speaks in whispers. Something we usually*
*interrupt with our grand plans or selfishness.*

I'd missed more than enough opportunities to stay silent with Suzanne;
I wouldn't miss this one. Eric, like my father, was a master practitioner. He
didn't look at people. He studied, interpreted, analyzed them. He'd locked
onto Suzanne, and it was as if she'd been given truth serum.

"I've discovered I don't much like what I became in our home. Rather
than something good becoming a part of me, I lost parts of myself." She
paused, embarrassed, but Eric's piercing eyes held her steady. "I don't think
I even want to go back. I don't think I'd miss it in the way I believe I would
miss Cornwall if we leave."

I felt all the possibility those words held. I heeded Eleanor's warning,
and so was slow to work out the next question that must be asked. Eric,
however, stayed true to himself. "You might stay? Make this your home?"
I held my breath.

She sighed, visibly relaxed. "Yes, though I must decide soon."

"That's a big decision. To leave what you know. Call a foreign place
home. It would take great courage, wouldn't it?"

Her laugh was bitter. "And that's something I'm not known for."

"Ach, that can't be right. Look what you've already done. The hardest
thing of all. Looked deep inside and found something true about yourself."
His face grew soft, as if his great, big heart melted away all those craggy
wrinkles. He looked at us a moment. "You know, there's something similar
in your stories."

I felt a freeze of fear. Eric knew a lot about me that I'd not yet told
Suzanne. "Both leaving what you know, searching for truth. Peter didn't
have to cross the ocean to do it, but he left his home in search of something
true. You've discovered something true that could compel you to find a
new home. It intrigues me."

This day was turning out like a race on the autobahn. Full throttle,
careful maneuvering, slowing down could result in a crash with casualties.
The school term was approaching and show season for my riding pupils
was gearing up. With a well-constructed list in hand, my efficiency was
impressive. I'd gotten to Truro by noon, and was in need of fuel to remain
at peak performance. I ducked inside the closest pub and screeched to a
halt. In the dimly lit room, I saw that Jillian and Ian occupied a table

against the wall. Turned so their backs were to me, I had a difficult choice. I chose the less noble one, pretending not to see them. Glancing around, I decided to order at the bar, then take an empty booth against the opposite wall. While I waited for the bartender, Jillian's voices rose above the steady murmurings that filled the room. I snuck a look at them over my shoulder.

"You really can be quite dim." She stared at Ian, dumbfounded. "Haven't you ever heard of the expression 'you can get more flies with honey than vinegar' or some such nonsense?"

"What are you trying to say, Jillian?" he asked impatiently.

"That you've got to be smarter. There's no point in antagonizing anyone. You acted like a bull in a china shop. Smashed to bits any good you had done wasting the day with that child." She picked up her fork and pushed a piece of broiled chicken around her plate.

"The child's name is Blair, and I actually found myself enjoying the time with her."

"Hurrah for you. But what about Suzanne? You'll scare her if you act victorious too soon."

"I'll go see Eleanor in the morning. Get her to speak to her."

"I thought you said she didn't want to interfere."

"Oh, she said that once, but surely she'll want to help. Especially now. Strike while the iron's hot. I will ask her to subtly convince Suzanne of it. Tell me again her exact words. I'll want to have it right when I talk to Eleanor."

Jillian's face darkened. "She told me Peter said I was right. He and Laura reconciled. I always thought that was why he wouldn't commit to me. He's obviously still been in love with her this whole time."

What was Jillian talking about? That wasn't what I said to Suzanne. Not exactly, anyway. Should I march over, put them right? Humiliated that I'd listened to their gossip, I didn't know what to do. "Yes," Ian was saying, "Eleanor should sing my praises; I'll stop by and have done with it."

"Tidy as a package, huh?"

"I should think so," he said, all smugness and confidence.

I headed for the door. It would be appalling if they saw me now. I had to think beyond the pounding in my head. Suzanne talking to Jillian? When, where would that have happened? But really, that didn't matter. Focusing on how we got here was a distraction from what to do now. Eleanor knew the truth. She would sort Ian out. But what about Suzanne?

Nothing that had happened since Blair's show indicated she thought I was in love with Laura. So why would she have let Jillian think that?

# 17

# *Suzanne*

Peter surprised me with an invitation to meet his family in York. Hillary agreed to keep Blair, knowing, I'm sure, that her children would be as happy at the news as Blair.

"Yippee," Blair cried, circling round and round, then falling into a heap of rapturous delight in the middle of the floor.

And so I departed, free of guilt, but full of apprehension. Archie and Frannie were delightful; I knew I had sure allies in them both. Peter's description of his mother brought back memories of my own and warmed me to the thought of meeting her. It was Thomas that made me nervous. From what I'd heard, it seemed impossible to imagine that I could win his approval. What I would need it for, I didn't know. But that didn't matter right now. All I knew was that his opinion held sway.

It was going to be a long day of driving. Since coming to England, I'd only traveled from London to Cornwall and around the West Country. We began our trip on four-lane divided highways. Dual carriageways, they called them here - a term that tickled me every time, conjuring up images of coaches and horsemen. Finally, at Exeter, we pulled onto the M5 heading northeast. Peter was an easy companion, equally comfortable with silence or conversation. He tuned into a classical station, keeping the volume low. I kept feeling like he was on the verge of saying something serious to me, but he never did.

We stopped off at a few Little Chefs along the way. The roadside restaurants were as varied as the people inside them. Some were new and fancy with a full menu to choose from. Others were stuck in the year they were constructed, presumably sometime around 1956, with the menu choices to show for it. Although Peter seemed bothered, embarrassed even, by the provincialism, I found something to like everyplace we stopped.

By the time we reached York, I was regretting the decision to come. Meeting people required talking about myself, the last thing I should be doing right now. What would I say? My life was so upside down that I felt like a stranger to myself. I wasn't even sure I could answer the simplest of questions. How are you? How long are you staying? Tell us about your life in America. Conversations were like chess games. I'd learned over the years to think five moves ahead. I don't know how I'd let Eric checkmate me.

Peter looked over, alarmed, and I realized my breathing had turned quick and shallow. I pulled down the visor and looked in the mirror. My face looked as pale and frightened as I felt.

"They aren't as terrifying as all that," he said with a reassuring smile.

"No, of course not. I'll be fine." My smile felt pathetic.

"More than fine. I think you'll really enjoy yourself. And I know Fran and Arch are chuffed about seeing you again." He chuckled when I gave him a nod that meant I was done talking about it.

Evening light had just faded to dark when we arrived. Lights shone through the windows, allowing us a glimpse of their family. Thomas was wrestling Lily. She broke away, running to Gemma's arms for safety. Everyone was laughing and smiling back and forth. Peter turned to me. "What is it?" he asked, taking my hand.

"I...I don't belong here."

"What do you mean?

But before I could answer, Archie was running to the car. A tidal wave of welcomes followed. The family ushered us into the kitchen, mugs of hot tea thrust into our hands. Lily immediately climbed into Peter's arms. The kids asked about Blair's show. They let me know, in no uncertain terms, how disappointed they were she wasn't with us. Gemma got busy laying out the trifle she'd made in honor of our coming. Peter monitored me with concern, relaxing when he saw me setting the table with Gemma.

The adults held our talk for later, letting Frannie and Archie dominate the conversation for the moment. They wanted to know everything. How Fergie was, if Margaret was jumping over the brush box, if we'd had another picnic near Kynance Cove. And then, in that direct way of his, Archie scored a bulls-eye.

"Mrs. Morgan, are you and Blair going to stay in England?"

I'm guessing I turned as red as the cherry he'd just popped in his mouth. "We haven't decided yet. There would be a lot of arrangements to make if we did."

"Right. Like at your store. But I thought you didn't really like working there. That's what Blair told me."

I could see Peter and Thomas tense up. Thomas scowled and looked ready to scold him. I didn't want that to happen, so I tried diffusing the question with a grin. "Trust you, Archie, to have your finger on the pulse on things." I could feel some of the air return to the room. "Blair's right in some ways. I'd always rather be at home. But sometimes you find yourself somewhere that you didn't really plan. I would have to do something with the company. And, right now, I'm not sure what that would be."

"Is that the only reason you'd go back? To go to the store? Gosh, seems like there's lots more reasons to stay here than to go back there."

Thomas pulled his son close. "Archie, you forget it's her home. Home always has a strong pull, doesn't it?"

Archie shrugged. "I guess. If you like it."

I could either wait for the earth to open and swallow me up, or I could answer him plainly, again. "That's true. Sure there are things about home I miss. Blair does too. So you can see why it's a hard thing to decide." I avoided looking at Peter, since we both knew I'd just lied.

Messing his son's hair, Thomas said, "You'll have more time to grill Mrs. Morgan tomorrow. For now, it's bed time." Looking at Lily in Peter's lap, he said, "And you too, Miss. Give Uncle Pete your biggest hug." Lily buried her head in Peter's chest until he peeled her off, laughing.

Archie broke from his father's arms. "But they just got here."

"I know. But we can't wear 'em out the first night. Off with you. I'll be just behind to tuck you in."

With an exaggerated frown, Archie took Lily's hand and led her up the stairs. Thomas watched him until he turned the corner. "He's been as excited for your visit as he is for Christmas. We all have been." He slapped his hands on his legs, stood, and followed the children.

Peter turned to me. "I'm sorry Archie put you on the spot."

I shook my head. "Archie's directness is part of his charm. He didn't say anything wrong. In fact, he was quite right about everything he said."

Before long, Thomas, Gemma, and Jean joined us in the living room. I watched and listened as they talked and laughed and interrupted each other. It was living, breathing love. I felt better just being in its presence.

I marveled at how well Gemma fit in, knowing she'd been in the family less than two months.

It had been a long day. Gemma must have sensed this. She looked over and, noticing my fatigue, suggested we retire for the night. She walked me to Frannie's room, who had kindly agreed to bunk with her brother during our visit. Before I could finish looking at the posters plastering her walls, I fell into a deep and restful sleep.

⌇

I woke the next morning feeling refreshed, though not quite ready to meet the crowd downstairs. A hot shower would be just the thing to buy me a little transition time. A little later, the sizzle of frying sausages drew me downstairs. Last night, Jean announced she'd be making a full English breakfast. Gemma and Lily had run to the market to get a few things for lunch, but everyone else was helping in the kitchen. I stopped on the last stair, hesitant to break into the sweet scene before me. Jean's tender care for her family was so like my mother's that I ached at the sight of it. Peter must have sensed my presence because he turned around, jumped up from the table, and came to stand directly in front of me.

"Is everything all right?" he asked quietly.

I nodded, though my moist eyes betrayed me. Calling past him, I said, "Good morning, everyone."

Jean left the stove to give me a hug, then quickly returned to add more eggs into the skillet of hot grease. The kitchen turned wild with activity, everyone filling their plates and pulling up chairs around the big wooden table. After breakfast, it was like watching a live comedy troupe- they ran about assembling their gear for the day, making multiple trips into the house to retrieve forgotten items. All the laughter and fun made them less frightening to me. It didn't take me long to realize we would have to take two cars. The whole clan launched into traveling negotiations began. Peter demanded that I ride with him, immediately putting me in the middle of a tug-of-war. We agreed we would rearrange for the trip home.

It took some time to work our way to the edge of Yorkshire Dales National Park. The view out my window came straight from a storybook; I wanted to jump inside the pages. Verdant hillsides and snaking stone fences made crazy quilts in shades of green. A village nestled down into the crease of a landscape. From a distance, it looked like stones had rolled down the knoll and landed in a pile. It thrilled me, made me wish we could turn toward it for a closer look.

We entered the park and stopped at a tiny stone house now serving as the information center. I envied the English their tradition of walking as a part of country life. We donned hats and sunglasses before Thomas lined us up for a photograph. Archie, anxious to be off, attempted an escape, but Peter collared him, and Thomas got his picture between exasperated sighs.

Clumps of purple heather sat amid wild grasses at our feet. Lily gathered a handful, passing sprigs all around, which we dutifully placed behind our ears. The heather gave way as we rounded downhill, coming upon a low stone wall that separated us from several bored sheep. I hesitated, but Thomas quickly explained the right of way system and assured me we weren't trespassing. I relaxed after that and really began to take in the beauty around me. I wished, for the thousandth time since I'd come to this corner of the world, to be an artist, able to capture a fraction of all this loveliness. The wildflowers that leaned out of tumbling down stone walls. Weather-worn wooden fences leaning on each other for support. And grey stone houses with dark slate roofs, brought to life by window boxes overflowing in a spectrum of color. I got lost in the beauty until a cry from Lily roused my attention.

She'd grown tired and tripped on a rock. Thomas kissed her knee and went to hug her, but she reached for Gemma. It was moving to see this motherless child being comforted by her new mother. Which made me think of Blair. And then, of course, Peter.

Peter. Suddenly, I was overrun with memories of him since that first day at Oakton. Peter. The only man I could imagine being with. The only man I would want to be a father to my fatherless child. I was smothered by an avalanche of emotion. Peter. The man I loved.

Exhilarating, wonderful, terrible—and dangerous. Immediately I felt exposed, as if my thoughts were there for all to read. I had to tell myself not to speak. Not a word for fear this would spill out of me. I stopped walking and tried to focus, but instead only managed to arouse suspicion.

"Mrs. Morgan, what's wrong? Do you have a blister? I think Gemma has plasters in her backpack." Frannie had come up from behind me.

Peter turned around. I shook my head, hoping to deflect the attention, but I felt like I might explode. Using every ounce of control I had, I began to ask her questions about herself. As in Cornwall, she answered slowly and thoughtfully. Every time she paused, I felt the rising pressure of new emotions. Fighting to keep them at bay, we talked awhile about her upcoming school term until it was time to eat.

Any English family worth its salt knows how to have a picnic, I learned. Necessities include blankets, fold-up chairs, plates, glassware, silverware, chilled beverages. What followed from the hamper called into question my whole concept of a picnic lunch. No peanut butter and jelly sandwiches, no potato chips, grapes or cookies. Instead, Gemma unpacked cheese, bread, meat pies, thick relish and a cellophane wrapped cake. This was a hearty, satisfying meal; meant to be eaten slowly and enjoyed, along with the view.

"Gather in," said Thomas, once everyone had settled down with full plates, then proceeded to entertain us with recitations from Keats and Byron. When he asked me if I had any poems I wanted to recite, I felt the distinct disadvantage of my American public school education.

"Don't be too impressed," he teased. "English school children have it drilled into them along with simple sums."

I listened to their friendly banter awhile, then drifted away, daydreaming. The view spread out before me like a mural. Off in the distance, the sky turned hazy. All was still awhile, then one lone car poked its way down a road hardly wider than our footpath. I followed it with my eyes and imagined I was its driver, on my way to the village market. I felt, again, that yearning for a simpler life. How realistic was it to think that a woman whose whole life had been spent in American suburbia could adapt to English rural life? It seemed more the stuff of dreams than real life.

I turned my attention back to the Stewarts. Gemma had started the clean-up. The children were playing tag. Thomas and Jean were leaned in close, talking, occasionally stopping to remind Frannie or Archie to watch out for Lily. Peter, it turned out, was watching me watch everyone else. When I'd made the rounds and finally got to him, he mouthed, "I've caught you." I burst out laughing.

He tapped the blanket beside him. I moved over, and we leaned back to look up at the sky. The blue was growing fainter, and gray edges were crowding in from the north and east. The soft white clouds from earlier had turned thick and angry. I closed my eyes, immediately assailed with thoughts of Peter and what to do. His feelings were the same as mine, I was fairly certain. Yet he was holding back. After Blair's show. Even at Eric's. And who could blame him? I could only imagine how confused I'd left him, running hot and cold like a broken faucet. How could I let him know it was different now? How could I let him know I was sure of my feelings?

Time disappeared awhile, until a raindrop landed on my cheek. I opened my eyes and sat up. The haze in the distance had turned dark; a storm was moving in. One raindrop became many, and a mad scramble ensued as we raced to get everything into the cars. Earlier seat assignments were abandoned in favor of keeping everyone as dry as possible. We'd just pulled out of the park when Thomas signaled to Peter to pull over and roll down his window. As he did, the heavens opened up, and the rain came down hard and fast.

"Have you got Lily?" Thomas shouted through the noise. Peter shook his head. Tires screeched as both cars turned around, racing towards the car park. We poured out of the doors, running in all directions and calling Lily's name. Gemma ran into the information center but came out empty handed. Peter and I searched a thicket that started at the edge of the path and covered the side of the hill. Jean had gone to where a large clump of heather grew. Frannie and Archie darted to and fro across the car park and along the perimeter.

The looking grew more frantic while the rain gushed from the sky. And then, like the thunder itself, Thomas' booming voice could be heard above the cacophony of the storm. Everyone turned to see him raging at Frannie and Archie.

"I trusted you to mind her. How could you have been so stupid? How could you not look after her? Your mum would have expected you to, and so do I. You're daft if you think this will go unpunished. I'll sort you out once we've found her. And if she's hurt...it'll be unforgivable."

Everyone stopped in his tracks, but Frannie and Archie stood rigid with the shock of their father's blame. "Go on, keep looking," he bellowed.

"Thomas," Gemma shouted as she ran to him. "Stop it straight away. You don't know what you're saying. You're over the top."

Thomas looked at once wild-eyed and eerily calm. She reached out for him, but he turned away. Then she reached again, grabbed him, and pulled him toward her. Just then, we heard a scream off in the distance. It was Jean. Everyone ran in the direction of her voice, where she and Lily struggled up a steep spot near the walking path. Everyone but me. I was frozen to the spot where I stood. Horrified, furious, remembering.

"Look Daddy, I got some heather for Blair. I forgot before." Lily held out a handful of bent sprigs. Thomas bent down, scooped her into his arms, and took inventory. There were cuts on her knees and chin.

"You've been cut. Does it hurt?"

"Not much. It hurt more when I fell on my bum." Thomas' laughter was tinged with hysteria and did nothing to relieve the tension. "And I'm cold," she said pulling at him. Peter put his arm around Archie and Gemma's went around Frannie, though both were still as rigid as if suffering from rigor mortis.

But then that would be right. Rigor mortis followed death.

Thomas ran to his car and began digging in the trunk for the picnic blankets. "Yes, we all are. We'll dry off as well as we can and get everybody home."

"Peter, you and Suzanne take Archie and Frannie back in your car." Gemma said, "And we'll talk about it later."

"No, we won't," Frannie said, to no one in particular.

Gemma hugged her tightly and whispered something in her ear.

"Wha'd she say?" asked Archie. Frannie just shook her head.

"Here, I got these," Lily said, looking at me. I gave a weak smile and reached toward her with a shaking hand. "They bended when I fell," she explained.

Peter pulled two blankets from his car. He gave one to Gemma. He took the other and wiped my dripping face. He reached for my arm, but I took it from him and turned to Frannie. I recognized her dull stare. Quickly but gently, I wiped her arms and legs. Gemma was doing the same with Archie. One by one, we dried off as much as we could and got into the cars. As we pulled away, the rain let up as quickly as it started. Except for an occasional observation by Archie, all was quiet. Except the sound of Thomas screaming in my head.

≈

Frannie and Archie disappeared upstairs the minute we got home. Thomas, after watching us go into the house, drove off without explanation. Peter, Gemma, and I emptied the car in silence. Jean took Lily up to see to her scrapes and warm her in the bath. The pall that hung over the house reminded me of the afternoon after Edward's funeral.

I emptied the hamper while Gemma put food away. Peter was sorting the other items into piles on the table when he broke into the quiet. "I've never seen him like that."

"No," Gemma agreed. "Nor have I seen a day when he wouldn't rush to apologize. He just left it all standing. That's as troubling as the words he spoke."

No, I thought. An apology can't make up for cruelty to your children.

"I'm worried for him," Peter continued. "To say such things—well, there has to be something else going on."

"Of course," Gemma rushed to answer. "There always is, in all of us. How can such an outburst ever just be one thing?"

Finished organizing, Peter started washing the dishes. "Do you have any idea where he might he might be?"

Closing the cabinet, she tilted her head. "Of course I do."

I watched and listened in unbelief. "You're worried about him?" I asked, my eyes boring into Peter's. "What about—?"

A cry came from the bath. Peter went running. I closed the basket lid and went to Frannie's room. I had just changed into dry clothes when there was a light rap at the door.

"Suzanne, may I come in?" Gemma called. I pulled open the door. "I wanted to see if you were feeling peckish. I could bring you something."

"I was actually thinking I needed to get out a bit, you know, to clear my head."

"Right." Gemma answered cautiously. "You'll need a driver. And I know just the place to go."

We talked pleasantly enough in the car. I felt tied up in knots and would have preferred quiet, but Gemma was a hard person to resist. Our talking slowed as the streets got busier and more developed. We turned into a residential area, and Gemma parked along a curb. The air was fresh after the rain. Flowers in every yard stood with their faces to the sun. Just seeing them brightened my mood. We walked several blocks, then came to an ancient wall with a wide gate cut into it. We walked through and turned the corner. Facing us was the hugest cathedral I'd ever seen.

"Are we going in?" I asked, awestruck.

"No. I thought you should see the Minster, but I have something else in mind." We walked back towards the gate. I followed Gemma through a narrow passageway, up dark steps. When we came back out into the light, we were standing on a walkway on top of the wall. Sometimes we were in a world of branches and leaves. At other times it opened up to give clear views of the residences below. I paused, looking at a particularly lovely home and manicured garden. "It's rather fun, isn't it, peeking into people's worlds like this?" Gemma said over my shoulder.

"I feel like I'm doing something I shouldn't, but I keep telling myself the wall was here before they were."

Twenty minutes later, we came to another gate and descended to street level again. A half block's walk brought us to the Minister Yard, a lovely park with benches tucked under trees and pigeons in search of scraps. We bought tea and pastries from an adjacent shop and found a seat in the sun. "I love this place," Gemma said, "to think and refresh."

"I can see why," I said, looking around. We sipped and nibbled, enjoying the easy silence. In the stillness of the moment, I began to sort through the day. From the wonder of realizing love for Peter, to my shock and horror at his judgment. The man revered by the family as its head spewing hatred at his children. Archie's confusion, Frannie's devastation. Less than 24 hours ago, I thought this was an idyllic family. That was laughable.

"Suzanne," Gemma said, interrupting the quiet, "I'm not in the habit of apologizing for others, but I want you to know that Thomas' outburst was a complete aberration. As was not immediately asking forgiveness from Frannie and Archie. I don't know the cause, but I know he won't rest until he's made it right with them."

How will he do that, I wanted to scream? I knew that every aspect, from the smell of the rain to the dimming light, would be forever etched into Frannie and Archie's minds, filling out the memory of their father's words.

"I imagine it seems odd to you that I'd defend him." She leaned forward to look me more fully in the face.

"No, of course not," I said, feeling the horror of all the times I'd done it for Edward. When he'd belittled Blair. When he'd disparaged me.

"I can do it because I've seen the fierce love he has for those children. And I know his character. I am not making excuses for him. Neither was Peter." I wouldn't be talking about Peter with her. Her allegiances were as skewed as his. "I know what it's like to make excuses for someone whose actions are always in need of covering. This is not the same thing."

Could she mean…?

"I know covering up for someone makes you ashamed. I don't feel shame, I feel love."

I would have laughed at this parade of loyalty if I didn't find it so compelling.

"Anger," she added gently, "that accuses, that tears at our soul and is never accounted for, strips us of our dignity. Then it robs us of truth. Brainwashes us." She paused, and then said in an even gentler voice, "Maybe your husband had that kind of anger. And you believed the lies."

I felt such shame, I couldn't move; the tea turned lukewarm in my hands

"The good things about my first husband were always ruined by his horrid, explosive anger. I learned quickly never to let my guard down, never to leave my vulnerability in plain sight. If I did, he used it against me. What makes living with a man like that so insidious is that we despair of ever being acceptable, of ever being free from the wrath of one who says we don't make muster."

"Why are you telling me this?" I faltered.

"I've watched you and Peter. It would be tragic to let your husband keep taking from you. He's already taken quite a lot, hasn't he?"

"How do you know?"

"Because I recognize it. I can see the despair that lives in you."

"That's ridiculous. We've known each other less than 24 hours."

"I know it seems crazy. But I've caught sight of you when you didn't know I was looking. Seen what you work so hard to keep covered up. And I saw how Thomas' explosion undid you. You barely reacted, but there was a haunted look you couldn't keep from your eyes." She touched my hand. "You don't have to own your husband's anger ever again."

# 18

# Peter

The look on Suzanne's face haunted me all afternoon. It held shock, to be sure. But also something else I couldn't name. Gemma and Suzanne had left without a word while I helped Mum. So besides being worried, I was also annoyed. I wanted to know where they'd gone. Thomas returned an hour later, altogether saner. "Don't say it," he said, beating me to the punch.

"Say what?"

"What a foul thing I am. For everything in me, I didn't know I was capable of saying such things to my own dear children. Believe me, I was as horrified as all of you."

"Fran and Arch will be okay. They've got big hearts." He nodded at me then went straight up to them, not returning for an hour.

It was nearly 4 o'clock. by the time Suzanne and Gemma arrived home. I was sitting on the floor playing cards with Lily and Archie. Strained and worn, Suzanne looked no better now than she had after the hike. And, I noticed, she wouldn't look directly at me. Or Thomas.

"Where have you been?" Thomas asked Gemma.

"I took Suzanne to one of my special thinking spots, so you'll appreciate it if we don't say exactly where." Gemma smiled kindly at her, and I saw just the barest of softening in Suzanne's eyes.

"Oh, down at the Minster Yard?" Archie asked.

"How did you know my secret place, you rascal?" Gemma asked, tousling his hair.

"I saw you there once. I was with Patrick and his mum. You were sitting on one of those benches under a tree. Reading or something. So I guessed that was the place."

"Well done, Sherlock."

He beamed, full of pride, and returned to the card game. My attention, however, was still on Suzanne. "Would you like to join us?"

She shook her head. "I need to freshen up. I'll be down in a bit to help with dinner."

I looked to Gemma for explanation, but she escaped into the kitchen before I could make eye contact. Mum soon joined her. The familiar mingling of kitchen sounds and conversation flowed back to the living room. I realized how much I missed that, living alone.

Suzanne was subdued during dinner. It reminded me of when we met, when every response was measured and nothing seemed very real. Only Archie seemed able to provoke a genuine response from her; his jokes and antics entertained us all. Near the end of the meal, Lily moved from her place and leaned against Suzanne. She had little choice but to put her arm around Lily, yet even that seemed forced. I felt almost frantic to know what she was thinking.

"What's your plan for tomorrow?" Mum asked innocently, as she cleared the table.

"We don't know," Suzanne answered. "Might need to get back."

I snapped around. We weren't due to pick up Blair until the day after tomorrow. "How about a walk?" I asked.

I had a vague sense that it was a lovely evening, the kind I usually savored, full of gossamer light. But tonight all I could think about was Suzanne; her drawn, wary face suggested another storm might be brewing. I wanted to get her out of the house, hoping she might tell me what she was really feeling. We were halfway to the meadow when I realized this was her third outing today. She had to be tired, though she hadn't refused. As we neared the bridge, I let out a deep sigh.

"What?" Suzanne asked warily.

"Sorry?"

"Nothing."

I tried again. "It's been a rough day. You must be worn out. Thanks for coming out with me." She kept her eyes on her feet. "Did something happen with Gemma this afternoon?"

"What do you mean?"

"Before you went with her, we were planning to stay another day. Then tonight you told mum we didn't know."

"I wanted to talk to you first. I'm just anxious to get back. I don't like imposing on Eleanor."

"You'll have to come up with a better reason than that," I said, smiling, hoping to coax her good mood back. "I'm sure Blair is having a wonderful time, not a bit of trouble."

She scowled at me. "She might wear out her welcome."

"It's something else. You're angry with Thomas? Something Gemma said? Or both?" The question filled the space between us, growing wider with each step. We trudged on in painful silence. I didn't know how to break through.

"He's made it right with the children. You saw them at dinner."

"Make it right? He can't make that right." Her words were full of derision, contempt even. We got to the bridge. I leaned heavily onto the rails, closed my eyes, let the sound of the rushing water soothe me. I didn't want to fight. Whatever that unknown thing in her eyes had been was now audible in her voice. I thought how little I knew of her life. Of what caused this reaction.

"I'm saying he's apologized. He's talked about it with them. Tried to explain."

She looked aghast. "And that fixes it, does it?"

"What else can he do?" I asked, trying not to sound as disconcerted as I felt. What else could anyone do? "Fran and Arch must rest on the fact of who he is. How he's loved them every day of their lives. They've got to allow him not to be perfect. He didn't mean what he said."

"How do you know that?"

"Because I know him. The moment was terrible. It hurt them. But he loves them. And they know that. You want a full on condemnation of him, and I'll not give it to you."

"Why are you defending him?" She was accusing, not asking.

"I'm not defending him. What he did, what he said was wrong. But they have to be able to move on from it."

"Easier said than done."

"Sure," I acknowledged.

"Impossible."

⸻

Though no one said it out loud, the goodbyes after breakfast were brief, meant to ease everyone's discomfort. At the last moment, Archie ran up to Suzanne. "We'll see you the next time we come see Uncle Pete, won't we?"

"I would always be happy to see you, Archie," Suzanne said, and pulled her door shut.

The ride back to Cornwall seemed to have mysteriously doubled in length. We touched briefly on safe subjects: medieval cathedrals, the Tate Gallery, cream scones. I didn't always need to be pulling secrets out of someone's heart, but this fluff was draining the life from me. The truth was I felt cheated. I'd planned a trip where Suzanne would get to know my family, see where I'd come from; see, as Eric said "what became a part of me." I expected the trip to bring us closer, give us a nice memory to share. Instead she couldn't tolerate Thomas, seemed uncomfortable with Gemma, and was angry with me.

The long silences gave my mind room to wander. I found myself back in the pub in Truro, eavesdropping on Jillian and Ian. At the memory, a trace of the embarrassment over what I'd done returned. I continued to be troubled by Jillian's words. *Peter said I was right. He and Laura have reconciled.* Considering the source, I should have stopped myself right there.

"An odd thing. I saw Jillian the other day. She was telling Ian that she'd seen you."

Out of the corner of my eye, I saw Suzanne sit up straighter and cross her arms. "I was in St. Ives last week."

"Right." Good, a chance meeting. "Said my name came up."

"Huh," she said, turning to look at a passing lorrie.

"She seemed to think Laura and I had gotten back together. Actually said you told her she was right and that'd we'd reconciled. Is that right?"

As if a mason were fast at work in the car, so fast could I feel a wall go up between us. Her mouth was hard and set, her arms cemented across her. I don't know why I brought it up. I really didn't intend to make her angry. Or did I? Anger, at least, was a real feeling.

"I don't remember exactly. I'm sure I told her what you told me," she said half-heartedly.

"You understood what I meant, right? When I said we were reconciled? I didn't mean we'd decided to get together again. I don't love her." I stopped for emphasis. I wanted her to look at me. To see how seriously I meant this. I wanted her to know whom I loved. But she didn't look at me. She looked out the window, straight ahead, at her feet. Anywhere but at me. "I meant she accepted my apology. That she didn't harbor a grudge."

"Of course."

"That's strange, then."

"She just misunderstood."

&

With all the work that piled up, it seemed like we'd been gone longer than three days. But I didn't mind. I needed something to occupy the hours. I had never met anyone like Suzanne. Just when I thought I knew how she felt, a breeze blew and it changed. I had a poor track record predicting what she enjoyed doing, where she liked to go, and what subjects were safe. Like the *London A to Zed* helped me navigate the streets of central London, I needed something to help me steer through Suzanne's moods and reactions. Or someone. I would think about it. For the time being, I had loads of work to do. And, through it all, the hope of seeing her again soon.

It was Friday. Blair was due to spend the afternoon with me at Muirfield. Margaret had arranged to be there, too. The day dragged on. I checked my mobile every thirty minutes, afraid I'd missed a call. A conspiracy of inefficiency seemed to pervade all day; half the lessons started late, a horse threw a shoe, and tack inexplicably disappeared. I was obsessed with wanting to call Suzanne to remind her, but I was afraid I'd make her angry. Instead, my frustration grew and defined the entire day.

Finally, the last horse was groomed and put to pasture. It was 7:10 P.M. Ignoring my hunger pangs, I drove straight to Wisteria Cottage. Suzanne was weeding a flowerbed. Blair played nearby, pretending to jump plastic horses over stick jumps she'd erected.

"Hello," I called out, coming through the gate, mustering my best "nothing bothers me" face.

The reactions that greeted me were as far removed as the North and South Poles. Blair's looked as though the medicine she knew would cure her had arrived. Suzanne, on the other hand, looked as though I was the poison that would finally do her in.

Blair dropped her horses and came running. As she got closer, I saw apprehension mixed with joy. I looked her in the eye, winked, and said, "Margaret and I were expecting you at Muirfield today. I've saved some tack for you to clean."

"It wasn't a good day to come out," she answered, unable to maintain eye contact.

"Oh, I'm sorry to hear that. I guess it's understandable, what with having been gone a few days. There are always things to do to get caught up. Maybe tomorrow?" I suggested, looking at Suzanne.

"I don't think that will be convenient either," Suzanne said primly. I waited for an explanation. Hoped for one. Nothing came. I tried to question her with my eyes. I was met with a surprisingly cold stare.

"Blair, I'm a bit thirsty. May I have a glass of water?" I asked the friendlier face.

"Sure, I'll be right back."

"Take your time. I'm not in a panic for it." I gave her a faint smile, hoping she was reading between the lines. Suzanne breathed hard, annoyance mixing with the air. "Is something wrong?" I asked. I knew there was. But I hoped asking directly could draw out the answer.

"No, we're fine. It's just not a good time for Blair to fill her days at the barn. We have other things we need to do."

What other things? What could be more important than Blair's riding? Than me seeing you? "Of course. But surely you can work in an hour sometime soon."

"No, I don't think we can." She turned to go inside.

"Suzanne, what's going on? What have I done to offend you so? I know we disagree about Thomas."

She turned back and threw her arms up. "He has nothing to do with me. I'm tired of everyone telling me he does. I do not need people interfering all the time."

"I don't mean to interfere. I'm your friend. I…" Everything from my tired arms to my wounded pride wanted to finish that sentence.

"Please go. Leave us alone." She looked sad, defeated, and beautiful.

"Can't we talk about it? Won't you tell me how you feel?"

"Just go."

Her words seemed as heavy as her arms, which now hung limply at her side.

∽

Eleanor said I could run by after work. She was in her garden, tending to her dahlias. "They love the late summer. I do, too." She started to push up off the ground. I ran to her, extending a hand. She took it, laughing. "Gets harder every season. Next year, I may need to sleep out here."

We walked to her potting shed, and I watched her thrust the tools into planters full of sand. "Keeps them clean and sharp," she explained. Garden smock folded, gloves stowed in a drawer, hands wiped. "Now I can have a proper chat." She finished rubbing thick lotion on her hands as we went in the kitchen. She poured two tall glasses of lemonade.

"Your trip to York?"

"A shambles."

"I'm sorry. I could see Suzanne wasn't happy when she came to get Blair. Refused to say more than five words about the whole thing. Hillary and I wondered what went wrong."

I told her the story. When I got to Thomas's outburst, she flinched. "Surely that did her in."

I nodded. "And my unwillingness to suggest that something other than complete condemnation of Thomas was in order."

Eleanor put her glass down. "What did you say?"

I repeated our conversation. "I was just trying to help her. She was so upset with Thomas."

"But she thought you were defending him?"

"Yes. And now she's as angry at me as she was at Thomas. Angrier, even. I went to see her and she wouldn't talk. Just told me to go."

Eleanor looked pained. She went to the sink and stared out the window. "I feel very sad for her," she said.

"Eleanor, I'm struggling here. I don't expect to figure her out completely. Wouldn't want to. Couldn't. But some of her reactions are so confusing to me."

Fredericka and Martin came screaming in, doing their best banshee imitation. Wally came yapping in behind them. Hillary followed, calling in vain for them to remember they were at Gran's. The parade passed through the kitchen, into the dining room, and finally disbanded in the sitting room.

Eleanor smiled at me. "I'm the villain for all the behavior Hillary wants from the children but won't quite demand herself. She puts if off on me. Won't admit she'd like them to stop screaming, too. The funny thing is I don't think she's even aware of it. Andrew used to get rather ugly with her when she disciplined the children. Didn't like them growing up. So to keep peace she became lenient too. But their behavior bothers her."

"So now it's easier for her if she acts like you're the exacting one."

"Yes. Then she doesn't have to deal with herself."

"How do you know it bothers her? How do you know how she'd really like them to act?"

"I know her history. She worked as a nanny for a year. I remember how she talked about the kids. How it helped her know the kind of mother she wanted to be. And because I know that, I don't mind when she blames me. She's got a lot to work through after Andrew. I don't mind waiting for her to sort things out."

≈

The drive home was a blur of thoughts. I went inside, fed Winston, and heated a plate of Shepherd's Pie. I fell into my chair, threw my head back, and tried to fit the pieces together. Evening faded to night. Night grew deep black. Then a piece moved. And another piece. And a picture started to take form.

I picked up my mobile and dialed international information. I punched in the number.

"Cathy Lawrence? You don't know me. Peter Stewart here."

# 19

## *Suzanne*

"You look like you have something to say," I said to Hillary, who had stopped by to return a book Blair left at Penwylln.

Hillary blushed. "You're right. I do have something to tell you. I haven't even told mother yet. I overheard something last night. About Agnes." I stiffened and she hastily added, "I know your relationship is strained."

"I wish you'd stay out of it. I know you think you're helping, but you aren't. It's best to leave things as they are." I'd found the best course of action was to let the memory of hurt grow dim. With time, it was usually forgotten.

"I know you want me to mind my own business. But I think your way of handling it will hurt you worse in the end. You need to talk to her."

"Okay, just get it over with," I said, slumping against the car.

She spoke eagerly. "Last night, I overheard a fight between Agnes and Ian. They were eating dinner a few tables away from me at Le Jardin. I didn't notice them until Agnes stood up and began yelling at Ian. It was quite a scene." I hated to admit it, but now I was curious. "Anyway, I didn't hear what he'd said, but I heard her. She called him 'a user and a manipulator.' Said he wasn't 'capable of genuine affection.' As Vicar, she 'expected better behavior.' Then…" Hillary stopped and savored the memory. "…she said Peter was the opposite in every way." What? I felt slightly sick. Why did Agnes mention Peter? "And then, this is the best part," she exclaimed, "she said, 'Suzanne Morgan is someone who matters to me, for whom I want the best. She's better off with Peter Stewart than she'd ever be with you.'"

I gasped loudly. "How could she do that?"

Hillary was staring at me with her mouth agape. "I thought you'd be happy—."

"Happy? Are you crazy? It is no one's business what I do with my life. And besides, I'm not better off with anyone. My husband died. Can't any of you remember that? I've never seen such a bigger bunch of busybodies and meddlers. If I ever entertained any ideas of staying here, you've just convinced my why that's the stupidest thing I could do."

"But what about Agnes? I thought you'd be pleased."

"You thought I'd be pleased to hear she was yelling private things about me in a crowded restaurant?" I stopped to catch my breath.

Hillary looked as if she'd been slapped. "I'm sorry you feel that way. I found her defense of you to be very loving."

"Well, I don't." I held up the book as I opened the door. "Thanks for dropping this off."

◠

We'd managed to fill the day puttering in the cottage. Windows shone, sheets dried on the line, and the flowerbeds were pristine. And yet it hadn't been a day of joyful camaraderie working side by side. Blair was sullen. I was introspective. Our miseries kept us focused in our own personal universes, where the world was small, lonely and threatening. The afternoon waned and with it our energy. Blair grew restless and begged for a chance to get out of the house. Within the hour, we were driving to Lizard Point. We rolled down the windows and let the clean, salty air blow through us, giving each of us a chance to sit back and simply breathe. By the time we parked the car, Blair was laughing out loud and I could feel a smile overtaking my face.

We carefully spread the blanket on the ground, with Blair paying special attention to any wrinkles. Next, cards, books, a sketchpad, and various drawing implements were laid out with the order of surgical instruments in an operating room. Then dinner was taken out of the hamper and set up as a mini buffet. I was ready to start serving but Blair begged me to wait. She took off on a run and returned with a handful of wildflowers.

"Margaret's mom always has flowers on her table," she said, putting them in a cup. No matter how many times she adjusted them, the flowers kept falling to the sides. Finally, she accepted the arrangement and reached for a plate.

I filled mine too. "Margaret's a good friend, isn't she?"

Blair nodded wistfully. "Uh huh, she's really super. She's become my very best friend. But I don't want Freddie to know that cause it would hurt her feelings."

"What do you think makes a best friend?"

She took a big bite of chicken salad, giving her time to think. "Somebody who likes to do what you like. Or, at least, will do something you want to. And, I guess, somebody you can tell your secretest things to. And they won't tell anybody, even when somebody asks them." She stuck out her lip. "Like Rachel did. Before she changed. I thought we'd be best friends forever. I thought we were like sisters. I didn't think she could ever be mean to me."

"It hurts when people let you down, doesn't it? Especially when you shared your heart with them."

"Yeah. And it can feel kinda scary when you make a new friend. You wonder if they'll do the same thing, too."

I nodded, then realized how much I didn't want to be talking about this right now.

"Let's take a walk."

My suggestion was met with a quick clean up. Blair neared the edge of the cliffs several times to watch the waves lap against the rocks; each time I held my breath a little less. By the time we returned to the blanket, the weight on my heart had lifted and I took my first deep breath in days. I lay down and looked up at the slow emergence of stars in the sky. Blair sat beside me and drew a map of the constellations. Her clear voice broke into the quiet.

"Mom, why are you so mad at everyone right now?"

"I'm not."

❧

"Eleanor, this is a surprise." I came home from a quick trip to the bank to find her sitting at the kitchen table, enjoying a plate of cookies with Blair.

"I hope you don't mind. Blair offered me tea while I waited for you."

I guessed she was here to talk about Agnes. Frankly, I didn't want to hear it. I was pretty content with feeling annoyed and wasn't in the mood to change. Blair, on the other hand, was even chattier than usual, ignoring my non-verbal cues about wanting this to be a short visit. When Eleanor asked Blair about her riding, she looked disturbed. "I haven't ridden for a couple of weeks, but I'm anxious to get back at it."

"Why ever not? Have you been ill?"

I interrupted Blair before could answer. "She's fine. We've just been busy."

Eleanor took a sip of tea while Blair mindlessly fingered the fringe of a pillow, her eyes fixed on the floor. Abruptly, Eleanor stood and put her cup on the tray. "Ladies, I have a plan for tonight. Blair, pack your bag. Fredericka and Martin are renting a film tonight and would love to have you join them. Plan to stay over. Suzanne, get showered. I'm taking us out for a ladies evening. I know just the perfect spot. I'll not take no from either of you. I'll be back at half six to gather you. We'll deposit Blair at Penwylln and be on our way." She marched out the door before either of us said a word. Blair bounded up the stairs, already calling out a list of things she planned to take. I trailed behind her; a growing list in my head of all I couldn't, wouldn't say.

$\backsim$

"Take a sip of your wine and unclench your jaw," Eleanor said. It reminded me of the days after Edward's funeral when Cathy had to tell me to eat.

I looked at Eleanor's kind eyes and began, ever so slightly, to let my guard down. We sat on the terrace of the Dartmoor Arms, a lovely restored hotel perched high along the coast. The chill in the evening breeze was a pleasant reminder that autumn wasn't far behind. "I think you're angry with me," I ventured.

"I'm nothing of the sort. Should I be?"

"I don't know. Anyway, I'm angry enough at myself for both of us."

Eleanor nodded and took a bite of her appetizer. "Is that why you've not called or come by for so long?"

I wanted to pour my heart out to her and have her tell me everything would be okay. I wanted to tell her how Thomas's actions unnerved me. How Gemma's words got too close. And how Peter disappointed me. How he didn't stand up for the kids. How he sided with his brother's harshness. How that made me afraid to trust him with Blair. I nodded. "Partly," I said, squirming in my seat. "Of course, I was gone for a bit, a couple of weeks ago."

"To York, with Peter."

"Yes." I swirled a piece of bread in the plate of olive oil absentmindedly and looked toward the sea. "Have you met Peter's sister-in-law, Gemma?" Eleanor shook her head. "She's interesting." Gemma's words still swirled around my head, like bats inside a cave – crowding, darting, threatening.

"Suzanne," Eleanor said in a voice both firm and tender, "something is different. Something happened, didn't it? I wish you'd tell me. I'm your friend. I care about you."

What's different? Nothing and everything. I forced myself to look into Eleanor's wise eyes. "I appreciate that. You've always been lovely to me, but I can't think what—."

"The scene in Le Jardin, to start with," Eleanor said sharply. "Hillary told me. You must be glad to have a friend like Agnes."

I pulled back as if I'd been punched in the stomach. "No, I'm not. I can't imagine how you could say that," I said, my voice rising. "Agnes managed to take what was a private conversation between Ian and her and make it into a public spectacle. That's not my idea of friendship. Still, it isn't surprising."

"What do you mean?"

"That's not the first time Agnes has discussed my life with people she had no business to. Actually, I've been keeping my distance from her for a while. You know, with friends like that…"

"That doesn't sound like the Agnes that I know."

"She told me about it herself." I winced, remembering how she'd asked for forgiveness. Or was it remembering my refusal to give it?

"What happened?" Eleanor asked, still surprised.

"I don't want to rehash it. Let's just say Agnes has shown her true colors more than once."

"Maybe. Or maybe you're color blind."

"I don't think spouting off to Jillian about something I told her in confidence is blindness on my part."

"You say she told you about it herself? Did she realize she was wrong to break your confidence?"

"She apologized, yes. But…"

"And she asked your forgiveness?"

"Yes," I said more quietly.

"I understand why you'd be so angry at her, and your anger is perfectly justified. But usually when someone has the humility to apologize and ask forgiveness, he is truly sorry and sees he was wrong. Hasn't that ever happened to you? Wouldn't you want to be forgiven for something that you now regret?" She paused, waiting for an answer I didn't plan to give. "We can't keep people in the prisons of their mistakes. And especially not when they know they've been wrong. You wouldn't want to be treated that way, would you?" Again she paused. "You didn't like being treated that way, did you?"

My throat grew tight and I fought back tears. I shook my head, trying to dislodge memories of Edward parading my mistakes in front of me and anyone else who would listen. I coughed, clearing the emotion out. "But that doesn't change the fact of what she did at Le Jardin."

"From what I heard, she acted out of loyalty to you."

"Hillary thought so, too. But I can't see how broadcasting her opinions of my social life to a room full of strangers can be characterized as loyalty."

"I think it's the dressing down of Ian that can be characterized that way, as well as declaring her desire for you to have the best."

"You mean..."

Eleanor shrugged. "That's a different issue."

My voice rose, again, to meet the anger I felt. "Really, Eleanor, what gives you the right to tell me how to live my life?"

People on either side of us turned in interest. "You can see how easily that happens when you're angry, can't you?" Eleanor said matter-of-factly.

I glared in helplessness, but before she could say anything the waiter arrived with dinner. By the time he finished serving us, I was looking out of the window again. I followed a boat as it made its way out to sea and into the darkening night. How lovely it would be to sail away from my problems. But then it climbed a big swell and heeled strongly to the side. Even the escape wasn't without problems, I admitted to myself with a deep sigh.

"I can appreciate that you care about these people - Agnes, Hillary, Peter - and that you are unhappy with how I am treating them. But I'm an adult and I resent your interference on their behalf."

"I'm not interfering on their behalf; I'm interfering on yours. Didn't you hear me say I care about you? I've felt a special connection to you since that day you picked up my hat in Thom's Cove." She bore down on me with those twinkling eyes until I had to smile in return. "I sense that you need an older woman in your life who loves you. One who isn't afraid to speak the truth. I brought you here tonight because of you. Because I care about you and am worried about *you*. I'm willing to risk having you angry at me if it will help you look at things differently, make better choices."

Her love was irresistible. It wrapped around my sore heart like a bandage. By the time we ordered dessert, I'd agreed to try and work things out with Agnes. Remembering my nervousness when I asked Blair for forgiveness, I finally accepted how difficult it must have been for Agnes.

We chatted about Fredericka and Martin and the upcoming school term. In typical fashion, Fredericka was excited, adding personal touches to her school uniform and shopping for fun school supplies. Martin, on the other hand, turned grumpy at the mere mention of school. He told his mum to get whatever supplies he needed, just so he didn't have to pick them out himself. "Fredericka is just like her mum. A new school year is as exciting as Boxing Day." She lost herself for a moment in happy memories. "Blair's like that, isn't she?"

I nodded. "Yes, she's always loved school." I felt a stab in the pit of my stomach and stopped eating.

"Are you alright?" Eleanor asked, looking at me curiously.

"Hmm," I cleared my throat. "I'm fine."

"No you aren't. What is it?"

I took a deep breath and put my fork down. Worry spread through me like a virus.

"I've got to tell Blair my decision. The school year is around the corner and the last thing she needs is to start late and get behind the other children."

"I was going to ask you about that. What are you thinking?"

"We're going back. The company is my responsibility. Edward would be appalled that I've left Morgan's in someone else's hand for this long. And my father is expecting me back. He's angry that I've stayed as long as I have. What would it look like if I stayed away longer? Edward put so much attention into the house, and now it's like I've abandoned it and our life. What does that say to everyone? I don't think I have a choice." It was a wonder I got through that under Eleanor's penetrating eye. We both knew I wasn't telling her everything.

"Listen to yourself. You've talked about Edward, your father, the store and everyone else, who ever 'they' are. What about you? What do you want to do? What is best for you and Blair? What does Blair want to do?"

"She wants to stay."

"And you?" Eleanor prodded.

I winced. "Until recently, I wanted to stay too."

"What happened?" Eleanor asked, her voice gentle.

I started shaking inside. "I realized I was better off back in Virginia."

～

Agnes was filling in the Back to School display when the door closed with a thud. She almost dropped the books when she saw me standing there. "Suzanne. What can I help you find?"

"My way back to my friend." I smiled at her sheepishly.

"Sorry?"

"I need to ask you something. Tell you something…Well, both, I guess. I should have accepted your apology for talking to Jillian long before this. I'm embarrassed that I didn't. And even though I'm not happy about the scene with Ian, Eleanor convinced me that you meant well. I've missed you and I've been wrong to hold a grudge. I'm sorry."

It took a few seconds before Agnes reacted. Then, rushing toward me with arms open, she said, "I'm so sorry, too, for betraying you to Jillian. I've hated myself for that."

Remembering the lie I told Jillian, I said, "It's over. She brings out the worst in people. Can I ask you something now, without Blair around to hear it?"

"Sure, anything."

"Why were you having dinner with Ian to begin with? What did he want?"

The smiling Agnes of a moment ago disappeared. "He tricked me into thinking he wanted to go out with me. I didn't realize how lonely I'd become. Anyway, he only took me out because he thought I could influence you. He thought you were falling for Peter and that you should be falling for him. He wanted me to keep you from making the biggest mistake of your life. I believe that's how he put it. That's why I told him, in no uncertain terms, that you were far better off with Peter than you'd ever be with him."

"I just can't understand it."

"What?"

"How you've all have been so blind about Peter?"

～

The ringing phone startled me. I stuffed a bookmark between the pages and found my cell phone.

"It's me, Cathy," she said in her familiar warm voice. It seemed natural to ask her about Morgan's, but I found I quickly tired of the details. I didn't really care what sportswear line was setting records. I did, however, perk up when Cathy said things with Mark were serious.

"Serious, as in marriage?" I asked hopefully.

"He hasn't asked me yet. But I think he's going to."

"What will you say?"

"I'll say yes, of course. I can't imagine my life without him." Yes. I do know. I couldn't say anything. For several seconds. "Suz, is everything okay?"

"Yes. Fine. Everything's great. I'm so happy for you both. When do you think he'll ask?"

"Soon. He's hinted at starting the year as man and wife. Maybe just before New Year's."

"Oh good, then I'd be there."

"I thought you were staying. Has something happened?"

"Why does everyone keep asking me that?"

"I don't know who everyone is, but I'm asking because you thought you were going to stay. You told me Peter Stewart—."

"I know what I told you. I've changed my mind. That's all."

"I don't believe that's all for a minute." I didn't understand why she sounded so upset. I thought she'd be thrilled to have me back. "Is it Blair? Does she want to come back?" Cathy asked, more gently this time.

"Not at all. In fact, I haven't broken the news to her yet. But I will. Soon. Maybe tomorrow morning." I dreaded her reaction. But I needed to view it like a doctor giving a shot. The short-term pain was worth a long, healthy life.

"Don't do it yet, please. Take another couple of days."

"Why?" I asked, feeling cornered. "It's my decision."

"Of course it is, Suz. I just feel like you're rushing it. Just two weeks ago you told me you were falling in love."

I began to pace around the room. A path to nowhere. "The decision's made." My voice sounded cold. "School starts soon. We'll be back in two weeks." It made me want to cry.

"Just tell me you'll be absolutely sure. That you'll only do this if you feel completely peaceful about your decision."

After I hung up, I wondered what it would be like to feel peaceful about anything.

~

The cool morning breeze carried all the promises of autumn. For me, it was September, not January, which spoke of new beginnings. Each fall, with its clean notebooks and newly sharpened pencils, brought the hope of something new. The calendar said it was still summer, but the air whispered something different.

My heart was heavy with confusion and regret as I pondered the past couple of weeks, particularly Blair's question. Why was I suddenly mad at everyone? It was obvious. Because they all thought they knew something, and they were wrong. They all thought Peter was different than he was. I was there when he defended Thomas. They weren't. Defending that kind of behavior is only one step from actually doing it. I could never risk living with that kind of anger again. The truth was widowhood brought with it a kind of freedom. At first I despised it, but then I tried to embrace it. I almost laughed out loud. Embraced it? What kind of psycho-babble was that? All that meant was to accept reality. I accepted reality. A reality that led to decisions I had to make, decisions that would shape our lives. And I'd made this one. It is what made getting out of bed so hard. I pulled the covers tighter around my neck and waited to drift back to sleep. Then I heard the door to the bathroom close. Blair was up.

I roused myself from bed, threw on my robe, and went into the kitchen. By the time Blair finished in the bathroom, I was stirring flour and eggs in the bowl. "Are pancakes okay?"

"I don't want you to go to any trouble," Blair said softly. She got silverware out and carried it to the table.

The defeated look in her eyes as she quietly performed her duties transported me back in time. Two September's ago, Blair looked like this most of the time. It hadn't been quite so shocking then because I hadn't known how different she could look. Now that I knew the real Blair, happy and engaged and full of youthful exuberance, this déjà vu was devastating to see. And it was even more devastating to risk a return to it again.

I rested the spoon against the side of the bowl and walked over to her. I took the forks from her hands, and guided her to the couch. "Blair, I need you to listen to me."

She nodded.

"Okay, mommy," Blair responded automatically.

"No, it isn't, honey." I sighed, pulling her to my chest and rubbing her hair. "Blair, you have been cursed with a very selfish parent. I should have been more decisive about this. Not let it go on this long, unsettled. I've let my own confusion and fear control me and that hasn't been fair to you."

"I don't understand."

"Blair, we can't stay. We have to go home."

"No, Mom." She pushed me away and started crying. "I don't want to. I'm happy here. This is home now."

"No, it's not. It's all been a fantasy. We wanted things to be a certain way. But wanting them that way doesn't make it real. My most important job is to protect you. I didn't do that well when Daddy was alive. I refuse to fail you again."

"But what about all our friends? Margaret, Freddie, Peter? I love Peter."

"You don't. You can't."

"He loves me," she shouted. "He always takes care of me. He doesn't yell at me." She was becoming hysterical. Crying, shouting, flailing. I'd never seen her this upset. Never. Not even... I grabbed her by the arms. She wrenched herself from my grip.

"You can't do this. It's wrong. We belong here. With Peter. And Fergie. And everyone."

"Blair," I shouted back. Startled, she stopped everything but the crying. Tears streamed from her eyes uncontrollably. Inconsolably. "I've been wrong about a lot of things before. But you have to believe me now. You don't know what you're talking about. You don't know what I know."

Blair looked up at her mom. "What do you know?"

Hesitatingly, I said, "I know the truth." But not an ounce of peace.

# 20

# Peter

I clicked off the mobile and sat down, having been unsuccessful at reaching both Eleanor and Thomas. Winston, sensing my dejection, waddled over, acknowledged me with a snort, and then returned to his bed by the hearth. With a new school term approaching, my days were full at Oakton and my evenings at Muirfield, but the joy I usually felt was missing. I was still waiting to find out if Blair would be enrolling. And I was still trying to figure out how to break through Suzanne's fortress of anger.

Forty minutes later, I ordered dinner at The Curry Shoppe. Then I went next door to Blockbuster, in search of a distraction. Finding a series on the RAF, I picked up two DVD's and went to queue up at the till. Just then Ian entered. In no mood to talk to him, I pretended to be engrossed reading the backs of the cases.

"Stewart, shouldn't you be mucking somewhere?" he said derisively.

"I'm not in the mood tonight, Ian."

At this, he came over to the queue, suddenly bright and interested. "Tightly sewn world showing signs of rips at the seams, is it?"

"Like I said…"

"Right. Well, I'll just have to check in with, let me see, the one who's better off with you. Maybe she'll fill me in." I looked at him blankly. "I must admit that dumb look you are giving me is quite convincing," he sneered.

I felt the muscles in my neck and shoulder tighten. I stretched my head from side to side to work out the kinks. Less likely to punch him now, I simply said, "Right-ho."

Ian considered me for a moment and walked off.

Back at home, the RAF was trouncing the Luftwaffe over the Channel, but I couldn't concentrate. Ian's usual mean spirit had turned rancid, and I felt poisoned by it. I couldn't get what he said out of my mind. What did he mean *the one who's better off* with me? Since I didn't know the context, I was left with the face value of the words. And that could only be Suzanne. Surely Ian would never refer to her that way. But then I remembered his mocking tone. Maybe that was exactly who he meant. I had to find out.

⌒

I could hear the television as I knocked on the bright yellow door. "Hallo, Peter. This is a surprise."

I cleared my throat. "Hello Jillian. It's been a while since I've seen you."

Abruptly she cut in. "Your choice, I believe. What do you want? As I recall, you've made it clear I'm not one of your favorite people."

"I think you misread me," I said. "I never stopped considering you a friend." Met with silence, I persevered. "I was hoping to catch up. It's been a while since we've talked."

"Right," she said. I shifted nervously on my feet while she eyed me up and down, then stepped aside. "I guess there's no harm in it. I'll make some tea."

I followed her into the kitchen and leaned in the doorway. "Some new paintings, I see."

She followed my eyes. "Good, too, don't you think? I need three more and then we'll be showing the collection in London."

"That really is terrific. Well done, you."

She looked genuinely pleased. "Yes, my prospects are improving. I hope you drink chai. It's really become the thing." She poured our cups and sat beside me on the couch. Then she took a sip, made a face, and put the cup down.

"Don't you like it?" I asked.

"Of course. It's very popular." She raised the cup slowly to her mouth and took a smaller sip. "It's so unusual," she declared, smiling.

I took a sip. "Dodgy, if you ask me." I tried engaging her in conversation about her day, but she was reticent to answer and things were slow going. She seemed preoccupied, getting up to straighten a picture on the wall and picking at lint on her skirt.

"I came over to see you, Jillian, but you don't seem the least bit interested in visiting with me."

"I'm not sure why I should be, Peter. The last time we spoke you were rather harsh. Do you remember?"

"That seems forever ago. And as I recall, you were not in the friendliest of moods that evening. Can't we let bygones be bygones?"

She scrunched her nose up. "Not really in my nature, is it?" she quipped.

I laughed. "No, generally not. But I was hoping you'd make an exception for me tonight."

Something flickered in her eyes and she returned to the couch. "If it would make you happy," she paused, "then alright." We fell into conversation about everything Jillian: art, fashion, the need to get to London more frequently, tiresome tourists, and the suffocating life in Cornwall.

"This fishbowl existence is terribly wearing. You know what I mean, don't you? I mean, in light of recent events and all?"

"Sorry? What recent events?"

"Don't toy with me," she said playfully. "It had to annoy you. My goodness! You who guard your privacy as though you were a member of the royal family." She was finding something delicious in all this.

"I really don't know what you're referring to." She was making me uneasy; I actually caught myself squirming in my seat. "Just tell me. Clearly, I've missed something important."

She gasped. "You're not lying. You haven't heard."

"Heard what?" My unease grew.

"Calm down. Do you want more tea? I've got a great story for you."

In a measured voice, I said, "No, I don't want tea, Jillian. I want to know what you find so amusing and what it has to do with me."

"I guess I shouldn't keep you in suspense." She took a biscuit from the plate and nibbled the edges. "It seems that, recently, our vicar had a scathingly brilliant plan to, how shall I say it, garner support for his camp. And so he took our shy, retiring librarian out to dinner. He thought he could turn her into Mata Hari. Planned to persuade her to help him win the fair widow Morgan."

"He told you this?" I asked, still confused.

"Oh, no. No, no. It's better than that." She took another bite of biscuit and sipped her tea. "It seems his reconnaissance was faulty. For whatever reason, he felt sure she would eagerly agree."

"She didn't?"

"Not only didn't she. She stood up and declared to everyone in Le Jardin that Ian was practically a reincarnation of Hitler, that you were a saint of some kind, and that you were meant to be the widow Morgan's knight in shining armor. I think the only thing missing from the scene was Agnes tossing her drink in his face."

"I guess Suzanne's heard about all this." It was more a question than a statement.

"How could she not? The whole county's talking about it." She rose from the couch. "But then you didn't know. Maybe, like you, she's playing the recluse."

"I work two jobs. I don't purposely avoid people, you know. This is just an especially—."

She cut me off. "I know, busy time of year." She picked up the tray and carried it into the kitchen, looking satisfied with herself.

I had my car keys in hand when she returned. I'd found out what I needed. After an awkward goodbye, I walked towards my car and reached for my mobile. "I can't believe you knew and didn't say anything to me," I groaned into the phone.

"I can barely hear you. Come over and we'll have it out face to face."

Twenty minutes later, I was knocking loudly on another door. Eleanor answered. "I think you owe me an explanation," I said, pushing my way in. "I thought you were on my side."

She led me into the morning room and sat down. "Sit down so we can have a civil conversation. I'll not be bullied by you."

"Bullied by me? I've never bullied you in my life. But I can't understand why you kept something as important as this from me."

"I kept nothing from you, Peter. I just didn't call you to tell you about it. Those are two very different things."

"They don't feel that way," I said, hearing the pathetic pout in my voice. I sighed down to my toes.

"In the adult world they are," she replied firmly. My head snapped up. I felt as though I'd been slapped. Eleanor's firm gaze was tinged with compassion. "Peter, you know I think you're a wonderful match for Suzanne, in every way except one." I felt a chill.

"I know," I said, hanging my head. "And there's nothing I can do about it."

"Except to keep on loving her and giving her the time and space she needs." She put her hand on mine. "I took Suzanne out for dinner just after she heard about the incident. All we talked about was how she felt about Agnes' behavior. We never even discussed you or Ian. She was already confused, and I think this paralyzed her. I could see how distraught she was, but she wouldn't discuss it with me."

"Why? Why is she reacting this way? If she cared for me at all, wouldn't she agree with Agnes?" I stood up, but instead of pacing, I just stood there. "She's mad with me about Thomas. But now she won't even talk to me. She treats me like the enemy."

"Aren't you?"

"What?" I sat back down with a heavy landing.

"Aren't you the enemy to her neatly ordered world?" Eleanor asked gently.

"No, I'd say the death of her husband was that enemy."

"Not to her." Eleanor paused a moment to let me consider this. "Peter, if she returns to America, to Morgan's, to the life she used to live, the only difference will be the absence of Edward. She'll still be living her life for everyone except herself. She'll still be sad, lost and alone. But at least she knows how to do that. She's done it for years." A faint light dawned in my thick head. "But if she stays here and accepts all the love being offered her… can't you see the upheaval that would cause? She'd actually have to start living for herself. If the prospect of that isn't enough to terrify her, then I don't know what is."

I leaned forward and put my head in my hands. "She'll go. I know she will."

Eleanor grabbed my hands and forced me to look at her. "Stop it. You aren't God. You can't tell the future." She watched my face, waiting as the truth of her words sunk in. I relaxed and got a grip on myself. "Come, you need tea."

"You're not making chai, are you?"

"Why do you ask that?"

"Jillian made some for me earlier and it was awful. Tasted like sugary moss."

Eleanor stopped and turned around. "What were you doing at Jillian's?"

I told her about running into Ian. "And I figured there was only one person who had her pulse on the local gossip, so I rang her. Said I wanted to catch up. And just as I expected, she was eager to tell me the story. Though she skipped the part where Agnes says Suzanne is better off with me. She was rather caught up in her amusement at the embarrassment the whole scene brought to Agnes and Ian."

I expected her to join in my laughter. Instead, she glowered at me. "I'm quite shocked, really."

"At what?" I said, crossing my arms.

"At you."

"Why? I didn't do anything wrong."

"You don't think it was wrong to use Jillian like that? She may be a lot of things we don't like, but she does have feelings." Eleanor's anger was increasing by the minute, as was mine.

"Eleanor, you're not my mum."

"Of course not," she said quietly.

"I don't have to stand for correction from you. I did nothing against my conscience, and I'll not have you falsely accusing me." I strode from the room, toward the door, keenly aware of what a liar I was.

～

This kind of anger made me want to be reckless. I drove the car out of Penwylln, nearly missing a stone pillar as I turned onto the road. I didn't much care where I ended up, as long as I could drive like the wind to get there. I took the turns too quickly, more than once pulling out of a ditch just before catching a tire in it. Still, it didn't slow me down. On the next turn, I overcorrected and narrowly missed a century old oak tree, instead driving into a thick hedgerow. The car stopped with a jolt, flinging my head forward and narrowly missing the steering wheel.

I got out of the car and walked round to the bonnet, swallowed up by a thick tangle of bushes and vines. Enraged, I got back in the car and shoved the gear into reverse. As I listened to the branches and brush scratch the car, the absurdness of my situation settled over me. I stopped the car, put my head back, and closed my eyes. My mind raced with accusations until, finally, all the stones I had to throw at myself had been launched. Ahh, I'm the fool, I thought, and laughed out loud. And then, suddenly, my amusement turned to sadness. Quietly and stealthily, without my noticing it, loneliness had crept into my car. It surrounded me, and I breathed it in. I shook my head sadly, turned the car around, and motored off.

It was dark when I arrived on the edge of the moor. I took the torch from the boot of the car. I knew I could shine it straight ahead and illume much of the path, but I aimed at my feet, brightening my way one step at a time. A little while later, I came upon a wide stone table, almost hidden among summer flowers dim in the moonlight. White Sea Campions, azure Bluebells, and pink Thrift shone out like a pale rainbow. From here I had an expansive view of the sea. A full moon came out from behind passing clouds, shedding a silver, luminous light. I turned off my torch and sat down. And, in so doing, my mind, like stones on the water, finally stopped its skipping and found a place to go deep.

My thoughts quickly found their way to Da, as they usually did when I felt this way. A sudden hollowness overtook me, reminding me how keenly I still felt his absence from my life. From comic relief to sounding board, he'd filled practically every role. But what I missed most of all was the way he used to look me in the eye and point out the truth. Because everything about him, his eyes, his face, his whole demeanor, spoke of a forceful, unshakeable love for me. I never felt diminished when we talked of my shortcomings, because I knew that his love for me was so much more than anything I could do wrong. I'd known it as sure as the sun rose each morning.

I sat there a long while, letting my thoughts run the gamut. From Da to Thomas and Gemma, to Eleanor and Jillian, and back to Suzanne and Blair. I grew tired and ready for sleep. Rogue clouds reappeared and shrouded the moon, so I pushed the button on my torch. No light appeared. I shook it hard, thinking to encourage the batteries to do their work, but again, no light. I had to laugh as I stumbled along the path in the dark, using my memory to navigate- surely an apt picture of me tonight.

As I thought back on the evening, my heart stirred and some things felt suddenly very clear. I saw that Eleanor was right. I'd deceived myself into thinking there was nothing wrong with visiting Jillian, but I'd used her. And I'd been short, proud with Eleanor. I'd been blinded by my fear of losing Suzanne. Hah. I don't even know if I'd ever had her. I thought of the times when she was sweet and vulnerable, when she seemed open to me and was willing to show it. But as quickly as those times came, they disappeared, and she turned guarded and aloof, almost hostile. I wanted to understand her. I meant to be patient. Then we went to York. And whatever had been warming in her heart toward me was extinguished. She misunderstood my care of Thomas, and I didn't understand why she reacted to it so violently.

It didn't change my feelings for her. They continued to grow. In every situation, every interaction. But as my affection for her grew, so did the thread of desperation I felt when she shut me out. And look what it had led to. I was ashamed, and even a little shocked at myself. I could mend things with Eleanor and apologize to Jillian.

But there was not one thing I could do to earn the love of Suzanne Morgan.

# 21

## *Suzanne*

Approaching London by car was a different experience than departing by train. I sat white-knuckled through the confusion of motorways, roundabouts, and lay-bys. Agnes maneuvered deftly through the chaos and easily found the hotel I'd booked for us in Kensington. We spent the afternoon shopping in the city, then found our way to a corner bistro for dinner. I was happy to talk about everything except why we were here. Later, sounds from the street below filled our room. We lay on our beds, listening as the evening noises turned to a comfortable, background hum. I was a moment from sleep when Agnes spoke from her bed.

"Are you nervous about seeing your friends? Shall I come with you tomorrow?"

"If they're here to bring bad news, I don't want to hear it alone."

"What are you afraid of?"

I couldn't say it out loud. That Morgan's is failing. That all I have to go back to is a big, empty house.

The next morning, Cathy greeted me with a fierce hug. "I've missed you. You look wonderful. Something here agrees with you." More reticent, Mark kissed me on the cheek.

"Marrying my best friend warrants more than that," I said, reaching for his shoulders.

The hotel restaurant opened onto a veranda, surrounded by big pots of glorious blue and white flowers. It was more like being in a garden than in the heart of the city. Before getting to business, I wanted to hear about them. With a glowing face, Cathy eagerly answered my questions. She told of their early working relationship, the growing romance, and the struggle to keep personal and professional worlds separate.

"We ended more than one date with a disagreement about how to deal with a new vendor or promote a sale. After a few times, we had to set some boundaries," Cathy laughed.

"Smartest thing we did," Mark added. "And I'm sure there'll be more after we're married."

And then, feeling as if I was stepping off a cliff, I asked about Morgan's. As they painted the picture of a strong business, two questions nagged at me. Why wasn't I happier to hear it? And why had they come? Mark sat straighter and reached for Cathy's hand. "It was much easier to step into the roles of interim managers than we'd expected," he explained. "You and Edward built a wonderful company, and your diligence after his death paid off in huge ways. It's been marvelous for both of us. And it's helped us see what we want out for ourselves."

"To own a store like Morgan's?"

Cathy shook her head. "Not exactly." She withdrew her hand from Mark's and reached for mine. "What we want—is to own Morgan's. We want to buy you out."

I pulled away from her. "I don't understand. Morgan's isn't for sale."

"I know. That's why we came to talk face to face."

"I don't know how you can ask me about it at all," I said, my voice sounding small to my ears.

"Because I believe it would be good for you."

"How could selling Edward's store be good for me?" I said, staring into my lap. I tried to ignore the fact that when I first came to England I was considering just that. Now the idea was preposterous.

Evenly, Cathy said, "It's not Edward's store any longer. It's yours. We'd like to buy *your* company from *you*." She waited until I looked up. Cathy had been with me at every critical moment of my adult life—my wedding, the day Blair was born, the night Edward died. I knew those eyes. And the person behind them. Though I was ashamed of my hostility, I couldn't understand her.

"I know how much Edward loved Morgan's. How you loved it, because of Edward. But Suzanne, ask yourself, is that what you would have chosen without him?" She paused. "Think of what this would mean for you and Blair. You'd have the freedom to do what you want. Doesn't that sound wonderful?" I closed my eyes. It might have if I had any idea what that was. "It would mean you could stay here. See if you can work things out with Peter."

The shock of her words forced open my eyes and propelled me to my feet. I threw my napkin down, and fled. In the ladies room, I swallowed air and held onto the marble vanity. Were there really no safe people in the world? I stayed in there until my head cleared, then straightened up and made for the door. This conversation needed to end as quickly as possible.

I took a sip of water and breathed deeply. "There are two issues. The first is whether or not I would sell Morgan's to you. The second is your presumption that you know what is best for me and my daughter."

"Suzanne, really, I can't take it. You sound like you're addressing your father. I'm your friend. Just talk to me."

I didn't know how to at this moment. This was Cathy, but… "The points you make about Morgan's are compelling. If you draft an offer, I'll show it to my attorney. Then I may be willing to enter negotiations. As for the second issue—."

"Stop it!" Cathy demanded. "I can't stand the coldness in your voice."

"And I can't stand the coldness in your heart," I blurted back.

She shrank back. "What do you mean?"

"How can you even think there could be someone else for me besides Edward?"

She looked at me. Through me. In me. "Edward is gone."

"His memory isn't. His daughter isn't," my voice rising.

"You don't betray him by moving on with your life. Your wedding vows said 'til death do us part," Cathy responded, her voice also rising.

"Slow down, both of you," Mark interrupted.

I assumed my fortress position- arms crossed, eyes and mouth hard. I couldn't begin to know what to say to her. Cathy tried again. "My motives are good. I love you and Blair. I believe buying the store is in both of our best interests. Just tell me how you feel, Suz."

The waiter appeared to clear the dishes, giving me a desperately needed moment to think. China cups tinkled nearby. Piano music wafted from discreet speakers. "How do I feel, Cathy? I feel confused. Hurt. Alone. I've told you a few things about Peter. You know he's been wonderful to Blair. But considering how very little that is, I don't understand why you'd want to see things work out between us. He's a stranger to you. How could you not be more protective?"

"We both know he's more than that to you. You told me yourself that you've never met anyone like him."

Furious, I turned to see Agnes smiling at me. "I…I could have meant a thousand things."

"But you didn't," Cathy continued. "And you know it." Actually, I didn't know what I thought anymore.

"But still, you haven't even—."

"Cathy talked to him," Mark said, cutting me off.

It felt like I'd been punched in the stomach. "When? Why didn't you tell me before?"

"It wasn't the right time," Mark answered for her. "This is."

"I see." I stared at them, feeling the hurt and resentment seeping from me.

"Maybe we should talk privately, Suzanne. Do you want to go to my room to finish this?" Cathy asked. I sank back in the chair and shook my head. It didn't matter anymore. "He called me because he needed help understanding you. He was very open about himself and his feelings." I know she wanted me to hear this as good news rather than the betrayal it was. "He loves you, Suzanne. In ways Edward wasn't capable of."

I couldn't look at any of them. I hated the weakness that allowed me to be hurt by them. I hated the truth of whom I'd chosen to marry. I hated the confusion I felt about Peter.

"He wants to love you well. He even asked me to check in on him. He didn't want to take the chance that he would use information about Edward, or your father, or anything else to manipulate you into loving him."

"What did you tell him?"

Tears sprang to her eyes. "I told him the truth."

I stood, thanked them for coming, and said they'd be hearing from me. I felt calm, controlled and detached. Just like the night Edward died.

⸾

Halfway to Mousehole, we stopped to stretch our legs. I hadn't said a word since leaving London. Agnes proved her friendship by letting me think. Shortly after getting back on the motorway, my phone rang. "Hallo, Suzanne. It's Hillary. Where are you?"

My heart started pounding. "Two, three hours away. Why? Did something happen to Blair?"

"She's okay. There was a sailing accident. She's at hospital, but just for observation."

My stomach turned. "Sailing? She wasn't sailing."

"It was planned for Fredericka and Martin. Mum gave Blair permission. Look, go straight to hospital. We'll meet you there." She hung up. I dropped the phone in my lap.

"What happened? Who was that?" Agnes demanded.

"Hillary. A sailing accident."

"Is Blair all right?"

"She's at the hospital." The words came out in a rush of sobs. Agnes looked over at me so often, I'm surprised she didn't wreck the car. Eventually, I calmed down enough to tell her what Hillary said.

"Observation? That sounds good, doesn't it? Not too serious…"

"Unless she's lying and doesn't want to tell me the truth until we get there."

"Oh." Agnes turned suddenly pale. "What about Fredericka and Martin? How are they?"

"I forgot to ask."

With trembling fingers, I called Penwylln but got no answer. I tried Eleanor's mobile, but the phone rang straight to messages. I called Peter. His phone was off. I tried Ian next. "Hamilton here."

I started crying again. "Ian. It's Suzanne. I'm so glad I got you."

"What's happened?"

"It's an emergency. I'm with Agnes, coming from London. Hillary called. Blair's been in an accident. Have you heard anything?"

"No."

"Blair's in the hospital. For observation, she said. Would you check on her and call me back? Please, Ian. I'm terrified."

"Of course I will. Don't worry." He hung up abruptly.

Limp with fear, I tried Eleanor and Peter several more times. It seemed like years before we saw the hospital entrance. I'd not heard from Ian and noticed my phone was dead.

The car screeched to a stop. We ran in, looking for anyone we knew, but settled for the information desk. The nurse directed us to the Critical Care Department; my knees buckled. Agnes caught me and held on until I could stand again. Trying to be helpful, the nurse called after us, "It doesn't look like a Blair Morgan was admitted." I clung to Agnes as she pulled me, stumbling, into the elevator. When the door opened, we came upon Eleanor, Hillary, Fredericka, Martin and Ian huddled in the waiting area. I heard myself moan, as if from a distance, and then everything went black.

⁓

Someone told me to wake up. I opened my eyes. I was in a hospital bed. Blair stood beside me, a purple bruise and several stitches blazoned across her forehead. "Mommy," she said, leaning into me. "Why did you faint? What's happened? Everyone was worried."

Seeing my confusion, Eleanor said, "You're in hospital. Agnes brought you. You fainted when you got off the lift."

Then I remembered. "I didn't see you," I said to Blair.

"Oh Suzanne, you thought Blair was..." She didn't finish the sentence. "No wonder. Oh my dear, I'm so sorry."

Agnes stepped into view. "All the nurse said was that Blair hadn't been admitted," she said.

"They didn't tell you she was fine," Eleanor said.

"I'm okay, Mom. It was scary. But I just got this cut on my head." Blair's chipper voice sounded forced.

Eleanor turned to Agnes. "Would you take Blair to the waiting area to sit down? We don't want her to tire out." Blair went too willingly. There was something I didn't know.

"You're scaring me," I said the moment the door closed.

"I don't mean to. Blair wants me to tell you the rest of the news."

I pulled up on my elbows. "What is it, Eleanor? I remember seeing Fredericka and Martin."

"It's Peter," Eleanor said softly, taking a firm hold of my arm.

My body went cold. "Is he dead?"

"He's...unconscious." She blew her nose, drew her hand across her eyes. This *couldn't* be happening again. I sunk back in the bed in a wave of nausea.

"The other day, when I told you Hillary had an outing planned, I didn't know Peter had offered to take the children on his boat. I didn't think you'd mind if she joined them." She paused again to dab her eyes. "I only have the children's explanation to go on. It appears they were having a wonderful sail, seas running high, good wind. They'd been out for several hours and were ready to head in. Peter was turning around to head back when something hit the side of the boat. Blair turned toward the noise. The boom hit her in the head, and she fell overboard."

Eleanor rubbed my trembling arms. "Peter yelled to Fredericka as he gave her the tiller and jumped in after Blair. She hadn't gotten far. Had a life jacket on. He reached her quickly and pulled her to the side of the boat. He shouted to Martin to lean down as far as he could. Peter pushed Blair up so Martin could grab her hands. When Fredericka saw Martin struggling to pull her in, she left the tiller to join him. Peter was telling her to get back and steer, but in the midst of all the confusion, she didn't understand.

"A gust filled the sails, but, without anyone at the tiller, the boat followed the wind. The turn caught Peter by surprise, and the boat hit him hard. He was tethered to the boat; he always did that when he was the only real sailor on board. He was fighting to stay conscious, but the wind was picking up, pulling the boat faster. All of a sudden, Fredericka realized she was supposed to be at the tiller and ran back. They could see something was wrong as Peter was dragged along. Martin and Blair tried to pull him up, but they couldn't do it. Mercifully, the wind finally died."

"It was a fishing pot that hit the boat. The fisherman, Billy Hawker, had been tying it when the rope broke. He'd come after it. Reached the sailboat just as the wind died. Pulled Peter in. The children don't know how long it all took. Billy's mate climbed aboard, moved the children into the fishing boat, and sailed her in.

"Billy radioed ahead to the harbor. Ambulances were waiting. Martin and Fredericka didn't have a scratch. The doctors examined Blair and stitched the cut on her forehead. Said to rest a few days."

"What's the prognosis?" I bit down hard on my trembling lip.

Eleanor stopped, overtaken by tears again. It must be grim. I held my breath, thinking of the vibrant man I knew. "They won't say. They're waiting for his brother to get here."

"Thomas?"

"He's coming from London."

"What do the children know?" I didn't even know which children I was asking about. Fredericka and Martin? Frannie and Archie? Blair?

"That he's unconscious. Not how serious it could be. Hillary's ready to take them home. Should she take Blair, too?"

I nodded. "I'll be right out." I rang the nurse and eased myself from the bed. I was shaking so hard, I could barely pull myself up. She checked my blood pressure, gave me a stern warning, and signed me out. In the waiting area, I went directly to Blair. She was worn out and offered no complaint about leaving. We nearly hugged the breath from each other.

Eleanor, Ian, and I sat on the green vinyl sofa in heavy silence; a TV droned in a corner. I was glad to hear Ian clear his throat. A few more minutes left to my own thoughts and I might really go mad. Eleanor's head was bent down. "Let me take you to the cafeteria," he suggested. "Strong tea would do you both good."

"I'd like to stay close," I said. Eleanor looked up and nodded.

"Of course you do. I'll bring it to you." Pensive, he hesitated. Then he kissed us each on the cheek. "I know he means a great deal to both of you. I'm truly sorry." Eleanor took his hand and squeezed it. I watched him walk away without an ounce of any of the usual attitude. I put my head back, trying to push out the eerie familiarity of this scene.

Eleanor touched my hand. "How were your friends this morning? What did they have to ask you that they couldn't do over the phone?"

This morning? That couldn't be right. Felt like days ago. "They want to buy Morgan's."

Delight flooded her face. "What did you say to that?"

"At first I refused. Then I told them to put a proposal together and that I'd consider it."

"And will you?"

I shook my head and shrugged. "I don't know." The next moment, Ian was running toward us.

"Thomas Stewart is here."

❧

He was talking to the doctors when I found him. Hugging me, he said, "I'm glad you're here. And Blair's all right?" I nodded, still brought to tears by the thought of what might have happened. "I wanted you here for the doctors' report," he said.

"That's for family only."

"But I know how Peter—."

"No," I cut him off. "I'll wait over there." I pulled away and joined Eleanor, who had followed me down the hall. Watching their expressionless conversation was agony, reminding me that doctors couldn't make promises. Finally, they finished.

"They don't know," he said; a sob escaped him. "He was in the water a long time. He's stable. They're watching him closely. Said the first 24 hours are the most important."

"Blair's doctor said that, too." He looked at me oddly. I wouldn't explain now.

"They also said sometimes people in comas hear voices. It's important for loved ones to talk to them." I nodded, again. Important to do, though I remembered how futile words spoken to Blair felt at the time. "So you'll sit with him?" Thomas asked.

"What?" Wait. I didn't mean…

"You'll sit with Peter. Talk to him."

"It should be you, Thomas. I'm the wrong person, you know that." I expected Eleanor to agree.

"Thomas is right," she said. "Suzanne, Peter is in love with you. It's your voice, above all others, that he'll respond to."

"You don't know what I…" I stopped and looked at them pleadingly. "I really think he would respond to you, Thomas. Yours is a voice he's known his whole life."

"He needs to hear both of us."

∾

Being in the room made me weak. The beeping of the machines, the smell of hospital disinfectant, the seemingly lifeless man in a bed brought a shudder to my whole body. Thomas saw, and pulled me to his side.

"Pray with me, Suzanne." I closed my eyes. This man talked to God in a mysterious way. I was completely out of place, yet I wanted him to continue. He finished, and then surprised me by saying, "We have unfinished business, you and I."

"I don't know of any." I didn't relish a conversation with him. He still scared me.

"It was because of me that you had a falling out with Peter. It's been hard on him. And hard on me, too, knowing I caused it. I wanted to explain myself. He wouldn't have it. But now…" He wiped his eyes. "I need to talk to you."

"It wasn't your fault. I was mad at…" It seemed so stupid at this moment. We didn't know if he'd live through the night. "Why does it matter now?"

"Truth always matters. And it did that miserable day, when the true man came out of me. Afterwards, Peter wasn't approving of me; he was making room for me. For my failings. For the worst in me. What you saw as defense, I felt as compassion. Mercy, even. I was guilty. Horrid. We all knew it. But Peter wasn't willing to stop there. If you'd all just been mad at me, and rightly so, an opportunity might have been lost."

"I don't understand. What opportunity?"

"Everything I shouted at Arch and Fran was meant for me," he explained. "I was responsible for Lily. I'd lost track of her. I felt stupid. I didn't want to be guilty of being a bad father in front of all of you."

"No one would have thought that."

"It didn't matter what you thought, don't you see? It was what I believed about myself." The sheer force of Thomas' sincerity drew me in. I looked at Peter in the bed. It was always true of him, too. Neither of them was perfect. But both were sincere, earnest, humble men. "When Lily couldn't be found, I reverted to the oldest trick in the book. I shifted the blame from myself. Surely, *I* wasn't guilty. It must have been Fran and Arch."

He stepped closer to the bed. I was stuck a few steps back. The machines, Peter's motionless body. I still couldn't walk right up to it.

"Liza would have been angry at me for losing track of Lily. She was always reminding me to watch her close." He picked up Peter's hand and started rubbing the back of it. "When I said if she was hurt it would be unforgivable, I meant I wouldn't forgive myself. What I did by putting that enormous responsibility and blame on my two dear children was cowardly and selfish. I was hiding behind them." He finished his story. I got lost in the beeping of the machine. "Shocking, isn't it?" he said in a broken voice.

"No." And it wasn't. My guilty ways may have played out differently in a different story, but I'd been cowardly and selfish when I hadn't protected Blair from Edward. No, I wasn't shocked at all. Not anymore.

"So Peter...?" I edged up a step.

"He knew I was playing God. That I still blamed myself for Liza's death. I should have known she was sick before she did. I should have found a better doctor. I should have been able to keep her alive. When we couldn't find Lily, it became about something more. No longer just my missing child, but my dead wife, too. And, more than anything else, my inability to keep my family safe."

I threw my head back. Oh my goodness. That was *me*. I thought I should have been able to predict the changes in Edward before they happened. I thought I should have been able to find a way to please my father. I thought I should have been able to protect Blair from days in a coma. From losing her father.

"He knew how quickly I would have accepted harsh judgment from everyone and not taken the time to understand. Understanding doesn't remove guilt. But sometimes, our guilt doesn't run deep enough. We settle for the most obvious issue. Something that, while still true, is not complete. My brother was trying to love me as well as he could."

I was mortified I'd never let him explain. "I'm sorry. I misjudged both of you. I should have listened to him." Still holding Peter's hand, he squeezed mine with his other one.

We settled in then, turning our attention back to Peter. Thomas told stories of their cherished father and reminisced about their boyhood. My head spun with all that was unfamiliar to me. But each time Thomas reminded Peter that he loved and needed him, something in me stirred. After an emotional time, he stepped out to call Jean.

The door closed, shutting out more than the noise of the nurse's station and doctor's voices. Outside that door, I could fool myself into believing I knew my own mind and heart. Inside this room, with Peter Stewart somewhere in the netherworld between life and death, I was as lost from myself as I'd ever been. This was too hard. Why was I here? I stopped looking at Peter and instead found a picture on the wall. Thomas had given me a job, so I steeled myself and got to work.

"Wake up," I said in an upbeat voice. "I need to thank you for saving Blair's life. You jumped in that water without a thought to yourself. Used your last bit of strength to get her to safety. You are a good man, a good friend." But the pretence quickly fell apart, and I began to weep. "You've been wonderful to both of us since the first day we met you," I said amidst tears. "Do you remember? Blair thought you were the janitor and you played along." It was a few minutes before I could continue. "You captured her heart from the first day. Wake up so she can thank you."

I stopped, unsure what to say next. This awful wooing back to life surely required someone stronger than me. I closed my eyes and tried to think of the right words. The door opened and I saw it was Eleanor.

"I just wanted to check on you," she said. She took one look at my tear-stained face and rushed towards me with open arms. "I'm right outside if you need me."

After she left, I pulled a chair beside the bed and carefully took his hand, calloused and brown. I knew this hand. It had held mine. Rubbed my back when I was sick. Fitted a saddle for Blair. Pushed her to safety. "I'm supposed to be talking to you, but I'm not sure what to say. Thank you is all I can think. You saved Blair by risking your life. If you don't—."

I stopped as suddenly as if I'd slammed into a wall. I couldn't say those words out loud. But it didn't stop them from filling my mind. I rubbed my temple. If you don't live, then you will have sacrificed your life. You will have given your life for hers.

I wanted to get up and run, and yet, at the same time fling my arms around him in gratitude. I never asked him to love me like this. I did the opposite; I pushed him away. And still he did this. He did it out of his love for me, not mine for him. He chose to love me. He chose me.

I sat back in the chair and rubbed my tired, gritty eyes. And I thought about the myriad of ways Peter had demonstrated his love for me. I turned them over like jewels in my mind. His patient kindness from our first meeting until now. When my emotions ran hot and cold; when I shut him out, not just from myself, but also from Blair; and when I misconstrued his love and loyalty for Thomas. He didn't demand that I listen to his defense, but waited, believing the truth would win out. He had a greater vision for us than we had for ourselves. He'd shown me that when he gave me his Da's old pen and the lovely journal and when he helped Blair get back on a horse and jump again.

He didn't get angry easily and was quick to apologize when he was wrong. I'd never met a man less guided by his ego. But he also possessed a strong and manly protective side. I'd seen it, albeit in retrospect, in how he cared for his brother, as well as in his warnings to me about Ian.

I thought about how he let me know he'd wait for me. He'd been willing to put up with my confusion and my guilt, to give me space to be unsure, even mean to him. What marked his love for me? Patience, kindness, humility, protection, perseverance. Suddenly, Cathy's words from this morning echoed with shocking clarity. *He didn't want to manipulate you into loving him. He wanted to love you well.* I wanted so badly to wake him up. I wanted, more than anything, a chance to tell him what my heart had finally realized. I wanted him to hear me say, "Peter, you *do* love me well."

Edward didn't understand this kind of love; he wasn't capable of it. Edward's love was always for himself first. All those years of believing I was unlovable. It was Edward who didn't know how to love. And Peter knew that.

A tremor ran from my head to my toes, welling up into a deep, heartfelt panic. Was I making this up? I wanted to get Eleanor, to ask her if this was true. But I couldn't leave this room. My mouth went dry. My right leg bounced uncontrollably. The chaos in my heart rose to a crescendo.

And then, suddenly, I understood. This was radical love, different than anything I had ever known. Love that is willing to die for another, in big ways and small. I didn't know much about this kind of love, but enough to realize it was larger and deeper than I could wrap my brain, or my heart, around. But that was all right. Because what I did know was that, finally, I was ready to receive it. And in the receiving, I knew something deep, true and mysterious. And then I experienced something unlike anything before. It was beyond happiness, greater than delight, more sustaining than pleasure.

I squeezed his hand, again. Why, Peter? Why do you think my voice is worth hearing? My heart worth knowing?

"I don't understand you," I said in a voice to rouse him. "You deserve someone better than me. I'm...I'm...not worth it. Don't you see? I'll fail at loving you. Like I have with Blair."

I thought of how his words touched me, as gently and honestly as I was touching his flesh right now. How my soul was stirred by his delight in me. How he asked questions and listened, hearing what I didn't say.

"You know me. You know where I belong." I thought about how much of my life I'd felt restless. Searching. "I love you, Peter. Please come... back... to me." Eternity passed, and then my fingers felt a faint squeeze.

Through my tears, I saw his smile.

Breinigsville, PA USA
01 August 2010
242795BV00002B/5/P